Brigid

Brigid

KIM CURRAN

MICHAEL JOSEPH

PENGUIN MICHAEL JOSEPH

UK | USA | Canada | Ireland | Australia
India | New Zealand | South Africa

Penguin Michael Joseph is part of the Penguin Random House group of companies whose addresses can be found at global.penguinrandomhouse.com

Penguin Random House UK,
One Embassy Gardens, 8 Viaduct Gardens, London SW11 7BW

penguin.co.uk

First published 2026

001

Copyright © Kim Curran, 2026

The moral right of the author has been asserted

Penguin Random House values and supports copyright.
Copyright fuels creativity, encourages diverse voices, promotes freedom of expression and supports a vibrant culture. Thank you for purchasing an authorized edition of this book and for respecting intellectual property laws by not reproducing, scanning or distributing any part of it by any means without permission. You are supporting authors and enabling Penguin Random House to continue to publish books for everyone.
No part of this book may be used or reproduced in any manner for the purpose of training artificial intelligence technologies or systems. In accordance with Article 4(3) of the DSM Directive 2019/790, Penguin Random House expressly reserves this work from the text and data mining exception

Set in 13.5/16pt Garamond MT
Typeset by Falcon Oast Graphic Art Ltd
Printed and bound in Great Britain by Clays Ltd, Elcograf S.p.A.

The authorized representative in the EEA is Penguin Random House Ireland, Morrison Chambers, 32 Nassau Street, Dublin D02 YH68

A CIP catalogue record for this book is available from the British Library

HARDBACK ISBN: 978–0–241–71305–1
PAPERBACK ISBN: 978–0–241–71306–8

Penguin Random House is committed to a sustainable future for our business, our readers and our planet. This book is made from Forest Stewardship Council® certified paper.

*Above all, this is a story about sisterhood.
So this one's for you, my sisters, Heidi and Natasha.*

Author's Note

The stories I was told in my youth about St Brigid were all about her kindness, her beauty, her endless patience and goodness. She was . . . well, saintly. So saintly I didn't know if I could write a book about her. But when I began my research, starting with the seventh-century *Vita Sanctae Brigidae*, it gave me a lovely shiver to learn there was more than a little darkness in her too. She healed the sick and gave everything she had to the poor. But she also made her brother's eyes explode. She turned water into ale and milked her cows three times in a day to provide a lake of milk for her guests. But she also turned the waters of the Liffey against her enemies. She was, like all real women, complex. Wonderfully so. Why then, have so many questions been asked about whether St Brigid ever even lived? In 1969, Pope Paul VI removed her from the Roman Catholic calendar due to insufficient evidence of her existence. And yet, we have more historical information about Brigid than anyone else from this period. Including St Patrick.

It was my hope in writing this book that I could find Brigid, the woman, in all her messy complexity and bring her to life.

A Note on Pronunciation:

Spoken Irish is a beautifully fluid language, as it does not have a standard, universally accepted pronunciation. Here is how I would pronounce the names and places, but if you're looking for more help, https://inirish.bitesize.irish and https://www.teanglann.ie/en/fuaim are great places to start.

People

Aillil: *al-il* – son of King Dunlaing
Áine: *awn-ya* – a young woman
Beccan: *beck-awn* – Brigid's youngest stepbrother
Breachnat: *brock-hnat* – Brigid's stepmother
Brigid: *bridge-id* – both the daughter of a slave and chieftain and the goddess of inspiration and healing
Brión: *bree-ohn* – one of King Dunlaing's men
Broicsech: *bruck-seck* – Brigid's mother
Brónach: *broh-nock* – a nun
Buach: *boo-ock* – a nun and cowherd
Caíndelbán: *kaw-een-del-vawn* – a leper
Ciara: *keer-a* – a slave girl and Brigid's oldest friend
Cinnia: *sin-ee-a* – a princess turned nun
Clodagh: *clow-dah* – a young blacksmith
Cuach: *coo-ock* – wife of King Dunlaing
Darlughdach: *dar-luch-ta* – bard and Brigid's anamchara (soul friend)
Dubhthach: *dou-ach* – Brigid's father
Dún Ailinne: *doon all-in-yah* – Dubhthach's fort

Dunlaing: *doon-lang* – a High King
Éces: *ay-kuss* – a master bard
Enna Niadh Mac Bressal: *ay-na nee-ah mock bress-al* – Dunlaing's father
Euhel: *uh-hell* – Brigid's eldest stepbrother
Fachtna: *fock-tna* – Brigid's second eldest stepbrother
Fiacc: *fee-uck* – a young bard
Flann O'Banain: *flan oh bon-in* – a cruel man
Fothairt: *fuh-hert* – the tribe of people to which Brigid belonged
Gráinne: *grawn-ni-ah* – King Dunlaing's daughter
Indiu: *in-dyoo* – a nun and twin
Induae: *in-doo-ay* – a twin and nun
Íte: *ee-ta* – a nun
Laoise: *lee-sha* – a nun
Lochru: *luck-roo* – a druid
Lóegaire mac Néill: *loh-gar-a mack nay-il* – High King of Tara
Lommán: *lo-man* – a leper in disguise
Lonan: *low-nan* – Brigid's second youngest stepbrother
Machta: *mack-ta* – Indiu and Induae's uncle
Maithgen: *mah-gen* – a great druid and Brigid's adoptive father
Mealla: *mal-la* – Indiu and Induae's mother
Melchu: *mell-coo* – a bishop
Moel: *moh-ell* – a bishop
Muirenn: *m-wir-inn* – Dubhthach's old wet nurse
Mullaghmast: *mull-ock-hmast* – King Dunlaing's fort
Myrna: *meer-nuh* – a tradeswoman
Rechtabra: *ray-uck-tab-rah* – Brigid's husband-to-be
Rian: *ree-awn* – a stable boy
Sinann: *shin-uhn* – a goddess
Tadhg: *tayg* – a leper and storyteller
Tlachtga: *clack-da* – druidess and Maithgen's wife
Trian: *tree-an* – Brigid's middle stepbrother
Ui Brolaig: *ee broh-lig* – Indiu and Induae's father

Gods and legends

Aengus: *awn-gus* – the god of love and youth
Balor: *bah-ler* – a giant with a poisonous eye
Brigid: *bridge-id* – both the goddess of inspiration and healing and the daughter of a slave and chieftain
Caer: *ka-re* – the goddess of dreams
Dagda: *dag-da* – 'the good father', a god
Deichtine: *dech-tin-e* – Sétanta's mother
Fionn mac Cumhaill: *fyun mack coo-all* – legendary hunter and warrior
Lugh: *lu* – the 'many-skilled' god of light
Manannán mac Lir: *mon-an-nawn mack ler* – god of the sea
Oisín: *oh-sheen* – legendary poet and warrior
Sétanta: *Shay-dan-da* – the boyhood name for the great hero, Cúchulainn
Tuatha Dé Danann: *too-ha day dan-nan* – the Tribe of Danu, the gods

Places

Baile Átha Cliath: *bal-ye ah-ha klee-ah* – 'town of the hurdled ford', present-day Dublin
Cill Dara: *kil-dara* – 'church of the oak tree', present-day Kildare
Curragh: *curr-ah* – a flat open plain in Kildare
Emain Macha: *evin mak-ha* – 'fort of Macha', a fort in the north of Ireland
Faughart: *fock-herd* – 'good field', an area in County Louth

Seasonal festivals and flowers

Beltane: *Bel-tayn* – the festival marking the beginning of summer

Caisearbhán: *kash-ar-uv-awn* – dandelion
Imbolc: *im-bulk* – the festival marking the beginning of spring
Lughnasadh: *lun-nah-sah* – the festival marking the beginning of autumn
Nóinín: *no-nee* – daisy
Samhain: *sow-win* – the festival marking the beginning of winter

I

The grove is damp with the smell of winter's end. Moss, mulching wood, the sharp tang of peat. The months of ice and rain have soaked the soil, turning the earth to marsh, and morning frost covers the ground. A sacred well bubbles up from the roots of an ancient oak. Beneath its creaking branches stands a girl, head veiled, shivering like the leaves overhead.

'Here,' her father throws a rough cloak over her shoulders. 'Can't have your new husband thinking you're frail.'

The girl accepts the cloak, wrapping it around her, though she does not tell her father that it is not the cold causing her to shake.

She has been waiting since before dawn, and with each passing moment her fear builds. For today, she is to be wed.

She did not know that it would be this day. She was woken in the dark, washed and dressed by rough hands.

'You look beautiful, Brigid,' they had said and held up a polished brass mirror so she could look at her reflection. She did not recognize the face staring back at her: lips painted red, eyebrows darkened with soot, her hair tightly bound for the first time in her life and her skin slathered in oils that stank of musk and rotting flowers. 'You look like a goddess.'

Brigid had pushed the mirror away and wanted to cry.

She has been told she is beautiful her whole life, as though it was the greatest gift she could ask for. After all, it was because he had heard tales of her beauty that Dubhthach, her father, had sent word to Maithgen that he was claiming the child for his own. Maithgen was the great druid who had bought her mother when Brigid was still in her belly, and by rights, the child would be his too. But Dubhthach was not a man to cross. And so Maithgen had given her up and Dubhthach had kept her under his watchful eye so that she would not go to waste, waiting for when he could get the highest price for her. That time, it seemed, has finally come.

On the journey to the grove, her father had said hardly a word. Her stepmother Breachnat would not stop talking. As though she was making up for the years she had ignored her stepdaughter by giving her every instruction she could think of on what it means to be a good wife.

'A husband is like a master. You must do everything Rechtabra tells you,' Breachnat had said.

Dubhthach had snorted at his wife, who rarely did anything he told her, though she had ignored him.

'Everything,' Breachnat said again. The word *everything* heavy with threat.

The girl has only glimpsed Rechtabra, her husband-to-be, once before, when he came to Dún Ailinne to bargain for her. She watched from behind a pillar as Rechtabra and her father traded words as other men trade blows. When at last Dubhthach and Rechtabra shook hands, she felt as though someone had put greasy fingers down her throat, and she had been sick.

'You should be happy, Brigid,' Breachnat had said, handing her a rag to clean up her vomit. 'You earned your father a fine price. Seven cumals' worth of gold. That's more than a girl like you could have hoped for.'

What is a girl like me? The nobody daughter of a Pict slave and an Irish chieftain with one duty. To marry well. To bear strong sons. She was born for this, she was told. Born to be bought and sold. And for a sum that could buy seven enslaved women – cumals – like her mother.

Brigid knows with bone-deep certainty she does not want to be a bride. And not because of the stories she has heard about Rechtabra: that he beats his horses and gives his slaves less than their due share of food. Or because he is old and ugly. Almost twenty years her senior and with a face that could turn milk sour. For even had Rechtabra been the kindest, sweetest, most beautiful man ever to walk Ireland's green grass, she would not want to marry him.

Brigid doesn't want to be married to any man. Ever. Yet the world does not care much for what a girl like her wants.

Brigid looks up as a flock of linnets pass overhead, their chittering sweet as children's laughter. As the sun warms the frost, water drips from the branches of the oak tree and down the back of Brigid's neck, though she hardly notices the cold over the creeping dread flowing up her body from the ground. She can feel her heart thudding against her chest, she has been clenching her teeth so hard, her jaw aches, and her hands, curled into fists, are white-knuckled. Fear is not new to her: she has been afraid every day since she first arrived at Dún Ailinne eight years ago, summoned by her father, torn from her mother's arms, and thrown into a life as a chieftain's daughter. But this fear feels different. As though she might drown in it. She stares at the twisted trunk, peeled open from a lightning strike like a wound, and thinks of lips and a dark mouth opening to devour her.

'All shall be well,' she says, mumbling to herself, trying to push the fear down inside her. 'All shall be well.' The last words her mother spoke to her. If only she could believe them.

All women marry. All free women, anyway. Why should she be any different? It's not as if she is special. She closes her eyes, tries to surrender rather than fight against the fear, for what use is that?

She wriggles her toes, trying to bring warmth back into them. The icy dew has soaked through her new linen slippers, turning the pink stitching red. As her breath moistens the cloth of the veil, it becomes harder and harder to breathe and her head begins to spin. The grass beneath her feet must be hungry for her spirit. They should not be atop this hill, with its ancient oak and magic well. Why could they not have met at Dún Ailinne? Or in Rechtabra's fort to the east? This a place where the gods once lived and where their magic still flowed, a place of stories, each layered around each other like the rings of a tree. It is not a place for mortals.

'Won't the god-folk be angry?' she had asked her father, when he pulled her off the cart and began the walk up the hill to the grove. 'If we trespass?'

'You listen to too many stories,' her father had said, dragging her behind him. 'Besides, what use would the god-folk have for a girl like you?'

A girl like her.

When she was younger, her half-brothers had pointed out this hill with the great oak tree on top, and told her that if she went up there on the eve of Samhain, the god-folk would come riding out of the mounds and they would take her away to their lands beneath the earth.

'They'll do things to you,' one brother had said.

'Because you're a girl,' another had added, pinching the flesh of her arm.

They wouldn't explain what things or why only a girl would suffer them, but had merely laughed and said, 'You'll see.'

The idea of these *things* filled her dreams. She saw bodies writhing in the darkness and sometimes she awoke to her skin slick with a hot sweat and she had to sink her face into the rainwater butt to cool it.

On the way here, Breachnat had told her what would

be expected on her first night as a wife. She had been told about her dark places and how she must give them up to her husband. There would be pain, she had been told. But Brigid was used to pain. Would it be like her monthly times, her 'shedding of petals', which she was still growing used to, having only started to bleed a few moons before? A pain deep and gnawing? Or would it be sharp, like when you cut yourself on a rusty nail? Or dull as a bruise after a beating?

After the pain, Breachnat told her, would come more pain and then babies. Babies she would love with all her being, giving all of herself to them, leaving nothing of herself, as her mother had done before her and her mother before her and all mothers, stretching back and back. Brigid wants more for herself than to be a spoke in a wheel of women's lives repeating over and over and over. She wants so much more. But what choice does she have? Her fate was decided the day she was born a girl.

There is still no sign of her husband-to-be. Breachnat wrings her hands. 'What if Rechtabra has changed his mind?'

'He won't have,' her father grunts.

'But if he's heard the stories, about how the girl gives everything away to any beggar that comes calling?'

Dubhthach gives only a snort for an answer.

Brigid has been told to keep all of this to herself. Her father had beaten a promise out of her. When she'd asked why, it had earned her another slap.

Her father paces, back and forth, each step heavier than the last. She knows him to be easily angry, easily violent, but she has never seen him nervous before and does not know the cause of it.

Brigid turns, opens her mouth to say that her husband isn't coming, but her father's heavy hand grasps her shoulder, thick fingers digging into her collarbone, and pushes her down on to her knees.

'You're going nowhere,' he says.

The damp soaks slowly into her skirts. There is a small stone digging into her kneecap, a single point of pain. But rather than move she leans harder on to it, the pain helping drive out the fear.

'Where is the bastard?' her father mutters, leaving her to go and look to the east. Her shoulder throbs as the blood rushes back into where his fingers gripped her. She imagines the white finger marks turning red beneath her tunic. She is alone. Now could be her chance.

Sight frosted by the sheer cloth of the veil, she looks through the gaps of a ragged whitethorn hedge, out at the forests covering the land around them. Even if she could run in her soft slippers and dragging dress, where could she go? Is there any fort or homestead that would take her in? How far would she get before her father caught her and knocked her to the ground? How bad would the beating be? No, there is no point in running. But there must be another way.

If only she had been blessed with something other than beauty. She would rather be blessed with wisdom or bravery or strength. Anything but beauty, for what use was something that didn't last and only existed in the eyes of others? Beauty can't warm the cold or feed the hungry. If stories are to be told about her, let them say more than she was beautiful. Let them say anything but that.

But what if she wasn't beautiful? What if she was ugly? Gloriously, monstrously ugly? What if her skin was as spoilt as the beggars she sneaked bread to, as withered as the hags she gave her father's milk to? What if her teeth were rotten as old bark and her hair thin as cobwebs? What if looking on her was like looking on Balor's poisonous eye?

The idea is delicious.

Ribbons tied to the low branches of the oak flutter in the wind. Wishes made to the old gods. She has no ribbons, but she makes her wish anyway.

'Make me ugly,' Brigid prays to whichever god will listen. Any single one of them would do if only they would grant her wish. 'Make me hideous.'

As soon as the words are whispered, a cold wind rushes through the grove, sending her veil dancing. She hears a soft slithering on the ground and feels a gentle brush against her ankle. A golden snake, with a soft brown line that zigzags down its back like the lazy stitching she tries to get away with when she has better things to do than sew. Brigid picks the snake up, it wraps around her wrist, tight and gentle as a hand leading her away. She has never held a snake before and had thought it would be cold and slimy, like the eels she helped catch in the rivers, but its skin is soft and warm and under it there is solid muscle. Red eyes stare at her, bright and cold as the gems in her father's sword. She brings it up to her face, for she has a sudden desire to press the hard flesh against her lips. The snake opens its jaw and strikes, needle-teeth punching into the soft flesh of her cheek. She gasps and drops the snake, which undulates away into the undergrowth.

Brigid's cheek pulsates with pain, and when she holds her fingers to where the snake has bitten her, they come away red with blood, like the day she dipped her fingers into the place between her legs, curious as to why she was wet. Her stepmother had seen and word had been sent to her father and he had been happy. A girl bleeds and men rejoice.

The skin of Brigid's face tightens, her lips swell and her tongue becomes thick in her mouth. She tries to speak, but the words are muffled, like trying to speak with a mouth full of dry bread.

'Rechtabra, bless the gods!' Breachnat says, clapping her hands.

'What took you so long?' Brigid hears her father say, though she doesn't hear the reply.

Her future husband come at last. Brigid stares straight ahead at the oak, not wanting to turn to see him, as if by not looking she can keep him away.

She smells him before she sees him. The stink of the drink and sweat coming off him in waves. A different hand on her shoulder turns her around, rougher than her father's. Even through her veil she sees the wet gleam of spittle on his lips, as though he were salivating before a meal.

'Come then,' Rechtabra says, his voice hoarse. 'Let me see what I have paid so much gold for.'

He rips the veil from her head with rough, stubby fingers and Brigid looks up into the face of the man who is to be her master. For a moment, he stares back at her, bloodshot eyes bursting out of his head. And then, he screams. He backs away, stumbling over the roots of the oak, hands held up as though warding off a beast about to eat him.

Breachnat steps forward, looks down at Brigid, and is the next to scream.

'What is all this screeching?' Dubhthach demands.

Rechtabra turns on Brigid's father. 'Thief. Liar. Cheat,' he roars, pointing a shaking finger at Brigid. He pushes past her stepmother, knocking her to the ground. Breachnat wails, begs Rechtabra to wait, says there must be some evil magic at work. Dubhthach curses all kinds of violence against the man for breaking his promise, swearing upon the gods he won't see a single grain of his gold back.

Dubhthach follows Rechtabra down the hill, the two men shouting all the way, Breachnat tripping after them, screeching still.

Brigid gets to her feet, pulls the skirts of her heavy, damp dress up, and walks towards the edge of the well. She looks into the still dark waters and sees not the pale, beautiful bride she saw that morning, but a foul creature with blotchy, bloated cheeks and swollen eyes. She sees not a goddess, but a monster. She smiles, her lips wonderfully fat and puffy, her cheeks stretched to bursting, for she knows that someone, at last, heard her prayer.

Me.

Girls and women pray to me, their goddess, every day. They pray to be married, to become mothers. They pray for their cows to be fertile and their husbands to be kind. But in the thousand years I have listened to the prayers of human women, none before had ever prayed to be ugly.

How could I resist?

2

When it had become clear that Rechtabra would not be returning, Dubhthach turned his ire on Brigid.

'What did you do, stupid girl?'

'It wasn't my fault. A snake . . .'

The blow comes hard and fast. A sharp blow to the face with the back of his hand. 'What did I tell you about lying to me, girl?'

Brigid refuses to look away. Refuses to back down, because she has not lied. She never lies. He has never hit her that hard before, but she can barely feel it over the throbbing pain from the snake bite. Over her own deep relief.

'Get in the cart,' Dubhthach says, shaking his hand.

Brigid hopes that hitting her has caused him pain.

The drive back to Dún Ailinne is silent except for Breachnat's hissing.

'Didn't I tell you the girl should not come to us? Didn't I tell you not to take her whore mother into your bed? You and your stupid prick,' Breachnat says through snapping teeth. 'Rechtabhra will demand his bride price repaid.'

'He's the one who walked,' Dubthach grumbles.

'Because you promised him a beauty. And look at her. A cursed girl who is now as ugly as she is stupid. No one will want her.'

Brigid likes the idea of not being wanted. She stares back at the hill with the ancient oak on top that grows smaller and smaller as they ride home. She hadn't truly known the weight of the burden she had carried on the morning's journey till it was lifted from her. She feels as though she might jump off the cart and fly up into the air. She remembers Caer, the swan maiden, who no one could compel to marry, and how the god Aengus had to transform himself into a swan to win her heart. If only she too could become a swan.

Brigid has a great memory for stories. Heard once, she can relay them word for word. When she was a child, when she lived with her mother in Maithgen's house, the greatest bards in Ireland would visit him and she would sit by their feet and drink in their tales as they drank Maithgen's wine. When she came to Dún Ailinne, there were no more bards, for Dubhthach had neither time for their fantasies nor wine to spare.

What story would a bard sing about this morning? Would they tell of Rechtabra's sorrow at having lost his beautiful bride, or of Brigid's joy in being set free?

The black walls of Dún Ailinne appear in the distance. Brigid has been told that Dún Ailinne was once a mighty fort, where the kings of Leinster were crowned. But all she sees is her own prison.

As they ride through the gates of the fort, eyes follow them and whispers soon after.

'What's she doing back?'

'Wasn't she to be wed to Rechtabra?'

'This will mean no good, just you wait and see.'

Rian, one of the stable boys, runs out and takes the reins. Breachnat doesn't even wait for her husband's hand before jumping off the cart, mud splashing beneath her feet, and stomping off into the fort.

Dubhthach follows, muttering. 'No such curse as a wife.'

Rian offers his hand to Brigid and gasps when he sees her swollen face. 'Did your new husband give you that?'

'Oh, this,' Brigid says, placing a hand against her cheek. 'I prayed for this.'

She refuses Rian's hand and slides down into the mud herself. Her feet sink in deep and when she pulls them free, the new slippers are swallowed up by the muck. Maybe when summer comes and the mud is dried, they'll be revealed and someone can have use of them. She makes her way to the kitchens, barefoot.

'And what in all the gods are you doing back here, Biddy?' Ciara, a blonde-haired slave girl and Brigid's only friend, stands in the doorway to the kitchen, fists pressed into her hips, head tilted. 'What did you do?'

'It wasn't my fault,' Brigid replies.

Ciara strokes Brigid's sore cheek with her rough hand. 'It never is.' She wraps her arms around Brigid. Brigid resists returning the hug, for she knows if she lets the girl's kindness touch her the river of tears she has been holding back will burst.

Ciara pulls away and runs her eyes across Brigid's face. 'Well, doesn't look like anything is broken.' Ciara knows a lot about broken bones and bruises.

'It was a snake,' Brigid says. She wants to tell Ciara about how her prayer was answered, but she dares not believe it herself. Goddesses do not go around saving girls from marriage: if they did, would men not tear down the standing stones raised for them, burn the groves? No, it was a coincidence and not one that will happen again.

OH, WE SHALL SEE ABOUT THAT, I say, but she doesn't yet have the ears to hear.

Ciara holds Brigid's chin and moves her face to catch the light, seeing a perfect red circle the size of a silver coin rising up on her cheekbone. 'Your snake wore a ring on its fist, did it?'

Brigid doesn't say anything.

'Sit. I'll get comfrey.'

Brigid sits in the doorway, resting her pounding cheek against the cool stone. From inside the main hall, she can hear the voices of her stepbrothers, talking over each other.

'She's a freak, no wonder Rechtabra didn't want her,' Euhel, the eldest and the loudest says.

'She's always staring into the sky, doing nothing.' This is Trian, the middle boy. His lisp gives him away.

'She gave my best hurley to a leper to use as a staff and you did nothing, father.' Lonan, the second-youngest, and most prone to whining.

'Sure, she gives everything away to any wretch that comes begging.' Fachtna, the second-eldest, who despite being sixteen still has the high voice of a girl.

Ciara returns with a mortar and an unguent that smells of horse piss. With swift, sure fingers, she starts to slather it on to Brigid's face.

'She has to go.' Breachnat's voice. Softer than the others, but its coldness carries further. 'I'll no longer have her in my house. There's something unnatural about her.'

'Not that bloody prophecy again?' Dubhthach scoffs. 'Druid's dreams is all.'

'I will not have her raised above my children.'

Brigid sighs. She has heard of this prophecy before, in snatches of whispers and snide comments. A foretelling by Maithgen, made before she was even born, that the children of Breachnat will one day kneel to her. She agrees with her father that it is nonsense.

'So, if you won't find her a husband,' Breachnat says, her cold words slicing through the wall of the hall like knives, 'then I will.'

Brigid stiffens. A writhing heat rises up from her belly to her throat, as though she has swallowed a mouthful of maggots.

Rechtabra was bad enough, but she can only imagine the kind of man Breachnat will choose for her.

Ciara finishes pressing the poultice into Brigid's wounds. 'There now, the swelling is already going down. By tomorrow, your face will be back to normal. Well, as normal as your face ever gets.'

'Thank you,' Brigid says, kissing her friend's hands. The only hands that have shown her kindness since she was taken from her mother.

The shouting starts up again, and Brigid flinches as something is smashed against a wall.

'The cows need milking,' Ciara says, placing a pail next to Brigid. 'Come on, you can help me.'

Brigid knows full well the cows were milked that morning and no more need milking than a bull. But she knows it's Ciara's way to get her away from the raised voices.

The girls walk hand in hand towards the field where Dubhthach keeps his finest cattle. With each step Brigid puts between her and the cold walls of the fort she feels better. Freer. The girls start to skip, swinging their hands back and forth as though they were still children rather than young women with futures that are not their own. Brigid always wonders at the leather toughness of Ciara's hands. A reminder of the hard work she does in the grey hours while Brigid still sleeps. If it were not for Ciara's hands, cracked and callused, Brigid could believe they were the same class. Brigid's marriage would have raised her up, made her a fully free woman. Why did that not excite her? Why did that repulse her? Ciara had said she would give anything to be free. Anything. But Brigid had prayed for a different kind of freedom and now feels a swirl of guilt within her relief, like a bitter herb mixed with butter. That relief would not last, for another marriage was sure to be arranged.

'Don't worry. Dubhthach won't let Breachnat hand you over to some monster. He loves you,' Ciara says, always seeming to be able to read the thoughts scudding through Brigid's mind.

'He has a peculiar way of showing it then,' Brigid says.

'Men don't know what to do with their love sometimes,' Ciara says, sounding older than her years. Though Brigid has no idea how old the girl is. Neither does Ciara. She was brought to Dún Ailinne when she was only a handful of years old and couldn't speak enough Irish to tell them her age or her name. She bit and fought like a cornered cat and they called her the little black one, though her hair was pale as straw.

Ciara stoops under the fence to get into the field, while Brigid, taller, pulls up the heavy cloth of her wedding tunic and climbs over. The cows moo at their approach, thinking food has come early.

'He'll find someone else to marry you, you'll see.'

Nóinín, Brigid's favourite cow, trundles closer, head bowed in greeting. Brigid rests her forehead against the velvet softness of her forelock. 'Why do I have to marry at all?'

'So you can have beautiful babies and I can help you bring them up,' Ciara says, giving a calf's rear a welcome scratch.

Brigid checks Nóinín's udder. She is surprised to find it full. She places the bucket in position, squats down and brushes dirt from the teats, and then gets to work, a steady squeezing and stretching that sends two jets of milk hissing into the bucket. Nóinín sighs with the relief.

Ciara walks through the herd, checking the other cows. It is only Nóinín who has an udder full for a second milking.

'There has to be another way, Ciara,' Brigid says. 'It can't be marriage or nothing. Couldn't I stay here and help run the fort like Muirenn? She has no husband. No babies.'

Muirenn was a hollow-eyed, grey-haired woman who had once been wet nurse to Dubhthach and later all his sons. When his sons no longer needed her milk, rather than sell her on, Dubhthach appointed her the head of his household.

'Oh, Biddy,' Ciara says, shaking her head. 'How do you think Muirenn had milk to give?'

Brigid already senses she will not like the answer.

'Because they took her babies away,' Ciara continues. 'One for each of Dubhthach's five boys, sold off before they could take a drop from her.'

Brigid stops her milking of Nóinín. She had never thought about how the only way to keep a cow in milk was to keep it calving every year. Or that the same would apply for a woman.

'There must be one woman. *You* are not being forced to marry,' Brigid says, desperately.

'Not marry, no,' Ciara says, and there is a tone sharp as shale that Brigid has not heard in her friend's voice before. 'But that doesn't mean I will be free of men. I am a slave, Biddy. My life is not my own. At least you are half free.'

Brigid's mother had been like Ciara: stolen from her home as a child and traded between men. The last time her mother had been sold for the price of two milch cows, Brigid was still in her belly, so she herself had been born a fuidir – half free. How can one be half free? she thinks, looking up at the sky. Isn't freedom all or nothing?

'And once you're married, you'll be a properly free woman,' Ciara says, her voice brittle as her smile.

If such a thing as a free woman exists, Brigid has not seen one. Every woman she knows is owned one way or another and as far as she can tell, there is little difference between a slave and a wife. She stares into the bucket, her future as clouded as the milk.

'Do you remember we used to talk of escape?' Brigid says. 'Of running away to live in the woods?'

'Or creep into the fairy rings and hope to be carried away?' Ciara laughs. 'Childish dreams.'

'Is that all they were?' Brigid asks, though Ciara doesn't answer.

'Are you done?' the girl asks, wiping her hands on her tunic.

'A few minutes more.'

When Nóinín has no more milk left to give, Brigid stands. The pail is too heavy for her to carry alone, and she and Ciara each place a hand on the handle. There is no skipping on the way back to the fort.

3

Brigid's skin has started to itch where the poultice has got to work. Must healing always hurt?

They pour the milk into the larger pails, ready to churn tomorrow, and walk back to the kitchen. Inside, Muirenn dozes by the fire, snoring gently, her mouth hanging open, revealing teeth like broken posts. A speared pig hangs over the fireplace, its skin cracking and spitting. The old woman always seemed so formidable to Brigid, as cold and unmoving as standing stones. But Brigid looks at her now with kinder eyes. *Where are your babies? Do you even know?*

Pig fat sizzles as it drips into the flames below and Muirenn twitches awake.

'You're not married then?' she says when she sees Brigid.

'Seems not.'

'I've been basting and turning this bloody pig every hour since dawn for your wedding feast. And now what will we do with it?'

'Eat it anyway?' Brigid suggests.

'Here,' Ciara says, stepping forward quickly before Muirenn can add to Brigid's bruises. The old woman has never let Brigid being Dubhthach's daughter stop her hand. 'You go and rest. Let us take over the roasting. It's nearly done anyway.'

Muirenn snorts, pulls herself to standing and hobbles away. 'A waste. What a waste.'

And Brigid doesn't know if she means herself or the pig.

'Get out, you filthy beast!'

Brigid turns at what has caused Ciara's outcry. It's a grey, shaggy dog, back bent, head lowered to the floor with hungry eyes fixed on Brigid.

Ciara picks up a stone from the ground and goes to throw it at the dog.

'Stop it!' Brigid says, grabbing Ciara's wrist. 'Look at the thing, it's starving.'

She can see the ridges of the dog's ribs under its fur, teats enlarged and heavy as though still feeding.

'I don't see how. It got into the sheep field and made off with one of the old ewes, scaring the pregnant gimmers so much that one of them miscarried.'

'It's not her fault.'

Brigid cuts a thick slice off the back of the roasting pig, the skin cracking like flint as her knife digs into the flesh. This might have been Rechtabra's portion. Better it goes to a dog than a beast. She turns the spit handle, so the missing slice is hidden from view, and throws a small scrap to the dog. The dog snatches it, despite the heat, and retreats to eat it.

Brigid throws more, each piece a little closer, till the dog is eating out of her hand.

'You wouldn't let that thing near you if you'd seen the mangled, monstrous lamb, fresh out of its mother's womb.'

'What happened to the gimmer?' Brigid asks, running a hand through the dog's matted fur.

'Survived,' Ciara says. 'They've put her back in with the rams, the blood from her baby not yet dry.'

Brigid shivers at the image.

'That will be you, soon enough.' A light, high voice.

The girls turn to see Beccan, Dubhthach's youngest son. The boy is so pale the blue lines of his veins show through his skin like marble. He has a constant cough, even in the summer months, and sure enough he coughs and spits on to the floor. Ciara curses under her breath – she's just scrubbed the flagstones.

'What do you mean?' Brigid asks, standing. She is taller than Beccan and likes to remind him of this.

'You'll be given over to a husband to mount you whenever he likes, just like the ewe.' He moves into the room. 'Do you know what happens during sex?'

Brigid stays silent.

'A man plunges his manhood inside a woman's belly.' At this, Beccan stabs his finger into a block of butter with surprising violence.

His finger goes in and out of the butter, till Ciara slaps it away.

'That won't happen to Brigid,' she says, though she is too afraid to meet the eyes of her master's son.

'Oh, it will. Mother has *plans*.' He walks closer to Brigid. His breath like rotten eggs on her face. 'She will trade her to a man who will use her up till she's old and worn. That's if she doesn't die in childbirth, the baby of some brute stuck inside her.' Beccan places his hands on Brigid's hips and shakes her. She shoves him away with more force than she intended. He trips and falls on the stone floor.

Brigid does not remember picking the knife back up, but she is holding it now, so tight the tendons in her hands burn. How easy it would be to plunge the blade into Beccan's belly, as she has seen herself do in her darkest dreams.

Ciara's rough fingers brush against her arm. A series of quick lines drawn on her hot skin. *Peace*.

Brigid taught Ciara how to write in ogham, passed on the way of it as it had been taught to her by the druid Maithgen. Within Dún Ailinne, only the two of them know its secrets. It has become their way to talk to each other without being heard.

She allows the knife to be taken from her hand and tries to

still her breath. Beccan smiles and his smile becomes a grin and his grin a laugh. He laughs and laughs and laughs.

Beccan hates her harder than any of her other brothers, with a sharpened cruelty that she does not understand. For didn't she once save his life?

Dubhthach had been visiting Maithgen, along with a pregnant Breachnat who, after the long journey, went into labour. At the same time, Brigid's mother was giving birth alone. And so Brigid and Beccan were birthed on the same day, mere hours apart. But whereas Brigid was born strong and glowing with life, Beccan had been born blue and near to death. Brigid had been brought to him, still slick with the blood from her mother, and laid next to the boy. The healing power of her blood and the warmth of her breath, they said, brought him back from the dead. The son of a noblewoman saved by the daughter of a slave.

'They should have let me die,' Brigid overheard him say once.

Beccan lies on the floor now, staring up at the wooden beams, unmoving. Brigid turns away from the boy and sits again in the doorway, feeding more of the pork to the dog. Between each strip of meat, it rests its head on her thigh, the white of its eyes shining.

'What are you doing on the floor?' Dubhthach has come to find them.

Beccan stutters an excuse. Somehow, him not getting up is her fault. Brigid does not turn around, she does not want to hear what her father has to say.

'Look,' Beccan says, 'Brigid's been feeding the best portion of the roast pig to a mutt.'

Brigid hears her father's footsteps and feels the presence of him behind her. She fixes her eyes on the dog. It has finished the meat. It is begging for more.

'Is that true?' Dubhthach asks. 'Have you been feeding our meat to the dogs?'

Brigid twists her head a little to look at her father and then turns away. If she does not speak, it will not be a lie.

Beccan points in outrage. 'I saw her! She fed it a whole side of the pig!'

Ciara shakes her head in warning. *Don't lie*, the gesture says. For Brigid should know that Dubhthach has a special anger reserved for liars.

'If I find that you are lying to me . . .' he says.

LET ME TAKE CARE OF THIS, SWEET CHILD, I whisper in her mind, YOU HAVE HAD ENOUGH BEATINGS FOR THE DAY.

A sudden certainty floods into Brigid. She is unafraid for the first time she can remember since coming to this place. 'See for yourself,' she replies.

Dubhthach looks to where Brigid has pointed with her chin at the pig, its skin brown and glistening. He spins the handle, around and around. The pig meat is untouched.

Brigid hears Ciara mutter a curse in her old tongue, or perhaps it is a prayer. She doesn't know how she has done this wonder, only that she had wanted the pig whole and it became whole. Just as she had wished for something to stop her wedding. She can feel her hands shake and does not know if it's fear that has sent them quaking or excitement. Perhaps she is not so powerless after all?

Dubhthach stares at his daughter. At the sheen of meat juices on her hands, at the dog licking its lips. 'I warned you once today about lying,' he says. 'Take that off.' He gestures at the heavy, embroidered tunic she had been dressed in for her wedding.

Brigid pulls it over her head and folds it in a neat square before placing it on a rough wooden table. Underneath, she is wearing a plain, yellow léine, no different from the one Ciara is wearing.

'Where are your shoes?' he asks.

'In the mud.'

'Ciara, give her yours.'

Ciara slips off her rough leather shoes and kicks them over to Brigid. 'I've just worn them in,' she mutters.

Brigid pushes her feet into the shoes, her hand still on the head of the dog. It's growling now. 'Where am I going?'

'To Dunlaing,' Dubhthach says. He takes her old blue cloak from a peg on the wall and throws it at her.

'The king?' Brigid asks, blinking the dust from her cloak out of her eyes. 'Why the king?'

She has never so much as laid eyes on the new king, only heard tales of his wisdom and strength. Though they are tales told by the king's own druids, so not to be believed. But perhaps Dubhthach is going to him to seek counsel.

'Because the king has gold. Which I will need when Rechtabra comes demanding his bride price back.'

'Can't you just repay it?'

Dubhthach snorts and looks at her as though she is witless.

'You've already spent it?' Brigid says.

'Of course I've fucking spent it,' Dubhthach spits. 'I had debts to pay and ungrateful daughters who give everything I own away.'

Heat burns in Brigid's stomach. She has never thought of the cost of her charity, only measuring her own little needs against the great pains of others.

'Please, Father, I will work to pay your debt off. I will spin cloth or make butter or brew beer.' She has seen other women do these things and believes she can learn how. 'Please, Father, I don't want to marry any man. Not even if that man is a king.'

Dubhthach snorts again, a great guffaw of laughter. It blows away the heat of her shame like a winter wind across a hearth fire. She tightens her fists, feels the nails dig into her flesh. Of all the cruelties her father and brothers bestow on her, she hates their laughter the most.

'What a fool you are,' Dubhthach says, shaking his head. 'I'm not taking you to the king to be married. I'm taking you to be sold.'

4

A slave. Like her mother. Passed between men and used up. Fear clutches her throat as tight as a hand. What a fool she has been not to consider that becoming a slave might be a path for her. She should never have prayed to be saved from marriage. What she thought had been a blessing was now a curse.

'Sold!' Beccan laughs even louder, as Brigid is dragged away. Ciara cries. The dog barks, snapping at Dubhthach's legs till a swift kick in the ribs sends it whimpering away.

'Please, Father,' Brigid says. She can hardly breathe for the panic. 'By all the gods, please, I will marry Rechtabra. I will marry anyone. Please not a slave.' She yanks herself free and falls to her knees. She prays now to her father, but he will not listen.

Dubhthach grunts and pulls her to her feet. The bones of her wrist crunch under his grip as she is dragged outside and bundled on to the cart.

Brigid calls out to her friend, her only friend. For all the times she stopped Dubhthach beating Ciara by taking his blows herself, for every skirt and shawl she gave over to her, every plate of food she brought her, now is the time for restoration. 'Ciara, help me.'

Ciara chases after her. But what can a slave do to help another slave?

Dubhthach flicks the reins and the horse moves forward. It takes an effort to get the wheels moving in the mud and Dubhthach whips the beast till it finds its strength.

Brigid looks back over her shoulder as they ride out. When she had left that morning to be married, she knew she would be returning for the celebrations afterwards. And after that, she would be expected to return for each of the festivals. She and Ciara had planned how Brigid might even convince her new husband to live in Dún Ailinne, for it was grander and richer than his own fort in Ballaghmore. Now she fears this is the last time she will look upon the walls of the place she has been forced to call home for eight long years.

Ciara raises a hand in farewell, tears streaking her face like finger marks.

Dubhthach follows the path of the river. Recent rains have caused it to swell and the rapids are too dangerous to cross. They will have to go via Áth Figile, meaning their journey will take twice as long. Brigid stares away from her father, refusing to let him see her fear. She presses it down deep inside herself, like a seed pushed into the soil, one she hopes will never take root. *Let it rot inside me. Let it be swallowed up.*

She knows talk won't change her father's mind. But if she's brave enough, there is a chance he might soften. Quiet enough. Obedient enough. If only she had been all of those things earlier, she would now be on her way to Rechtabra's fort, married and with a clear future, one carved out by generations of women before her. Now, she is on her way to Dunlaing and darkness.

Trust me, little one. We are only beginning.

Without knowing why, she feels a small flicker of hope in her heart.

'King Dunlaing's a good man,' Dubhthach says after they have ridden in silence for an hour.

'I'd rather be a wife to a bad man than a slave to a good one.'

She would rather be neither, but that feels like an impossible thought. Slave or wife. It seems there is no third way.

Dubhthach grunts. 'You know so little of the world.'

On this her father is right. She looks around at the landscape as it unfolds itself. The forests of their territories giving over to the stubble of the newly burned cattle fields of Killinane. This is the furthest she has been from Dún Ailinne in eight years.

They pass a field, workers bent-backed, sowing barley seeds. A woman stands to wipe sweat from her forehead, sharp eyes watching Brigid as they pass.

They arrive at last at the ford at Figile. Ahead, a gathering of people wait to cross on the ferry. Her father pulls the cart to a stop behind them. A sad, solemn bell rings out. Voices are raised. The group are wearing tattered cloaks, tunics that are more rag than not, and some have strips of material wrapped around their faces. Brigid sees red marks on the skin of some of the people. Others limp or drag bent feet behind them. Brigid has never seen a more wretched people in her life.

The ferryman is holding them back with the pole he uses to push the boat across, shouting at them to turn back.

'Why won't he let them cross?' Brigid asks.

'Lepers.'

Brigid has heard this word. Said as a curse, a warning. Once, lepers were spotted on the road to Dún Ailinne and Dubhthach and three of his men rode out, their swords and spears ready. The lepers did not come begging that day.

The lepers shout at the ferryman, surging forward, but they are pushed back again. One is knocked into the river; the fast-running water whips him away like a log in rapids.

A child dressed in rags runs after him, wailing. 'Father, hold on. Hold on, I am coming.'

The man in the water vanishes beneath the surface as the river turns a bend.

Brigid clutches at her heart. She can feel it pounding her chest like a punch. 'Do something!' she shouts, looking at her father. 'Help him.'

Dubhthach stares ahead, unmoving.

How had she thought she could change his heart? It is like stone.

The lepers back away and Dubhthach moves the cart forward and on to the ferry.

Cold eyes in scarred faces watch them. Brigid wishes she had something to give them. Anything. But she has only the cloak on her back.

5

Mullaghmast, King Dunlaing's fort, appears before them. The doors are open and a steady flow of people make their way in through the wooden walls. Shepherds droving sheep. Carts loaded with wood and cloth and grain.

A snatch of a song rises above the chatter and thrum of cartwheels. A woman's voice, though deep and strong, singing:

'There was grief on the company of women.
Here in the great plain at their fatal encounter,
For the loss of Maistiu.'

Brigid knows the words from an old poem recited about the fort, told only by women. A sad tale about a beautiful bride named Maistiu and how she was carried away from her beloved husband by an enemy warrior and driven mad by the jealous magics of an evil sorceress. Brigid turns in the cart, trying to find where the voice is coming from. A woman bard moves through the crowd, a harp strung over her back, her hand held out in hope of payment. Brigid has heard of women bards, but she has never seen one before. She has never seen so many people before. And all of them seem to be selling something.

As their cart passes the threshold into Mullaghmast, she is hit first by the noise: shouting, laughter, the bleating of animals, the ringing of hammers on anvils. And then the smell: rotting food, flowing effluence and woven through it all, the rusty tang of the blood of animals put to slaughter. She had imagined Mullaghmast would be a wondrous place, but it is much like other forts she has seen, only bigger.

'"There was grief on the company of women",' Brigid whispers as they reach the gates, repeating the first line of the song.

Her stepmother talked about Mullaghmast with envy and anger. She could, Breachnat had said more than once, have married Dunlaing when he was nothing but a warrior with pretty eyes. The king's sixth son and never destined to rule. She'd chosen Dubhthach, who was already chieftain, raised up by the old king Enna Niadh mac Bressal. But after Mac Bressal was sacrificed, the druids chose Dunlaing to rule.

'What a fool I was,' Breachnat had said many times, while staring at her husband in scorn.

At the heart of the fort is a roundhouse, raised up on a high mound of earth, with walls the height of three men, windows cut into the walls and a wide door at the base. Ragged standing stones circle the fort, so huge they must have been put in place by giants.

Brigid stands to get a better view over the heads of the throng. The wagon shakes as it is driven over a rock and Brigid stumbles. Her father grabs her wrist to stop her from falling.

'Sit down,' he snaps. 'You'll crack your head open.'

She sits, wondering at the contradictions of the man. Worried for his daughter's safety and yet about to sell her into slavery.

'Dubhthach!' A man holding a spear steps out of the crowd and comes to stand before their cart. He has his hair styled in the same way as her father – shaved at the sides with a long mane, matted into a single mass that falls between his shoulder blades. This and his grey-blue cloak mark him as one of the Fothairt tribe, one of Dubhthach's own people.

'Brión,' Dubhthach replies, and Brigid sees the skin around her father's eyes crinkle as he smiles.

'It's been some time,' Brión says, slapping Dubhthach on the shoulder.

'Ten years at least,' Dubhthach replies.

'You've got fat.'

Dubhthach laughs. 'Well, every time I fucked your mother, she gave me a slab of cheese.'

Brigid has never heard words like this from her father's mouth. She expects Brión to pierce his spear through her father's eye. And yet, both men are laughing now.

'Well, she does make very fine cheese,' Brión says. 'Who's this?' he asks, seeing Brigid for the first time.

'My daughter.'

His eyes drag across Brigid, taking in her rough cloak and poorly soled shoes.

'I thought you had only sons.'

Dubhthach doesn't answer.

'Is the king at home?'

'He is. And would you see him?' Brión asks.

'I would.'

'Then you'll have to leave that here,' Brión gestures to Dubhthach's sword with his spear. 'The king will have no weapons in the fort but his own.'

'Since when?'

'Since he became a Christian.'

Dubhthach curses under his breath. What is it about this word 'Christian' that causes him such ire? It is not the first time Brigid has heard it, and at first she thought it another tribe of people. When she asked her father who the Christian tribe were, she was told they were fools from the lands in the south, and that was that.

Dubhthach's hand rests on the ivory hilt of his sword. It

is carved with the head of a dragon with rubies for eyes and emeralds for scales. It is his most prized possession, won in the battle of Áth Dara. He hesitates, looking from the sword to Brigid. With a sigh, he unbuckles his belt and presses both sword and scabbard into Brigid's hands. 'Keep this safe.'

He steps off the cart and without looking back, walks up the mound to the roundhouse, followed by his kinsman.

Brigid runs her hands over the hilt; the ivory is warm, the jewels cool. Stories are told about the blade within. Death-dealer, widow-maker, head-lopper. It's said that if you listen closely, you will hear it sing the names of those it has killed. Brigid slips the sword free of the scabbard only an inch and holds it to her ear. She sees her eyes reflected, but hears nothing. The scabbard alone is worth five cumals. The sword itself four times as much.

An idea pricks at Brigid. If the sword could buy fifty slave women, could it buy the freedom of one fuidir, a half-free woman? Her eyes scan the crowds once more. Everyone is selling something, but that also means people are buying. Would someone buy this sword from her? For silver? Maybe even gold? The sword deals death, but could it also buy a life? It would be so easy for her to lose herself in the tide of people. To vanish for ever with enough gold to buy her freedom. But what would that freedom look like? Her memories of life before Dubhthach are like mist and fade with every year. But she was happy, she thinks, she was loved.

'Can you spare some food, sister?'

The voice snaps her out of the vision. It is a beggar woman, a baby clutched to her chest. Both look starved and wretched. The woman wears a red cloak that would once have been of fine quality, but now is faded and moth-eaten.

'I have no food,' Brigid says. 'I have nothing.'

'Then have my blessing,' the woman says. She moves her hand, touching first her forehead, then her stomach, then her shoulders, and at last places a hand on Brigid's. 'God be with you.'

Brigid has never seen this gesture before. She has seen the druids presiding over the festivals, waving their arms and calling to the wind. But never this gentle, subtle movement. And why would this woman want a god to be with Brigid? Gods are beings to be kept away through sacrifice or ritual. And yet, with the simple blessing, peace washes over Brigid like silk. There is magic in it.

She knows the tales. Goddesses disguised as hags, bringing good fortune to those who show kindness and destruction to those stupid enough to wrong them.

OR POWER TO THOSE WHO INTRIGUE THEM.

'Wait!' Brigid jumps down from the cart and runs after the woman. 'Here, have this.'

She hands over the sword. Her father's most beloved possession. Her own chance at freedom.

The woman stares at the gift she has been given, head shaking.

'Don't accept less than ten gold rings for it.'

Brigid walks back to the cart and waits for her fate.

It is not long before her father returns. 'Come,' he says. 'The king will see you.'

Brigid jumps down, eyes on the ground so that Dubhthach cannot see her tears.

'Where is my sword?'

She lifts her chin and meets Dubhthach's stare, defiant.

'What have you done, girl!'

Her whole life Dubhthach has hurt her, and now she sees that she has hurt him without even meaning to.

He raises a hand across his shoulder, ready to strike. She

doesn't turn away, for a strength has flooded into her she has not known before. She smiles. *This is what justice feels like.*

The strike does not come. Dubhthach grabs her by the arm and pulls her roughly towards the roundhouse.

'I'll let Dunlaing deal with you. You belong to him now.'

6

Dunlaing is not what Brigid had imagined a king would look like. He is older than her father, short, not especially handsome, and a small stain like spilt wine marks the side of his face. Kings, the stories say, must be perfectly beautiful, without flaw or blemish. And yet, here he is, King of Leinster. He has bright, keen eyes, which fix themselves on Brigid. She is not sure if it is permissible to look on the face of a king, but she does not look away.

Dubhthach throws her forward. She stumbles, but manages to stay on her feet.

'Take her,' he says. 'Have her work scrubbing your floors or grinding your corn or give her to your dogs for all I care. All I want is paying.'

The voice of the bard floats through the window. She is singing the goddess Brigid's lament for her son, a song bards love to sing, as it always brings tears to the eyes.

FOR HOW SWEET IS THE PAIN OF A GODDESS TO MORTALS.

Dunlaing beckons Brigid with curved fingers. She takes a step forward, into the path of a sunbeam cutting through a small window, and for a moment she is blinded. The king closes the gap between them, blocking the light, and now it seems as if he is glowing.

He looks at Brigid, his keen eyes taking her in. He reaches out a hand and she flinches.

'I won't hurt you, child.' He squeezes the top of her arm. 'She's skinny.'

His hand moves to her face and he pulls back her lips to

examine her teeth. A fleeting thought passes through her mind of biting the king's finger off. Would Dunlaing still be king with only four fingers?

Hold, little one. This man means you no harm.

'But healthy,' Dunlaing says, stepping back. 'So why sell her? Are you so desperate for money?'

Dubhthach flushes with shame. 'She is the cause of much vexation to my wife.'

Dunlaing raises an eyebrow, which is slashed through by a scar. 'From what I remember of Breachnat, a change in the weather is enough to cause vexation to her.'

Brigid fights back a smile. Breachnat loves to tell how she was adored by Dunlaing and could have married him. She sees now that the story was a lie, like so many things Breachnat says.

'The girl gives everything I own away to wretches who come to the kitchen door. She just gave away my best sword.'

Dunlaing looks again to Brigid.

'Is this true?' he asks.

Dubhthach goes to answer, but the king holds up a hand. 'I asked Brigid.'

Her name on a king's tongue sends a shiver over her skin. 'I give what can be spared to those who need it,' she answers.

'And if you were to join my household, would you give all of my belongings away?' Dunlaing asks.

She looks at the king. She has never seen a léine woven of so many colours, for only a king is permitted to wear cloth of seven colours. It is embroidered with intricate patterns and held by a silver brooch at his shoulder. A sword, its hilt even more extravagant than her father's, sits at his waist, in a scabbard of etched leather. She calculates the worth of what he is wearing. It would be enough to buy one hundred cumals. Gold rings dance across his fingers and a thick golden chain hangs around his neck. From the chain hangs a golden charm: two lines intersecting at their centre.

'I would, my lord. I would feed every beggar who asked for food, clothe every widow unable to provide for herself. I would starve myself before I allowed even a dog to go hungry. For no man should be rich, while even one man is poor.' The words flow out of her as birds flushed from brush. She has no more control over them than she does the beating of her heart.

Dubhthach grunts with such fierceness, Brigid can feel his breath on her skin. The leather of his gloves creaks as he makes fists behind her, ready to box her ears again. But the damage is done. She has spoken and now she must wait.

Dunlaing's expression remains calm, unmoved. Brigid senses the weight of this moment, a pause in the arc of a pendulum, which could swing either way. Two lives forking like a path, each leading to an unknown place. This man is a king and she has spoken to him as though he were an equal; worse, an underling. But she will not lie. She has spent her whole life surrounded by lies and half-truths. Even the stories she loves are another form of lying, ways of making the cruelty of life seem sweeter.

The equilibrium extends in stretching silence. Will the king ever speak?

Finally, he nods. 'Such kindness from one who I suspect has known little kindness herself.' His fingers play with the gold charm at his neck. 'Tell me, do you know what this is?' he asks, holding it up.

She pauses, for the only thing it reminds her of is the rune ailim, and she has never revealed her knowledge of ogham in front of her father. She is caught between the two men.

'Ailim,' she says, making her choice. 'The sixteenth letter.'

Dunlaing takes a step back, staring at her. 'You can read?'

'I can, my lord.'

'And write?'

'I can.'

Her father snorts with derision. 'I am sorry, my lord, for it seems that liar is to be added to her list of failures.'

Dunlaing ignores Dubhthach and walks over to his table. There is a small pile of papers. He picks one up along with a white feather. This he holds out to Brigid. 'Show me.'

She approaches and takes the feather from his hand. The tip has been cut off at an angle and it is stained with black. She does not know what she is supposed to do with it.

Dunlaing pushes over a small pot filled with dark liquid. 'Dip it in and write.'

Brigid has only carved letters into wood bark and earth before. Writing meant to be read and then brushed away. She follows his instruction.

The feather tip scratches on the parchment. Black specks scatter like freckles as she works through the letters. Beith, luis, fearn all the way to iodhadh. The lines are not straight, for her hand is shaking and she has to dip the feather into the liquid three times to complete it. When she is done, she lays the feather down.

Dunlaing lets out a small laugh of wonder. 'And the new alphabet, from Rome, do you know that too?' he asks.

Brigid shakes her head.

'It's only good for Latin anyway,' Dunlaing says, looking down at her writing.

Brigid bites her lips. She has kept so many secrets since she arrived at Dún Ailinne, warned by her mother and by Maithgen to hide her cleverness to keep her safe. But she is beyond safety now.

She has to fight to remember the words, for she has only spoken them in her head for the past eight years.

'*Latine loqui.*'

The words echo against the cold stone walls of Mullaghmast. Dunlaing stares at her, not unlike the way Rechtabra stared at her this morning. As though he were looking upon something unnatural. She does not know if she has cursed herself by speaking.

Dunlaing's open mouth snaps shut. His lips curl up in a smile. 'You speak Latin? Well, well, it seems we have a scholar among us.'

Dubhthach grabs Brigid's shoulder, digging his fingers once again into her flesh, bruises on bruises. 'I don't know what trick you are playing, girl, but tell the truth.'

'I am,' Brigid says. 'Maithgen taught me the Latin he knew from the Romans of his youth in Wales. He taught me to write ogham. I do not lie.'

Dubhthach raises his hand ready to strike her.

'Hold your hand!' Dunlaing roars, and for the first time he sounds like the king he is. 'Or by the gods I will have your head.'

Dubhthach lowers his arm and steps away from Brigid. Dunlaing brushes down the cloths of his robes, steadying his breathing. His fingers find once more the golden cross around his neck.

'By God,' he says quietly to himself, before turning back to Brigid. 'I asked you what this meant. It is the symbol of my faith. Faith in the new Christian God. Those who follow him pledge to live a life of humility. Something I forget all too easily, but which you have reminded me of today.'

He turns now to Dubhthach. 'I would buy your daughter from you. However, to pay her true price would leave me a pauper. But perhaps . . .' He draws his sword.

Brigid has never seen a thing so beautiful. Tiny jewels glitter in the beams of light, the blade's edge patterned like a wave. It is a champion's sword, too beautiful for human hands. The smith who made it must have been a god.

'This belonged to my father. He killed a thousand men and took the throne of Leinster with it. There is no finer blade in my kingdom. Your daughter gave away your sword, Dubhthach. So take this one in payment.'

Dubhthach brushes past Brigid, his hand already outstretched. He stops, hesitant. Is this a test? The king's sword is worth more than a thousand girls. If Dubhthach goes to take it, will the king strike him down for his greed?

Dunlaing flips the sword around and hands it to Dubhthach, hilt first, blade resting on his forearm. 'Take it.'

Dubhthach does not wait to be told twice. He takes the sword and bows, backing away before the king can change his mind. 'She is yours, my lord.'

And that is it. Brigid is a slave.

She feels something inside her crush like an eggshell. Something once precious now destroyed. Could freedom be a sense as essential as sight, one that some can be born without and others have robbed from them in battle or through sickness? For it is as though something has been taken from her, as keenly as though a hot poker has been pushed through her eye.

What will the king do with her now she belongs to him? She tries to force herself to hope. She could become a maid, like Ciara. She is skinny but strong and doesn't tire easily. She pulls her shoulders back, hoping the king will see her strength and decide she is fit to be put to work out in his kitchen or in the fields. If not . . . she looks out of his window at the clouds scudding by. They are high up, as high as a cliff top. The windows are small, but so is she. She could easily squeeze through one and hurl herself out into that sky. Perhaps a cloud would catch her, or she could swing on a sunbeam. Or perhaps she would fall, and crush her skull on one of the standing stones below. And would that be so bad? Perhaps that was the only freedom open to a girl like her.

All of these thoughts stampede through her head in a matter of seconds.

'And now, sweet Brigid of the Fothairt, I have something for you.' Dunlaing reaches out and takes her hand.

She wants to slap it away. To scratch it with her nails. If only she had the skill, she would grab the sword from her father and use it to slice the king's hand off. She has never in her life hurt a living thing, and the anger that burns in her chest feels as though she has swallowed a hot coal. If she does not spit it out, it will sear through her flesh.

HOLD.

'Your freedom,' Dunlaing says.

In the distance, a bell rings, calling a lost sheep back to its flock.

'What?' Dubhthach says.

For once, Brigid is grateful to her father for she too wishes the king would repeat himself.

'I grant Brigid her freedom.' He lets go of her hands, as though he has set a falcon loose.

'You . . . you can't,' her father stutters.

'I bought her from you, Dubhthach, or is your memory so faulty? Lest you forget, I am king. All peoples in Leinster ultimately belong to me, slaves and freemen alike. I could have freed her without paying you at all. Would you rather I take my sword back?'

Dubhthach's hand tightens on the hilt of the sword. There is a gentle scrape of wood from the back of the hall. Brión has been standing guard this whole time, his spear ready. How loyal is he to his kinsman? Would he make it a clean kill?

Dubhthach removes his hand from the sword hilt and bows, so low that the ends of his long hair brush the floor. 'No, my lord. It is as you will it.'

Freedom, Brigid thinks. *Freedom.*

The word strikes like a flint and sets light to her heart. She could burst into flames.

Yes, my little one, let that fire burn.

7

'And what will you do now that you are free?' Dunlaing asks.

This is not a question Brigid has dared to ask herself. Any time she has tried to imagine her future, she has seen only clouds and darkness. But now, there is a patch of clear blue sky.

'You could stay with us here in Mullaghmast. My wife has need of a clever maid and you may be a soothing influence on my wild daughter. As for my son, Aillil, well, he could certainly learn from your selflessness.'

Now she has her freedom, she does not know what to do with it. Could she become a bard like the one singing outside the fort walls and rise to become the king's own poet, and one day wear cloth of six colours, almost as many as the king himself? But no, she has no skills for storytelling. She could run away and live in the woods and feed off fallen fruit and roots. Or become a warrior, for hadn't women been warriors once and gone to war screaming alongside their men? She could go anywhere. Be anyone. All of a sudden, she is dizzy with the vast sea of possibilities.

COME TO ME, YOUR MOTHER GODDESS, FOR I HAVE SECRETS TO SHARE.

She tilts her head as if trying to hear a song caught on the wind. But she is not yet ready to listen. She is not yet ready to receive. A single word appears in her mind. *Mother.*

'I want to go to Faughart to see my mother, Broicsech,' she says.

'You'll do no such thing,' Dubhthach says.

'I was taken from her eight years ago.' Brigid ignores her father and talks only to the king. 'And my heart has ached for her every day.'

'And hers for you, no doubt,' Dunlaing says.

A figure slides into the room from a door hidden in the corner. A man wearing the ankle-length tunic of a cleric, the hems and cuffs skilfully embroidered with intricate patterns. The cleric coughs, and it speaks louder than any words. The king has business and this silly family drama has kept him from it.

'Take the girl to see her mother,' Dunlaing says, with a wave of his hand, dismissing them both. 'And blessings on you, young Brigid.'

Brión appears next to them. He gestures with his empty hand towards the doorway, while his other hand tightens around the staff. They can leave, or they can die.

She and Dubhthach bow and allow Brión to lead them out. They walk through the narrow doorway in silence, shoulders brushing against each other, down the slope of the mound and back into the bustle of the crowd. Dubhthach's face is burning red and Brigid can feel the heat of anger coming off him like the stink of sweat. She should be afraid of him, terrified. But she is giddy and light-headed, as though she has drunk too much mead.

Once outside, Brión and Dubhthach part ways, their hands gripping the other's elbows.

'Your visits are always eventful,' Brión says. 'But maybe leave it another ten years before you return.'

'Gods willing, I'll never look on these cursed walls again.'

Dubhthach pushes aside a hopeful cloth merchant and climbs back on to his cart. Brigid does not move.

'Well, come on then,' he says.

'Will you take me to my mother?'

'I will in your arse. I swore I would never lay eyes on Broicsech again. No, we're returning to Dún Ailinne and once Breachnat finds out what has occurred, the chances are only one of us will see the sun rise tomorrow.'

Brigid stays standing. 'The king told you to take me to my mother.'

'And what, will you run back up and tell on me? You're as foolish as he is, girl,' he shakes his head. 'Don't think any of that was about you. It simply amused him to vex me for we have grudges older than you.'

She does not like to think that she was only a piece in the game between men.

She clenches her jaw, pulls her shoulders back. She is a free woman now and will not cower as a slave. 'If you won't take me, then I will go myself.'

Dubhthach pauses, mouth open, and then begins to laugh. He slaps his thigh and rocks back and forth, hardly able to catch his breath. People around them stop to see what has caused such mirth.

'You?' Dubhthach says at last, wiping tears from his eyes. 'Walk all the way to Faughart?'

'If I have to.'

'It's two days' hard travel north. You won't make it to Baile Átha Cliath before you're taken by slavers or eaten by wolves.'

The cart is in the way and people around are shouting and complaining at Dubhthach to move.

'What do you care what happens to me?' Brigid asks. 'You sold me.'

Dubhthach goes to say something but swallows the words as if forcing down a mouthful of gristle. 'I don't care,' he snaps. And with a whip of the reins, he drives the cart on.

Brigid watches him go, the crowd closing in behind him like a stone sinking into a bog.

What have I done? She has nothing; even the shoes she wears don't belong to her and have already started to pinch. She spins around, trying to find her bearings. *I don't even know which way is north.*

'Excuse me,' she says, stopping a woman carrying a bundle of wheat. 'How would I get to Faughart?'

The woman looks down at the spot between them. 'Well, I wouldn't be starting from here,' she says, before moving on.

The noise around Brigid grows louder, the smells stronger. Her stomach roils, greasy and heavy. She pushes her way through the mass of people, ignoring the hands tugging at her wanting to show her something, sell her something. She heads towards the singing, for that is her only way of knowing the way out of Mullaghmast. She barely makes it through the gates before she is sick, bringing up only foam and bile.

When the heaving has passed, she wipes her mouth with the back of her hand and straightens. A calmness settles on her, like a soft cape.

'Here.' A hand passes her a leather flask.

Brigid looks up to see the bard, her cloak of ribbons and feathers dragging through the dirt. She is younger than Brigid had thought when seeing her from afar. Her face looks no older than Brigid's own, though she is tall as a man and has shoulders as broad too. Eyes as blue and deep as a lake shine above cheekbones so sharp they could have been carved in stone. Her hair is as dark as a crow's wing. Brigid knows that the gods sometimes walk the lands above and thinks this girl must have some of their blood in her. She is not fully of this world.

Brigid pulls out the stopper and drinks. She had been expecting water, but her mouth is filled with the taste of stale bread and burnt hops.

'Ale,' the bard says. 'Not the good stuff, alas, but as I am banished to outside the walls, so I must make do with whatever the traders have left as they leave after market day.'

Brigid hands the flask back. 'Thank you—' She waits for the bard to give her name.

'Darlughdach.'

Daughter of Lugh. Brigid sees a silver charm hanging around the young woman's neck, a spearhead suspended within a circle. A follower of the old god of light? Or something even more?

'Thank you, Darlughdach. I am . . .'

'Uh-uh,' Darlughdach says, holding her finger to Brigid's lips. 'Don't ever give a bard your true name. You never know what stories they might tell about you, what magic they might make with the words of power. Words to heal. Words to protect. And words to wound. No, never give a bard your name.' The bard winks and her angular face breaks into a warm smile.

Brigid smiles back. She likes this bard. 'Why were you banished?'

Darlughdach drains what is left in the flask. 'I wrote a poem about the king's son that was less than flattering. And now, not only am I not allowed to set foot inside the walls, but I have been told that should I ever so much as compose a ditty again, the king will cut out my tongue. So I am lowered to reciting only the words of others.'

Brigid is awed by this woman's boldness. 'Satirizing the king's son is a dangerous act. I am surprised you are still able to talk.'

'I told the king if he could prove one word of my poem a lie, I would cut out my own tongue. He could not, and so.' She sticks her tongue out and blows on it.

Brigid finds herself laughing.

'There,' Darlughdach says. 'That is better. You shouldn't carry so much sadness on you. Even slaves should laugh every day.'

'I'm no slave!' Brigid says.

'You're not?' Darlughdach picks at the rough fabric of Brigid's faded white tunic. 'Your dress says otherwise.'

'The king has freed me.'

Darlughdach steps back, as if looking at a miracle. 'Well, well. Isn't that a thing. And what service did you do him?'

Brigid blinks as she considers this. 'I told him the truth.'

Darlughdach laughs, but it is not the type of laughter Brigid has heard for much of her life. Cruel and sharp. Darlughdach's laugh is sweet as music, and laughter of her own bubbles up in Brigid's belly.

'I tell my truth and the king banishes me, you tell your truth and he frees you. What a slippery thing the truth is. Well, free woman, I wish you well with your freedom. Make fine use of it. If I was only permitted to compose a song about the truth-telling slave, I would ask your name and sing it across the land. But, as I can only sing the words of others, I will send you on your way to . . .'

'To Faughart. Though I do not know the way.' Brigid bites down on her lips to stop their shaking. She will not cry.

'Faughart, I know it well enough, for the old druid who lives there has a hunger for new stories. But it is a long way from here,' Darlughdach says.

'So I have been told.'

Darlughdach looks down at Brigid's feet, chews on the inside of her cheek. 'You'll not make it far in those.'

Brigid looks at the shoes she is wearing. They were not made for her and they already pinch and bite. A cart trundles past them, leaving the fort. An old woman sits hunched in the front seat, holding the reins, driving a weary-looking horse.

'Myrna,' Darlughdach shouts up at her. 'Are you heading out to Baile Átha Cliath?'

'I am at that. And what business is it of yours?' the old woman replies, spitting over her shoulder.

Brigid can see now that her eyes are foggy with age.

'Would you care for some company?' the bard asks, nudging Brigid.

'I've heard all of your tales already, bard.'

'Not me. We have a young free woman here, on her way to Faughart.'

'Faughart,' Myrna repeats. 'I wouldn't be starting here if I were wanting to get to Faughart.'

Brigid closes her eyes. Will someone not just tell her the way?

'Take her as far as Baile Átha Cliath and there's a copper piece in it for you.'

Brigid opens her mouth to protest. She has nothing to trade. But Darlughdach winks.

'Two,' Myrna says.

Darlughdach sucks air through her teeth and then nods. 'All right, then.'

The old woman sucks on toothless gums. 'Payment in advance?'

Darlughdach dips her hand into her pouch and pulls out two copper pieces. 'Half now,' she says, flicking one with her thumb towards the woman. It catches the light as it spins. With a hand as quick as a cat's paw, Myrna snatches it out of the air.

'Half on safe arrival.' Darlughdach pushes the other piece into Brigid's hand.

Brigid looks down at the small round disc. She has never held money before; she was never trusted with it. Even now, her temptation is to throw it away as though it were burning iron. But she forces herself to close her hand around it.

'Thank you. I don't know how to repay you,' Brigid says.

'Fear not. The gods will find a way,' Darlughdach says. 'They always do. Now, get on.'

Darlughdach helps Brigid up on to the back of the cart. There is a solitary goat chewing on straw. It bleats, angrily. Myrna makes a clicking noise and the horse begins to walk.

Darlughdach keeps pace for a while. 'I will send you on your way to the great old hill of Faughart and the great old goat who lives there with a song. Any song you choose.'

'Do you know the "Song of Sinann"?'

'Do I know the "Song of Sinann"?' the bard says, with a shaking of her head. 'What kind of a bard would I be if I did not?'

Darlughdach strums her harp and starts to sing, her voice deep as sleep.

'A poetess there was, with a thirst so fierce,
All the rivers of the land it could not quench.
She hungered for more than her humble life, saying,
"All knowledge of the world shall I possess."'

Brigid watches the bard weave in and out of the flow of people passing through the gates, bowing and winking at both men and women. Some join in the song, for it fills the heart. The ringing sound of metal being dropped in the bard's bowl makes Brigid smile as the cart carries her away.

8

Mullaghmast grows smaller and smaller before being swallowed by the forests. Brigid wonders if she will ever lay eyes on the dark walls again. She arrived thinking her life as she knew it was over, and she leaves not knowing what her life will be going forward.

'So, are you a bard?' Myrna asks.

'Me?' Brigid says, shocked at the idea. 'Oh, no. I have no gift for storytelling. I always want to rush to the end.'

Myrna chuckles. 'When you're older, you'll be less keen to get to the end, believe me. Besides, it's often the journey that is more interesting than the destination.'

Brigid wriggles forward in the cart, so that she is closer to the woman. 'Do you make this journey often then, from Mullaghmast to Baile Átha Cliath?'

'From Mullaghmast to Baile Átha Cliath. Tara to Emain Macha. North, south, east, west. There is not one river in this land I have not crossed nor fort where I haven't sold my wares.'

'What is it you sell?' Brigid asks, looking at the goat.

It watches her warily with its sideways eyes. Looking into the eyes of a goat always makes Brigid feel as though she is looking at the world askew.

'Whatever needs selling,' Myrna says. 'It was sheepskins to Mullaghmast, which I traded at a good profit. I'll use that to buy prawns at Baile Átha Cliath, which I will take on to Cashel to trade for charcoal. Though I might rest there a day or so, as there's an old friend of mine I haven't seen in many a year, and she's always good for a few meals and a warm bed. And then I'll see where the winds take me.'

The woman reaches into her cloak and pulls out a handful of hazelnuts which she throws into her mouth and bites down, cracking the shells with her teeth.

'And you do all of this on your own?' Brigid asks in wonder.

She spits out a shell. 'I have Fionn. And Macha.'

It takes a moment for Brigid to realize the woman is referring to the goat and the horse.

'I mean, do you not have a husband?'

Another shell flies out of her mouth in a neat arc. 'I had me one of them once.' Her old body shivers as though caught in a chill. 'Never again.'

'What happened?'

Myrna looks over her shoulder at Brigid. 'You really want to know?'

Brigid nods. 'I do.'

They ride on for a while, Myrna chewing on the nuts, Brigid waiting for the story to come. She wasn't lying when she said she had no gift for telling stories herself, but she has always had a way of coaxing them out of others.

'My parents arranged for the marriage,' Myrna says at last. 'My people are descended from the Uí Liatháin, big in battle, big in cattle, or we were once. You've heard of us?'

'I have not, I'm sorry,' Brigid says.

'Well, the name is not what it once was. There was a time when we were counted as high as chieftains. Our names are in the roll of high kings.'

'Impressive,' Brigid says, though she does not know what the roll of high kings is.

Myrna waves her hand. 'Anyway. What matters is that my da was a big deal and as his only daughter, I was sought after. You wouldn't think it to look at me now, but I was beautiful back then. Or so they said. When my father let it be known I was available for marriage, men came day and night to the fort to make offers. At last, my parents settled on one man. My parents thought it was a good match. That it would make the family stronger. He was a strong man and at thirteen, I was ready to bear him strong children.'

Brigid gasps. She thought she was young being married off at sixteen. 'You were just a child,' she says.

'Was I? I suppose I didn't know any different.'

Myrna stares out at the road ahead, silent again for a while, and Brigid is worried she has lost the thread of the story in her memories.

'Was he a good husband?'

'What?' Myrna says, blinking and pulling her focus back to Brigid. 'Oh, I suppose. He never beat me with a stick thicker than his thumb and his appetites were no more than a normal man. But I wasn't made to be a wife.'

A strange feeling flutters in Brigid's chest. It is as though this woman is speaking a truth that she had thought belonged only to her. Her whole life, she has been told that being a wife is the highest a woman could hope for.

'What did you do?'

'I waited. He was much older than me, and I knew that time would free me eventually. He died the fourth winter after our marriage, and I have been travelling the land ever since.'

'You're a free woman then?'

Myrna's smile wrinkles her face and her eyes shine like gems. 'In the truest sense.'

Dusk has crept up on them as Myrna was talking and the sky has turned the deep grey of the pebbles of the river that runs through Dún Ailinne. She used to wade through the water with Ciara to try to find the smoothest stones for skimming. Though Brigid often came home with them still in her skirts as she hated to throw them away.

'Take Fionn's blanket,' Myrna says. 'He'll only eat it given half the chance.'

Brigid reaches out for the rough, dirt-covered blanket the goat is sitting on. She tugs it and the goat stamps his foot down, pinning it in place.

'It's all right; I have my cloak.' She knows she has met a match for her own strong will in the goat.

It lets out a satisfied huff and curls up on its blanket, tucking its bony legs under it. Though it keeps its yellow eyes on Brigid.

Myrna ties the reins to the front of the cart, wraps her shawl around her and lies down on the seat.

'Should I drive the cart?' Brigid asks, looking at the winding road ahead leading into the darkness.

Myrna snorts. 'Macha knows the way.'

And it seems that she does not lie, for the horse continues to trundle on, heavy hooves finding solid ground. Even the goat closes its eyes and sleeps. Brigid did not know that goats snored.

Soon, she is lulled by the rocking of the cart and the warmth of her cloak and though she fights it, sleep comes.

Loud shouting snaps Brigid awake. At first, she thinks it is her father, and that she is still at home in Dún Ailinne. But as she takes in her surroundings, the cart, the goat, she remembers where she is and that Dún Ailinne is not her home.

'It never was,' Brigid says.

'You're awake then?' Myrna says. 'We're here.'

'Here' is a small market, bustling with people buying and selling fish. She sees huge, slippery grey salmon and piles of grey prawns, green and grey crabs and lobsters still snapping in their baskets. The sellers shout about the quality of their produce, promising their buyers that they will never have seen fish as fresh as these. Though judging by the stink, Brigid doubts the truth of that. Not only can she smell the fish, she can taste them in the back of her throat and almost feels the slick of oil on her skin.

She shuffles her way to the back of the cart and jumps down. Her legs are stiff and she has to shake life into them. She reaches into the waistband of her skirt where she has kept Darlughdach's copper piece safe.

'Thank you,' she says, handing it over to Myrna.

The woman looks between Brigid and the coin. 'Keep it,' Myrna says, wrapping her hand around Brigid's and pushing it away. 'You were good company.'

'But I didn't tell any stories.'

'Sometimes it is good to hear stories,' Myrna says. 'And sometimes, it is good to tell them.' She pats Brigid on the hand. 'Now, you'll want to be following the Midluachra Way north till you reach the sea at Balbriggan. You'll know it by the black rock pools. From there, it's another day's walk north, following the coast. If anyone tries to bother you, say you're King Dunlaing's slave—'

'But I'm not—!' Brigid tries to protest.

'A simple lie that will keep you safe. From Balbriggan, you may find a boat to take you to Dundalk, if you're lucky. A slaver's ship to carry you off to England if you're not.' Myrna clambers back on to her cart, twitches the reins and leaves Brigid standing alone.

'Move!' a man bellows in Brigid's ear.

Before she has a chance to react, she is shouldered out of the way by a man carrying a tray of black mussels on his head and knocked into a stall of nets and ropes.

'Watch it!' the man behind the stall shouts.

Brigid spins around, trying to untangle herself from the nets, only to get caught in more ropes. The net seller rushes out from behind his stall, grabs her to stop her moving and yanks ropes free.

He pushes her away. 'Clear off before I catch you for real, girl.'

She staggers back and tries to give her apology, but the man has already turned away.

She ducks and weaves her way through the flow of people until she finds a break from the stalls and piles of fish and shouting men, provided by the shade of a rowan tree. Here she stands to get her breath, clambering up on to the feet of the roots, and squatting down against the trunk. She tries to make herself small, unseen, hoping that no more will shout at her. She has been to bigger markets, but never louder ones. Everyone seems in a fierce rush to be somewhere else.

'Oi! You little shit!'

Brigid sees a blur of movement as a child rushes towards the rowan tree. It does not pause when it sees her but scrambles up the tree trunk and vanishes into the branches above. Brigid can make out two wide eyes staring down at her from amid the branches.

The child's pursuer appears, pushing people aside to try and find his prey. It is the man she saw earlier with the tray of mussels. His hair is a thick thatch of black curls and his face blotched with red.

His nostrils flare like a bull's as his eyes meet hers. 'You see a boy come by?'

Brigid can hear an intake of breath from above. 'Have you looked over there?' she says, pointing into the thickest part of the market.

The man stomps off, body swaying back and forth as he pushes through the people, bellowing murder as he does.

She waits, to make sure he is not going to turn back. 'I think you're safe now.'

After a moment, there is a rustling and snapping of twigs. The child shimmies down the tree and sits behind Brigid.

He smiles up at her and she sees he is missing most of his front teeth, with the hint of new teeth pushing through his pink gums. The boy can't be older than seven. He looks as though he hasn't washed or eaten in half as many years. Dark purple circles ring his eyes and his cheekbones shine through his pale skin. And yet, he is still grinning.

'What did you steal?' she asks in a whisper.

The boy holds out a clenched fist. Finger by finger, he opens his hand to reveal a single shining black mussel.

All of that for one mouthful of flesh. If he is even able to get the thing open.

'It's for my sister,' he says, snapping his hand closed again. 'She loves them.'

'Nothing for you?'

The boy shrugs with one shoulder. 'Nah. Maybe tomorrow.'

The boy peers around Brigid, checking the man is well gone, then scampers away.

'Wait,' she says, before he is swallowed up in the crowd. She digs inside the waistband of her skirt and pulls out the piece of copper. She tosses it towards the boy. It spins a slow, glittering arc before being snatched out of the air by the child. He does not even stop to thank her before he is away. And yet, somehow, she feels light. As though she has been carrying a heavy load and has at last put it down.

Brigid looks up to the sky. The sun is already a quarter of the way towards its zenith. She positions herself north and starts to walk.

9

Brigid's feet are bleeding. She has been walking longer than she has ever walked before. The blisters burst a mile back, and now it feels as though the shoes are rubbing against bone. But pain is just a feeling, she tells herself. And feelings can be ignored.

The terrain becomes more undulating, and she has no sooner made it up one hill than she must come down it again, only to find herself at the foot of another, higher hill to climb. The rocks are black and grey and covered with orange lichen that stains her hands as she grabs hold of them to help drag her forward. But after a while, all begins to slope downwards. The grass under her feet becomes like dry straw and the wet black soil turns to a soft yellow sand.

Above, there is a high keening cry she has not heard before. A white bird with curved wings cuts through the skies. She finds energy in her tired feet to follow it and soon she is running, skipping over molehills, pulling free of yellow gorse, chasing the white bird towards the sun. The ground slopes downwards and as she runs, it feels like she is flying too. A root catches her foot and she falls flat on her belly, her face pressed into a bracken bush. When she looks up, she sees how close she came to running off the edge of a cliff, which falls away, straight down to jagged black rocks beaten by waves below. The sea. She cannot remember seeing the sea before, though she must have passed this way on her first journey to Dún Ailinne. It stretches out and out to the curved ends of the world. She had been told the sea was blue and had imagined it a reflection of the sky. But it is grey and green and black in parts, topped by white; frothy, foamy white like cuckoo spit on morning grass. Tiny brown boats dip and bob on the waves like acorns caught in the skirts of an ancient goddess. They will return later with fish or more slaves for the markets.

She counts the crests of the waves. Beyond the ninth, she knows, lies the otherworld, where the old gods live. Only the very bravest ever make it beyond the ninth wave.

There is evidence on the shoreline of life. Ropes and baskets for catching and keeping of fish and shellfish. She scans the cliff looking for a way down and sees a narrow path snaking back and forth to the beach. It is hard to stay upright so instead she slides down on her backside, shuffling forward like a baby not yet able to walk. When the rocks turn to sand, she stands again and runs, rolls and spins her way towards the water's edge.

She kicks off the torturous shoes and sinks her feet into the grey sand. Cold waves dance around her ankles and she shrieks with the joyous thrill of it. Soon her feet are so deep in the grasp of the sand that she has to drag them free or risk toppling over. How long, she wonders, would it take for the earth to swallow her whole? The two dark spaces where her feet once were are quickly filled by another incoming wave, and when it flows back out, there is no sign that Brigid was ever there.

Moving far enough up the beach so that the edges of the waves just tickle at her toes, she sits, breathing in the unfamiliar scents of the sea: it smells of life and death at the same time and like nothing she has ever known. She licks the taste of salt on her lips. Salt is highly prized, given as a gift by guests in thanks for hospitality. And yet here it is, all around her.

A pair of the loud white birds swoop out of the sky and

land behind her. They squawk and flap their wings at each other and Brigid sees the cause of their enmity: a fish the size of a newborn child lying on the sand. Flies circle its white eyes and chunks have already been snatched from its silver belly. The fight ends and one bird takes to the air again, while the other stands over the fish, yellow feet holding it in place as its sharp orange beak tears at the flesh. It *keows* at her, a warning to stay away.

'I don't want your fish,' she says. 'Though I do envy your meal.'

A bell sounds in the distance. Steady, sad. She has heard this bell before. And sure enough, when she turns to see the source of it, there is a line of lepers flowing down the cliff edge towards the shore. She counts six figures, no, seven, for one lags behind the others. They are dressed in tattered grey tunics, their faces covered by cloths, and hands wrapped in stained bandages. Some drag their feet while walking, others stride unburdened.

They have come, it seems, for the rock pools and whatever fish have been left by the retreating of the tide. They squat, hands dipping into the water, snatching shimmering silver fish, red crabs, black mussels and green oysters. Some they crack against the rocks and put to their mouths, sucking the flesh out. Others they throw into a wooden bowl, for later.

Brigid approaches, carefully. Her hunger overcoming her fear. She has not eaten in a full day now, and whatever was in her stomach from the morning lies by the gates of Mullaghmast.

One of the lepers raises their head from their work and watches her. Sharp blue eyes meet hers. The figure, for she cannot tell if it is a man or a woman, nudges the leper next to them, and on, till all are looking at her.

'Can I help?' she asks, pointing to the rock pool.

'I don't know,' the blue-eyed leper, a man, replies. 'Can you?' There is no cruelty in his question. A playful teasing perhaps.

Brigid approaches. She can see them better now: their scarred skin and gnarled limbs. An instinct against ugliness turns her stomach, but she forces that away. Instead, she imagines them as part tree: gall-like lumps across their faces, fingers bent or missing like snapped branches, patterns like moss across their skin. Men becoming nature.

'Here,' a hand reaches out holding half a white shell. A plump scallop sits in the middle, quivering in liquid. Brigid takes the shell and sucks the flesh into her mouth. It tastes briny and sweet.

She smiles at the group. There is laughter and another scallop shell is pushed into her hand.

'There's plenty to go around,' one of the lepers says. 'The great sea god, Manannán mac Lir, provides.'

Brigid has eaten shellfish before, but always cooked in a broth and tasting slightly of dirt.

When she has eaten her fill, she waves away the last morsel offered to her. 'Thank you.'

She wants to pay them for their kindness, though she has no money, no belongings. She looks down and sees the dirty bandages wrapped around their wounded feet.

'Let me wash your feet. Give you fresh bandages.' She slips her cloak off her shoulders. It is long and she can spare enough cloth for them.

The men – they are all men, she sees now – hesitate. Though those with missing fingers seem more interested. One man watches her from the back. He has kept himself away from the group, fishing in his own pools.

'Please, it is the least I can do.'

She gestures towards a smooth stone next to a deep rock

pool. The first leper, the man with the blue eyes, comes and sits.

'I am Caíndelbán.' The name means beauty and Brigid sees that he could once have been handsome.

'Brigid,' she says.

'And where are you from, little Brigid?' Caíndelbán asks.

'Where I'm from is not as important as where I am going. Which is to Faughart.'

The man looks to his left, at the coastal path rising up and up and beyond. 'You've a fair walk to go.'

'So I keep being told. But I'm in no rush,' she says, though this is not the truth. She has to force herself to be patient and finish the job she has promised to these men.

With gentle hands, Brigid unties the cloths covering his feet. She forces herself not to turn away from the sight of his missing toes and the oozing sores, or the stench of rotting flesh. She scoops up the water in her hands and lets it fall over his feet, one foot after the other. The cloth of her cloak itches against her teeth as she bites into it, making the first cut. She tears off two strips and wraps them around the man's feet.

'Good job,' he says, when she has finished.

The next leper takes his place and she gets to work once more.

Brigid's cloak only comes down to her waist by the time she has washed and bound the feet of the sixth leper.

'And you?' she calls out to the last man.

'That's Lommán,' Caíndelbán says. 'He keeps to himself.'

'Lommán,' Brigid says. 'Will you not rest awhile?'

The group all call Lommán forward, teasing and cajoling him. He seems unwilling to be washed as the others have been and is dragged towards Brigid. Hands oozing with sores push him down on to the stone. The man squirms, desperate to be free.

'Don't be afraid. I will be gentle.' She lays a hand on his foot, and at last he is still.

As she has with the others, she begins to unwrap the strips of filthy cloth woven around his feet. There is none of the choking, ulcerous smell coming from this man and when at last Brigid pulls away the last scrap of cloth, it reveals pink, healthy flesh. She holds the foot in her hand. It is small, almost as small as her own, though Lommán is tall enough. Not perhaps as tall as the other men. The ankles are delicate, the calf muscular but slim. Almost the leg belonging to a . . .

Brigid looks up into eyes soft and green as moss, eyes begging for mercy. These are not the eyes of a man.

Brigid moves quickly, throwing the cloth she has been using to wash the men over this woman's feet.

'Have you been with the group long?' Brigid asks, for she has chatted with the other men and wishes all to seem normal.

'Five years,' Lommán replies, her voice a rough whisper.

Brigid meets Lommán's eyes again. The pain of sympathy grips like a fist in her chest. 'So long. You must be so lonely.'

'There are worse places.'

Brigid's hands pause in their work. 'I suppose there must be.' She finishes binding one foot and moves on to the other. 'Will you stay with them?'

'Perhaps,' Lommán says. 'Until my path takes me somewhere else.'

Brigid glances over at the group. They are busy looking for more food, or watching the sea. Caíndelbán and two of the others are striking flint into a pile of driftwood.

'I want you to know, you can trust me,' Brigid says, keeping her voice low. 'Your secret is safe with me.'

Lommán hesitates, lips opening to speak and shutting again. 'Thank you,' she says at last.

'There,' Brigid says loudly. 'I am done.'

Lommán stands and returns to her position at the back of the group. Even now, knowing the truth, Brigid sees only another man, cursed by illness, hiding from cruel eyes. There are so many things she does not understand about this world. What could push a woman to this life is only one. She thought she had known cruelty, but senses with dread that she has only touched the surface of the depths of brutality that is possible.

She bends, her back stiff from the long sitting, and washes her hands in the briny water. The sun is no longer beating on her back. She has been with the lepers for longer than she realized.

'I have to go now. I wish you all well.'

'You won't be going anywhere for a while, little one,' Caíndelbán says. He points behind her.

The tide has come in, almost to the foot of the cliff. Her path back is cut off. A dull panic creeps up her: she is trapped. She will not reach Faughart this night. In their plans of escape, she and Ciara had imagined sleeping under the stars. But the skies overhead are cloud-covered and rain-heavy.

'Come, sit,' Caíndelbán says. 'Now is the time for stories.'

The squirming creature that had been bristling in her belly quietens a little. 'Stories?' she asks, her eyes glistening like the pools around them.

'Ah-ha,' Caíndelbán chuckles. 'We have found young Brigid's weakness, it seems. We have many fine storytellers here, but none finer than our Tadhg. Isn't that so?'

Tadhg is one of the oldest men in the group, with skin like tanned leather, grey hair and cloudy eyes. 'It has been said, it has been said,' he replies, bowing down as though he were greeting a king.

'And what tale will have us transported from our woes tonight?' Caíndelbán clambers up a black boulder and takes a seat under an arch formed out of the cliff face by waves of old. Framed by the jagged flint, he looks like a king on his throne.

Brigid finds a smooth rock to sit on below him, her feet pulled in tight to her body, her arms wrapped around her legs for warmth. Their small fire gives off a little heat and the woodsmoke wraps around her like a blanket.

'Well, now, what tale, what tale? What tale for a misty evening such as this?' Tadhg considers Brigid. And I consider Tadhg. A gentle breeze blows off the land, tickling the hairs around what remains of his ears as I whisper my name.

'Ah!' Inspiration strikes. 'Have you heard the one about your namesake, the goddess Brigid, and how her cloak revealed the world?'

Brigid has heard it, many times, but says she has not, for she wishes to hear this man tell it. She sits, chin resting on her fists, as the man weaves a world with his words.

'Brigid was one of the Tuatha Dé Danann, the tribe of gods who once walked this land. Daughter of the great god, the Dagda, and never a more beautiful being has stepped foot on the green grass of Ireland.'

I listen too, and remember when I was young and this land I love was just a dream.

'She was filled with joy and light,' Tadhg continues. 'Just to look on her was to feel sunshine warm your bones. Her laugh alone was enough to spark a fire. That was, till the day her son died.'

10

The sky has turned grey by the time Tadhg finishes my tale. The tide has released them: the black sands are revealed once more. Brigid stands to leave and as she makes her goodbyes, the lepers press more shellfish, wrapped in flattened leaves of seaweed, into her hands.

'Thank you,' Brigid says, and looking to Lommán adds, 'And be safe.'

Brigid thanks them all, and scrambles back up the bank and on to the path heading north. She knows she is almost home now. Can almost taste the change in the air, as the fertile grazing lands give over to rocky soil. She believes she recognizes the landscape, though she knows this must be a trick of the mind for when she made her journey south to Dún Ailinne, it was by cart and she slept most of the way, her young body exhausted by the crying. But she knows that each step she takes brings her closer to home.

Night comes quickly and the chill creeps into her bones. The moon is close to full and she can see by the grey-blue light, so she keeps walking, a sleeping, trance walk, one foot in front of the other, in front of the other, in front of the other. She trips, falls, but pulls herself to standing again. The nourishment of the shellfish has only lasted so long and hunger returns, biting, sapping what little strength the cold hasn't already taken from her. She has only a handful of food left, but she will need that for the day ahead.

SLEEP, I say, my voice the murmur of wind in the trees.

She shakes her head. 'I have to keep going. I can't stop.'

Sleep.

An oak tree, like the one she knelt before on the morning of her wedding, shines in the moonlight. Small, fresh leaves quiver in the cold breeze. She wants to keep going, but her body is not as strong as her mind.

Here, child, I say, I am here.

Roots like clasped arms twist around each other and between them, a space just big enough to fit her. She squeezes herself inside and finds a bed of soft leaves and fur tufts. The tang of musk burns her nose. An animal once made their home in this place. But for tonight, it is her bed. She closes her eyes and sleeps in my arms more safely, more soundly than she has ever known.

Barely an hour has passed when she awakes to a low grunting and opens her eyes to see a sharp black snout, nostrils twitching, eyes like molten gold. A wolf. A young one judging by its size. It stands frozen, head low, eyes fixed on her.

'Don't be afraid,' she says, pressing her back against the inner bark of the tree. Whether she is talking to the wolf or herself, she cannot be certain.

It replies with a low growl from deep in its belly.

Brigid has never met a beast that she cannot bring to love her. Humans, she finds, are harder. She reaches for the small bundle of food tucked in beside her, trying to keep her movements slow. Fingers find a lump of flesh. Scales catch at her skin.

She tosses the fish away from the tree. The throw is weak, but the fish lands far enough away. The wolf's head whips around. It follows its nose, snuffling towards the fish, and buries its soft snout in the silver skin. Teeth sharp as daggers tear at the flesh. Brigid throws the rest of what is in her bundle – she can worry about hunger later – and slides out of the hole, almost as slippery as a fish herself, and begins to crawl away on her belly.

Before she is even a yard away from the tree, she knows from the prickling of the hair on the back of her neck that she has not made it. Paws crunch on leaves. The beast is behind her. If she moves too quickly, it will attack and make of her what it did of the fish.

She can feel her heart thudding against her chest as fear takes hold. She can smell the decay of the leaves beneath her, hear the breathing of the wolf, taste the bile rising in her throat. Every other fear she has experienced crept up on her like damp. This has struck like lightning. She forces herself to roll over and face the wolf. Bright yellow eyes meet hers and she sees in them a sharp intelligence. It is only doing what is in its nature, she tells herself, trying to quieten her racing mind; she must feel no anger towards the creature. It twitches its nostrils, lowers its head and takes one step closer. She remembers the wild dog back at Dún Ailinne, of how it rested in her lap. Of the piglets she had hand-reared, who would follow her around snuffling and nipping at her heels. This wolf looks beyond starved and has not learned how to rely on the scraps of humans for its survival. She also thinks of the roasted piglet, slaughtered and ready for the feast. Now she has become the feast.

The wolf charges. Brigid closes her eyes and bites back a scream, for what good will that do her here in the darkness.

There is a heavy thud, and a yelping. Brigid dares open her eyes to see a figure dressed in grey rags standing in front of her, a heavy branch in their hands.

The wolf cowers from the branch, which the person swings back and forth like a scythe. Each swing pushes the beast further back. In one last attempt to assert itself, the wolf howls. The person howls in return, a wild, screeching wail as of a mad person. Beast versus beast. The wolf yelps and runs out into the darkness.

'You didn't need to hurt it,' Brigid says, clambering to her feet. 'It was only hungry.'

'I didn't take you for a fool. It could have killed you.'

'Lommán?' Brigid says, recognizing the soft voice. 'You followed me?'

The woman pulls her wrapping from her face. It is a square face, strong, handsome. Brigid can see how she has got away with her pretence for so long.

'I only meant to follow you a little while. I didn't think the roads were safe for a woman alone, and I was right. You're only lucky it was a wolf that found you and not a man.'

'Are you not a woman?' Brigid asks, brushing sticks and moss from her clothes and hair. 'Is the road not as dangerous for you as for me?'

'I have not been a woman for some time. You are the first person in five years who has . . . seen me.' She hesitates, then coughs. 'I . . . wanted to thank you for not revealing me.'

Brigid waves Lommán's words away. 'It was nothing. Sure, for all I know, you could be a goddess in disguise.'

Lommán laughs, a snuffling snorting laugh, not unlike the sound of the wolf. 'Me, a goddess. That's a good one. I'll be off to the land of youth and beauty then.' She walks on the spot, arms swinging as though she were marching away. 'A goddess.' She laughs again.

'Stranger things have happened.' Brigid takes a seat on a tree trunk. As the fear drains away, a dizziness takes its place. She fears she might be sick again, but swallows the bile down.

Lommán sits in a tight crouch opposite. She looks ready to spring away at any point. 'To you?'

'Well, not to me. But in stories.'

'Ah, stories,' Lommán says. She rocks forward on to her knees and begins to lay sticks and twigs and leaves from the ground in a careful pile. Her hand dips into a leather pouch tied to a girdle around her waist and from it she pulls a steel and a wad of wool. With her other hand, she draws a dagger from her belt. It shimmers a dark grey in the moonlight. A flick of her wrist, blade against steel, and sparks catch the wool. Lommán carries the flame in her hand and places it within the pile of wood she has made. She lies, head close to the smoking tinder, and blows gently. The fire blooms to life.

Brigid watches all of this in fascination. Fires burned in almost every room in Dún Ailinne, and yet she herself had never started one. Tending to fire was the job of slaves.

Satisfied with her work, Lommán returns to her ready crouch and tucks the kit back into her girdle pouch.

'I could do with one of them,' Brigid says.

'A flint?'

'Well, yes, but no, I meant your pouch. I have no means of carrying anything.'

Lommán looks down at her belt, fingers hovering over the clasp. 'It was my mother's.'

'And I will ask my mother to make me one,' Brigid says quickly, suddenly afraid that Lommán was about to gift her this precious thing. She has already taken too much from her and the other lepers and feels the weight of their charity like a yoke.

'Is that where you are off to, your mother?'

Brigid nods. 'I haven't seen her in eight years.'

'She will be happy to see you.'

Brigid hasn't even thought about this. Whether her mother, after these long years, will be glad to have her daughter returned to her. 'I hope so.'

Lommán pulls out another bundle from within the depths of her robes and slowly unwraps a small stack of oatcakes. She passes one to Brigid, who takes it with both hands. She holds it for a while, not wishing to eat it. She is so used to being the one who gives and has never thought of the cost of being the one who receives. She bites into the oatcake. It is dry and coats her teeth, but she forces it down anyway.

'Will the others not miss you?' Brigid asks.

'I come and go as I please.'

Silence. An owl hoots in the tree overhead. Brigid inches nearer to the fire and stretches her hands towards it, as though she could draw the heat into her bones through her skin. She pulls off the shoes that have tormented her so, wincing at the pain. But it feels good to be free of them.

'You're not going to ask then?' Lommán says.

'Would you like me to ask?' Brigid says, rubbing her hands together for warmth.

'I think I would like to tell someone.'

Brigid drops her hands to her lap. 'Tell me, Lommán, why are you disguised as a leper living among men?'

Lommán opens her mouth, but her hand rushes to her lips, as though trying to hold the words in. She must have carried this secret for so long.

'I never knew my father,' Lommán starts, forcing her lips to move. 'For he died before I was born. My mother died a few years after. I was raised by the tribe, a little wild, I suppose. But the blacksmith took a special interest in me.' She pauses, scratches in the dirt with the tip of her knife. 'He was a giant of a man, just one of his fingers was as thick as my arm. I adored him and would spend every hour I wasn't at chores in the forge. I wanted to do what he did.'

'Be a smith?'

Lommán nods. 'But he told me girls were not allowed to know the secrets of smiths.' She pauses, hand rubbing against her chin. 'I begged him, promised I wouldn't tell anyone. He refused. But told me he had other secrets he could share. If I was a good girl.' The last word catches in Lommán's throat.

She spits into the fire, her phlegm causing it to hiss. And now, the words come flowing out of her, as though a dam had been let loose.

Brigid listens to Lommán's story, though it is not a story in the way Brigid thinks of them. Lommán does not try to thrill or excite, or even pull tears from Brigid's eyes. It is simply the truth.

'I was twelve the first time he came to my bed at night,' Lommán says, voice as cold and hard as quenched iron. 'Afterwards, he told me it was my fault, that I had seduced him. And that if I told anyone, they wouldn't believe me anyway.'

Brigid swallows the taste of sick that has risen in her mouth again.

'For two years, he would come with sweet words at night, and beat me in the morning. I had nowhere to go. But I knew that if I stayed, I would die. So, one night, I poured him more ale than usual, piled his plate high with food and waited till he fell asleep. I took the hammer I had been forbidden to touch and hit his skull over and over and over as though I was striking nails.' She slams her fist into her empty palm, then looks down at her shaking hands. 'The leper group had passed by our fort, ringing their bell and asking for food. No one even looked at them. I so desperately wished never to be looked at again. So I wrapped myself in rags and caught up with them.'

Many of the stories Brigid knows end in death. Beautiful women dashing themselves against rocks or being lost under the waves. She has heard fewer stories about women fighting back, of surviving, and for some reason she cannot explain, it feels dangerous. Seditious. If more women heard this story, how many men's heads would be smashed open?

'You can stop running,' Brigid says after a while. 'You can come with me to Faughart. My mother, Broicsech, would care for you. My stepfather . . .' She pauses. She wants to say he would not hurt her, but she cannot be sure what he would do. 'He is a great druid,' she says instead.

'Well, you see, I've become quite accustomed to life as a leper. And as a man for that matter,' Lommán says. 'There is freedom in it.'

'Then come as a man and a leper. I will keep your secret.'

Lommán smiles. 'I'll think on it.'

The smoke from the fire stings Brigid's eyes and upon closing them, she struggles to open them again.

'You should sleep,' Lommán says. 'You need your strength for the last part of your journey. You're nearly home.'

Brigid lowers her head to the soft ground and as the warmth of the flickering flames dies away, she falls into sleep.

She awakes again, but this time to dawn. The sky is on fire with colours, some she does not even know the name of. Birds call out, their voices sweeter than any harp. Brigid wonders if they are sharing the news of the night past or predicting the day to come.

Lommán has gone. The spot where she sat overnight is empty, and if it were not for the broken branch resting nearby and the taste of oats still in her mouth, it could all have been a dream.

'You're nearly home.'

Brigid stretches her stiff limbs, considers the shoes by her feet, and instead decides to walk the rest of the way barefoot.

11

She sees it at last: the hill of Faughart. And although it has been eight years since she set eyes on it, she knows it as an old friend. A turf-covered mound of earth rising up like the swell of a woman's body. On top, the fort; home of the druid Maithgen, shelter of her mother, place of her own birth.

Her legs find new strength as she starts the climb upward, taking a narrow pathway that spirals around the hill. She does not feel the pain any more and as the land falls away beneath her, she starts to run. Only a few steps more. The very last drops of her strength are spent and she falls to her hands and knees and crawls the last few paces to the top. She rolls over on to the grass and laughs, breathless and giddy, as though this has all been a game and it has ended: chase or hide-and-go-seek. She closes her eyes and feels the morning sun beat on her face, warm and gentle.

She sees through the velum thinness of her eyelids a shadow passing.

'What took you so long?'

She opens her eyes to see a man leaning over her. He holds a wooden staff with gnarled fingers and a tunic that was once of many colours but they have now all faded into each other. He has long grey hair that has been shaved at the sides and a beard that has been woven into plaits and bound with rings of gold and silver. He is so much older than she remembers and she has to squint to see the face of the man she once knew behind the wrinkles. He smiles and she knows it is him. Maithgen.

He reaches out a hand and pulls Brigid to her feet. 'I expected you yesterday.' His grip is as strong as she remembered. His scent too. He smells of mushrooms and musk and woodsmoke. She remembers how she would sit on the floor by his side while he told her the old stories. When she stands, she sees that he is the same height as her. How can that be possible? The man she remembers was a giant. For much of her life, she believed he was her father, for he would lie with her mother at night and she knew that was how children were made. The day she learned her father was another man, a man who had sold Broicsech to Maithgen, was the day she learned what a slave was. And the day she felt anger for the first time: for Dubhthach, the father she didn't know, and for Maithgen, the father she no longer had. For the death of innocence and the pain of knowledge. She had buried that anger deep inside her, for what good was it?

'How did you know I was coming?' she asks Maithgen.

He taps the space between his eyebrows on his forehead. 'I see everything.'

'Ignore him,' a woman says. 'We saw you approach from the tower an hour ago.' Brigid does not know this woman. She is small, small as a child, with overly large hands and feet. Her skin is wrinkled as bark but her eyes shine as bright and curious as gems.

'Shush, woman,' Maithgen says. 'How am I supposed to shroud myself in an air of mystery with you giving all my secrets away?'

The woman snorts. 'You have plenty of secrets left over, some might say too many secrets.'

'But did I not say that Brigid would be returning to us? Did I not say it!'

'You did indeed. At least once a month, for the last eight years. You were right about one thing though; she is radiant.

Or at least will be when she's washed and fed. I am Tlachtga,' the woman says. 'Come into the fort. We will have the girls heat water for you.'

Brigid looks down at her muddy bare feet and the dirt around her ankles. 'A bath would be most welcome. But I would see my mother first.'

'She is in the dairy,' Tlachtga says. 'We did not tell her you were coming.'

The dairy is a new building made of heavy grey stone with a sloping slate roof. It smells of sour milk and fresh hay.

If Brigid thought that Maithgen looked older than her memory, it is nothing compared to the sight of her mother. The Broicsech she remembers had soft hair the colour of ripe barley and skin like golden honey. This woman's hair is brown as mouse fur and her skin is dull as day-old porridge. And yet it is her mother; she knows her movements, knows her voice. She is singing as she churns the butter, back to the door. Brigid watches Broicsech at work, unaware that her daughter has returned.

'Mother?' she says at last.

Broicsech's back straightens. She stops the work of the wooden dash she had been using to churn. Slowly, she turns, eyes closed as though unwilling to see what is waiting for her. Her eyes open and they are shining with love. The fear that had been growing in Brigid's chest that her mother would not know her, or would not be happy to see her, evaporates as quickly as morning mist.

She runs into her mother's arms, tears already flowing.

'My Brigid. My Brigid. My Brigid.' Broicsech smothers her in kisses, her forehead, her face, her lips. She cups Brigid's face in her hands. They are rough as pumice stone and warm as sunshine. 'You have returned to me.'

Brigid lets the tears flow at last. 'I have.'

'But how? Dubhthach sent word that you were to be married. He told me he had made you a good match.' She runs her hands over Brigid's tunic, over her torn cloak. 'And why is the daughter of a chief dressed like a slave?'

'I'm not a slave. Not a wife either,' Brigid says. 'I am a free woman.'

Her mother shakes her head, her brows drawn together in confusion, and Brigid takes in the new map of her mother's face: the unfamiliar lines and pathways.

'Did Dubhthach free you at last?' Broicsech asks. 'Has he come with you?' She looks over Brigid's shoulder, eyes wide and shining with hope.

A ball of heat swells in Brigid's chest, as though she has gulped broth before letting it cool. 'No, he is not with me!' she says, fingers curling into tight fists. 'I had to walk the many miles alone.' She is surprised at the bitterness in her own voice. She did not believe that she had the capacity for hate, but whatever this feeling is towards her father, it is close to it.

Broicsech's eyes find Brigid's again and perhaps it is a cloud passing over the sun, but Brigid imagines that they have dulled a little.

'Oh, my sweet child. Come, sit, you must be worn out.'

Brigid and her mother sit in the doorway of the dairy, hand in hand. Chickens peck at the ground, not knowing the difference between corn and pebbles. A sow waddles through a patch of mud, her piglet following after, its mouth opening and closing and reaching for her teats but as soon as it is close to latching on, the sow waddles forward, leaving the piglet snapping at air.

'Do you remember Faughart at all?' Broicsech asks.

'Some. I remember the smell.'

Broicsech laughs and Brigid is suddenly a young child again, helping her mother with her chores.

'You were always a sensitive child. When you were a baby, you refused to drink any milk. Whether from my breast or a cow's udder, you refused it all. We thought you were going to die. But one day, a red-eared cow wandered on to the land, and I milked it and you drank and drank. Only from that one cow.'

Brigid has not heard this story about herself. Though she knows that red-eared cows come from the other world.

'God sent us that cow,' Broicsech says, and surely she must mean the gods. She moves her hands across her body as Brigid had seen the beggar at Mullaghmast do. Touching her head, stomach and shoulders.

'What is that?'

'The sign of the cross,' Broicsech says. 'I am a Christian now. A man called Patrick came and showed me the way.'

Broicsech reaches her hand inside her tunic and pulls out a strip of leather, to which is attached a charm: two twigs tied together at their centre. Brigid holds the charm in her hand, rubs her thumb against the rough wood. King Dunlaing wore a similar charm, though his is made from gold.

'What does it mean?' she asks.

'It's a way for us to remember Christ. He was nailed to a cross like this one, through his hands and feet.' Her mother slips the necklace back under her clothes.

'Nailed?' Brigid says, a shudder passing through her body at the thought of the violence. She used to watch the blacksmith at Dún Ailinne as he drove an iron nail into a block of oak with one strike of his hammer. How could someone do that to another living thing? 'Why? What did he do?'

'Nothing. He sacrificed himself for us.'

Brigid is familiar with sacrifice. Dubhthach had taken her and his sons to watch as Mac Bressal, the old King of Leinster, was led into a bog by the druids, wearing only a léine, his hands tied. One of the druids had raised a club above his head and she'd turned away so as not to see the blow. But she had heard it. A heavy, wet sound that sometimes haunted her dreams. The harvest that summer had been the best in a generation.

'And was the harvest good, after your Christ was sacrificed?'

'It's not like the old ways,' Broicsech says, looking up to the sky. 'That was all superstition and stories. Christ is a new god. He sacrificed himself so that we all might have salvation.'

Her mother speaks these words in a rush, her voice high-pitched and giddy, though Brigid suspects Broicsech does not truly understand them, like a bard reciting snippets of a poem they only half-remember.

'Salvation from what?' Brigid asks. *Are they under threat? Is this Christ a warrior God who will protect them in battle as Lugh once protected his people?*

Her mother looks to her, a strange, serene smile dancing across her lips. 'Salvation from sin.'

Brigid does not know this word. 'What is sin?'

Broicsech looks down at her hands, which are twisted in the cloth of her skirt. 'Sin is . . . shame.'

'What do you have to be ashamed of?' Brigid asks.

'I have given my body to men,' Broicsech says. The cloth twists tighter.

Brigid leans away, looking at her mother. And suddenly she sees her, in the darkness, a man lying over her, pressing her screams back into her mouth with his hand. Images which she thought were only dreams, she now realizes were memories.

'Given?' Brigid says, the heat rising in her chest once more. 'Or was it taken?'

'It makes no difference now,' Broicsech says, shaking her hands free. 'For Patrick has freed me of my sin. He was a slave too, once. Taken from England by raiders and brought here as a young boy, just like me. He escaped and he could have lived a life of luxury, but he came back to Ireland.'

'Why?'

'To save us all! To free us all!' She lays a hand on her daughter's arm and pinches it tightly. There will be bruises there later, for in her fervour, her mother does not know her own strength.

'You are free?' Brigid asks.

She is confused by everything her mother is saying. The rush of words sound more like a story told by a child; half-remembered and garbled. But there is a fire in her mother's eyes that both delights and scares her. Brigid has seen that same fire in the eyes of druids after chewing on the raw flesh of a pig to bring on Imbas – the fire of inspiration.

'I am still a slave in this life,' Broicsech says, placing her hand on her chest. 'But in my heart, I am free.'

'That is not enough,' Brigid says, taking her mother's hand. 'You should be free in body, heart and soul.'

'One day, my child.' Broicsech slips free of Brigid's grasp and pats her daughter's hand. 'If God wills it.'

Brigid looks down at her empty hands, feels her jaw tighten. Her mother should not wait for some god to give her freedom, she should take it, fight for it.

'It's a fine day,' Broicsech says, turning her face to the sky, her eyes closed.

It is true. It is unusually mild and the rain has held off, though grey cloud hangs on the horizon like a promise. It will rain, the wind will blow, and after there will be sun again. And on and on. Brigid copies her mother and closes her eyes. She has heard tell of places where the weather changes with the seasons, each day the same for a quarter of a year, rather than changing from one hour to the next. Would she love the warmth of the sun as much if she knew it would not be snatched away by a hungry cloud within moments? Would she resent the rain if it fell all day long, rather than in bursts?

Feet crunch on stones and Brigid opens her eyes to see Maithgen, beaming at her.

'Didn't I tell you she would return, Broicsech?' he says. 'What a waste of all your tears when she was sent away, hey? All those silly prayers to your new god. He must have been bored listening to you! And wasn't I right?'

Broicsech looks down, not wanting to contradict her master. Anger flares in Brigid's chest. She too had cried herself to sleep night after night when she had been taken from her mother. She too had been told she was being silly and had had the tears beaten out of her.

'We were apart for eight years,' Brigid says. 'Eight painful years without my mother and she without me. That is worth a few tears.'

Maithgen waggles his head. 'Perhaps. Perhaps. But no more time to waste now, hey, Broicsech? That milk isn't going to churn itself and we have guests coming tonight. I've told them about you, about my prophecy that you would be a woman of power. And wasn't I right? Wasn't I right?' He leaves without waiting for a response.

Broicsech takes hold of the door frame and pulls against it, as she attempts to lever herself to her feet. Brigid sees how her knuckles are red and swollen, how slow she is to stand up.

She rests her hand on her mother's shoulder and guides her back to sitting. 'You rest. I can churn the milk.'

'But you've been walking all day.'

'I'm not tired.'

Her mother accepts her kindness and rests her head against the door frame. 'Then you must tell me everything.'

'There is little to tell,' Brigid says, dipping the dash into milk. 'Dubhthach sold me first as a bride to a brute and second as a slave to a king.'

'I am sure your father only wanted the best for you,' Broicsech says, her words muffled by a yawn.

Brigid's hands tighten on the dash, twisting against the rough wood. 'You think well of a man who never showed you any kindness.'

'Oh, Dubhthach could be kind. In his own way.'

Brigid resists a sudden urge to spit into the milk and continues to stir it in silence. It has only started to thicken and it will be two hours' work before the butter forms. She gazes into the churn. Images form in the blue-touched liquid. She sees a man nailed to a cross, blood pouring from his head. As the image clears, his face becomes that of her father and for a moment, she is glad to see his pain.

'Is the butter ready? Our guests are nearly here.' It is Tlachtga.

The clouds have darkened, the sun sailed further west across the sky. Brigid has been stood over the churn for an hour at least. Brigid blinks and stares down. The churn is still filled with milk, for in her daydreams, she forgot to stir. Tlachtga leans over her shoulder and looks down.

'What have you been doing? Broicsech, wake up! Curse you, woman, have you slept all morning? Why did you leave this job for your daughter? Oh, useless woman. Maithgen!' she bellows. 'Broicsech has slept all morning and there is no butter for our guests.'

Maithgen comes running. Brigid puts the lid on the churn and tries to hide the evidence from the old druid.

'What's this about no butter?'

Broicsech is panicked, her cheeks flushed red as she mutters an apology. 'I am sorry, master.'

A stab of shame twists in Brigid's stomach, for she is the

one to blame. She took on this responsibility and failed. And yet, there is anger there too. Anger that they can talk to her mother in this way, while they speak only soft words to Brigid. Anger at the way her mother says 'master', in the same tone of adoration that she said 'God'.

Brigid twists the dash in her fingers as she might twist the neck of a rooster for the pot.

YES, LITTLE ONE. USE THAT ANGER.

When the dash moves in the churn, there is resistance, the telltale drag that the butter is ready.

'There is more than enough butter for your guests. There would be enough butter for fifty guests,' Brigid says, stepping away from the churn.

'Oh, come now!' Tlachtga says. She lifts the lid off the churn and gestures towards it with an empty palm. 'See, there's nothing but—'

The churn is filled with smooth, thick butter. Maithgen stands beside his wife and dips a finger into it.

'Perfection!' Maithgen says, sucking his finger clean. 'The best butter we have ever had.'

'But how . . .' Tlachtga staggers. 'A moment ago, it was milk. What trickery is this?'

'Not a trick,' Maithgen says, eyeing Brigid with a strange mix of pride and greed that makes gooseflesh ripple down Brigid's arms. 'Magic. Didn't I tell you she would be a woman of power? Didn't I tell you? A sorceress of the old sort. She must have the blood of the gods in her veins! Is Dubhthach her true father?' Maithgen turns, asking Broicsech. She has been staring at her daughter with her mouth wide open, as though she was looking at a stranger. 'Were you visited by one of the gods. In a dream maybe?'

'No, I . . .' Broicsech looks down at the ground, head bowed, shoulders rounded as though trying to fold in on herself. 'I lay with a man and I became pregnant. No gods, no magic. Just Dubhthach.'

And there is a sweetness in the way Broicsech says her father's name that makes the bile rise in Brigid's throat.

'Tell me, blessed exalted woman,' Maithgen says, taking Brigid's hands. 'What can I give you in return for this gift? Anything you want.' He gazes at her as though she were something precious.

Brigid's head is spinning. She doesn't understand how the milk became butter any more than she knows how the sun appears in the sky. Only that she willed it so.

'Gold, cattle, horses, anything!'

There is only one thing she wants in the world.

'My mother's freedom.'

Maithgen pauses, then laughs. He looks to his wife. 'She could have enough wealth to buy a hundred cumals and she asks for just one! Didn't I tell you? Didn't I tell you?' He claps his hands together. 'Done.'

'I'm free?' Broicsech asks.

'What?' Maithgen says, as though he has already forgotten about Broicsech. 'Oh, yes.'

'But . . .' Broicsech asks, her face almost grey. 'What will I do?'

Brigid rushes over to her mother. 'Anything you want to do! That is what freedom means.'

Broicsech does not seem to understand. Her brow is wrinkled and she stares at her hands as though they did not belong to her.

'It will be all right,' Brigid says. 'I will show you the way.'

'Well, we can't be standing around here all day; our guests are arriving,' Maithgen says, clapping his hands together. 'Brigid, go and bath, for you will join us as our guest of honour.'

Brigid would rather eat alone with her mother than under the eyes of Maithgen's many guests. But it was not a question. She nods. 'I will.'

'It is decided then!' Maithgen shouts, throwing his hands up to the sky as though he was unleashing a spell.

'I will help get the food ready,' Broicsech says, turning to go to the stores.

Brigid takes her hand. 'No, Mother. You will join us at the feast.'

Her mother looks confused, as though Brigid had told her she might fly. 'But . . .' She looks down at her tunic. Pale grey, almost white with age and the single colour of a slave.

'I have some clothes that do not fit me any longer, for I have grown fat with age,' Tlachtga says, taking Broicsech's hand. 'They will look much better on you.'

Broicsech allows herself to be led away.

12

It is hot in the hall. Too hot. The fires are blazing with firewood and turf, and trickles of sweat fall down Brigid's back. It is loud too. So loud that her ears ring. The tables are heavy with food, which all seems to Brigid to smell of fat, even the fruit. She has not been able to bring herself to eat more than a mouthful of grain.

She had attended Maithgen's feasts as a child, a quiet onlooker hiding in the corners. For her, they had been wondrous evenings of magic and stories and music. Now, as a woman, she sees them with clear eyes. The feast is raucous, and everyone is drunk. How did she ever hear the bards tell their stories over the pounding of the drums or the booming laughter of the guests?

'Are we having fun?' Maithgen leans over and shouts into Brigid's ear. 'Are we having fun?' He shouts again, this time to the gathering, waving his over-full goblet around and spilling wine into Brigid's lap. She is wearing a new tunic, given to her by Tlachtga. It is woven of heavy blue and yellow threads and scratches Brigid's skin. And now, it has been ruined.

The group cheer their response. Broicsech, who sits on Brigid's left, shouts loudest of all, for she has been drinking more than any of the others.

'I'm glad we only have this gathering once a year,' Tlachtga says with a sigh. She sits on Brigid's right, sipping her wine at a much slower pace than her husband. 'But it is good for all our neighbours to get together like this.'

'It is?' Brigid asks, wondering what purpose this could serve. All she can see are sore heads in the morning.

Tlachtga nods. 'They drink, they fight, they fuck. And in the morning, petty grievances that have built up over the past year seem smaller. It bonds them.'

Brigid considers this, looking at the men and women around her. They are laughing, sharing food and drink. Even if small squabbles break out, they pass as quickly as a rain cloud.

'Dubhthach rarely had time for feasts,' Brigid said, remembering the cold halls of Dún Ailinne. 'Though he had one planned for my wedding.'

'Ah, yes, Maithgen said you were to be married,' Tlachtga says. 'But what, then, are you doing here?'

'When my husband-to-be set eyes on me,' Brigid says, remembering the taste of blood in her mouth and the sweet pain of her swollen skin, 'he decided he did not like what he saw.'

'How is that possible? The man must be a fool!' Tlachtga says. 'You're a beauty. Well, maybe we will find you a husband here tonight. Is there any man who takes your fancy?'

Brigid scans the crowd. The men all seem to look alike to her: red-faced and bearded. Some meet her gaze and grin back, mouths full of food. She shudders.

'Who is she?' Brigid asks, seeing for the first time a young woman dressed in white robes, with a pale yellow cloth covering her head. Around her neck, she wears a similar cross to Broicsech, though hers has been carved from a single piece of wood. She sits at the end of the table, gazing out at the crowd, a soft smile on her face.

'Ah, that is another of Patrick's new converts. Brónach of Carlingford. She is . . . fond of sailors.'

'Fond?' Brigid asks, wondering at the meaning behind

Tlachtga's pause. The young woman looks so innocent, so pure.

'Oh, not like that,' Tlachtga says, slapping Brigid's arm. She then tilts her head to look at the woman. 'Though it would explain . . . No, no, I am sure. She is, after all, a consecrated virgin. No, I mean she is building a hostel for sailors shipwrecked in the Lough.'

'*She* is?' Brigid asks. She has never heard of a woman building something before. Only men build forts and hostels and farms. The most a woman could hope to do is weave cloth.

'She nurses them back to health and in return, they dedicate themselves to her Christ god. Cheap trick if you ask me, getting a man when he's at his weakest. But this new god of theirs seems to be full of tricks. The woman next to her is another convert, Íte.'

Brigid moves to see a woman sitting on Brónach's right. She too is wearing a veil and cross. She has a sharp, pinched face and an expression of discomfort, as if she has eaten something that has made her ill. Though her plate and cup remain untouched in front of her, save for a chunk of bread that has been broken in two.

'And she's not married either?' Brigid feels as though she is glimpsing into another world, where the rules are not as she has been told.

Tlachtga shakes her head. 'When Íte was sixteen, she was supposed to marry the son of the King of Munster. Instead, she chose to live in the mountains in the south with a group of other Christian women. Not a bad idea if you ask me.'

'She chose not to marry? A woman can do that?'

'Oh, there was a lot of fighting about it. But she said she was the bride of Christ and could marry no other and so . . . For someone who harps on about humility, she is mighty sure of herself.'

A hand sneaks towards Íte's plate to grab the remaining chunk of bread and, without looking down, Íte slaps it away. The hand belongs to a young man, with a square face and large ears. His hair is the colour of peat turf and freckles cover his cheeks. He keeps glancing over at Brigid, then looking away when she catches him, as though stealing a look was as forbidden as stealing the bread.

'Is that her son?'

Tlachtga looks to where Brigid is pointing. 'Ah, no, that's Brendan. A Munster lad who was fostered to Íte. Strange if you ask me, for a woman who makes a vow not to have a child of her own going round raising other people's. But Patrick tasked her with the care of the boy, and so . . .' She leaves her sentence unfinished again.

'You were not tempted by this Patrick to become a . . .' Brigid struggles to remember the words Tlachtga used. 'A consecrated virgin?'

Tlachtga laughs. 'Oh, my virgin days are long gone. I hear Patrick can perform wonders, but I think even that is beyond him.' She winks, an action Brigid fails to understand.

Brigid looks over at Brónach and Íte. The women look ordinary enough. They have no halo of light around them, wear no gold or jewels. And yet they are the wives of a god and this means they will never have to be wife to a man.

Brigid's view of the women is blocked as Maithgen suddenly slides his stool back and stands up.

'I want to hear a story!' he yells. 'Come, bards, bring us your tales.'

A figure dressed in the reds, blues and greens of a bard stands up. 'I have a new song, though it is a sad one.' He throws his cloak back, pulls out a small harp and plucks a single string. The ringing vibrates through the crowd and a hush overcomes the gathering.

The man begins to sing:
'Hush, my love, do not weep.
For though my corpse lies far away
Beaten, bloody and unwashed
Embraced by none but worms
I have stayed true to my word
The tryst we made in summer's wane.
Has been kept by me come winter.'

As his voice fills the hall, Brigid is a child again, hiding in the corner, transported by the magic of the bards. Their stories would give her wings to fly places she saw only in her mind. They gave her hope.

When the bard finishes the last note, there is silence save for the sniffing of noses. Then an eruption of applause and banging of cups, calling for another sad song.

'How about him?' Tlachtga says, whispering in Brigid's ear. 'His name is Fiacc. The ladies call him Fiacc the Fair.'

Brigid considers him. He is handsome enough, and he has a sweet voice. Would a bard be a bad husband? She would never want for entertainment. 'He is very good,' she says.

Tlachtga nudges her and laughs again. It is starting to annoy Brigid.

The next to stand is a young druid. He is small and has to climb on a stool to be seen above the heads of the gathering.

'That's Lochru,' Tlachtga says. 'He's a bore!'

Though Lochru's voice is loud, he has none of Fiacc's craft. The story he tells is one Brigid has heard many times before, and even though it has many battles and many deaths, Lochru manages to make it a tedious tale. The rest of the gathering grow quickly bored with his story and start to talk over him. At which, he kicks over a cup and challenges the man nearest him to a fight.

All the noise and stupidity makes Brigid suddenly weary. 'Excuse me,' she says, standing.

She pushes through a gathering of men standing around Maithgen to reach her mother. 'I am tired.'

'Oh, Brigid!' Broicsech says, taking Brigid's face in her hands. 'Of course, it has been such a long day. You must go to sleep.' Her hands are hot and her teeth and lips are stained red with wine.

'Will you come with me?'

Broicsech looks around the room. 'I'd like to stay for a few more stories.'

'And in the morning . . . Will you come with me?'

Broicsech blinks, as though trying to focus on her daughter. 'Aren't we staying here?'

She takes Broicsech's hands in hers. 'You're a free woman, mother. You can go anywhere. You can return to England. Perhaps we can find your family? Would you like that?'

Broicsech's eyebrows knit together. 'I can't remember my family. I can't remember England.'

'Then where? You are free, mother. We are both free!'

'Dubhthach.'

The name drops like a hammer on an anvil: dark and crushing. 'What?' Brigid asks.

'I would return to Dubhthach.'

This must be a dream. How can her mother wish to return to Dubhthach, the man who beat her, used her as a sex slave, sold her when pregnant? Her mother could go anywhere in the land or any other land and she chooses him?

'Yes,' her mother says, a new energy in her voice. 'I would return to Dubhthach.'

Brigid leans away, as though her mother reeks of a foul stench. The hall is too hot, the smells too strong, the noises too loud. Her ears ring and above the buzzing she thinks she hears a woman's voice.

Come home, little one. I am waiting.

'If that's what you want,' Brigid says, trying to find a softness in her heart for her mother. 'But know this: I will not stay a single night under his roof again.'

'Then we will go for just a day,' Broicsech says, patting her daughter on the hand. 'Just a day.' She looks back to the bard. 'Now, off you go to sleep.'

Brigid walks out into the cold and makes for the dairy, but her cheeks still burn as though sitting next to the fire.

13

A halo hangs around the moon, and it is near bright as day. Brigid's whole body feels heavy as she walks back to the dairy, where she will rest. Not sleep, for she does not believe she will sleep tonight. She knows anger, has felt it every day at Dún Ailinne. But it is an easy thing to be angry with someone who you do not care about. To be angry with one you love, that has weight to it. She wants to scream. To throw herself to the ground and beat her fists against the dirt. Instead, she makes do with kicking a stone.

'Oi!'

She looks up to see someone sitting with their back against the wall of the dairy. It is Brendan, the young man with the freckles who was sitting between the two virgins. He is rubbing his shin where the stone struck him.

'Oh,' she says. 'That was not meant for you.'

'Who was it meant for then?'

Brigid approaches him. 'The world, I suppose.'

'Would you like some beer?' Brendan holds up a cup, half-filled with liquid that shines silver in the moon. 'I find it helps when you want to kick stones at the world.'

Brigid takes the cup and sits next to him. She takes a deep sip and hands it back. 'Thank you.'

'Welcome. Just don't tell Íte,' he says, taking another sip himself.

'She does not approve of beer?'

'She does not approve of most things, I find.'

Brigid laughs, and Brendan smiles at her, as though pleased to have entertained her. 'So you're Brigid,' he says.

'I am.'

'Maithgen talks about you. A lot. Says you hang your cloak on sunbeams and you will one day be the most powerful woman in Ireland.'

'Does he?' She leans back, pressing her head against the cool stone walls of the dairy.

'You should see Íte's face when he does. She goes all . . .' He purses his lips together and puffs out his cheeks.

Brigid laughs again. 'Well, I have never hung my cloak on anything but a nail, if that helps.'

'I will be sure to tell her.'

He passes the cup to her again and she drinks. It is strong, and she can feel warmth entering her chest.

'So you're a Christian?' she asks as she passes the cup back.

'I suppose.'

'You suppose?'

'The world is so big,' Brendan says, looking up to the night sky, his eyes wide as though seeing beyond even the stars. 'And there are so many gods. How do I know that this one is the right one? But I've been baptized now, so . . .' He looks down again and shrugs.

'By Patrick?'

'Oh, no, I've never met him. I was baptized by his nephew, Moel.'

'He must be . . . impressive?'

'Moel?' Brendan says. 'I suppose. He was quite short if I remember rightly.'

'No,' Brigid says, nudging Brendan with her elbow. 'Patrick.'

'Íte certainly has a lot of good to say about him. A lot.'

'She is educating you?'

He nods. 'She mainly has me read to her from the Bible. I like the stories about Jesus, but she likes St Paul the most.'

None of this means anything to Brigid, but she is impressed none the less. 'You can read?'

He nods again.

'The new Roman script?'

It is Brendan's turn to laugh now. 'You sound surprised. It's not that hard.'

'I can only read ogham.'

'Oh, well then, it's easy.' He presses the cup into her hand. 'Wait here.'

He runs off, his long limbs looking not entirely under his control.

Brigid sits and stares into the cup. The beer is almost gone and she can see a shimmer of her reflection in the bottom. Round cheeks, large eyes, a small, pointy chin. Hardly the face of someone destined to be the most powerful woman in Ireland.

'Here.' Brendan has returned. He holds a sheet of paper in his hand.

He sits next to Brigid once more and swaps the paper for the cup. In the grey light of the pulsating moon, she sees the ogham alphabet written in a long row. Next to each rune is another symbol made of both sharp and curved lines.

'Not all the letters have an opposite,' Brendan says, pointing at some of the Roman symbols which have a blank space next to them. 'We don't have letters for J, K, V, W, X or Y.'

Brigid mouths the strange sounds.

'But you'll work it out. And here.' He hands a small bound book to her. 'It's St Paul's Letters to the Corinthians.'

The cover is of soft brown leather, with black stitching. Brigid holds it in her hand for a moment as though she were holding a fledgling bird, as if it might open its pages and take flight.

'Won't you get in trouble with Íte for giving this to me?'

'Probably. But I think she likes having a reason to be angry with me. And besides, the look on your face makes it worth it.'

Brigid looks into his eyes. They are kind, intelligent, and they look back into hers as though trying to find the answer to something. She has never, she realized, looked into the eyes of a man before. Not really looked.

Brendan turns away, stares back out into the darkness, a soft smile at the edges of his mouth. 'I'd like to see Corinth for myself. And Rome of course, and Gaul. Some say that now Christianity has come to Ireland – Ireland being the furthest edges of the world – the end of times will be soon after. But I believe there is more world to find. And I intend to see it all!' He shouts this last part, as though throwing a wish out into the sky.

Brigid laughs again. And it is clear why this young man makes her feel so at ease – he has no desire to settle down and have a wife. He is as hungry for freedom as she is.

'Why is that so funny?' He looks back at her, a deep line creasing the space between his brows. 'Don't you want to see the world?'

Brigid shakes her head. 'All I want is a place to call home. Somewhere I feel safe.'

'A sanctuary,' Brendan says.

Brigid mouths this new word. 'Sanctuary.'

They sit and stare up at the moon for a while. The silence is knifed by a woman's voice.

'Brendan!'

He flinches as his name is called.

'Brendan, where are you?'

He drains what remains of the beer and passes the cup back to Brigid. 'Don't tell her you saw me drinking.' He stands.

'I won't.'

'I won't call again!' Íte's voice is harsh as an eagle's cry.

'She will,' Brendan says, with a sigh. 'I'd better go. It's been good to meet you, Brigid. I hope you find your sanctuary.'

'And I hope you get to see the world,' Brigid says.

Brigid watches Brendan run back towards the main round house. Hears Íte's raised voice, as she finds him at last.

'Sanctuary,' she says, rolling the word around her mouth again. Yes, she likes the sound of this.

She stands and ducks her head under the doorway of the dairy. She unclasps her cloak and holds it out before her for a moment, thinking of what Brendan has said. A shaft of moonlight breaks through the roof. She holds the hood up and hangs the cloak on the beam. It hovers in the air for a moment, before falling to the floor. But of course, the moon is not as strong as the sun.

14

At the first glimmer of dawn Brigid and her mother rise, wash and dress in new clothes, woven from the multicoloured threads permitted to free women, and new shoes made of soft leather.

'It's so beautiful,' Broicsech says, stroking her wrapped skirt as gently as stroking a bird. As though it might fly away at any moment.

'You make it beautiful,' Brigid says, hugging Broicsech. She is trying not to be vexed with her mother for her desire to return to Dubhthach, and has to fight against the urge to shake the idea out of her.

The cows moo as they pass, and Broicsech pauses. 'Who will milk them if I am gone?'

'Maithgen has a household of slaves for that,' Brigid says, pulling her mother forward.

'But none who know how to milk.'

She remembers a donkey they had at Dún Ailinne. It had been tied to a post and used to grind corn. When its legs became lame, they released it from the work. But the donkey, having never known any other life, continued to walk in small circles around the post till it died. Freedom does not come as easy to some as to others.

She pats her mother's hand. 'They will learn. Now come.'

As they approach the gates, their names are called. Brigid forces herself not to grab her mother's hand and run.

It is Tlachtga. Hair loose and wild, face still pillow-creased. 'I thought you might try to sneak out without saying goodbye,' she says when she catches up.

'We have a long way to go,' Brigid says, standing between herself and her mother, in case Tlachtga may have changed her mind about letting Broicsech go.

'You have indeed. Take this.' She hands over a leather bag. Brigid peers inside to see it is full of food, oatcakes, wrapped butter, dried meats and fruits, all left over from last night's feast.

'And this,' Tlachtga says, slipping a gold torc from around her neck, and placing it around Brigid's.

Brigid's neck is too slim for it and the torc slips from her shoulders and into her hands. The gold is warm and heavy and she senses power thrumming in it.

THAT IS OLD MAGIC YOU HOLD.

She wonders if she should let her mother carry it, fearing she will be compelled to give it away to the first person in need. She slips it into the folds of her skirt.

'It has been enlightening meeting you, Brigid,' Tlachtga says, tucking a strand of Brigid's hair behind her ear. 'This will always be your home. Return any time.'

Brigid meets Tlachtga's eye. She does not have the gift of lying. 'I will never return.'

Tlachtga lets out a small huff of amusement. 'I suspect you are right. Well, safe journeys then. I hope you find what you are looking for.'

She waves them out of the gate and closes it behind them.

'What are we looking for?' her mother asks as they wind their way down the path.

Brigid does not answer, for the truth is she does not know. She only hopes she will when she finds it.

At the edge of the forest, a figure emerges as though it had been a part of the tangled undergrowth. Lommán, veil pulled up revealing only her eyes.

Broicsech pinches her daughter's arm to pull her out of

the leper's path, though she smiles through clenched teeth. 'I am sorry, brother,' she says. 'We have nothing.'

'It's all right, mother. This is my . . .' Is friend the word she is looking for? Would protector be a better word? She settles on what she does know. 'This is Lommán.'

'Oh,' her mother says, the fixed smile slipping.

'Will you join us?' Brigid asks.

'I thought you were staying here?' Lommán's voice is deeper, rougher, than it was last night.

Brigid sighs. 'No, we are returning to my father's home in Dún Ailinne. For a while.'

'That's a long way. The roads may not be safe for two women alone.'

'We will have you to protect us,' Brigid says, patting Lommán on the arm. 'If you will come.' She ignores her mother's gasp. Touching a leper is a curse.

'I will come.'

Brigid believes that she could have said they were going beyond the ninth wave and Lommán would have still said yes.

The way south is quicker, for Broicsech has a way of smiling at men driving carts and gaining free passage. The roads they take are busier than the wandering coastal path Brigid followed on the way, for with the Imbolc festivities only a day away, there is much trading to do and there are plenty of men with carts to choose from.

On each new ride, Brigid and Lommán sit on the back, quiet, trying to remain unseen, while Broicsech sits up front, laughing at bad jokes. Unease squirms in Brigid's chest with every high-pitched giggle. She does not, she realizes with a cold clarity, know her mother. The woman in her head was a fantasy created in the dark nights of sorrow, one who was as desperate to be reunited as she was. But she never came to find her. *Did she ever even try?*

She forces herself to remember that her mother was a true slave, with no choice at all even to see her daughter. But she senses a resentment growing in her own heart. Sure, didn't Broicsech tell her that Patrick, her beloved Patrick, escaped his slavery? Why could she not have done the same? Brigid tries to snuff the emotion out, but she can feel it smouldering in her belly.

To distract her, she pulls out the page Brendan gave her and begins to work on learning the new alphabet. The sharp clean lines of ogham becoming the curved, elongated shapes of the Roman letters.

By early nightfall, she has trapped the new shapes and sounds in her mind. When she closes her eyes, she can see them dancing.

'Here you are,' the latest driver says. 'Baile Átha Cliath is that way. Dún Ailinne that way.' He points first to the east and then to the south.

'A million thank-yous,' Broicsech says, as they jump off.

'Ah, the company of a pretty lady like yourself is thanks enough.'

Broicsech covers her mouth and giggles like a young girl. She waves to the driver, before turning back to Brigid and Lommán, all sign of the blushing girl gone.

'Urgh, he stank,' she says. 'And feck me, so boring.'

'Then why do you do that?' Brigid asks.

They have to get out of the way for a cartload of squawking chickens.

'Do what?' Broicsech asks, smiling at the man driving the cart. The journey has been good for her and the colour has returned to her cheeks.

'Smile at the men on the road?'

'Do you still give everything away?' her mother replies, meeting Brigid's question with one of her own.

Brigid is surprised at her mother's evasion. 'For the most part.'

'I smile for the same reason. They're going to take it anyway, better be willing than fight it.'

Is that why I give? To save myself the pain of having it ripped away?

'And besides,' Broicsech continues, talking through her teeth now as she smiles at yet another man passing by. 'If you smile, they are less likely to hit you.'

Brigid remembers all the blows her father and brothers have given her and suspects her mother is right, but she would rather a bruise than the chill that passes through her when men rake their eyes across her body like tongues.

'Where might you be going to, my ladies?' a drover with a cartload of pigs asks, looking at both Brigid and her mother.

Broicsech tosses her hair and smiles again. 'We're on our way home to Dún Ailinne for Imbolc.'

The man sucks at toothless gums. 'Well, I'm going as far as Maigh Nuadhad.'

'Oh, thank you,' Broicsech says, jumping up next to him before he has a chance to change his mind. 'You are ever so kind.'

'Your . . . friend there will have to go in the back with the pigs,' the man says, nodding at Lommán. 'Though there *is* space up here for two,' he adds with an oily smile at Brigid.

'I'd rather be in with the pigs,' Brigid replies.

She and Lommán clamber into the back. The pigs accept their presence with little fuss, and soon they are travelling southward under dark, starless skies.

15

The morning is grey and wet. They disembark the pig farmer's cart and walk away before he can ask for payment, for Brigid knows what kind of payment he would have in mind.

All travel now is heading north, and no amount of smiling from Broicsech will get them transport in the other direction.

'Let's walk,' Brigid says, wanting to be away from carts and their drivers.

'It's a half-day's travel still,' Broicsech says.

'Then we'd better get started,' Brigid says.

Lommán takes the lead, Brigid and her mother follow behind. They walk in silence for some time, and Brigid cannot think of what to say to her mother. She has already told her about her failed attempt at marriage and how King Dunlaing set her free. But other than that, nothing. Many years of life have passed, and now that she comes to speak of it, there is not one story worth recounting.

The road becomes a mud track and the trees thicken as they take a path through the woods. The air smells of moss and pine and the rich tang of decay. Brigid stops and breathes deeply, filling her lungs with the scents of life and death.

'I could live here,' she says softly. 'I have everything I need right here.'

'What's that?' her mother asks, stopping to turn around.

Brigid walks on. 'Oh, nothing,' she says.

'Come on, we'll be through the forest soon', Broicsech says. 'This place feels as though a curse is on it.'

A large black-brown bird bursts out of the undergrowth in

front of them, making Brigid jump and her mother scream. Large wings beat against the air as it breaks for the sky above the tree canopy.

'It's just a buzzard,' Brigid says, looking down to see that her mother has grasped her hand in fear. *Was it to protect me, or herself?*

Lommán runs towards them, dagger already out. 'What happened?'

'It was a bird,' Brigid said.

Her mother laughs, hand pressed against her chest. 'It scared the living—'

Before she has a chance to finish, a man appears from amid the trees. He almost crashes into them but stops just in time. His eyes are wild, as though in a frenzy of fear or delight. He is clutching something to his chest. Gold glints between his fingers.

He lets out a crazed 'Whoo-hoo', leaps up, his legs bent like a toad, and runs on, deeper into the forest.

The sound of muffled voices drifts through the trees, from the same direction he came from.

Brigid steps off the path, up on to a mound of moss and mud, to try and see.

'Don't,' Lommán says. 'We should stick to the path.'

'There are people.' Brigid can see movement between the trees, flashes of colours against the greens and browns and the sound of trickling water. 'I think it's a well.'

Ignoring Lommán's protesting, she follows the sounds, stepping over tangles of brambles and ducking under branches. She was right. The trees clear and open up to a pool of water, trickling over blueish-grey rocks. A willow hangs over the water, its leaves breaking the surface like fingers. Ribbons and trinkets have been tied to the branches: wishes and offerings to the god of the well, though she does not know which deity this well belongs to. Two men, each dressed in the warm, thick clothing of those of the free classes, rip the offerings from the branches, while a boy wades in the water, bending over to pluck something from between the cracks of the rocks.

'What are you doing?' Brigid says. 'This is a holy place.'

'Not any more,' one of the men says, tearing a small stone figure from one of the branches.

'It's been . . . what's the word?' the other, shorter man says, turning to the first. 'Sainted?'

'No. Sained.' The first man looks at the figure and throws it over his shoulder. It lands by Brigid's feet.

'Yes, sained. By your man Patrick. He drove out the god that used to live here, along with all of the snakes that did its bidding. So there.'

'Patrick was here?' Broicsech has followed Brigid to the well, Lommán a few steps behind her.

Broicsech's eyes glisten in the light breaking through the canopy and her hands flutter together like the closed wings of a butterfly.

'Not a day gone,' the taller man says. 'We're lucky there's anything left to take.'

Broicsech kneels before the water and dips her hand into the pool. Water trickles between her fingers as she brings them to her lips, kissing her slick palms.

'Yes!' the boy shouts, holding his hand up. It is closed in a fist.

The shorter man runs over and grabs the boy. The lad tries to hide his catch from the man behind his back, but it earns him a smack around the head.

'Give it.'

Blubbering now, the boy opens his hand. Gold shimmers in his palm.

'Roman,' the man says, snatching the coin from the boy's hand. It vanishes into his pocket.

'You can't take these things. They are prayers,' Brigid says, picking up the stone figure the man had thrown to the ground. It is a rough figure of a woman with a large belly and curled hair. Brigid can see the marks of fingerprints dragged across the clay. A woman's hope was baked into this figure and brought to this place.

'Prayers to a dead god. Who has no need of them any more.'

THIS PLACE BELONGED TO ONE OF MY TRIBE. HER NAME IS FORGOTTEN, HER POWER GONE. ALL BECAUSE OF THE EGO OF ONE MAN.

Brigid tightens her fingers around the stone figure. Seeing these men strip this place feels like a wound.

'Let's go,' Lommán says, touching Brigid on the wrist. 'It won't be long before they get hungry for more than gold.'

Brigid stands for a moment, then places the stone figure into the waters of the well, before allowing herself to be led back to the path.

'I can't believe Patrick was here!' Broicsech says, looking around as though he might step out from the treeline at any moment. 'Oh, you should see him, Brigid. He is tall as a giant, but gentle. That he walked this very path, it's a sign, don't you see? A sign that we were right to take this journey. That God leads our way!'

'Tell me more of your new god,' Brigid says, for she would rather hear of him than this Patrick.

Broicsech is only too happy to oblige. She starts slowly at first, warming up as she goes. 'It is said Jesus was born in a barn, a god, born beside the cows and sheep, he was born pure, to a pure mother, Mary. She was unwed—'

'Like you?' Brigid says, interrupting.

Her mother shakes her head. 'Nothing like me. Hers was a virgin birth.'

'How can a woman be a virgin and give birth?'

'Because God willed it,' Broicsech says, as though that were an answer.

Brigid knows that the gods can stop the sun, or make it speed up, that they can impregnate a woman with a word. 'Like how Lugh put Sétanta into the belly of Deichtine?'

'I told you, those are just stories. This was a true miracle!' Broicsech throws her hands into the air, as though she had flung a handful of leaves to the wind.

Brigid sees no difference between this new magic and the old. But she stops asking questions and listens to her mother as they walk, Lommán leading the way. Brigid learns how the man, who was also a god, called Jesus gave fish and bread to the poor, brought dead men back to life. Broicsech tells her other stories, older ones, about a place called Eden and a woman called Eve who was tempted by a snake towards knowledge and sin. She thinks of her own snake, who saved her from Rechtabra, and wonders if this Eden snake had not in fact saved Eve from a life of stupidity.

'And there is a promised land. Not the one below as the druids say, but above us. In the heavens.' Broicsech bends her head back and turns her face to the sky.

Brigid wants to ask her mother how anyone can get to this land without growing wings, but she remains silent.

She likes the stories, though her mother doesn't tell them well and forgets parts, though she waves the gaps away as though they don't matter. 'That's not what's important. What is important is that God loves us as though we were his own children.'

Brigid's experiences with her father do not make this a comforting thought. But a mother's love, *that* she remembers. Or had it only ever been a dream?

'How is Dubhthach?' Broicsech asks, for it seems her mind has also been brought to the matter of fathers.

Brigid starts at her father's name. 'Why would you care?' she asks. 'After what he did to you?'

'He cared for me,' Broicsech says. 'In his way.'

Brigid's nostrils flare as she struggles to control her angered breathing. She has to bite down on her lips to stop them trembling. 'But he threw you away, as though you were nothing. Did he know you were pregnant when he sold you to another man to do with as he wished?'

Broicsech stops walking and stares at Brigid. 'That was Breachnat's doing. She demanded I be sent away for she could not stand how dearly Dubhthach cared for me.'

Brigid knows Dubhthach feared Breachnat's wrath. But he was ruler in the home. Had he truly wished to keep her mother, he wouldn't have let anyone stop him. *Just as if he had wished to keep me.*

'One day, when you are older,' Broicsech says, running a lock of Brigid's hair through her fingers, 'you will understand.'

Brigid does not believe she will ever understand, but she does not want to argue with her mother so she holds her tongue.

'Do you remember when I used to brush the tangles out of your hair?' Broicsech says, changing the subject.

'You would sing as you brushed it,' Brigid says, smiling at the memory of sitting before her mother, pretending it did not hurt.

Broicsech pushes Brigid's hair over her shoulder. 'I swear you used to tangle it yourself because you liked to have it combed.'

'I liked when you sang.'

'It's been many years since I sang for anyone.'

'Will you sing now?'

And she does. Her voice is weak at first, trembling and uncertain, but it grows in strength with each new verse. She only stops as they ascend a hill on the border of Druim Craig, needing her breath for the climb.

At the top, they can see fields and forests laid out before them, as the setting sun fights to break through the rain clouds. To the west there is the smoking stubble of a forest that has been cleared for cattle and beyond that, new pastures growing winter barley. Broicsech throws her arms open as though they were wings and she could soar all the way down the hill. Brigid looks back the way they have come and thinks that it is more than distance they have put between them and Faughart.

The light rain that has followed them all day grows heavier, turning cold and biting.

'There,' Lommán says, pointing at a small hut.

They run for the shelter and crawl inside. The shack looks to be an old roost for chickens. The birds are long gone, but their smell remains.

'We should stop here for the night,' Lommán says, pushing against the walls to test their strength.

'It's not much further, and the rain will soon pass,' Broicsech says, squeezing the water from her skirts. Brigid believes her mother would walk all through the night, for the closer they get to Dún Ailinne the more alive she seems.

They have been walking since sunrise and Brigid is glad to sit. The pain in her feet has radiated to her shins and up her knees.

'Please, mother, it has been eight years. We can wait one more night.'

Broicsech looks out the doorway at the road ahead, but then nods. They make a small fire and Brigid and Broicsech sit next to each other, bodies pressed close for warmth.

Lommán sits as far away as she can, knees pulled up under her chin, back pressed against the wall. In the flickering shadows from the fire, she could be a bundle of rags waiting to be washed.

'It will be good to be in Dún Ailinne for Imbolc,' Broicsech says, wriggling her toes near the fire.

'Does your new god still believe in Imbolc?' Brigid asks. 'For isn't Imbolc the day for the old goddess?'

Broicsech hesitates to answer. 'It's fierce rain tonight. Would you listen to it howling?' she says, changing the conversation again. Brigid senses a slipperiness in her mother she did not see before. But perhaps this is because they are now meeting as women.

'It will be a fine morning then,' Lommán says.

Sleep comes fast to Brigid. She is safe, she is warm, and she is with her mother again.

And in her sleep, I find her.

I bring dreams of fire and figures dancing, becoming like flames themselves. A baby, with a golden crown, held in the arms of a woman who feeds it milk from her breast as a snake curls around her neck and a flame dances over her head. A woman crying over the body of her dead son. The images flicker back and forth and the woman is both red-haired and pale-skinned, dressed in cloak and léine, and also dark-skinned, dark-eyed, wearing a light blue veil over dark hair and long, flowing robes that fall to her bare feet. The son is both a boy of ten years or so, with russet hair and soft round lips, a spear piercing his throat, and at the same time a grown man, with dark hair and brown skin, wounds in his hands and feet and side, a crown of thorns around his head. Brigid recognizes the dead boy from the old stories and the dying man from her mother's new tales. She reaches out, to touch the dead child, who is also the dying man, and her hand burns as though she has thrust it into fire. The flame spreads up her arm, her neck, through her jaw and bursts into life in the space behind her eyes. Light, all is light. Bright, burning, cleansing light. She is bathed in it, her whole body glowing. She looks at her hand, which ends not in fingers, but in flames. Power courses through her. With a touch she could harm or heal.

The flame splutters as though water has been thrown on it, and goes out. She is in darkness, deeper than any she has known, and cold sharper than the depth of winter.

COME, BRIGID. YOU MUST TEND TO THE FIRE.

Brigid awakes to a crack of lightning that calls her name. In the after-image of the strike she rises, pulls her ragged cloak back around her shoulders and makes her way to the door.

'Where are you going?' Lommán mutters, stirring as Brigid clambers over her.

'I must tend to the fire,' Brigid says, stepping out into the darkness.

Lommán looks at the fire. It has gone out long ago.

The rain has passed and taken some of the chill of the night with it.

'There is firewood here,' Lommán says, pointing at a pile she had gathered earlier to feed the fire.

Brigid does not seem to hear Lommán. She repeats the only thought in her mind. 'I must tend to the fire.'

I have called her to me and she has no choice but to come.

16

There is a forest close by: yew, ash and oak trees standing side by side. In the gloom, their waving branches are arms reaching out for Brigid, the snap of sticks under her feet the clapping of hands. She is barefoot, though she feels no pain from the twigs and thorns as she walks across them, deeper and deeper into the forest. Ahead, warm red lights flicker. It is the flame that has been calling to her, the one she must tend. Fallen trees block her path, but she clambers over them, moving ever forward following the light, till she breaks free of the forest. There is a grass-covered barrow and a fallen stone lying in the long grass. She rests her hand on it and traces swirling patterns and the faint crossed lines of ogham. A resting place of a hero of long ago. All that remains are the words 'Son of F'. Of all the stones she has read, most bear the name of a man. What of all the women? Do their names not deserve to be remembered?

Up and over the stone she goes and up the slope of the barrow. There is singing ahead, laughter, and a steady heartbeat *boom, boom, boom* of a drum.

She is running now, tripping and skipping towards the drum and the light, the weariness of the days' long travel easing with every step. The clouds have cleared and the moon, its fullest self now, lights up the night like dawn. On top of the barrow, she sees the flame that has called to her: a bonfire lit before an old oak tree.

I know this place. I know this tree.

She has approached from the north side, but this is the

same hill she climbed on the day she was to be married; this is the same oak tree she prayed under.

Around the oak women are dancing. They are dressed in red robes that drift and float with their movements as though they were in water. Around and around the fire they dance, arms swinging wildly, their heads thrown back, hair long and dancing too. Many of the women have grey or white hair, and yet they dance like children. There is such joy in their movements, such lightness. They are laughing, whooping, screeching at the top of their lungs.

This is freedom. A kind she has never seen before. Those she has known who called themselves free women – Broicsech, Tlachtga, even Lommán – only dared take up as much space as men permitted. But here, she is looking at truly free women.

'Brigid!' they call out to her, waving her towards them. 'Brigid, we have been waiting.'

She had almost forgotten her own name. How do they know it?

A young woman stops her spinning to wrap her arms around Brigid, squeezing in a hug so tight the bones of her ribs crack. She does not resist it, she melts into it, breathing in the scent of this woman: burnt wood and honey.

'We have been waiting for you,' the woman says when she lets Brigid go.

Upon parting, Brigid recognizes her angular face, the frost-blue eyes and crow-black hair. It is Darlughdach the bard.

Warmth washes over Brigid as though she has sunk into a hot spring. There are so many things she wants to ask. How are you here? What are you doing? But all she manages is, 'How do you know my name?'

'The goddess told us.' Darlughdach smiles and takes Brigid's hands in her own and now she is dancing too, spinning around and around the fire till she feels as though her feet no longer touch the soil. She and the other women weave in and out of each other, hands grasping hands, hair flowing. She laughs with the heady joy of it. There is nothing but this moment and these women who, though she does not know them, have become like sisters. She loves each and every one of them, dearer than her own blood. The beat gets faster, faster, her heart pounding in time, her breath in and out, in and out, building and building and building till she and Darlughdach and all the women fall to the floor in release.

And out from beneath the oak tree, I emerge.

The women raise their heads from the ground to see a golden snake, thick as the trunk of the oak, slither out from a hole beneath the tree. I coil, round and round, spiralling upwards till I tower over them, shimmering like an ancient monument of gold.

I shake off my snakeskin and step out in the form of a woman, naked. I am sumptuously, gloriously, beautifully fat, with hips wide enough to birth the world and breasts heavy enough to feed it. Fat as a mother before birth, fat as a baby newly born, fat as butter and as golden too. My rolls of flesh fall like undulating hills, and long red hair cascades around my shoulders like water crashing over waterfall rocks.

'My daughters,' I say.

The women kneel before me, arms outstretched. Only Brigid stares, unable to take her eyes from me.

'Goddess,' she says, staggering forward as though in a trance and falling to her knees.

'I wondered if you would ever make it, my little one,' I say, laying my hand on her head.

She closes her eyes as tears fall down her cheeks. 'It was you calling to me?'

I reach my hands down to her, large as lakes, soft as wind. 'I have so much to show you, my sweet Brigid.'

'Why? Why me?' she says, as I raise her to her feet.

'Why not you?' I run a knuckle against her cheek, wiping away a tear. 'Are you willing though? What I have to show you will not be easy. Once you have seen, the world as you know it will not be the same. It will splinter.'

Brigid nods.

'Then come.'

I take her hand and lead her, away from the fire, away from the other women, and down into the earth. Into the darkness.

It is dark the like of which Brigid has never known. Blacker than black. She cannot tell when her eyes are open and when they are shut. But I can see clear as a star-filled night.

'Take a deep breath,' I say. I do not know if she will survive this.

There is light and there is pain. And then, there is only me.

I begin my tale.

'I was born of light.'

17

'I was born of light and made of dreams. Poets called out to me and I blessed them with inspiration. Warriors prayed to me, and I gave them bravery and strength. I was in every sunrise and star fall. In every hearth and every bonfire. I was the spark in every strike of hammer on anvil. The fire of creation. The joy of birth.

'My people, the Tuatha Dé Danann, came to this land in a time beyond remembering. We are older than the rivers and the mountains, older than the oak forests and the standing stones. We brought magic and treasures. And we brought war.

'The first battle we fought was brutal, but swift. We drove our enemies out and sang songs for our victory. I believed we would only know peace from then to the end of time. I gave birth to a son, who I loved with a fire that could scorch the fields.

'But battle came again and my son was taken from me, pierced through the heart by a spear, a wound beyond even my power to heal. I held him in my arms and watched the love in his eyes turn to darkness.

'When he died, all light left the world. I wailed and all the women of the land wailed with me. I sang my sorrow and they sang with me. When I had no more tears to cry, I crept into the darkness and waited for death to take me too. And in the dark, I heard the screams of women. I heard their pain as they too lost their sons, their daughters, as they were beaten and broken for the pleasure of men. I told them to bring me their pain and I would swallow it all for them, bring me their sorrow and I would bathe in it. And they gave it to me, all of their hurt, their hope, and I ate it all. Drank it in like an ocean.

'When I thought I could take no more, when there was nothing left of me but their pain, it became a burning. An itch at first, like holding your hand over a candle. Slowly, it burned and burned. Agony. And it burned away my pain and the pain of the women I had carried. It cracked open my mind and into it poured an ancient wisdom, an ancient power, older even than my people. As old as the land herself. I came to life once again in that wisdom and I have held it all these long centuries, passing it on to those who are worthy.

'But it is fading. As belief in the old ways is fading, so too is my magic. I can no longer hold it. Perhaps no person, not even a goddess, can hold it alone. This wisdom must be protected. This light must be carried. It must never go out. For if it does, darkness will descend and everything I am, everything I was, will be lost.

'Light, love, inspiration, creation, all of it will fade into nothing. My flame must be tended.'

'The flame must be tended,' Brigid says, with the voice of the thousands of women who have been given this task before her and those who are to come.

She breathes deeply, raising her head up, her shoulders back. She wants to look ready for this task, but she is still so afraid.

'The flame must be tended,' I say, nodding softly. 'A new guardian must be found, one that can harness the power of the new god to protect the flame.'

'The Christ god?' Brigid says. 'My mother follows him.'

'As mothers must. He died so that their sons would live. So that the sacrifices given to make the crops grow and the rain fall would end. One sacrifice to end all. Even I could never give them that.'

'It is true, then.' Brigid's breath catches in her chest. 'He is a god?'

'A god. *The* God. That does not matter. What matters is that belief in him has given his followers a kind of power I have not seen before. And that power will sweep these lands and drive me and my kind deeper into the darkness.'

'Should we not fight him?' Brigid asks. 'Protect the old ways?'

'Our time will come again. For now, I would have you follow him. His strength will protect you.'

'But what if I don't want it? What if I don't want any of this?' Brigid asks, looking up at me, her pupils wide and black, sucking in all light.

I lean forward and kiss her on the forehead. 'Then you will stay here with me. In the darkness. And we will fade away together.'

18

When Brigid returns, a fire glows in her eyes. Power that was once promise is now ablaze. Her whole life she has been seeking something without knowing what it was. She has been told her thirst, her curiosity, was a weakness to be squashed, a hunger to ignore. But now she can see, it is the source of her promised power. She has been given purpose and she will bend the world to achieve it.

She touches her forehead where a mark glows: the kiss of a goddess. Her hands seem strange to her as she holds them out, stretching the fingers. Has she ever truly looked at her hands? Her arms, chest, belly, legs, feet. She runs her hands over her skin, feeling the giving hardness of her flesh, her bones. It is as if her whole body has never truly belonged to her before. *Have I always been this strong? This alive?*

She spins, leaps and feels that she could fly.

Of the women, only Darlughdach remains, still tending to the fire. It flickers still, low, weak, but alive. She sits cross-legged, head dropping as she fights off sleep, her cloak of ribbons wrapped around her for warmth.

'Awake,' Brigid says.

Darlughdach's eyes snap open. 'I was awake,' she says, wiping a streak of drool away from her chin.

She stands, stretches out her arms and arches her body like a cat. As her cloak falls open, Brigid notices the swell of her small breasts pushing against her shift. She blames my lingering presence for the strange flutter in her belly.

Brigid approaches the flame. It bursts back into life, as

though just lit. Darlughdach looks from Brigid to the fire to Brigid again.

'Oh,' she says. 'So you . . . Oh.' Finally, fully awake, she falls to her knees, her head bowed.

'Get up,' Brigid says, though not unkindly, 'there is work to be done.'

She walks to the edge of the barrow and looks out at the land below. The sky above is black as coal and yet, she sees as clear as if it were noon on a summer's day.

'I will build my city here,' she says, holding her hand out over the landscape, as though she were placing a rock down. 'It will stretch out for miles like the roots of this great oak tree. A low ditch and a high wall to protect us. And there, I will build a . . . holy fort . . . a place of worship.' She does not know the right word.

'A church?' Darlughdach says.

'A church,' Brigid replies. 'The church of the oak tree.'

'A church for the goddess?' Darlughdach asks.

Brigid shakes her head. 'A church for the new Christ god.'

Darlughdach's eyes tighten, her lips pull back in a snarl. 'Followers of this Christ god are hounding druids and bards out of the land. Why would I kneel to him?'

'Because,' Brigid says, grasping Darlughdach's hand in a grip like a vice, 'in bowing to one man, to Christ, we will be free of all men.' Her eyes glow as though the flame were burning within them. She looks back out across the land.

'Beside the church, I will build a tower.' She points at a deeper shade of darkness, beside the snaking curve of a river. 'A library, filled with scrolls and books, oh, Darlughdach, the books. Works of art each one. Every scrap of knowledge from across the world will be transcribed and protected so that as darkness falls across the rest of Europe, it will not fall here.'

'I cannot read,' Darlughdach says.

'I will teach you. I will teach every woman who comes here. To the outside world, it will be a place where we worship one God, but inside the walls, we will create a sanctuary where women can come and be safe. Lost, broken women everywhere will find a home within these walls. A community of women, protected, powerful. A community the likes of which this land has never seen. And together, we will keep the flame alight.'

The two young women stand, hand in hand, looking out into the night.

'I will not follow this new god,' Darlughdach says at last. 'But I will follow you.'

'As will I.'

They turn to see Lommán, who had been waiting in the shadows beneath the crest of the hill.

Darlughdach stiffens. 'You cannot come near the flame! It is sure death to any man who comes close.'

'But this is no man,' Brigid says, holding out her hand for Lommán to take.

Lommán kneels before Brigid as a warrior before a king.

'Tell me, mistress, what do you need?' Lommán says.

'For you not to call me mistress for a start,' Brigid says, pulling Lommán to her feet. 'There will be no slaves here. Call me sister.'

'Well then, sister, what do you need?'

Brigid looks back out into the darkness. The red glow of the flame behind her turns her hair to flowing lava. She smiles, the smile of a goddess, and I swear if I haven't seen that smile in my own reflection.

'I need land,' she says. 'Lots of land.'

19

Brigid shakes her mother awake. She is sweating and out of breath from the run back to the hut, her hair tangled and her dress torn. She has never felt more beautiful.

'No! No! Leave me,' Broicsech shouts, hands batting her nightmares away. She blinks, waking at last. 'Where have you been? I woke and you were gone.'

'I have to speak to Dunlaing,' Brigid says, not answering her mother. She has no time for questions, only action.

'The king?' Broicsech says, rubbing at her weary eyes. 'What do you need to speak . . .' her voice falters as she looks at her daughter. 'What happened to you?' She grabs her daughter's wrist, examines scratches along her arms that Brigid had not even been aware of. 'Did someone hurt you?'

Brigid pauses, wonders if her mother would understand if she told her she had met a goddess and been transformed. She decides not.

'No, nothing. I am well. Better than well. But I need to see the king.'

'Why? What can you have to speak to a king about?'

'Enough questions. I must see the king!' Brigid shouts, stamping her feet on the hay-covered floor. She has never raised her voice before and it shakes her.

Her mother stares at Brigid as though she does not know her. And for that moment, Brigid does not know herself.

'There are other kings,' Darlughdach says. 'Does it have to be Dunlaing?'

'It does,' Brigid replies.

'Who is this?' Broicsech asks, noticing the bard for the first time.

Darlughdach bows low before the woman. 'Darlughdach, my lady. A great pleasure to meet you.'

'I'm no lady,' Broicsech says, pulling her shawl around her, as though Darlughdach were teasing her.

'Well, we have a woman who is not a lady and a man who is not . . .' Darlughdach looks to Lommán, who tugs at the veil covering her face. 'A man who is not like other men,' the bard finishes. 'What a group we are.'

'Where are you finding these people, Brigid?' Broicsech whispers, stepping behind her daughter.

'They find me.' She gathers up her mother's things and presses them into her arms. 'Come on.'

'You can't just walk into Mullaghmast and demand to see the king.'

'Why not?' Brigid says. 'Dubhthach did.'

Broicsech takes a deep breath in and lets it out slowly. Brigid remembers this sigh of old, from when she was a child and she would ask her mother endless questions about the whys and the whats of the world. Broicsech would shake her head and sigh and Brigid learned to be silent and unsatisfied. It annoyed her then – it infuriates her now.

'But Dubhthach is a man.'

'So?' Brigid says, for she has seen a world where men are not the only ones with power.

'He will have requested an audience with Dunlaing. They are not easy things to come by.'

'Then I will ask him to request one for me,' Brigid says.

Her mother laughs. 'And you think he'll do that for you, do you? His bastard daughter?'

Brigid looks at her mother, head tilted as though she had been speaking another language. Why can't her mother see?

Anything Brigid asks for she will be given. 'I do not think it,' she says. 'I know it.'

They arrive at Dún Ailinne as the first fingers of dawn stretch out across the sky, turning grey clouds pink and orange. Brigid leads, Darlughdach beside her and Broicsech and Lommán behind. Broicsech's yearning for return had faded with the night and over the last mile, she struggled to keep up with Brigid's fierce pace. But Brigid had no time for rest.

The gates swing open with the slightest push of her hands, sending chickens and piglets scuttling away. Only the slaves are awake. They watch Brigid stride across the courtyard, mouths open and eyes wide. None dare speak. She pauses before the doors. Despite this being her home for eight years, she had always entered the roundhouse through one of the side doorways, as the slaves and other workers did, and realizes that this is the first time she will be entering as a free woman. The wooden doors groan as she pushes against them. The inner chamber is dark and cool and smells of damp and stale beer. The reeds on the floor need replacing. A single oil lamp flickers out as the breeze blows through the doors, throwing the room into shadows. Brigid walks across the stone floor, moving around the long wooden table and chairs, knowing the way even in the dark. She finds a flint next to the lamp and with a flick of sparks, sets it alight again.

'What is this?'

Dubhthach has awoken. Brigid doesn't turn at first to look at her father, instead she carries the oil lamp and uses it to light the others around the room. She can hear her father's heavy, angry breathing. At last, she faces him.

'I have returned.'

'Well, I can fucking see that.'

'As have I.' Broicsech steps out of one of the shadows.

Dubhthach staggers back, as though he has been struck. 'Broicsech?' He stares at the woman, and Brigid glimpses something she has never seen in her father's eyes before. A softness. 'Why are you here?'

'Are you not pleased to see me?' Broicsech answers.

'I . . . no, you cannot be here.' He looks over his shoulder. 'You have to go. Now!'

Can he really fear his wife that much?

'I claim the right of hospitality,' Broicsech says, her voice stronger than Brigid has ever heard it.

Despite his anxiety, Dubhthach laughs. 'A slave can't claim the right . . .'

'I am no longer a slave, Dubhthach,' Broicsech says.

Dubhthach looks from Brigid to her mother. 'Since when?'

'Since Maithgen freed her,' Brigid says. 'And as a free woman, you can't refuse her. You can't refuse any of us. You swore to offer hospitality to all. To deny us would be to lose your status.'

Dubhthach sees Brigid's other companions now. 'You expect me to welcome these people into my home? A leper and a . . . a . . .' He looks Darlughdach up and down, taking in the tatters of her ribbon cloak. 'A whore?'

Darlughdach laughs at the insult, but Brigid will not stand for it.

'She is a bard. One of the greatest in the land,' Brigid says. 'Be careful how you speak to her!'

'Don't fret, Brigid,' Darlughdach says, laying her hand on Brigid's. 'It is not the first time a man has called me a whore and I doubt it will be the last. Besides, there are worse things to be called. Better a whore than a fool.' She smiles at Dubhthach as though her words were a knife.

'I should smack that smile off—'

'They are welcome!' Breachnat walks into the hallway, her

words cutting Dubhthach off before he can finish his threat. She wears a pale orange robe that shimmers in the low light, and her brown hair is loose around her shoulders. She is beautiful, Brigid sees for perhaps the first time; a cold, harsh beauty. And yet, she is so frail. Brigid had always thought Breachnat an indomitable force, but seeing her with new eyes, she is just a woman. And a weak one at that.

'The girl is right. We cannot deny anyone the right of hospitality,' Breachnat says, though never has such a declaration sounded so unwelcoming.

Breachnat's five sons stand behind her, like a row of warriors ready to go to battle at the first word. For the first time in her life, Brigid has no fear of any one of them. She knows with a certainty that fills her lungs and makes her spine feel as though it was made of iron, that never again will one of them lay a finger on her.

'It has been a long journey and we are hungry,' Brigid says.

'And thirsty,' Darlughdach adds.

'Then sit.' Breachnat points to the table, where plates and scraps of food are still scattered from last night's feast. 'Ciara!' she shouts. 'Bring porridge and beer.'

They sit, Brigid and her party on one side of the table, Breachnat and her sons on the other. Dubhthach hesitates before joining them, but at last sits at the head of the table.

There is silence as they watch, each one waiting for another to speak. It is Broicsech who finally breaks the quiet.

'Much has changed since I was last here,' she says, looking around the hall and at the long cloths that hang on the walls. 'I don't remember the painted linens.'

'Oh, not much has been done,' Breachnat says. 'But of course, you wouldn't have spent much time in the hall, would you? You will have spent most of your time in the fields. Or the bedchambers.'

'As I said,' Broicsech answers, her expression still as a lake in winter, 'much has changed.'

Before the two women stop with the words and move to tearing each other to shreds with their nails, Brigid addresses her father.

'The reason I am here is a simple one. I wish to speak to the king and I need you to arrange it.'

'You hoping he'll marry you?' Euhel, the eldest, says.

'Or take her as his mistress?' Trian adds, laughing.

Dubhthach doesn't smile. 'What business have you with Dunlaing? Wasn't his freeing of you enough?'

'I am going to ask him for some land to build a church.'

There is a silence, followed by laughter that ripples first between the brothers and is then picked up by Dubhthach. Soon the men are slapping their thighs and laughing, barely able to breathe, as though this is the greatest jest ever.

'A church, is it now? And since when were you a Christian?' Dubhthach says.

Brigid doesn't answer this. 'Will you intervene or not?' She has never spoken to her father this bluntly before.

'I can send Rian with a message, what good may it do you. King Dunlaing is at Tara, trying to negotiate with Lóegaire mac Néill.'

'When will he return?'

Her father grunts, noncommittal. 'A week. Maybe more.'

'Then I will wait for him.'

'Here?' Breachnat says, all her pretend calmness gone.

Brigid is about to answer that she would rather wait out the time in the open jaws of a bear than stay here one second longer than she has to, but it is then that Brigid sees Ciara. She is carrying a large bowl of porridge and struggling with the weight. There are dark bruises under her eyes and angry red marks on her neck, as though a hand has wrapped itself around her throat.

Brigid stands, rage setting her blood alight.

'Which one of them hurt you?' Brigid says through clenched teeth.

She stares at the brothers, imagining their heads torn from their necks, their guts spilt on the ground. She has never known anger like this before and has to fight it back down, knowing that if she gives in to it, it will consume her.

THEIR TIME WILL COME, MY LITTLE ONE, I say, soothing her. THEY WILL BOW TO YOU AND IT WILL PAIN THEM MORE THAN ANY WOUND YOU CAN INFLICT. BE PATIENT. BE READY.

Ciara looks up, sees Brigid and drops the bowl to the ground. It cracks and splits in three, spilling porridge on the black flagstones.

'You stupid girl,' Breachnat shouts. She pushes back her chair and in three quick strides has closed the gap between herself and the slave girl. Ciara cowers, raising her arms to protect herself from the blows to come.

Darlughdach is on her feet. 'Don't you dare,' she shouts.

The sheer cheek of it is enough to stay Breachnat's hand. 'You would talk to me like that in my house? I will have the girl beaten and there is not a thing you can do about it.'

'You will not touch her,' Darlughdach says.

Lommán stands too, and throws aside her cloak, revealing the knife at her belt.

'Peace,' Brigid says, raising her hand, feeling a thrill in this small act of control. Violence befell her every day of her life in Dún Ailinne, whether delivered by words or fists, and she could choose to repay that violence in kind. But she chooses peace. For now.

Brigid steps out from behind the table and approaches

Ciara. Tears are streaming down the girl's face and she is sobbing too hard to speak. Brigid lays a hand on her face and wipes the tears away. 'All will be well, my friend.'

She bends down next to Ciara and gathers up the three broken shards of the bowl, wrapping them in her arms, like a mother cradling a newborn.

LET US SHOW THEM A LITTLE OF YOUR POWER.

'This is like the human spirit,' Brigid says, breathing the words over the bowl. 'It may be easily broken, but it can be restored.'

She places the bowl on the table. It is unbroken.

Chairs scratch loudly against the flagstones as the brothers all stand and back away from Brigid. They shout, cry, point fingers at her. Witch. Fairy. None say the word, but all are thinking it. Goddess.

20

'Get out!' Dubhthach shouts, grabbing a knife from the table and jabbing it in Brigid's direction.

Darlughdach and Lommán come to stand beside Brigid, her protectors. Her mother has not moved. She sits, chewing on a strip of meat, smiling as though she has always known that her daughter had these powers. As though she was responsible for it.

Brigid looks at her shaking hands, at the mended bowl. Like the butter and the roast pig, she had simply seen it whole and that had been enough to shape reality.

This power does not belong to me, and yet it is mine to use.

How far can she push it? Could she heal people? Could she break them?

'Wait,' Breachnat says still sitting, back straight in the chair. 'Brigid will stay.'

'No,' Dubhthach says, 'I will not have a witch in my house.'

'She will stay,' Breachnat says again, louder, sharper. 'And we will find her a husband who will pay even more than Rechtabra. Perhaps three, four times her weight in gold.'

'You gave up all rights when you sold me,' Brigid says. 'You cannot make me marry.'

'You are a girl,' Breachnat says, standing at last. 'A daughter. And free or not, you are still your father's property. And we will marry you to the highest bidder and you will at last be of some worth to your father.'

Brigid can feel the anger rising once more. They are speaking of her as though she were a cow to be sold, but she is a free woman. Freed by the king himself. And at last, she knows there is another path.

Brigid closes her eyes as Dubhthach and his sons begin to argue, quibbling over who they could marry her to, what price they might get.

'I will marry,' Brigid says, her voice cutting through the squabbling.

'Oh, yes, and who do you have in mind?' her eldest brother, Trian, asks.

'Christ,' Brigid says. 'I will dedicate my life in service to him and him alone.'

There is shocked silence followed by that laughter again. The cruel laughter she has heard all her life.

'She thinks she can marry the son of a god!' Euhel says.

'He's been dead for over four hundred years, so she'll have a tough time consummating the wedding!' Fachtna scoffs.

Brigid wants to press her hands over her ears to block it out. She wants to tear out their throats so that they can never laugh again.

'What a waste that will be,' Beccan says, walking towards her. He is the only one not laughing, he has been watching, eyes tight and sharp as a blade. 'For she has beautiful eyes, does she not? Eyes like that should be pressed deep into a husband's pillow as he ploughs into her.' His mouth twists like a gnarled branch.

OH, NO, WE CANNOT BE HAVING THAT.

Brigid stares back into Beccan's eyes, meeting his gaze properly for the first time. She always looked away before, afraid of the twisted desire she saw in them. She remembers all the cruelties he has bestowed on her, the harsh, disgusting words, the pinches and strikes, the threat always on the edge that he would do more than hurt her if he could. Never again will he look at her like flesh, never again will he drag those eyes across her skin and leave her shivering.

Words to heal.
Words to protect.
And words to wound.

Words rise up in her mind, as though she were remembering a snatch of a song learned long ago. She speaks them in a whisper.

A single red tear falls from Beccan's eye. He holds his hand up to wipe it away and looks at the dark stain on his fingertips. Blood. Another tear traces down his cheek before falling to the stone floor. Drip after drip falling like rain. Soon blood is pouring from his eyes like a waterfall. Beccan screeches, holds his hands to his face, but the blood continues to pour through the sieve of his fingers.

'Stop it,' Breachnat shouts. 'Stop it now and you can have anything you want!'

A hand rests on Brigid's shoulder, a cool touch cutting through the fire that threatens to consume her. 'Enough, Brigid,' Darlughdach says. 'Enough.'

She closes her eyes. Beccan falls to the floor, as though he had been held up by invisible strings just cut.

Brigid's body shakes like she has been plunged in ice. She cannot control the chattering of her teeth or the quaking of her limbs. Nor the fear of what she has done. In the past, she had secret fantasies of hurting Beccan, of punishing him for every wrong he had done to her or Ciara, but they had been only that: daydreams and nothing more. She had never truly *wanted* to cause him pain. She had never thought she was capable of it. She had always chosen to be kind, in all things.

ARE YOU SURE ABOUT THAT?

'I never.' She covers her eyes, as though afraid that looking on anyone else would do to them what she had done to Beccan. But she cannot drown out his wailing.

WHY SHOULDN'T MEN LIKE HIM SUFFER AS WE WOMEN HAVE DONE? WHY SHOULDN'T YOU USE THE POWER I HAVE GIVEN YOU ANY WAY YOU CHOOSE?

'No,' Brigid whispers. She will not kill her brother, for all he has done to her, she will not take a life.

'No!' Brigid shouts now, and all in the hall turn to her again, eyes wide in horror.

SEE HOW THEY FEAR YOU. FEAST ON IT.

Is this what it feels like to be powerful, to have all quake before you? If so, it is not a power she wants. She has been trapped in a cycle of oppression and pain. It is time for the cycle to end. There is another way, there has to be.

'No,' she says to herself.

SO BE IT. BUT YOU MAY REGRET IT.

'Brigid,' Darlughdach says softly. 'Are you with us?'

A hand holds hers and she feels as though her feet have found the ground after being out of her depth. She dares to meet Darlughdach's eyes. 'I am here.'

She turns then to the people who are her family by blood, but by blood only. 'You will arrange for my meeting with the king,' she tells Dubhthach. 'And then we shall be free of each other once and for all.'

21

Outside, the wind is picking up. In the distance, she can see great oak trees bowing in its path. An invisible force that can bend nature to its will. Is that God? Is it in everything? Is it even in her?

The anger that set her alight has passed, leaving only tears in its path. What good are a woman's tears? The last resort of weaklings. She will not be weak. She will not give in to her emotions. She stands with her back to the fort, letting the cold spring wind whip her tears away.

I will never again set foot here. I swear it.

The slaves will not look at her, for fear that one glance from her and their eyes might burst out of their heads. But they are already whispering, stories travelling from lips to lips. Stories can travel faster than horses, they say. How far will this story travel? Will people think her monstrous or godlike?

Is there a difference?

The slaves of Dún Ailinne bend, almost double, twisting their bodies away, and scatter before her as she walks for the walls.

'Are you all right?' Darlughdach asks, catching up with her, Lommán by her side.

'I will be once I'm away from this place.'

'Then let's be going,' Lommán says.

The three women walk, side by side away from the looming weight of Dún Ailinne. Brigid is struck by a sudden desire to reach out and take their hands, to feel their strength as her own drains away with every step. She balls her hands into fists, for she believes she must do this alone.

'Wait! Biddy, wait!' It is Ciara.

Brigid stops, fighting the instinct of her muscles to turn back and embrace her friend. Instead, she tells her bones to stand still as stone, for they will not betray her.

Wet footsteps getting closer. A warm hand on her shoulder. Ciara stands before her and throws her arms around Brigid, pulls her tight.

'Take me with you,' Ciara says, breathless from the tightness of Brigid's embrace.

Brigid steps back and looks at the girl. How young she seems to her now. Her wide, blue eyes that once seemed to hide secrets are now like clear pools. In the girl's eyes she sees fear and loneliness, all buried beneath a gossamer-thin layer of hope that Brigid can do something, anything, to free her from this life of pain. And deep, deep within her soul, a shimmering resentment that at last Brigid understands, for Ciara must resent all free people. As she herself would have done had she become enslaved.

'I . . .' There is so much Brigid wants to say.

'Ciara, get back here.'

Ciara's fingers tighten on Brigid's arm. 'You can't leave me. Your brothers . . .' Brigid knows what her brothers will have been doing to the girl. Perhaps what they have been doing for years but she was too blind to see.

Brigid does not want to look back. Fears that if she does, she will lose her friend for ever. But she forces herself to turn and face her stepmother. Broicsech is a pace behind, her head bowed so as to be sure to be smaller than Breachnat. Her mother is a free woman and yet she stands like a slave. It sickens Brigid. She needs to get them all away from here, away from the oppression of this place before its corruption seeps into them like mould.

Brigid makes her mind up. 'How much for the girl?' she says.

'What?' Breachnat says, closing the space between them.

'I said, how much for the girl? You always claimed you were a master negotiator, Breachnat.' She realizes that this is the first time she has spoken the woman's name aloud and she enjoys how it feels like hacking up phlegm. As if by speaking it she has rid herself of something poisonous. 'So, negotiate.'

Breachnat looks Brigid up and down. The torn tunic, the muddy cloak. Brigid has nothing and this is her last chance to beat her, if not with her palms as she has so readily done in the past, then with commerce.

'I won't accept less than three cumals of gold.'

It is an outrageous price. Three times what any slave would be worth. Brigid reaches into her skirt and from it pulls the torc Tlachtga gave her.

'No,' her mother hisses. 'That is all you have.'

'I think this will more than cover that.'

Brigid throws it at Breachnat's feet and fights to keep the smile off her face as it lands in the mud. Brigid watches, tries to read the thoughts flickering across the face of this woman she has never understood. She knows she has trapped her, between her love of gold and her love of winning. She regrets using her friend as bait, for she fears Breachnat will choose victory.

Breachnat's love of gold wins out. She bends down and snatches up the torc before anyone can take it away. She wipes it clean on her dress, leaving a dark streak of mud across her belly.

'Take her then,' Breachnat says.

'You are witness,' Brigid says to the onlookers. 'Ciara is freed.'

A resentful agreement is murmured.

Ciara closes her eyes and groans with relief, a deep heartfelt moaning as though freed from a great pain.

'Come on,' Darlughdach says. 'Let's get out of here before they change their minds and decide to take us all as slaves.'

She's right. They must be fast before the magic of the gold wears off.

Brigid refuses to break into a run, though she desperately wants to. She takes slow, deliberate steps, her head held high. They are at the gates when Brigid realizes her mother is not with them.

Broicsech is still standing in the middle of the courtyard.

'Mother, come on,' Brigid shouts, holding her hand out to her.

'I am staying.'

The words pierce Brigid like arrows.

'You will come with us now.' Brigid stamps her foot, but the mud swallows up the impact.

Broicsech walks slowly towards her daughter and with every step Brigid feels a swell of relief: her mother has chosen her.

Broicsech kisses her on both cheeks. 'Go in God,' she says.

Brigid cannot believe this. She looks at the fort, at the small, dark windows and sees movement within. 'You would stay here, with him?'

Broicsech nods. 'I would.'

'Then you will never be free. Not while you live under a man's roof.'

The heat rises again, the hatred. *I would rather see my mother dead than stay here.*

'I am too old for freedom,' Broicsech says. 'And Patrick

told me, a wife should be subject to her husband. Dubhthach is still my husband.'

Brigid thought she hated her father. She thought she hated her stepmother and all her snivelling stepbrothers. But in this moment, she has discovered a new depth of hatred for her mother.

'Stay then,' she says, turning her back on her mother. *And rot.*

22

Days become weeks and still King Dunlaing has not returned from Tara. Brigid has learned that his negotiations with Lóegaire mac Néill failed and now he is preparing for battle. Brigid wanders the lands of Leinster with her three companions. The stories of her power race ahead of them on the road.

One morning, they approach a small crannóg: a falling-down homestead perched at the end of a rickety bridge over a stinking bog. A gathering of women and children is already waiting on the bridge. Their clothes are barely more than rags, their cheeks hollow and bodies lean. And yet, as Brigid approaches, the children run forward, dancing around her, and the women offer her and her sisters what meagre food they have. Dried fish, dock leaves, mushrooms. They have so little and yet they would give it all to her.

'Please, Holy Mother,' one of the women says. 'Stay a while.'

Holy mother? Brigid shudders, though she keeps her face still. *But I am still just a child.*

'We can't take your food,' Ciara says, pushing the wicker plates away.

For Ciara to say no is proof of how desperate these women's lives are.

'But we thank you for your kindness,' Brigid says, for she knows there is pride in giving, even when you have nothing.

'Will you stay a while then?' another of the women asks, the youngest of the group.

'The whole place stinks,' Ciara whispers, though not quietly enough. 'We'd be better off staying in a ditch.'

'A little while,' Brigid says, taking the young woman's hand, ignoring Ciara's grunt of annoyance.

Brigid likes how the young woman's face glows as her thin, cracked lips break into a broad smile. Kindness given is better than kindness received.

It is like this in most of the villages and forts they pass. The women welcome Brigid and her sisters in, offering them rest or respite, and in return she listens to their pain. The men do not welcome her approach. They watch her, wary, their slaves kept behind closed doors in case she takes it upon herself to free every slave she crosses.

Lommán leads the way, for she knows the roads and paths, knows which places are likely to welcome them and which are likely to turn them away.

'There's a fort a day's walk from here,' she says one day, after they have spent the night sleeping in the woods, huddled together for warmth. 'Where the wife makes the best rabbit stew I have ever tasted in my life.'

When they arrive, the woman is gone. Dead a year since. And all that remains of her home is a pile of stones that have been pillaged by her neighbours, and a colony of rabbits running wild. Lommán catches two brace of rabbits and does her best to make a stew in the ruined hearth of the woman's home. It tastes of salt and earth.

For a month, this is their life. Nomads, passing from place to place. Brigid no longer notices the blisters on her feet, for they have turned hard and callused. Like Lommán, Darlughdach is used to this life. She keeps their spirits up with songs and stories. She knows a thousand of them and Brigid loves to sit hidden in the shadows away from the small fires they make at night and watch the bard's sharp face shift and morph as she becomes the many characters in her tales.

Ciara has taken to freedom as an eagle to the sky, wanting more and more of it. And yet she is also the one who complains the most, about the walking and the hunger and tiredness.

'If I'd known being a free woman would have meant starving,' Ciara says, massaging her feet one day as they rest by a small creek, 'I might have stayed a slave.'

Brigid is on her feet, ready to box Ciara around the ears, before she can take control of herself. 'Never say that,' she snarls, standing over a cowering Ciara. 'Never.'

'She was joking,' Darlughdach says, stepping between the two.

The bard places a hand on Brigid's shoulder, gentle yet resolute.

How dare she stop me? How dare anyone?

The heat passes as quickly as it came, draining out of her like water from a dry swamp. Brigid walks away, head hanging in shame. She catches her reflection in the surface of the water and sees her father staring back.

The days blur into one another, each one much like the last. And so she does not know if it is two or three days later that they meet a man on the road.

'He looks wealthy,' Darlughdach says under her breath as they approach. 'Look at his tunic.'

'He looks well fed,' Ciara says with the hint of a sigh.

He is like many of the men Brigid has seen in these weary days of waiting: average height and build. A forgettable face. His only feature that stands out are squinting, watery eyes, that put Brigid in mind of a pig.

Lommán's body tightens, as she reaches for the dagger hidden beneath her cloak. She trusts no men around Brigid.

'Well met, blessed Brigid,' the man says, lowering himself to his knees as Brigid approaches, though he is careful to hitch his tunic up so as to keep it clean.

'Rise,' Brigid says. 'We are all equal in God for we are all equally blessed.'

'Ah, but if only that were true,' the man says, pressing his hands into the ground to help him as he gets stiffly to his feet. 'For I am cursed.'

I know this man. I have heard his prayers at night and those of his wife in the day. I have not answered, for they already have gifts enough that they neglect.

BE WARY.

'Tell me your woes,' Brigid says, my words of warning tempering her usual warmth. 'And perhaps we can help lift this curse.'

'I pray that you can succeed where others have failed. Even Patrick could do nothing, and they say he's blessed by God.'

'Patrick has been here?' Brigid asks. She has not heard his name since parting with her mother, and hearing it now sends a shiver down her spine.

'Come, I have a hostel,' the man says. 'It is not far and my wife is waiting for you. We have food and drink for you and your companions. When you have eaten and rested, we will tell you our sad tale.'

The promise of food is enticing. As is rest. The initial headiness of their wanderings has faded a little in the past days. They are hungry, having lived off the scraps of charity of the women they have met and what Lommán has been able to hunt. It has been over a week since Brigid slept in a bed and the last bath she had was the morning she was meant to marry Rechtabra. She and her women have washed in rivers and wells, and she cannot deny that they have smelt better.

She sees caution in the eyes of Lommán. Hunger in the eyes of Ciara. While Darlughdach's eyes shine only with hope as they always do.

'Very well,' Brigid says. 'Lead the way.'

The man claps his hands together as though a deal has been struck. 'Good! My wife will be so glad. So glad. I,' he clears his throat, 'am Ui Brolaig. You have heard of me? No? Really? You haven't heard of the raid on Uíbh Fhailí? Ah, well, perhaps I will tell you that tale too? Come, it is not much further.'

The man talks without breathing, without waiting for any answers to the many questions he fires at them like hailstones. And loudly too, as though used to making himself heard in a hostel. Brigid wants to put her hands to her ears to mute his noise, but does not wish to be rude. Kindness in all things, she reminds herself. Even when listening to the effluent chat of a stranger on the road. She smiles, nods along, and hopes he was not lying when he said his home was nearby.

Her women drop back as they walk and she can hear them whispering and giggling, though luckily Ui Brolaig cannot. Perhaps he is nearly deaf, and that is why he feels the need to shout? This idea needles her with guilt for the cruel thoughts she had about him, for if he is afflicted then it is not his fault.

His hostel is further than she hoped but not as far as she feared. A long ten minutes' walk and they arrive at a small farmstead. A herd of cattle graze in the field nearby and the cows lift their heavy heads as they pass, deep brown eyes watching them.

'We have fewer guests than we would like,' Ui Brolaig says. 'When I was first married and given this hostel I imagined we would have feasts every night. But my wife . . .'

He doesn't finish this thought and is silent for the first moment since they met.

'Ah, here she is! My wife, what a vision!'

A woman stands in the doorway, her body a mere silhouette in the arched darkness. She steps forward into the light, though she raises her hand to cover her eyes, as though the sun causes her pain. Her cheekbones sit high on her face and the skin hangs off them, all plumpness of youth long gone. She is frail and her steps hesitant. Following her through the doorway come two young women, who take up positions either side of the door. They are mirrors of one another, each small in height and slim, both with long dark hair woven into thick plaits that fall over their shoulders. Should their hair be let loose, Brigid estimates it would fall to the ground by their feet. They also have the high cheekbones of Ui Brolaig's wife, though theirs give them a sharp beauty.

'Mealla,' Ui Brolaig says, in a soft, gentle voice, addressing his wife. 'I have brought her, as I promised you. Brigid, this is my wife, Mealla. Mealla, this is she.'

Mealla reaches out arms thin as sticks, her hands palm upward. Brigid takes the woman's hands and flinches at the coldness of them.

'Brigid,' Mealla says. 'I prayed that you would come. The women in the village say your touch makes any woman fertile. That there is healing in your blood.' She yanks Brigid's hand and places it on her belly. For a weak woman, she has a strong grip. 'My husband and I have been unable to have children. But now that you are here . . .'

Protruding dark eyes stare at Brigid, flicking from one side to the other.

'You said there would be food?' Ciara says behind her.

'Yes! Food. Come, Mealla, let's get our guests in out of the cold, shall we?'

'Of course.' Mealla does not let go of Brigid's hand until they are inside, and Brigid has to shake the life back into her fingers once it has been released.

A table has been laid and a fire burns in the centre of the hall, though the weak flames do little to warm the room. Cold seeps up through the flagstones and moisture drips down the dark walls.

'No wonder they don't have any guests,' Ciara says. 'This place looks like a hovel.'

The food, though humble, is surprisingly good. And there is plenty of it. Roast pigeon and rabbit stew. Hard cheeses and soft fruit. Ciara does not wait before grabbing a whole pigeon for her plate and Darlughdach and Lommán follow quickly after. Brigid eats slowly, savouring every mouthful.

'Is it to your taste?' Mealla asks, perhaps worried that Brigid's slowness belies lack of enthusiasm.

'It might be the best food I have ever eaten,' Brigid replies. 'You must have the most prized cook in all of Leinster.'

'Oh, we have no cook,' Ui Brolaig says, his mouth full of cheese. 'My daughters do all the cooking.'

'Your daughters?' Brigid asks, looking to the dark-haired girls. She assumed they must be servants or slaves, what with the way they were treated. 'But you said you could not have children?'

'No sons,' Mealla says quickly. 'We have been unable to have sons.'

Brigid places her fork beside her platter, suddenly unable to eat.

'Well, I'm surprised a man has not snapped up your daughters for wives then,' Darlughdach says. 'For this food would please the gods.'

The two girls hide their smiles.

'No man would want them,' Mealla says. 'For Induae and

Indiu are mute and between them they haven't the sense of a sheep.'

Induae and Indiu's mirror smiles turn to ice and Brigid winces at the easy cruelty of their mother.

'Even more reason a man would want them,' Ciara says quietly. For perhaps she understands men better than Mealla does.

'Have they been mute since birth?' Darlughdach asks.

'They were born bright as any child but then when their blood came in, with it came the curse of stupidity,' Mealla says.

'And they weren't injured in any way?' Ciara asks, licking her fingers clean of pigeon. 'I knew a woman who was kicked in the head by a cow and after that she was as simple as a child.'

Brigid has not heard this story and wonders who this woman could have been.

'No.' Mealla shakes her head. 'No injury. There was no earthly cause. It is part of the curse; I am sure of it.'

The girls stare down at their laps, small hands knitted together, though Brigid sees their knuckles whiten as their mother speaks.

'People are not cursed for nothing,' Darlughdach says. 'Did you offend a passing poet? Dig up a whitethorn tree?'

'Nothing,' Ui Brolaig says. 'We have done nothing.'

'Then tell us.' Brigid leans back in her chair.

Ui Brolaig, who has not looked at his daughters throughout the meal, clears his throat as though about to speak, but it is his wife who begins the tale.

'It began when my brother, Machta, came to stay with us after our mother died. He used to play with the girls, and how they would laugh and sing all day.' Mealla smiles at the memory, though her daughter's expressions are like stone.

'Then the day after they bled for the first time, they stopped speaking. Just as they became women and we could start looking for husbands for them . . . this.' She waves her hand at her daughters, as though they were a pile of muck that needed clearing.

Brigid senses the depth of wrongness here. There are lies within lies, though whether Mealla and Ui Brolaig are lying to her, or just lying to themselves, she will only know if she can speak to the girls alone.

She coughs, as though her throat were dry. Mealla reaches over and fills her cup from a pewter jug, but Brigid pushes it away. 'No, alas I may only quench my thirst with flowing water.'

Darlughdach raises an eyebrow in Brigid's direction and she can read the meaning of it sure enough. *What game are you playing?* And yet, she plays along.

'Is there a stream nearby? A brook would do,' Darlughdach says.

Ui Brolaig jumps to his feet. 'Of course, we heard stories that you may only drink the milk of blessed cows, but we didn't think about water. I will take you.'

'No, please,' Brigid says. 'You stay here and look after your guests. I can go alone. Perhaps Induae and Indiu could guide me?'

'Yes. Girls, take Brigid to the stream,' Mealla says, flicking her hand at her daughters. 'And don't be going wandering now.'

Both girls stand in unison and wait for Brigid. She follows them as they walk out of the fort, step in step, as though they share one mind and soul.

'Which of you is Induae?' she asks.

The girls look to each other as though confused by the question, as though the idea of one of them being separate from the other is not a thought that has occurred to them. But after a while, one of the girls points a finger to her chest.

'And so, you are Indiu?' Brigid says, addressing the other.

Up close, she can see the tiniest of differences between them. The shape of their eyes, their jaws, a tiny scar on Indiu's upper lip, a mole on Induae's temple. They can be no older than Brigid herself, and in fact may be younger.

'How old are you?'

They do not answer.

'I am nearly sixteen,' Brigid says. 'Are you older than that?'

The slightest head shake from Induae.

'Fifteen?'

Another shake of the head from Induae, though Indiu has remained completely still, only her eyes moving, darting between Brigid and her sister.

'Fourteen then?'

A nod.

Brigid hears the stream before she can see it. It is hidden from sight by tall willow trees which the girls weave through, ducking under the low hanging branches and stepping over the roots.

The water is flowing quickly over dark boulders. Brigid takes a step forward and feels the ground beneath her feet give way. She is falling forward, arms wheeling wildly, as though she could catch the air to stop her fall. A dull thud and then pain exploding in her forehead. The water is icy and the shock of the cold hurts almost as much as the pain.

She gets to her knees in the fast-flowing water and tries to stand, but the current and her spinning head cause her to fall again.

A strong hand takes her elbow. She blinks away the dancing lights to see Induae, crouching next to her in the water, sharp eyes full of concern.

'Are you all right?' Induae says.

Indiu hisses from her place on the riverbank.

Induae, realizing her mistake, covers her small mouth with her hand, as though trying to push the words back in.

'Help me up,' Brigid says. 'Please.'

Induae does as instructed, though she does not meet Brigid's eyes.

Back on the safety of the bank, Brigid sits. She reaches her hand to her forehead and it comes away red. The pain is sharp and keen, but she does not think the cut is deep.

'So,' she says. 'You do speak?'

Induae looks to her sister.

'We do,' Indiu says at last.

'Do your parents know?'

'They do not,' Induae says, her voice almost drowned by the rushing of the water.

'But why? Why all this story about curses?'

'Because we were cursed. But not as our mother and father believe,' Indiu says. There is a directness to her that Brigid admires. A solidity.

'But we cannot tell you,' Induae says. 'We have been sworn on pain of death to silence. Even speaking as we are now...' Her hand again flutters to her lips.

'And tell me, who placed this geas on you?'

The girls look to one another, and Brigid sees that perhaps they have had no need of speech for it is as if each can read the other's mind.

THE YOUNGEST BROTHER, I whisper, my voice a gurgle of the stream.

'Machta, your uncle?' Brigid says.

Four eyes snap to her.

'How?'

'Mother was right. She is blessed.'

The dizziness has passed enough for Brigid to risk standing. 'Tell me,' she says. 'And perhaps we can break this curse.'

The story is an old one, known by many women. Their uncle did sing and dance with them all day. But at night, when the guests had gone to sleep and the fires put out, he would come to their rooms.

'We tried to tell our mother,' Induae says. 'But she said we must be soft in the head. When Machta found out we had tried to tell, he said if I breathed a word of it, he would kill Indiu.'

'And he told me, that if I spoke,' Indiu says, 'he would kill Induae.'

'So you stopped speaking at all?' Brigid asks.

They nod.

'But he has gone now. So why keep your silence?'

'Because if he learns that we can speak he will return. Our silence keeps us safe,' Induae says.

'It has become our armour,' Indiu says. 'As long as we stay small and stupid, they hardly think of us at all.'

'If we are lucky, we can vanish altogether. And then, at last, we shall be—'

Induae stops speaking, her head whipping around at the sound of a branch snapping.

'Whose voices do I hear?' It is Mealla, come to seek them out.

The twins freeze, their mouths perfect Os of shock and fear.

When their mother finds them, she will know that their being mute has been a lie. But perhaps she should know what her brother has done. That then at last justice can be served. If only this was a world where young women could find justice.

Brigid remembers what Mealla said. *"There is healing in your blood."*

She presses her hands against the cut on her head, first the right and then the left, pushing hard against the wound to make the blood flow once more. Then she places her bloodied hand around the throats of the twins, leaving an imprint of red finger-marks.

Mealla sweeps aside the branches of the willow like opening a curtain. Her sharp eyes scanning for any other sources of sound.

'Indiu, Induae. It was your voices I heard?' she says to her daughters. 'But how can this be?'

Brigid stands, placing her body between the mother and her daughters, as impassable as any fort wall. These girls are under her protection now and no harm will come to them while she lives. 'I have healed them.'

Mealla gasps and falls to her knees, bowing back and forth, her arms flying up and down like a wave. 'All praise the new god. All praise the new god and his messenger on earth.'

Their new god had nothing to do with this. The only miracle here is the wilful blindness of a mother. The only marvel that Brigid saw the girls' pain when their parents had turned away.

There is a rustling and stamping of feet. Ui Brolaig crashes through the undergrowth, with Darlughdach, Ciara and Lommán behind him. Lommán has her dagger drawn, ready to strike any that dare hurt Brigid.

'What is this screaming? Wife, why are you wailing?' Ui Brolaig says, trying to get his wife to stand.

She continues to rock back and forth; her praying has become a gibberish of sobbing and praise.

Lommán rushes forward and grabs Brigid's chin, moving her face to see the cut on her forehead.

Darlughdach is next by her side. 'Are you hurt? Did they hurt you?'

'Why the fussing? Sure, Brigid's taken worse than that little cut,' Ciara says.

Brigid raises her hand to silence the three. 'All is well.' She approaches Ui Brolaig. 'This curse you spoke of has been lifted and your daughters are well.'

'Is this true?' he asks.

Indiu's lips tighten like walnuts as she swallows. Brigid imagines the sour taste the girl must have in her throat. For two years, she has bitten her tongue and accepted the vile things said around her. For two years, she has protected herself and her sister in the only way she knows how, because her father failed to protect them as a father should. Now that she is free to speak, what will she say?

It is Induae who speaks first. She lays a hand on her sister's arm. 'It is, Father.'

'Oh, a miracle. It's a miracle. I knew it. I knew it! You . . .' he waggles a finger in Brigid's direction, 'are a wonder-worker! My daughters returned to me and surely a son must follow. Do you hear that, Mealla? A son, you will surely bear me a son at last!'

Brigid doesn't disavow him of his hope.

'Come, come, back to the fort,' Ui Brolaig says. 'We must feast.'

'No,' Brigid says. 'We must go.'

'Must we?' Ciara whines, her bottom lip hanging low. She is still holding a leg of rabbit.

'Yes.'

'Well, if you're sure,' Ui Brolaig says, and Brigid notices there is none of the usual protestation of a good host. 'Come then, daughters. Now you are in your wits again, we can start to look for husbands for you. Perhaps your uncle, Machta, knows of a good man?'

The twins flinch. They look to Brigid with pleading eyes.

'No,' Brigid says again, turning to their parents. 'They will come with me. They are now my sisters in God.'

Mealla's mouth flaps open and closed like a landed trout, while her husband splutters.

'But . . . their bride price?' Ui Brolaig says, blinking his small pig eyes. 'I've fed and clothed them for years.'

'You would dare quibble with God?' Brigid says softly and yet the leaves around her quiver as though afraid.

Mealla gets to her feet. 'Of course, take them. Go in peace.' She places her hands over her empty womb. 'Fear not, husband, for we will not be alone for long. I can feel life growing within me.'

There will be no boy born to this woman, no son to inherit this man's land and cattle. I will be sure of it.

Brigid leaves, her covenant of sisters now five strong.

23

Brigid and her women (*her* women, she thinks and cannot deny the shudder of delight that comes from that) sit by the river that marks the borders to King Dunlaing's land. It has been close to two months since Brigid demanded a meeting with the king, and there has been no reply.

It is an unusually hot day, as have been all the days of this summer.

'Thank Lugh,' Ciara says, holding her face to the warm sky like a sunflower. 'Or, I mean . . . thank Christ?' she says, looking to Brigid.

'You can thank Lugh,' Brigid says.

'I wouldn't,' Darlughdach says darkly. 'If he had anything to do with this weather, it will have been for his own purposes. He cares little for the concerns of us.'

Brigid has been meaning to ask Darlughdach about her relationship to Lugh. Her name, daughter of Lugh; she has never heard of anyone called this before. Was she his follower or . . . a suspicion rises in her when she watches Darlughdach, as the sun catches her face just so, and wonders that any human could be so beautiful.

The bard is weaving strands of fresh green reeds together, folding them back and forth, around and around with swift fingers.

'What are you making?' Brigid asks her.

Darlughdach holds up the weaving. It has four arms reaching out from a central square. 'A sun wheel. Éces taught us how to make them at Tuam. Here.' She hands it to Brigid. 'It will protect you.'

Brigid takes it with delicate hands, careful not to break it. 'It's like Dunlaing's cross,' she says.

'Don't let Éces hear you say that. He'd sooner snap off his own arms than have anything to do with the new religion.'

'You studied under Éces?' Lommán asks.

'I did indeed,' Darlughdach preens. 'Only the greatest bard the land has known. Until I came along anyway.'

Brigid had heard of the great bard Torna Éces, but had not known he was her friend's teacher. *All this time together, and we are only just scratching the surface.*

'We should wash,' Darlughdach says, changing the subject. 'We all stink. Our linens too for the sun will have them dry again in no time. Come on.'

Darlughdach peels her clothes off and throws them to the ground in a pile. Her body is lean, with strong shoulders and small breasts. She pulls her coal-black hair free of its binding and shakes it loose.

'Last one in's a rotten plum.'

With three leaping strides, worthy of a warrior's battle feat, she launches herself into the water and lands with a splash that catches them all.

'It's c-cold,' she says, as her head breaks the surface of the water. 'But so good.'

Darlughdach throws her arms up and falls back on to the water, floating on her back with her face to the sky. Her hair drifts around her reminding Brigid of the Selkie women, who can shapeshift into seals.

The twins cannot resist. They strip off their clothing, and hand in hand, they run, leap and splash into the river, letting out a warbling cry of joy. Ciara follows, though unlike the other women, she walks slowly into the water, wincing as the cold creeps up her naked body. Brigid closes her eyes as she sees wounds, only starting to heal, across Ciara's back, and curses her brothers once more.

'It's fucking freezing,' Ciara says, as she is at last submerged.

With a strange hesitation, Brigid places the woven sun wheel on the ground and begins to undress, unpinning her skirts and cloak and peeling her linens off. Unlike Ciara who shared rooms and bathwater with other slaves, Brigid was always afforded a room and a washtub of her own. The day she was bathed for her wedding was the first time she had been naked in front of another person since childhood.

She walks to the edge of the water, clumsy on the wet rocks and sharp stones. The first dip of her toe in the cold water is like a bite. She retracts her foot.

'Coward!' Darlughdach shouts, splashing Brigid with a handful of water.

She turns in time so the spray hits her back. She squeals with the shock of it, a sound she is sure she has never made before. A play at fear, rather than fear itself.

Emboldened by Darlughdach's taunting, Brigid launches herself into the water, arms and legs flailing as though she could fly, till she plunges into the water. At first, the cold is like a punch to the chest, squeezing her breath out of her lungs. She lets the instinct to fight against it pass and allows herself to surrender to it. Soon her body feels as warm as though heated from within. She pauses in the glittering darkness beneath the surface and hears the water-distorted sounds of the women above. Laughter. Screeches of delight. She thinks of Sinann becoming one with the river Shannon and for a moment wonders how peaceful that would be, skin becoming reeds, limbs darting away like salmon, the last breath in your lungs becoming bubbles on the surface. When the hunger in her lungs for air becomes too much, she pushes off the slimy surface of the riverbed and returns to the world above.

Lommán is last to join them. The women know her secret, though none but Brigid have seen beneath her bandages. Instead of undressing, she walks fully clothed into the river.

'Might as well wash my clothes too.'

Brigid lets the water take her weight and rises up and down in the gentle waves caused by the movement of the women around her. Unseen eels dart between her legs and soft reeds brush against her arms.

Lommán stands in the shallows, back bent as she stares into the water below. Her hand darts into the water quick as a kingfisher, and returns holding a brown trout, which dances in her hand. She slips her finger under its gills and with a small snap, the fish goes still. She throws it on to the bank behind her and returns to staring into the water.

Darlughdach swims towards Brigid, her long arms cutting through the water.

She floats in the river, only her head and shoulders above the ripples. 'You look happy.'

'I think I am.'

Darlughdach laughs. And it's like the gurgling of the water over the rocks.

The two drift side by side. The gentle tide spins them so they are feet to feet and then slowly pulls them apart, but Darlughdach wraps her feet around Brigid's ankle, keeping them close. They float like that till their fingers wrinkle and their lips go numb from the cold.

'We should get out before we turn into trout,' Darlughdach says.

Back on the grass bank, Brigid goes to pull her linen on again.

'Give it here,' Darlughdach says, beckoning for the clothing with bent fingers. 'I'll wash them first.'

Brigid wraps herself in her cloak. It smells too, but not as bad as her dress. This she hands to Darlughdach who gathers up the clothing of the other women.

As Darlughdach beats the linens against the rocks, Lommán gets to work preparing the trout she has caught, deftly emptying their guts into the water and scraping them free of scales and fins.

'Shall we resume our lesson?' Brigid asks Ciara.

Brigid has been attempting to teach the women to read from the book Brendan gave her.

The twins have taken to reading as they had taken to silence. With a fervour. They have also taken to the new religion, believing it was Christ working through Brigid that had saved them. But Ciara has been slower to embrace this new craft and Darlughdach has downright refused.

'Go on then.' Ciara sits beside her, head resting against Brigid's shoulder, as Brigid reads with a low voice, tracing her fingers across the letters and sounding the words. Holy. Glory. Sin. Innocence. Bliss.

She pauses in her reading to look at the women around her. All are happy in their ways. Darlughdach entertains them with stories at night. The old tales of gods and goddesses and heroes and warrior queens. Free at last to tell the stories her way, without having to bend them to appease the ears of men. Even Lommán, stoic, watchful Lommán, has begun to soften and reveals more of herself each day.

Brigid too, is happy, she realizes. A gentle kind of happiness that has crept up on her like spring. Had she watched for it, she couldn't have caught the point between before and after. Once she speaks to the king and gets the land she needs, everything will be complete.

Brigid returns to the passage, reading each word out slowly, tracing her finger under each letter, so that Ciara can follow along.

"If I give all I possess to the poor and give over my body to hardship that I may boast, but do not have love, I gain nothing."

Brigid looks up at the women around her in the sunshine. *I have love. I have everything.*

'I'll never get it,' Ciara says, throwing herself back so that she stretches her body out on the cool grass. 'Whenever I close my eyes, all I see are spiders crawling across a page. That's what your letters are to me. Spiders.'

'It takes time,' Brigid says, looking away from her friend's nakedness.

Ciara sits up. 'But why do I need to learn? Isn't it enough I've learned to speak Latin? Why must I read it? You haven't made Darlughdach.'

'And she never will,' Darlughdach says. 'Stories are wild things. If you write them down, you trap them.'

Brigid and Darlughdach have had long conversations about reading. And no manner of persuasion will change Darlughdach's mind. Her art is that of the memory, not the eye, and she will not be moved.

'See!' Ciara says. 'Besides, you or the twins can read it to me while I get on with better things.'

'Such as your chores?' Darlughdach says slyly.

Since becoming a free woman, Ciara has largely refused to do her part in wood-gathering or cooking. Brigid, knowing that her friend has worked harder than any of them will do in their lifetimes, has let it pass. Ciara's body has softened, but her hands remain tough as boiled leather.

'I was thinking more along the lines of lying here on this riverbank and letting the sun mark my skin with more little kisses.'

It is true, Brigid notices now, that Ciara's arms and shoulders are freckled and her cheeks that were once gaunt and pale are now full and rosy. Freedom looks good on her.

'Here,' Lommán says, as she drops a silver fish on to Ciara's bare belly. 'Gut this.'

Ciara screeches and jumps to standing, dropping the still-flapping fish to the ground.

Darlughdach laughs, a braying hee-haw that only comes out when Darlughdach cannot contain it. Ciara stops in her hopping to grab the fish and throw it at Darlughdach's head. The bard ducks to the side and the fish plops back into the stream and whips away.

'Uh-uh! *Love is not easily angered*,' Darlughdach says, quoting from later in the passage Brigid was reading. She may have refused to learn to read, but her memory is sharper than any. '*It keeps no record of wrongs.*'

There is a moment between the women where it could become an argument. Tension has been brewing over Ciara's laziness and Brigid's unwillingness to chastise her oldest friend. She readies herself to step in, to remind them of Ciara's life before. But instead of anger, Lommán breaks the tension by laughing. A deep, booming laugh from deep within her chest. Darlughdach, always quick to mirth, is laughing again. Then the twins, each covering their mouths with their delicate hands as giggles escape through the cracks in their fingers. And at last, Ciara catches the laughter as though it is a ball passed from one to the other and soon she is rocking back and forth. Ciara falls to the ground by Darlughdach's feet. They can hardly breathe for the laughter, and tears roll down their cheeks. This is the first time Brigid has seen someone cry with happiness. Joy bubbles deep in her stomach and she wonders if these tears taste of salt, as those from sorrow do, or do they taste of honey?

Lommán is the first to stop laughing. Her head snaps around.

'Someone is watching us.'

The women scramble to cover their nakedness. Brigid wraps her cloak tighter around her body, its roughness scratching at her sun-touched flesh. The long grass of the bank rustles, and through it comes a young man.

Lommán's knife is at his throat before Brigid realizes she knows his face.

'Oh, it's only Rian,' Ciara says.

'Put your blade down,' Brigid instructs. 'I know this boy and he will do us no harm.'

Lommán is hesitant, but frees the young man. He coughs and rubs at the red mark her knife has left at his throat.

'Yeah, don't worry, girls,' Ciara says. 'Rian's more used to bothering sheep than he is women.'

Rian blushes all the way to his hairline.

'How did you find us?' Brigid asks.

'You leave a trail of stories like a deer leaves its scat. Healing this woman, freeing that one. They say you wrapped the baby Jesus in your cloak, and that you can turn water to beer.'

Ciara laughs. 'If that were true, we'd all be drunk by breakfast and dead by midwinter.'

'And why have you come?' Brigid asks, uncomfortable with these tales of her miracles.

'To let you know that King Dunlaing has returned to Mullaghmast. Dubhthach was true to his word and has requested an audience for you, Brigid.'

'And will he see me?'

'He will. In two days' time.'

Brigid jumps to her feet. At last, the weeks of waiting, of wandering, are over. 'Darlughdach, my dress, quick, we cannot spare any time.'

Darlughdach retrieves Brigid's linen from the rock on which she had laid it to dry and throws it back to her. 'You can't go to the king dressed in that.'

Brigid considers the faded yellow linen. 'Why not? It's what I wore when I last saw him.'

'Exactly. You can't remind him that you were once a slave.'

'Yes, you should go dressed in gold and embroidery,' Ciara says.

'First,' Lommán says, 'where exactly are we getting this gold from? And second, he will then think her rich and in no need of his help.'

'Lommán is right,' Brigid says. 'We must appear before the king as virgin brides.'

There is a hesitation. A cough.

'I hate to break this to you, Biddy,' Ciara says, 'but I am no virgin.'

'Me neither,' Darlughdach says.

The twins look to their feet, their hands twisting in the cloth of their skirts. But of course, women don't always get to choose.

'I have never lain with a man,' Lommán says, but with a flutter of her eyes that Brigid infuriatingly cannot read, as though these women are sharing a secret between them she will never know.

Brigid feels her sense of the world shifting. Sex was something done within marriage; none of her women are married, and yet she is the only virgin among them.

'Don't worry,' Ciara says. 'You're not missing much.'

'You are unmarried women,' Brigid says, lifting her chin. 'You are pure. And that is all there is to it.'

Brigid slips her hand into her pouch and pulls out a silver ring she was given by a woman in gratitude for a healing Brigid had performed on her. She hands it to Rian.

'Go and buy me a dress of white. No, buy five dresses and a man's fine cloak and staff, and return before dark. In the morning, I will meet the king.'

The women watch Rian leave.

'This had better work,' Darlughdach says.

'It will,' Brigid says.

It has to, she says only to me.

24

Brigid arrives at the gates to Mullaghmast dressed in glowing white. Her sisters behind her shine like swans. Lommán, dressed in a black hooded cloak, leads the way, her staff kicking up dust as she dents the ground ahead with each strike. Come near these women, each thud says, and that will be your skull dented.

They have gathered a small group of people in their wake; travellers and traders pulled off their paths by the magnetic draw of Brigid and her virgins.

'Why has she come?'

'Do you think it's true what they say about her?'

'Let's see if she really can perform a wonder. She might be another liar.'

Their whispers swirl like a whirlwind.

Darlughdach pauses before the gates, staring up at the spikes around the fort wall.

'Are you all right?' Brigid asks.

'The king told me he would have my head on one of them if I returned.'

Brigid takes her hand and squeezes. 'You are with me now. Nothing will harm you.'

The gates open and Brigid leads the way through.

The sounds of the crowd stop in an instant, like birdsong when danger sends a flock scattering to the sky. All eyes turn to them. All movement stops. A man steps forward. He is stout, with the soft round belly and fine clothing of a cattle lord.

'If you think you can walk in here and free our slaves and run off with our daughters,' the man shouts, 'you'd better think again, Brigid of the Fothairt.'

'Yeah, you can't go around, like, taking people,' another man says, stepping beside the first. Behind him, Brigid can see other men, putting down the tasks at hand and gathering around her. Their grumbling anger rolls like thunder.

'Why not?' a woman's voice sounds from the crowd. 'Sure weren't the slaves taken in the first place?'

'I don't know what you're worried about, Cormac,' another woman shouts. 'You've no slaves and no daughters either as the gods wouldn't be so cruel as to curse a girl with you for a father.'

The women of Mullaghmast have come to stand around Brigid and her sisters, and though the men are stronger, with thick arms and fists like cudgels, the women outnumber them. They shout taunts at the men, jeering and teasing. The heat of bodies presses in on Brigid, her heart beats faster and faster, she has to get away.

The crowd is parted as a man pushes his way through and stands before her, his heavy feet stamping on the mud. His face is mottled with red, breath huffing from his nose like a bull. It stinks like rotting apples. It takes her a moment to recognize him, for she only saw him through the haze of her veil. It is Rechtabra, the man who was to have been her husband.

'You tricked me,' Rechtabra roars, and she turns away from the shower of spittle. 'Look at you, all beautiful. What is to stop me from throwing you over my shoulder and taking you as the bride you were promised?'

Brigid can sense the tension in the crowd, perfectly balanced; one step wrong and there will be violence.

'You touch her, and you will die.' Lommán takes a step

forward and places her staff in the space between Brigid and Rechtabra.

'Who do you think you are, little man, to shake your stick at me?' Rechtabra grabs hold of the staff and yanks Lommán forward.

It is one thing to set his ire on her, but to direct it at one of her sisters? She cannot allow this. Brigid grabs hold of the staff in a grip like stone. Heat comes up through her body, from her feet to the top of her head, as though she were standing on hot coals. The wood beneath her hand begins to pop and blister. She stares at Rechtabra and imagines it is his skin.

'Now, now,' Darlughdach says, coming to stand beside Brigid. She lays a hand on Rechtabra's chest. 'Look at you. A big man, trying to scare a little lad. Is that what you want? To fight him? Oh, what a tale the bards will weave of the great cattle lord Rechtabra and his mighty battle against the ickle boy. Oh, how your name will echo through the ages.'

The crowd laugh. Rechtabra's cheeks burn red and he seems to shrink before Brigid's eyes. Mockery striking him like a sword.

'Forget about Brigid,' Darlughdach says. 'Go and find yourself a great, fat woman. One with an arse as big as a cow. The bull and the cow. What a couple you'd make – two great big arses together.'

More laughter. Rechtabra glares at the crowd, as though daring any of them to fight him, his face going purple now, his nose flaring wider with each breath.

'He does look like a bull!' a woman shouts.

Rechtabra snorts, snot spraying from his nose. This causes even more hilarity. The crowd start to snort and moo at him, holding fingers up to their heads, in imitation of horns.

Brigid watches Rechtabra's face, as his eye twitches, his

jaw clenches. He wants to fight, someone, anyone. But that would mean fighting every man here.

At last, he lets go of Lommán's staff and steps back. He sniffs in Brigid's direction, forces a smile as though he is in on the jest and not the butt of it.

'Yeah,' he says. 'She's too skinny for my tastes, anyway.'

Brigid gazes at Darlughdach. The woman knew just what was needed. Knew how to choose her words, in order to bend people. To turn tension into laughter, to shame a man's anger away. This is a skill Brigid does not have and she wonders if she will ever have it; for she has only ever been able to tell the truth.

People are still gathered around, waiting to see what Brigid will do next. She herself does not know, only that she feels trapped, and if she cannot move soon, she may burst.

'Please let me pass,' she says. 'I am here to see the king.'

Silence ripples through the crowd like a wave as every trader and thief, warrior and widow, stops to watch Brigid and her women as they pass.

They climb the mound to the king's roundhouse, and enter into the darkness. The sound of fort life returns behind them as though a spell has been lifted.

King Dunlaing is waiting for them inside, two spear-carriers standing behind him and a young woman and girl to one side. Judging by the wealth of their clothing, these two must be the king's wife and daughter. The woman's hair is so pale it looks almost white, and her skin is the colour of the inside of an eggshell. She looks as frail as an egg too, as though the slightest brush could bruise her. The girl hiding behind her mother's skirts takes after her father: dark and broad-faced.

'Well met, Brigid,' the woman says.

Brigid bows, low and graceful. Her women follow her

example. Brigid tries to see them all through the king's eyes. Sacred virgins, not slaves and lepers and abandoned girls.

King Dunlaing steps forward to get a better look at her. 'I can hardly believe that you are the same girl who came before me only two months gone. You look . . .' He struggles to find the word. He settles on, 'Different.'

'A lot can happen in two months, my king. I hear you won even more land in battle.'

He tilts his head in acknowledgement. Such a subtle movement for such a mighty deed. He too has changed. He looks older, though it has only been a few months since they last met. A new scar cuts down the side of his face, tracing the line of his cheekbones. She heard he fought bravely alongside his men in the battle against Lóegaire mac Néill, the King of Tara.

'You have been fighting your own battles, I hear. So have you come to free all of my slaves?' he says.

'Not today,' she answers.

Dunlaing chuckles and repeats her words under his breath. 'Not today. But not never, hey?'

A rustling of cloth brings Brigid's attention back to the people with them.

'Oh, this is my wife, Cuach.'

Cuach bows also, though she does not take her eyes off Brigid's face. Her eyes are curious, not wary.

'And my daughter, Gráinne,' Dunlaing says, ruffling the girl's dark hair. She pushes her father's hand away and flattens her hair down again. 'My son, Aillil, is off causing trouble somewhere, no doubt.'

The queen's blonde hair is woven into intricate patterns and entwined with gold thread. She cannot be much more than ten years older than Brigid. In her late twenties at the most. Gráinne comes to just below her shoulder; eleven, perhaps twelve. Her son, Aillil, Brigid has heard is her own age, and she marvels at how young Cuach must have been when she birthed him.

'So, then, what is it that brings you here today? Have you changed your mind about joining my household?'

'I have one small request.'

'If it is in my power to give it to you, you shall have it. What do you ask of me?'

'Land,' Brigid says.

Dunlaing pauses, as if waiting for the rest of a joke. When it does not come, he blinks. 'And what, may I ask, does a girl like you need with land?'

Brigid flinches, but controls the stab of anger that twists in her stomach. She steps forward, into a beam of light breaking through the window, remembering the trick. 'To build a community. Where women can be safe from the world. Where we can live as we decide without the interference of men. Not wives, not slaves. Only women.' Anger sizzles in her voice.

There is the smallest of coughs from behind her. Darlughdach, reminding her of herself. Reminding her of how they had practised this request on the way here.

'Appeal to his faith,' Darlughdach had said. 'He wants the world to know he is no longer a pagan savage. And if that doesn't work, appeal to his vanity.'

Brigid looks to the gold cross glinting around Dunlaing's neck.

'A community dedicated to Christ,' she adds, touching her forehead, chest and shoulders as she has seen other followers of Christ do. It's a clumsy, unpractised movement that she still doesn't fully understand, but hopes Dunlaing will see it as a sign.

He gasps in delight and Brigid suppresses a smile that her plan has worked. 'You are a Christian now?'

Brigid does not want to lie. 'I have been shown the way,' she says, bowing her head.

Dunlaing presses his hands together and holds them up to his lips. 'This fills my heart with joy, Brigid, for I believed I saw the light of the Lord in you on our first meeting. But your duty as a Christian woman should be to marry, have children. Not build communities. That is a man's role, to protect and guide.'

Brigid bites down on her lip, fighting back the instinct to argue. If appealing to his faith has not worked, then she will appeal to his vanity.

'But of course, you would be our protector, King Dunlaing. I would merely be the handmaiden of God's work.'

The king raises an eyebrow. 'How much land?'

'A scrap,' Brigid says. 'Barely more than my cloak could cover.'

This seems to appease him. 'Follow me.'

'"Barely more than my cloak could cover,"' Ciara mutters under her breath, mocking Brigid's soft tones. 'What are you on about?'

'Be patient,' Brigid replies.

'Ciara's not wrong though. We'll need more than a scrap of land,' Darlughdach says.

It pleases Brigid to see her two dearest friends on the same side for once. Even if it is united against herself. 'Patience,' she says again.

Brigid, her sisters and Cuach follow Dunlaing out of the fort and away to a mound that rises behind it, the Hill of Almu. They clamber to the top and Brigid finds that her breath is taken from her by the effort.

'Behold,' Dunlaing says, stretching his arms out. 'The Curragh.'

The sun shines across a plain that stretches for five

thousand acres, the river Liffey to the east, the river Barrow to the west. Cows, horses and sheep graze on the lush green grass and lapwings swoop and dive in the blue skies above.

'Fionn mac Cumhaill trained his warriors on this very land,' Dunlaing says. 'They say he is buried here.'

Across the plain, Brigid sees another raised hill of earth, and on top of it, a familiar, twisted oak tree, older than even the mound they are standing on and the bodies buried beneath it.

YES, MY CHILD. THIS IS THE PLACE.

In the rippling heat haze, Brigid can see her future. She can see herds of cows giving rich milk churned into butter by laughing women. Yellow barley fields swaying in the wind, seeds sown by nimble hands on Imbolc, crops harvested by strong arms at Lughnasa. She sees the barley added to the fresh water from the stream and brewed into spiced beer to quench the thirst of her sisters. Rooms for women, where they can sleep, safe. At the heart, she sees a tower, round and strong and filled with backs bent over desks, fingertips stained blue and purple and gold as they transcribe the knowledge of the world and bring illumination.

Atop the hill with the oak tree, she will relight the flame of the goddess and will set a virgin to watching over it each and every night, and on the twenty-first night she will take the watch. And around it all, she will build a wall of brambles and whitethorn and any man that dares cross over into their sanctuary will burn. She sees it all as if it were there before her, hears the laughter, voices joined in prayer, the scritching of quill on parchment, smells the beer, the butter, the sweat of labour. They will call it a church, but it will be so much more than that. It will be a *convent* – a meeting place. A community.

In her mind, the Curragh becomes a blank parchment

waiting for her ink. She will create a whole world on that page. All she need do is make her mark.

You are so close now.

'Lay your cloak, Brigid,' Dunlaing says, 'and I will give you an acre around it.'

Brigid blinks and sees again the low grass and rolling hills. She unclasps her blue cloak and holds it in her hands. She walks down the hill, and out across the plain, dragging her cloak behind her. She stops every now and then, bending to pluck a blade of grass and bite down on it or to grab a handful of soil and rub it between her fingers as though testing for the fertility of the ground beneath her feet. She looks up to the sky, one eye closed against the beams of the sun which is close to its zenith and back to the earth below.

'Each acre is much like the other,' Dunlaing says, his patience wearing.

When Brigid has walked for ten minutes, she stops and looks down. A small snake slithers through the grass.

'Here.' She turns to the others. 'Darlughdach, Ciara,' she says, handing over her cloak. 'Take a corner each. And Indiu and Induae, do the same also.'

The four women each take a corner and stand facing each other.

'Are we going to play toss the pig?' Ciara asks.

There was a game Brigid played with Ciara and some of the girls from Dún Ailinne when she was young. Four would hold a heavy blanket between them; a fifth would lie in the middle and be thrown into the air. Brigid would always fly the highest, as though she weighed nothing at all, and would be tossed so high it scared the others and the game would end. She longs to fly like that again.

'No,' Brigid says to her women. 'I want you to run.'

There is a moment as the women look from Brigid to each other, confused. Darlughdach is the first to move, taking a step away. The cloak moves with her, stretching as though made of dough. She steps back and back and back again, the corner of the cloak in her hand still.

Darlughdach laughs in delight. As one, the four women take flight, running in opposite directions, skipping and leaping as children let out to play. The cloak stretches out between them, growing and growing as they run as fast as they can, their feet kicking up the soft turf, legs pumping, white skirts kicking up around their thighs, as their laughter and yells of joy float on the wind.

The blue cloak covers an acre. Two. Three. It grows and grows and billows in the light wind like a wave, over the heads of the cows and the sheep and the horses. Over the oak tree. By the time the sun is overhead, the cloak covers every lush acre of the Curragh like a new sky.

'Stop!' Dunlaing calls out. He tugs at handfuls of hair as though about to tear them from his head. 'You will take all of my land.'

'You made a binding promise,' Brigid reminds him.

For a king to break his promise would be to mark himself an unworthy king. Everything Dunlaing has fought to gain could be taken from him. What is five thousand acres against a whole kingdom?

His chest heaves, his pale skin is mottled with red anger, and his fists open and close, open and close in rhythm with his unsettled breathing.

A small hand, no bigger than a child's, takes his. Cuach steps out from behind her husband and looks up at him. She places her second hand over his heart. His breathing slows and the fierce anger drains from his cheeks.

How many cool hands of women have stopped the rage of

men? How many wars have been saved by a simple touch of love?

'And I hold to my word,' Dunlaing says, with a long sigh. He steps back, hand in hand with his wife. 'The Curragh is yours.'

Brigid waves her hands above her head, calling her sisters back. They come running, skipping back through the long grass. She does not need to tell them they have won, for her smile is enough.

She opens her arms and they embrace, foreheads pressed together in a huddled circle, as Brigid's cloak shrinks to become a simple cape once more. Their eyes sparkle with the thrill of what they have done, of the magic they have performed together.

Together, yes, we did this together. Power is better shared.

A moment later, the excitement passes. They stand looking across at the land that is theirs. Seemingly endless. A blank page waiting to be written on.

25

Brigid has so many plans for the land she can hardly sleep at night for seeing them. A roundhouse to start, with beds – actual beds – for them all to sleep in. A kitchen. A kiln, for drying corn, and a barn to store it. Behind her eyes, she sees stone buildings, reaching to the sky, though she does not know the use of them. Only that they shall be built. And the fields, she sees them golden with rape and barley. And lush green pastures for cattle to graze. She will have her very own herd of cows that she will milk two even three times a day to make more butter than they can dream of eating. What is left, they will sell or give to those in need.

But first, the flame.

Brigid sends Ciara and Lommán to Mullaghmast on market day to get a cauldron. They do not return till evening, dragging behind them a large bronze bowl, engraved with delicate looping patterns.

'It's beautiful,' Brigid says.

'It had better be,' Ciara says. 'We had to promise him a calf come spring in return.'

'We don't even have a cow yet,' Induae says, eyes wide in shock at the lie.

'He doesn't know that,' Ciara replies, stretching out her back.

Brigid places a stack of soft, thin sticks over a pile of wood shavings. She says a prayer and with a strike of flint on stone, makes a spark.

I take pity on her. It bursts into a strong, warm flame.

'And so it begins.'
AND SO IT BEGINS.

They pass another night sleeping huddled together under the branches of the oak tree. The heat from the flame hardly able to warm them.

'Enough of this,' Darlughdach says in the morning, as she wrings the damp out of her tunic. 'We need somewhere warm to sleep or we will all die and all you have won will have been for nothing.'

'Even a hut would do,' Ciara says.

Ciara has been careful not to complain too much about their life of freedom since the riverside. But Brigid can see the misery pinch at her old friend's face.

'No,' Brigid says softly.

The pronouncement is met with looks of sharp shock and anger. Even the twins' soft features crumple in annoyance.

'Do you want us to suffer?' Darlughdach says, her brow wrinkled like the bark of the tree she leans against. 'Just because your Christ did? Because if so, you can take your religion and f—'

Brigid cuts Darlughdach off with a raised hand. 'I only mean that we will need more than just a hut. We will need to build a roundhouse.' She picks up a stick and draws a circle in the dirt, with lines for windows and a door. 'At least twenty-seven feet in diameter. With cubicles for each of us to sleep.'

'Has anyone built a house before?' Darlughdach asks.

All the women shake their heads.

'It can't be too hard,' Ciara says, standing skirts pulled up, fists thrust deep into her hips. 'I saw some men do it at Dún Ailinne and it only took them a day.'

'But we don't have any tools,' Indiu says.

'Or any good timber,' Induae says, pointing at the pile of wood they have gathered. The logs are bent and covered with green moss.

Brigid sees that the twins are right. The confidence that has kept her going these last weeks – her surety that once they had the land they needed, nothing else would stand in their way – falters. She fights to keep her face still, not to let the sudden fear that creeps up her spine show in her expression. What was she doing, thinking she could build a home for these women with nothing but hope? What if she has condemned them all to a life of misery?

Darlughdach comes to stand behind Brigid. She rests her chin on Brigid's shoulder and looks down at the wobbly circle drawn in dust.

'Then ours will be a round-ish house,' Darlughdach says. 'Perfection is overrated anyway.'

Brigid squeezes her friend's hand and feels strength flowing up from her fingertips, pushing out the fear. As long as they are together, all will be well.

'We will call it Cill Dara,' Brigid says.

CHURCH OF THE OAK. YES. THIS WILL DO.

They get to work and mostly they fail. The soil gives way under their feet. The walls won't stay up. And the reeds they have gathered for a roof are too wet and bend limply inward. But as they fail, they learn. They move to higher ground, near a natural well. They dig deeper holes for the posts, leave reeds out to dry. It takes them six days – six days of sleeping under the stars and working in the rain, six days of cut hands and empty stomachs, of singing to lift spirits and laughing when it all goes wrong – but they build their home. A roundhouse, barely fourteen feet across and six feet high. Two walls of hazel wattle, one tucked inside the other, and the tight space between them filled with moss and leaves for warmth, and heather for the scent. For the roof, more woven hazel strips, topped with a thatch of reeds.

As she lies inside it for the first night, pressed up against the other women, dry at last, the sweet smell of hay gathered for bedding filling her senses, peace settles over her.

This is happiness. Nothing more than this.

And yet, when she closes her eyes, she sees not small houses, but great stone buildings, not a simple fire flickering, smoke curling through a hole in the roof, but a great fireplace and candles, so many candles dripping on to stone floors as women write and write and write their way to immortality. Happiness isn't enough. She wants it all.

Darlughdach moves next to her, throwing an arm across Brigid's waist, and pulls her tight, bringing her back to the present.

'Sleep,' Darlughdach whispers.

'How did you know I was awake?'

'I can hear your brain working,' she says. 'Like a tide mill.'

'I have much to think about.'

'It can wait,' Darlughdach says, wriggling closer. 'It can all wait.'

Each day gets colder, and each day more women find them. Broken, lost, abused women who pass her name from one to the other, whispered away from the ears of men. She is the Holy Mother who can heal them. Mary of the Gaels who can save them. Some stay only for a few hours to hear Brigid speak, or to ask her advice, before returning home with heads full of dangerous ideas about freedom. But many stay.

Soon the roundhouse is full to bursting – they will need to build another. And around it, a wall. Men have been seen gathering at the edges of their settlement to watch the women work, and even from far away Brigid can see the hunger and anger in their eyes. How dare these women choose not to marry? How bold of them to believe they could live outside the protection of men. How long before they do more than watch?

The endless chatter of the women and the presence of so many people presses in on Brigid. Despite the cold, she escapes to the oak tree and sits by the flame seeking solace from the constant noise. But the new women follow her even here. They sit bundled up in blankets and cloaks, and pretend to watch the fire. But she knows they are watching her, as though waiting to see if she too might burst into flames.

Lommán builds a small forge to the east of the roundhouse, remembering the smithing skills she learned from the man who hurt her. She passes these skills on to Brigid, who has taken to the heating and hammering of metal with delight. She sees in the soft red metal the world that she can bend to her will. Each ringing strike of hammer on anvil is a mark made on the earth. All it takes is persistence and effort and she has more than enough of both.

She looks for any excuse to work in the forge, the heat of the fire warming her ice-cold fingers. Part of her thinks she should give the job to another, one less able to bear the punishment of this cruel winter. And yet, working with metal is one of the rare times her mind is blissfully free of the concerns of keeping the convent safe and fed, so she allows herself this one indulgence, for the greater good.

She is working on a carving knife when her name is called between the beatings of the hammer. She cannot stop, for she must get the shape right before the metal cools and shatters.

'Tell whoever is shouting I will be with them soon,' Brigid says to Lommán who is easing the bellows up and down with her lean arms.

Lommán brushes sawdust from her hands and goes out to pass the message on. Brigid hears an exchange of voices outside, raised and impatient.

'She is needed now.'

The distraction is too much. Brigid misses a strike and the telltale ringing ping tells her the cast is ruined.

'Here.' She passes the tongs over to Clodagh, a thin, dark-haired girl who joined them in the summer. The bruises that covered her body told Brigid all she needed to know about the life she had left behind. 'Melt it down and start again.'

The contrast from the heat of the forge to the brutal cold of outside is like a punch. She sees it is Ciara who has come to summon her.

'What is it?' she asks, standing and joining her friend.

'A woman has come,' Ciara says.

'Women come every day.'

'This one needs your help now, or it will be too late. Come.' Ciara grabs her sleeve and leads her away.

In the small yard outside the roundhouse, a woman is sitting on an upturned milk pail. A soft scattering of snow falls and settles on the ground. The woman is wearing only a light cloak and her body trembles like a leaf.

Ciara taps the woman gently on the shoulder, and Brigid is struck by the unusual softness in her friend's touch. 'Orla, she is here.'

The woman turns. Her right eye is swollen shut and her cheek and jaw blackened by bruises. Around her mouth, dry blood. All Brigid's irritation at being taken from her task evaporates, replaced with a furious sympathy.

'Who did this to you?' she says, kneeling by the woman.

'The man who I am to marry.' The woman's words are slurred by her swollen lip and it causes her pain to speak.

'Come,' Brigid says, helping the woman to her feet.

Every step causes Orla to wince in pain, as Brigid leads her into the forge and sits her by the fire to warm herself.

'Go and get her some spiced beer,' Brigid tells Clodagh.

They have only just brewed it, and it will be bitter but strong. The girl throws the broken knife blade into the fire and runs off. When she returns carrying a large jug, others have followed to see the newcomer. They hover about the doorway of the forge to peer in.

'God love her,' one of them says, making the sign of the cross.

Many women have come bearing bruises, but none so beaten as this one.

'What happened?' Brigid asks, after Orla has drained half of her beer.

'There is a man,' Orla says, so softly Brigid has to lean in to hear. 'Ever since I was a child, he has pursued me. Desired me.' She swallows, as if the idea of this is bitter, and drinks more to take away the taste. 'Each year, he offered my father a larger and larger bride price. But my father, knowing my feelings for him, refused.' She drains her cup and sets it aside with shaking hands. 'Two weeks ago, my father died.'

Orla's chest shudders as she tries to catch her breath and stop the tears flowing. Brigid squeezes her hand. There are not many at Cill Dara who weep over the death of their fathers.

'The man came to pay his respects, but I knew why he was truly there. He offered me a golden brooch. I have never seen a thing of such worth, or such ugliness. He said it was a symbol of his love.' She winces, holds her hand to her lip. It has split again, and bright blood trickles down her chin. Brigid wipes it away with the cuff of her dress. Orla is quite beautiful, which Brigid knows can be a curse to a woman in a man's world.

'Did you take his brooch?' Brigid asks, for she would not blame her if she had.

'No!' Orla shouts. 'I refused it, told him to take it away and give it to another. But he left it on the floor. Said I should think it over and that he would return the next day.'

'He may have thought gold would weaken your will,' Ciara says.

'Not even the gold stores of Tara would tempt me,' Orla says. 'I left the brooch where it was. But when the man returned the next day, it was gone. And he beat me. I thought he was going to kill me. It might have been better if he had.'

'Do not say such things,' Brigid says.

'I would rather be dead than marry him. But he says if I cannot return the brooch to him, he will take it as my bride price and then he will take me.' She breaks down in desperate sobs.

'Hush, you are safe now,' Brigid says. 'Ciara, take her to wash and find her some clothes and a bed.'

Ciara, who has taken to grumbling each time a new woman must be found space for, says not a word. She takes the woman's hand and leads her to the wash house.

The other women gathered make way, brushing Orla's shoulders and back with gentle hands. 'Welcome, sister,' they say.

Orla stops outside the roundhouse and looks back. 'He will come for me.'

'HE CAN TRY,' Brigid and I say as one.

The man comes that very night.

The women are woken by his yelling and wrap themselves in their cloaks and stand huddled together. The door to the roundhouse is made of solid oak and bolted with a thick drawbar. But the walls are nothing more than sticks and clay.

'Orla,' a man bellows from outside. 'Come out to me, girl, or I will come in.'

Orla looks from the door to Brigid, her eyes wide in terror. Her whole body shakes as a branch in a storm. 'I should not have come,' she says. 'I should not have brought my woe to your home.'

'The woe of one is the woe of all,' Brigid says. 'Stay here. Place pallets from your beds in front of the door, and do not come out.'

Orla goes to protest, but Ciara grabs her hand, and drags her away to get to work. The other women join them, upturning their beds to gather wood.

Darlughdach and Lommán come to stand with Brigid. Lommán holds a hammer over her shoulder while Darlughdach holds two staves; one she passes to Brigid, the other she grasps in both hands.

There is a thudding, followed by a roar. 'Orla! You are mine!'

Another thud, and the door shakes. Brigid feared this day would come, when the men would turn on them. But she is not ready. The door is battered once more. The wood cracks. It will not hold.

'Open it,' Brigid says softly.

Lommán hesitates, then lifts the drawbar.

The man is not alone. Fifteen others, each armed with a heavy cudgel or a spear, stand around him.

'Welcome to Cill Dara,' Brigid says, her voice soft as eider and sweet as honey.

'I am Flann O'Banain and I have come for my wife.'

He is as tall as most men, slim, with small eyes and a crooked nose. He looks weak enough, but even a weak man can beat a woman when his rage gives him strength.

'And who might that be?' Brigid says, forcing herself to

step forward. Lommán and Darlughdach follow, closing the door behind them. Wood scrapes as the drawbar is replaced. They are trapped now, between this man and a bolted door.

'Orla,' Flann spits the woman's name.

Brigid lifts her chin. 'Orla is not married. And she has no wish to be.'

'You've seduced our women,' a man shouts.

'We've come to take them home,' another adds.

'Who are you to stand against the law of man?' Flann bellows in Brigid's face.

The men around him grumble their agreement, some shaking their weapons, others their fists. Thick, greasy fear, the kind she has not felt since she left her father's house, rises up from the darkness within her. Her heart thuds in her chest with every shallow breath she takes, like a fist against a door. If she does not give them what they want, they will kill her and her sisters. But not before handing out punishment first. She could step aside, let them take the woman and save herself. Save them all.

'I paid my bride price,' Flann roars. 'A golden brooch worth four cumals. Now I will have my bride.'

'No,' Brigid and I say, sharing one voice.

Flann lurches forward but Brigid stops him with a raised hand against his chest. It is as though he has slammed into a wall, for he recoils from her touch and staggers away. She will not allow him so much as to lay a finger on Orla or any of the women here.

There is muttering, and Brigid hears the word 'witch' passed between the men.

'Orla says that she does not have the brooch you are seeking.'

'She lies,' Flann says, though an uncertainty has crept into his voice.

IT IS HE WHO LIES. FOR I SAW HIM. HE STOLE THE BROOCH AND THREW IT IN THE RIVER.

'I wonder,' Brigid says, 'if perhaps you didn't misplace it. Or drop it in the river maybe?'

The man's jaw drops open. He splutters protestations, but they come out as the sound of a farting mule. Some of the men around him look at his discomfort and lower their weapons.

THEY KNOW AS WELL AS I DO THAT HE IS NOT TO BE TRUSTED.

'Let us see if we cannot find this brooch of yours.'

Brigid steps towards the huddle of men, who part in her wake like barley stalks. Darlughdach and Lommán stay close behind, whether for her protection or theirs she is unsure. She only knows that the spell she has woven – if a spell it is – is all that is keeping the men from attacking. And that the magic is cobweb thin.

She walks away from the roundhouse, leading the men from the other women hiding inside, and down the hill. The snow is falling heavily now and their feet leave black marks that are soon swallowed. She leads them to the river. A thick layer of ice covers the water but beneath the surface, a dark shape moves slowly.

'This river is heavy with salmon in spring,' Brigid says. 'But they have the sense to go upstream in winter.'

With her staff, she strikes at the thin ice that covers the surface. Cracks spread out like a spider's web. She strikes again; the shards give way and float off, leaving a dark hole.

'But a few of the older, slower salmon stay put.'

Brigid lowers herself to the snowy bank and lies down.

'Brigid,' Lommán gasps, 'let me, you will catch your death.'

Brigid waves Lommán's protests away, pulls up her sleeve and plunges her arm into the water. Pain knifes deep into her bone, but she ignores it. She forces her stiff fingers to wiggle and feels the brush of soft skin against her palm. The hint of a movement, feather-like fins tickling her wrist. Carefully, she curls her fingers around the thick, heavy body of a salmon and lets it settle in her palm, as though she were part of the riverbed. When the fish is still, she yanks her arm free, sending it flying into the air and on to the bank.

She shakes the cold water from her hand. 'What do you think, Lommán?' she asks.

'Better than I could have done myself.'

Brigid grins. 'Now, let us see what secrets this salmon hides. Lommán?'

Lommán picks up the floundering fish and with a practised flick, breaks its neck. She pulls out a knife and plunges it deep into the fish's belly.

'What is this?' Flann demands to know. 'Fortune telling?'

Brigid laughs. 'No, I cannot see the future any more than I can see in the dark. But as for fortunes . . .'

There is a flash of gold amid the red blood and black guts of the fish. Lommán plucks a golden brooch from the sucking flesh. It glimmers in the sparkling light of the snowfall.

Brigid takes the brooch from Lommán's hand and holds it up for all to see. 'Is this your brooch?'

Flann once again spits and stutters, like a fire going out. 'But . . . But . . .'

BUT YOU THOUGHT YOU COULD TRICK EVERYONE. AND NOW THEY SEE THE TRUTH.

'Explain yourself, Flann,' one man shouts.

'What the fuck are you playing at?' another calls out.

'You're a cheating shit, Flann O'Banain.'

Brigid drops the brooch by Flann's feet. It sinks into the snow.

She leaves the men as they start to squabble. By the time she is at the top of the hill, she can hear the sound of sticks thudding against bones.

That could have been my bones. It could have been any of us. The next time men come—

AND THEY WILL COME.

—we may not be so lucky. And what if they had come for the flame?

YOU MUST KEEP IT SAFE.

26

'What kind of wall?' asks Lommán. 'We have hardly enough materials to build the second roundhouse you wanted, and what of the shelter for the animals? Why waste good wood protecting a tree?'

'It's not the oak that needs our protection, but the flame.' Brigid looks around and sees a whitethorn bush bursting with flowers, flowers that hide barbs. She remembers the vision she had when she first looked over the Curragh. 'There,' she says, pointing at the shrub. 'Transplant that, and it will grow.'

It is hard work and takes all day, pulling up the gnarled roots of the whitethorn and digging a new trench for it around the oak tree. When they press the last handful of soil over the roots, the women are exhausted, hungry and covered in scratches.

'It looks as though we lost a fight with a clowder of cats,' Darlughdach says, licking the blood from a scratch on her arm.

'Don't lick at it,' Ciara says. 'Here.' She dips a cloth into a small bowl and dabs the substance within on Darlughdach's arm.

Darlughdach screeches like a cat herself. 'What is that? It stings like the Dagda's piss.'

'Figwort and honey.'

Ciara has appointed herself the convent's beekeeper, building a row of small hives behind the roundhouse. Only she seems able to approach the bees without getting stung.

'That does not smell like honey,' Darlughdach says, sniffing at her arm and wrinkling her nose.

'Consider yourself lucky – that was meant for my breakfast.'

Darlughdach pushes her arm into Ciara's face. 'By all means, help yourself.'

Ciara yowls and spins away. Darlughdach takes chase, weaving in and out of the women, and soon they are all shrieking and laughing and chasing each other as though everyone were a child again.

Brigid looks at the whitethorn hedge now surrounding the flame. It is weak and most of the flowers were shaken off in the transport. But it will grow stronger each day. As will they.

By the time Beltane approaches, seventy women have joined Brigid's community, dedicating their lives to protecting the flame. It burns still, watched each night by one of Brigid's sisters, and the whitethorn hedge surrounding it grows thicker and sharper.

'We're running out of places to put everyone,' Ciara says, one morning after a restless night. It was cold and there were not enough blankets to go around.

'And we're struggling to keep everyone fed,' Indiu says.

Induae nods. 'The cows can only be milked once a day.'

They have been feeding themselves through foraging and with whatever food the women have brought with them as offerings. One woman brought a small herd of cows, though with each milking they give less and less.

'Then we must ask the land to give,' Brigid says. 'We must start farming. Barley. Wheat. Apples. And pigs, we will raise pigs.'

'And where will we get the money for all these pigs and apples?' Ciara asks.

'We don't need money,' she says. 'The seeds are already within the ground, I will ask it to grow.'

'And the pigs?' Lommán asks. She has borne the brunt of the hunting and gathering, keeping her away from the rest of the convent for days on end.

'Wild boars live in the woods. Build an enclosure. They will come.'

And come they do. Out of the woods, snuffling their way through the fences built for them. And once the women have prepared the soil, bright green shoots appear within days and unfurl their heads. It takes a season of hard work and hunger and hope, but the land becomes fertile and soon they have more than enough grain for the stores, salted bacon sits in barrels rows deep, and what they cannot store they trade. For livestock, vegetables, cloth, wood and iron.

As Brigid moves through the women, going about her daily chores, hands reach out to brush her skirts, as though even the touch of cloth that has touched her skin can cure them of all the world's ills. They have taken to calling her 'Abbess Brigid', or 'Mother Brigid'. She smiles, but behind the smile is a growing irritation that even going to feed the chickens takes three times as long as it should for all the tugging on her skirts.

Brigid never ceases in her work. If she is not planting, she is picking, if she is not building, she is forging. But most of all, she is writing. She has built a small hut between the roundhouse and the forge, just three walls and a roof of hay, but it is enough to keep the weather off the parchment as she works. She dips her quill into a small stone pot and returns to the work at hand. She has set herself the task of making a careful copy of Paul's letters.

A barking catches her attention. She turns to see a dog pounding towards her, chasing before it a red squirrel. The squirrel leaps and bounces, the dog has no chance of catching it. It runs straight towards Brigid, up her skirts and before she can stop it, it runs across her page, and then bounds on to the roof and up and away. The dog follows it, leaping and snapping at the air.

Brigid looks down to see tiny footprints tracking across the page. She takes a fresh sheet of parchment and begins again.

'Abbess Brigid,' a voice says.

'What?' She does not look up, for she hates being disturbed at work.

'I wondered if you might like this.'

Brigid puts the quill down and looks up at the woman. Her name does not come to her at first, though she knows her to be a princess, the daughter of King Echu of Ulster.

The woman is holding a rectangular object, wrapped in fine cloth. Brigid reaches out and takes it from her. It is a book. Slightly larger than a man's hand, covered in the softest leather she has ever touched. A delicate, swirling pattern of a tree has been carved into the front. She opens the first page.

'*In principio erat Verbum*' is written in exquisite script of deep black ink, except for the first letter, which is painted in a vivid ruby red. 'In the beginning was the Word,' she translates.

'I was told it is the Gospel of St John,' the woman says. Cinnia, her name comes back to Brigid now.

'How do you have this?'

'Patrick gave it to my father, who gave it to me on the day I became a Christian.'

The story Brigid has heard about Cinnia is that her father traded his daughter's soul for his own, agreeing with Patrick that she would become Christian as long as he did not have to. Many of the women who have come to her have had dealings with this man Patrick. Her own mother was brought to Christ through him. He seems to weave in and out of Brigid's life, without ever touching her. But one day, their paths will have to meet. *And what then?*

'Would you . . . would you teach me to read from it?' Cinnia asks.

Brigid pushes the thoughts of Patrick from her mind and looks at the woman, smiling. 'I will, Cinnia. I will teach you all to read.'

Cinnia's face breaks into a grin, revealing tiny, pearl-like teeth. 'How can I ever thank you? For everything you have given me?'

'This beautiful book is more than enough,' Brigid says. She returns to the pages, scanning the words and turning the Latin to Irish in her mind.

She reads all through the night, and by the time the sun is rising, the life of the man Jesus has revealed itself in the pages. And yet, she knows, this is only part of the story.

'I must have more books,' she says to the dawn. 'More stories and somewhere to keep them.'

As she sits, gazing at the sun breaking through the clouds, a single bee settles on the cover of the book, as though mistaking the engraved tree for a real one. Brigid's thoughts return to Dún Ailinne. She has not thought of the place in many months, has tried to scrub it from her mind as she might scrub writing from vellum. But a memory returns to her now. One summer day, she was sent to collect honey from the hives, something she did often. She opened the hive, dipped her hand in and pulled out a wax comb, dripping with golden honey. She placed this in a clay pot she had been carrying and was about to return to the kitchens when she saw a single bee, struggling to free itself of the thick liquid. She looked for something to help rescue her, and found a single white goose feather on the ground. She dipped it in, breaking the surface, and waited as the bee climbed on to the feather, wings glued together, the soft fur of her body glistening with the weight of the honey.

Brigid was sure the bee would die and thought it might be kinder simply to crush her body under her foot. But instead, she gently laid the bee on a leaf and closed her eyes to whisper a blessing over it, not knowing if any gods cared for a creature as small as a bee. When she opened her eyes, the bee was surrounded; ten maybe twenty sister bees huddled around, tending to her. Cleaning her wings, her fur. And as Brigid watched, the bee opened her wings and shook. They shimmered in the light. She circled around, face nuzzling against the bodies of her sisters. Brigid knew that bees cannot think in the way that humans do, knew this must be instinct and not a deeper form of communication. But she swore there was gratitude in the bee's touch. Then, as one, all the bees took flight.

She opens her eyes and thinks she can see the bees before her now, flying through the smoke from the dying fire, up and out into the dawn sky.

A single bee lived because she wasn't alone, because her sisters tended to her and didn't give up on her. *We must be like bees: we must protect each other.*

She takes up a page and starts drawing the images she has been seeing behind her eyes.

At last, she returns to the roundhouse, where the women are sharing food around the cooking fire. She finds Darlughdach, Ciara and the others, and throws her drawing down before them. Ciara peers down at it first.

'A beehive?'

'An oratory,' Brigid says, smiling at her friend. For indeed, it was Ciara's beehives that inspired her. 'Large enough to house the whole community. With stone walls and seats, so we can worship out of the wind and the rain.'

'And this?' Darlughdach says, pointing to a drawing of a tower.

'A library. Where we can gather and transcribe all the books of the world. And here,' Brigid points at the page, 'a dormitory, with beds for at least one hundred and fifty women. Three hundred if they share two a bed.'

'And where will we get the materials for all of this?'

Brigid stops. This she had not thought of. She can coax wild pigs from the woods and shoots from the ground. But stone and wood at the scale she needs must be bought.

'How much gold do we have?' she asks Ciara, keeper of their purse.

'Not enough.'

'We could trade meat and cheeses,' Indiu suggests.

'We'd need a mountain of meat,' Darlughdach says.

'And what will we do for food if all our stocks go on stone?' Ciara says. 'We can't eat rocks.'

'The land will provide,' Brigid says.

Let me see what I can do.

The answer to Brigid's problem comes. But as a threat.

'Men!' Lommán shouts, running into the roundhouse, her face red and sweat-covered. 'Men, on the western border.'

Some of the women scream and clutch each other's hands for safety. Others stand still, frozen, staring out into the trees from where Lommán has come.

'Are they coming for us?' one asks. 'Should we run?'

Lommán catches her breath. 'I don't think so. They are building.'

'Building?' Brigid asks.

'It is Aillil, the king's son, and about a hundred of his men and horses. I was out hunting and I saw them arrive on the Curragh. They have wood and stone and have already begun work digging a ditch.'

'They are building on *our* land?' Brigid asks.

Lommán nods.

Brigid smiles. 'How kind of him to bring us what we needed.'

'You should be wary of Aillil,' Darlughdach says. 'He's not like his father. He has a cold heart and a tight fist. Don't forget he's the reason I was thrown out of Mullaghmast.'

'Then we shall see if we can't melt that heart of his.'

27

Brigid hears the noise of industry before she summits the hill. Men shouting, the buzz of sawing and the thudding of hammers ring in the air.

'Sounds like someone is busy,' Darlughdach says.

Brigid has brought Darlughdach and Ciara with her. Ciara to do the bargaining and Darlughdach to stand by her side.

Below them, men work like ants, swarming across dark soil. The wooden frame of a huge roundhouse stands, bringing to mind the skeleton of a giant auroch Brigid came upon once. Around the frame, stones have been piled, ready to raise up around the wooden structure. It will be a mighty fort when finished, one to rival Dunlaing's own.

Brigid counts fifty men at work and one hundred horses, walking in a slow procession towards the site, each beast laden with timber and stone. Sitting hunched on a bay horse, watching it all, a young man dressed in a tunic of red and gold and blue. Aillil. The king's foolish son.

Just how foolish? Brigid wonders.

'Go and tell him that we will permit him to build on our land, if he gives us some of the timber,' she says. 'He has more than enough there to complete his fort three times over.'

'He might be just a lad, but his ego is three times the size of any man,' Darlughdach says. 'He won't give us so much as a stick without knowing what's in it for him.'

'We can't fight him,' Ciara says. 'Look at the men he has with him.'

'Say it is to be done in Christ's honour.'

'Christ himself might have to come down here and ask, if we're to have a chance,' Darlughdach says, spitting on the ground.

'We shall see,' Brigid says.

'Do you know how annoying it is when you go all mystic like that, Biddy?' Ciara says, but she doesn't wait for an answer. She makes her way down the hill, walking in slow zigzags back and forth to counter the steepness.

Brigid watches as Ciara approaches the working men. Sees the men stop and lay down tools, elbows digging into ribs, fingers pointing at the figure in white approaching. The men peel away, giving room to Ciara who makes a path straight for Aillil on his horse.

She speaks, pointing first to the pile of materials and then back up to the hill at Brigid. Aillil's eyes follow her finger and Brigid sees him seeing her.

GLOW, MY LITTLE ONE. GLOW.

Sunbeams reflect off Brigid's hair and she shines like burnished bronze. Aillil's hand turns, palm facing towards her, no longer shading his eyes, but as if trying to push the brightness away.

He looks back to Ciara. More talking. More gesturing. After a while, Aillil throws back his head and laughs, exaggerated and ridiculous, a mummer's version of laughter.

He walks his horse forward, its hooves stepping up high before planting back on the ground. One more step and it will trample Ciara. But she does not move and at last, with a wave of his hand, Aillil dismisses her.

It's a slow walk back up the hill. Ciara's face is red, not with the effort but with frustration.

'What did you say?' Brigid asks.

'What you told me to,' Ciara says. 'That this is our land and if he wants to build here, the price will be a third of his timber, in Christ's name, and so on.'

'And what did he say?'

Ciara pauses, as though unsure if she should pass on his words.

'What did he say?' Brigid asks again.

'That your greed outstrips your grace, and while his father might be a fool to bestow his charity upon you, he isn't.'

'*My* greed?' Brigid says, shocked. '*My* greed?'

Brigid has been called many things, good and bad, but greedy? It's as though she has been called a fish or a bird. Something utterly not of her nature.

Ciara shrugs. 'That's what he said.'

'I told you he was a little shit,' Darlughdach says. 'Just give it to him. We have plenty of land.' Darlughdach takes Brigid's elbow to lead her away, but Brigid stands, unmoving as a standing stone.

She looks at the horses, trudging in the hot sun. Sees the men whipping their hinds to force them onwards. Their pain becomes her pain.

'His horses look weary. They should not work them so.'

Brigid blinks and every one of the horses lies down, long legs folded under them, their heavy loads still on their backs. Even the horse Aillil rides sits down, throwing the prince to the muddy ground.

He jumps up and looks around, as though checking that none saw his fall. Then turns his ire on the horse, kicking it. It rolls over and lies down, stretching out its legs and head.

The other men round on their beasts, tugging at their reins, trying to force them to their feet. When this will not work, they take to whipping them. Brigid flinches with every lash of a switch against a horse's flesh as though she were taking the blows on her own back. But the horses still will not stand. Aillil whips his horse hardest of all, but to no avail. It is like thrashing a rock for the good it is doing him.

His shouts carry up the hill to where Brigid and her women stand. He curses the horses. Curses the men for not being able to control them. More tugging and whipping. And still the horses sit, relaxed and chewing on grass as though waiting for a rain to pass. Not a mark on their russet hides.

Aillil draws his sword and holds it over the head of his horse.

'Whatever you're doing, Brigid, stop it,' Darlughdach says, pulling on Brigid's elbow. 'He'll kill the horses.'

'Wait,' Brigid says, yanking her arm free.

Darlughdach hisses her frustration but she waits. Aillil slides his sword back into its scabbard and steps away from the horse. Instead, he shouts at the men, who quickly get to work to free the horses of their loads. But still they will not stand.

Aillil then turns once more to Brigid, staring up the hill. He begins his walk up towards her, taking the most direct but hardest path, so that by the time he reaches her, he is out of breath and red of face. He has his father's strong jaw and broad forehead, but his mouth has none of the king's softness. He is small, like his mother, broad like his father, and dark like his sister. A soft fuzz of hair lines his upper lip, which is thin and puckered, and his eyes are a touch too close together for him to be handsome. When he talks, his voice is pitchy, as though his balls are yet to drop.

'This is your doing,' he shouts at Brigid, shaking his fist before her face.

She lowers her gaze, as is right when talking to a royal-born son, but she does not move back. 'You are trespassing on my land.'

He snorts. 'This is my father's land. And as his heir, it is my land.'

'He gave it to me.'

'You tricked it from him, with your . . . magic! And

I am taking it back. Now, break your spell over my horses, or I will break your skull!' He shakes a fist at her.

Brigid does not flinch. 'You overloaded your horses on a hot day,' she replies. 'It is your pride that has done this.'

'They have worked all week no problem, then you turn up and—'

'Days of being worked into the ground. All the more reason they need rest. Perhaps if you were to lighten their load. By, say, a third?' Brigid's voice is pure honey.

Aillil backs away, blinking, as if her cheek is a physical blow. 'Who do you think you are, to speak to the son of the king so? You should be on your knees.'

'I kneel to only one king. The King of Kings.'

Aillil throws his hands up. 'You sound like my father. God this, Christ that. It's all he goes on about these days. I remember when I was a boy, we sacrificed our enemies' heads to the old gods and now we can't even strike a slave. All because of this god of yours!'

'You like hitting slaves, do you?' Ciara asks. Her fingers flex into fists, as though she might begin to hand out the blows.

'A man should be allowed to do what he likes to his property. Horses or women both.' He turns once more to Brigid. 'They say you were once a slave.' Aillil's eyes slowly scan Brigid's body, up and down, and settle on her breasts. It reminds her of how Beccan would look at her. Desire and disgust in one. For a moment, she considers causing Aillil's dark eyes to burst like ripe grapes. The moment passes and Brigid's face remains a lake of stillness; not so much as a ripple passes.

'Leave now or your father will hear of it.'

Aillil lets out a huff of contempt at his father's actions. 'My father is a fool!'

'What do you think your father might say if he knew you spoke of him so?' Darlughdach says.

'I know you,' Aillil says, pointing a shaking finger into Darlughdach's face. 'You're that bard.'

'Then you know what I can do with just a few words,' she says, looking at him through one eye. 'I can cause pustules to burst out on your pretty face, can make your manhood wilt and fall off like a leaf in autumn.'

Aillil's hand reflexively goes to his groin.

'If you do not leave now, no woman will sleep with you, no man drink with you. And your father will be so ashamed of you that he will no longer call you his son.' A herring gull flies overhead, its piercing cry like laughter. 'Hear how even the birds mock you,' Darlughdach says.

Brigid stares at him, can feel the swirling fear within him. Her eyes burn through his, digging deep into his brain, and there she plants words, as though she were etching on his skull. *If you do not leave now, the sound of laughter will follow you every day of your life.*

The colour drains from his cheeks, the apple of his throat juts out as he forces a swallow. Brigid wants to laugh, but forces herself to be still.

He is afraid. He is just a boy and he is afraid.

'Fine,' Aillil says. 'I'll go.'

A collective whinnying rises up from below, as one hundred horses get to their feet.

'Leave a third of the timber as payment,' Brigid says, as Aillil turns.

Aillil goes to protest, his lips pulled back over his teeth like a snarling dog. Above, the gull caws again and Aillil flinches.

Aillil spits on the ground before Brigid's feet. 'Have it.'

Brigid watches Aillil leave with his men.

'I don't know how long that will keep him away,' Darlughdach says.

Brigid nods. 'When we build the walls,' she says, 'we will need to make them high.'

28

'It seems the Lord's work is never done.'

Brigid looks up from sawing wood to see King Dunlaing on horseback. The day is hot, the work hard, and she has laboured through the night since Aillil left.

She wipes sweat from her brow with the sleeve of her tunic. 'So it would seem, my lord.'

'At least you have plenty of hands to help.' Dunlaing slides off his horse and comes to look at the wood Brigid has been cutting.

She and seventy of her sisters have been toiling alongside a handful of labourers she has lured from Aillil's employ with promises of salvation. Women who were weavers or farmers or who had no skills at all, have all become builders, learning how to work with wood and stone. Hands that were smooth have become hard as leather, and the women's soft bodies have become etched with muscles.

'Would you care to join us?' Brigid says, offering him her saw.

The king laughs and holds out his hands, palms forward. 'Alas, my hands are not made for labour.'

Brigid sees they are soft and pink, as hers once were. Blisters have turned to calluses, and now her hands feel like leather. Her body too has hardened, as she has become stronger. Each day, she can carry more than the day before, and soon she will be as strong as any of the men. *How robbed we have been by being told we are the weaker sex. How small they tried to keep us.*

'Then perhaps you would join me in a drink of water,' she says, placing her tool down.

The king nods and the two walk towards the small river that cuts through the land. She squats and scoops up a handful of water and brings it to her lips.

'I came to talk to you about my son,' Dunlaing says, squatting beside her and dipping his fingers into the water. 'I wanted you to know, he will not trouble you again. I have sent him to be fostered by Lóegaire.'

'The King of Tara?' Brigid asks. 'I thought he was your enemy.'

He shakes the water from his fingers. 'He is. But these kinds of trades can help avoid war. Peace from compromise.'

'Ah,' Brigid says, as though she understands. But she knows little of compromise.

'I have also sent word throughout Leinster and beyond that you are under my protection,' Dunlaing says, standing. 'That it is God's work you do here.'

'Thank you,' Brigid says, straightening.

He steps forward and takes her hands in his. 'I thought once that God had given me a purpose, that he had chosen me because I was a king. A man. But I now see that it was not me he chose. God has chosen you.'

NOT YOUR GOD.

'I do not understand what God's purpose for you is, Brigid, but perhaps that is not my role. For as it says in the Bible, *"God's ways are as mysterious as the pathway of the wind."'*

Brigid looks to the oak tree that stands high above them. She does not find the ways of the Christian God all that mysterious. He desires that people worship him, much like any man.

'Indeed,' she answers, for she knows something is expected of her.

'I will leave you to your work.' Dunlaing gazes across at the land, at the women working, backs bent in the heat of midday.

He clambers on to his horse once more and points it back to Mullaghmast. 'I wish you well.'

'Go with God,' Brigid says.

'What did he want?' Ciara asks, coming to drink by the river.

Brigid watches Dunlaing ride out of sight. 'To let us know we are under his protection.'

Ciara swirls a mouthful of the water around her mouth, then spits it out. 'We'll need it,' she says.

Brigid hopes that King Dunlaing's word is enough to keep them safe. But what would it be like to have that power for herself? To not need a man's protection?

But for now, they work.

None work harder than Lommán. Her forge burns brighter than the sacred flame and there she melts and bends, hammers and quenches all day long, making posts and hinges and bolts. So many bolts, as if they alone can keep the world out.

'She's some woman, isn't she?' Darlughdach says, watching as Lommán swings a heavy hammer down on a slab of steaming iron.

Brigid agrees. 'I only wish she was ready for the world to see that.' For Lommán still dresses as a man, and only those in Brigid's inner circle know her secret.

'Maybe it's us who need to change what we think a woman is.'

'Perhaps,' Brigid says.

She and Darlughdach have been working all morning, digging a ditch to surround the fort, and her palms pulsate with pain. Brigid looks up at the sky. The sun is nearing the horizon and she hasn't stopped to eat.

'It's your turn,' Ciara says, passing by above them, dragging a wooden fence post.

'What?'

Ciara drops the post and stretches out her shoulders. 'To guard the flame. It's your turn. I did it last night. And it pissed down.'

'Already?' Brigid says. For it seems to her only a matter of days since she was up there.

'I would like to take the watch tonight,' Darlughdach says, laying her hand on Brigid's shoulder. 'If you would let me.'

'Of course, Dara. But are you sure?'

'I like the silence,' Darlughdach says. 'Gives me time to think. Without all the snoring and farting.' She looks pointedly in Ciara's direction.

'I never snore,' Ciara says. 'Fart, yes, but never snore.'

The women laugh and Darlughdach clambers up out of the ditch, and heads for the grove. Brigid watches her go in gratitude, for the idea of spending the night under the cold skies had filled her with dread.

'Take some sheepskins,' Ciara shouts after Darlughdach.

Darlughdach waves back at them.

Ciara sits, legs dangling into the ditch. 'What's going on with you two?' she asks, an upward nod of her chin pointing over at Darlughdach.

'What do you mean?' Brigid asks. 'She is my friend. As you are.'

Ciara laughs. 'We are friends, to be sure, but you and her . . . are something else. It's as though you can read each other's minds. She knows what you need without you saying it.'

Brigid cannot deny that she cares for Darlughdach in a different way than she does her other sisters. Needs her. Perhaps it is the goddess that has bound them together?

'Don't worry, Ciara,' Brigid says, reaching up to pat the other woman's cheek. 'You will always be my first friend.'

'Your first,' Ciara says, standing up and hefting the post once more. 'But not your best.'

The days ring with the sounds of sawing and hammering. And at night, they sit and drink beer and share their stories. They laugh, they cry. Hearts that were broken begin to mend; bodies that carried wounds start to heal. Brigid reads from the Bible, and at other times asks Darlughdach to tell one of the old tales. The same truths appear over and over. Eve and her apple, Sinann and her well, teach them about the pursuit of knowledge. Oisín returning from the underworld and Christ from the tomb, show that death is not the end. Jesus and Lugh are reflections of each other, proving that light can defeat the darkness.

They build a new roundhouse worthy of a cattle lord; thirty feet wide and with beds for one hundred. After that, they get to building a wooden round tower, the height of three forts, with a doorway placed in the middle that can only be accessed by a wooden ladder, and inside row upon row of shelves. She places the codex of Corinthians from Brendan and the Gospel of St John from Cinnia on one of the shelves. The first of many books to come.

It takes nearly two years of constant work, but the city she saw in her dreams has become reality. Cill Dara. And it is all hers.

They call what she has done a wonder. A miracle. The word has become almost mundane from use now.

'Oh, she turned the water into beer again? Someone fetch the cooper, we're already out of barrels.'

'More butter. The lot we have has already gone rancid. Feed it to the pigs.'

With each wonder she works, the weight of their expectations grows heavier.

Her beehive oratory proved the hardest to build. Gathering the stones – smooth, flat slabs – took months and the first two times they tried to build it, it collapsed, the carefully stacked stones not able to bear the weight of the roof. But at last, the slabs cooperated and the building rose.

The first day she stands beneath the arched stone roof of the oratory, all sound from the fort softened, the only light coming from a small window positioned in the east wall to welcome the rising sun, she feels a peace like lying under the outstretched arms of a tree. That even though this place was built by mortal hands, it feels blessed by something not human.

The peace is quickly broken, as the other women pour in after her, their excited chatter driving out the silence as a dog drives out birds.

'Will the roof not fall on our heads?' Indiu stands in the doorway, peering in at the curved roof.

'No,' Brigid says, 'it is strong.'

Strong enough, she hopes, to keep them safe. Every day she fears attack and every night, her dreams – when she sleeps, which is rarely – are filled with images of men with blades. Not since Aillil has anyone dared to test Dunlaing's word or, so the women say, the wrath of Brigid herself. Darlughdach has made sure that the stories of Brigid's powers have spread beyond the walls of Cill Dara. Exaggerated tales, no doubt, of what happens to those who stand against the Mary of the Gaels. But how long can stories protect them? She can sense something in the air, though perhaps it is only the promise of snow.

29

'Spring at last,' Darlughdach says, standing in the yard, head thrown back and arms outstretched. 'You can smell it.'

It has been a long time coming for it has been another bitter cold winter. The air has lost its bite and blades of grass have pushed their heads through the frosty earth.

'Look,' Indiu says, plucking a bright yellow flower from the ground by her feet and passing it to Brigid. 'An early dandelion.'

Brigid takes it and spins it between her fingers; the white liquid from the stem trickles down her hand. It won't be long before the sharp yellow petals turn to tufts of fluff and fly away.

'We used to collect these as girls, Ciara, do you remember?' she says. 'Though we called them bitter foot.'

'I do.' Ciara takes the flower and tickles Brigid under the chin with it. 'We said Breachnat must piss on them, to make them so bitter.'

Brigid laughs at the memory. Never before had she dared to laugh at her stepmother, but with the distance of time and land, she is no longer afraid of the woman.

'I saw watercress by the river,' Induae says. 'And nettles. I will gather them today and we can have some green with our grain.'

'What's the day?' Brigid asks, for she has not been counting the passing nights.

'How is it you can remember every line of scripture you read, Biddy, but you can't keep track of the days?' Ciara says, hitting Brigid playfully on the cheek with the flower. 'It's Imbolc eve.'

Brigid's eyes widen in shock. How could she have forgotten Imbolc? 'Why did none of you tell me? We must celebrate!'

As the sun begins to set, tools are laid down; cups are filled with what is left of their honeyed ale and the last stores of sloe wine are dug up and cracked open.

Brigid leads the women up the hill to the grove, Darlughdach by her side. They stop when they reach the top and look down at the fields below them: the cattle grazing, their small river glinting the last of sunlight, golden barley rippling like waves. At the foot of the hill stand the towers and houses of Cill Dara. It is Brigid's vision brought to life.

'It can't be five years since we first met here,' Darlughdach says.

'It feels like a hundred,' Brigid says, taking her friend's hand. It is rougher than when she first felt it. Darlughdach has worked almost as hard as Brigid herself building this future for them all.

Darlughdach smiles at her. 'You've achieved enough for a hundred years.'

'There is still so much to be done.'

'But not tonight,' Darlughdach says, starting to skip and taking Brigid's other hand to pull her forward. 'Tonight is for dancing.'

The women circle around the flame, slowly at first, huddled together and reaching their hands out towards the fire to keep them warm. But as the ale reaches their bellies and reddens their cheeks, the circling becomes faster, faster. Soon they are dancing, whirling around wildly, laughing freely. Someone pounds a rhythm on a drum, a steady *boom, boom, boom* that vibrates like thunder, and their hearts beat in time.

'Brigid. Brigid. Brigid.'

My name is chanted over and over again. Though only some of the women know they are calling to me. Most believe it is their abbess's name they shout like a prayer. Even I have lost sight of where she begins and I end.

'Who are they?' A breathless Ciara shouts over the drumming and chanting.

Brigid stops, mid-spin, her hair catching up and wrapping around her face and throat. She untangles it to see what Ciara is pointing at.

A group dressed in grey cloaks are gathered before the gates to Cill Dara. A tall figure at the front stands, head tilted, looking up. Even from this distance, Brigid senses power there. And danger.

'Has Flann returned for me?' Orla asks, her voice a croaking whisper.

'Or Aillil?' Darlughdach says.

'They don't look to be armed,' Lommán says, coming to stand beside them, her keen eyes squinting at the newcomers.

'They don't look like they're here to join the festivities, that's for sure,' Ciara says, raising her hand to shield her eyes from the setting sun.

A cold shiver passes through Brigid's body. 'I will go,' she says. 'You stay. Enjoy yourselves.'

'Not alone,' Lommán says. She has not taken part in the dancing, despite Darlughdach's attempts to drag her into the whirl in the centre. Though a gentle flush of her cheeks suggests that she has been enjoying the ale. Brigid is glad. She so rarely sees Lommán relax. But she is also glad to know she will have her strength beside her to greet these strangers.

Brigid pats her warrior on the arm. 'No, never alone.'

She and Lommán peel away from the gathering, and wind back down to the fort. They exit the wall via a hidden door, and walk to meet the strangers. When they are about ten or so yards away, the figure at the front lowers their hood.

It is a man. Sharp, angular features: nose like an eagle and jaw like a boulder. His skin is as wrinkled as an oak trunk and as dark as a hazelnut. Thin white hair shines like a halo around his head and reminds Brigid of a dandelion in the spring sun. He wears a long tunic dyed a faded blue and embroidered about the hem in gold, an engraved gold cross hangs around his neck and he carries a thick wooden staff, with a curled head like the ones she has seen shepherds use to guide their sheep. He stands with his back straight as a plank of wood, though Brigid can see that his knuckles around the staff are white with the effort of holding himself up.

The others with him also lower their hoods. She counts them now, three men and four women. The men have their heads shaved from ear to ear and wear simple tunics, tied at the waist with twisted ropes. The women are clad in long grey cloaks and black veils pulled tight across their heads and under their chins, so that only their pale faces shine out like the moon. They all look weary, as though it has been a long walk that has brought them to her gates.

'Greetings on this most blessed of days,' Brigid says.

'I was told you were followers of Our Lord and Saviour, Jesus Christ?' the man says. His voice is gruff and he chomps on the words as though they do not come easily to him. His accent reminds her a little of her mother's: he must be a Pict or a Roman from Britain.

'This convent is dedicated to Christ, yes. And who might I be speaking to?'

He does not answer her question. 'And yet . . .' He looks up to the hill above the fort, where Brigid's women can be seen dancing with ribbons trailing behind them, and if ears were strained, singing and laughing might be heard. 'You still carry out pagan rites?'

'It's Imbolc,' she says, as though it should need no more explanation.

The man's expression does not change from its scowl of disapproval, so Brigid continues. 'We celebrate the arrival of spring. *"For behold, the winter is past, the rain is over and gone. The flowers appear on the earth, the time of singing has come."* From the Song of Solomon,' she adds, when she sees no recognition of the verse in the man's face.

He grunts dismissively. 'I meditate on the words of Christ, King of Kings, not the mortal kings come before him.'

'May I know who I am talking to?' Brigid asks, though she suspects she knows the answer.

One of the women steps forward. She has small, sharp eyes and lips pursed so tight, it's a wonder she doesn't swallow them. 'This is his most holy Bishop Patrick.'

AT LAST.

Brigid has imagined Patrick so often. When she thought of him, she saw an image of Christ himself and looking on him now, there is something of the Nazarene on the cross in the man's hollowed cheeks and sunken eyes, something of the carpenter in his leathery hands. He is old, and yet his back has not bent and his grey eyes are sharp as flint. Power radiates from him like heat on a dry track in the peak of summer.

'He is Bishop of Armagh, envoy of Rome and the saviour of the men of Ireland,' the woman continues.

'And what do you say of her women?' Brigid asks.

The woman blinks, open-mouthed, as though Brigid has struck her. Patrick lets out a long, angry huff of air through his aquiline nose.

'We have come a long way. My men are weary and my women hungry,' Patrick says.

Brigid looks over her shoulder at the gates to Cill Dara. 'Men are not permitted inside the walls,' she says.

'That man was,' Patrick says, pointing at Lommán with his staff.

'This is Lommán, my . . . personal guard. He is the exception.'

This is not strictly true, for they have allowed craftsmen and labourers through the gates when needed. But she wants very much to keep this man away.

Patrick clears his throat with a wet, phlegmy cough. '"*Depart from me, you who are cursed, into the eternal fire prepared for the Devil and his angels. For I was hungry and you gave me nothing to eat, I was thirsty and you gave me nothing to drink, I was a stranger and you did not invite me in.*"'

Brigid hesitates. The laws of hospitality were part of this land long before Patrick and his Christ God arrived. 'Come,' she says. 'Let it not be said that I would turn away those in need.'

She nods at Lommán, who rushes back through the small doorway, and a moment later the gates are dragged open.

30

'Welcome to Cill Dara,' Brigid says, leading the group through the gates.

The woman who introduced Patrick chokes when she sees Brigid's city, though she covers her mouth quickly with her hand, as though trying to catch the sound that had escaped her lips. She is not alone in her wonder. Some of the other women and the men also let out sighs of surprise.

'I had heard much about your work here,' Patrick says, looking at the oratory and the tower. 'I had no idea that your ambition was so vast.'

It is not a compliment. Brigid decides to remain silent. A trick she learned from Lommán who stands beside her, still as one of the foundation stones of Cill Dara.

'I see your sisters have returned from their . . . revelry.'

Patrick nods at the women filing back down from the grove, their faces flushed and their voices high and chattering. They fall into sudden silence when they see the newcomers.

'My sisters,' Brigid says, 'we are truly blessed for we are joined by his dear lord Bishop Patrick and his brothers and sisters.'

There are gasps of delight from some of the women. Grunts of displeasure from others. All have heard of Patrick and his battle against the pagans of Ireland.

Ciara approaches and stands on one side of Brigid. Darlughdach on the other.

'Welcome, Bishop Patrick,' Darlughdach says, though there is none of the usual warmth in her voice.

'Yes, you are are most welcome,' Ciara says, her eyes scanning the men behind the bishop.

'Patrick and his people will join us for our celebration feast,' Brigid says, careful not to use the word Imbolc, for she fears what Patrick would think of the old ways still held tightly at Cill Dara.

'There's hardly enough food to call it a feast for us,' Ciara whispers in Brigid's ear, 'let alone enough to feed another eight. And barely enough ale as it is.'

'It will stretch,' Brigid says, patting Ciara's hand.

I WILL SEE THAT IT DOES.

They file into the refectory, where the tables are laid out ready for food. A black iron pot hisses over a fire at the end of the hall and from it comes the smell of sweet lamb flesh and herbs. Indiu and Induae get to work filling large bowls and passing them out. Despite only being half full, the pot does not empty, no matter how many bowls are filled. The twins, used to Brigid's wonder-working, barely raise an eyebrow.

'Sit,' Brigid says to Patrick.

'I and my men will eat alone,' Patrick says, his nose wrinkled as though the smells of cooking were turning his stomach. 'For it is not proper for unwed men and women to sit together.' He looks at the only woman to have spoken so far. 'Íte, you and your sisters may take your place with Brigid and the other women.'

Íte looks disappointed, but bows her head in submission as Patrick takes a seat at the end of the longest table and his men sit around him. Brigid can feel the eyes of her women on her, for that is her place he has taken. She forces the edges of her mouth up in a smile.

'Please, sit.' Brigid leads Íte and her women to a smaller table, where a large bowl of steaming stew has been placed.

Indiu and Induae are already seated and make room for the women in grey cloaks and dark veils.

Soon the room is filled with the chatter of women, and the scraping of spoons in bowls. Darlughdach takes a seat at the table beside Íte's women, who have yet to speak a word, and Brigid sits beside Íte. She soon wishes she had not.

'I am Íte of Killeedy,' the woman says, her voice lifting and falling like a songbird.

The woman waits, as though Brigid should know her. The name is familiar, but Brigid cannot place it and feels somehow as if this is her failing.

'We met once at the house of Maithgen,' the woman says.

'Íte! Ah, yes.' Brigid does not recognize the woman in front of her. But the name is familiar. 'It has been some time since we last dined together. Let me introduce you to my dearest friends, Darlughdach, Indiu and Induae.' Each woman nods in turn as they are introduced. 'And Clodagh, our youngest sister.'

Clodagh grins at them, her mouth already full of stew.

Íte does not introduce her own companions. They remain sitting in silence, staring down at their plates.

'Would you like some?' Indiu asks one of the women. 'We made it fresh today.'

The women look to Íte for permission.

'Only bread and ale, if you will spare it,' Íte replies.

'Are you sure? It's delicious.' Induae offers her bowl to the woman nearest her.

'We are sure.' Íte reaches across the table to push the bowl away.

Something about this woman makes Brigid feel small, scared. These are old feelings, and ones Brigid has fought to keep at bay, but this woman's presence has brought them back to her.

'Did you know, dear Brigid, that we are cousins? Yes, yes,

I learned of this only recently. My mother was sister to your mother, Breachnat, God bless my mother's soul.' Íte makes the sign of the cross, whispering the words. The three women sitting opposite her mirror her actions, like shadows cast from different candles.

And there Brigid has her answer. The blood of the most detested Breachnat runs in this woman's veins.

'Breachnat was not my mother,' Brigid answers, her jaw clenching.

'Ah, well, as good as a mother, I am sure.'

'Have you come to join our sisterhood?' Darlughdach asks quickly.

As ever, Brigid is grateful for the bard's skill in changing the topic of conversation.

Íte looks shocked. 'We have not. I am a head of my own order of nuns, and these women are my followers.'

'Your nuns can't speak for themselves?' Clodagh asks.

'They do not speak. We are a silent order,' Íte says. 'As Paul said, "*Let a woman learn in silence and with all submission.*"'

'You talk well for a silent nun,' Darlughdach says, into her bowl.

Íte's lips pucker like a flower bud closing. She lifts up in her seat, trying to raise herself above the women around her. 'I have permission to speak when we are travelling. And of course, when reading from the Works.'

'Oh, we love to read, too,' Indiu says.

'Your women read?' Íte asks, surprised.

'Most of them,' Brigid answers. 'And those that don't are learning.'

'How interesting,'

'We are an . . . order.' The word sits uncomfortably on Brigid's tongue, for although there is structure to their community, she would like to believe it is by choice for all involved.

'A sisterhood dedicated, above all, to the preservation of the written word.'

'And to prayer?' Íte's eyes tighten while her nostrils grow so large that Brigid can't help but stare into the dark holes.

'Of course,' Brigid says. She takes a mouthful of the stew. 'You're right, Induae, it is delicious. Are you sure you will not join us? Your women look hungry.' She hopes this will move the conversation on to safer grounds.

'We are full on the love of God.' Íte takes a sip of her ale, and places the cup back on the table.

'But you can't dip bread into the love of God,' Darlughdach says, reaching over and filling her bowl once more. Her elbow connects with Íte's arm, spilling ale on the woman's lap.

From the other table, raucous laughter erupts and hands are slapped against the boards.

'I have selected only the most chaste and humble women to be my nuns,' Íte says, her eyes daggers thrown at the laughter coming from Ciara and a group of her friends. They are staring over at the men with Patrick, sharing the kind of loud jokes that have made Brigid blush in the past. Now she is more grateful for Ciara's wild nature than she has ever been. If only for the look it has caused on Íte's prune-like face.

'The world has room for all kinds of nuns,' she says.

'You do call yourself a nun then? And yet, you have not taken the veil,' Íte says, looking at Brigid's flowing red hair, her nose wrinkling as though she were looking at something rotten. Brigid finds herself running her fingers through the tangles. She had only this morning been thinking she should cut it off. Now she thinks she will keep it long and unruly out of spite.

Again, Íte does not wait for an answer. 'I was given the veil by his holiness Bishop Patrick himself.'

'How do you come to be travelling with him?' Darlughdach asks.

'His holiness Bishop Patrick is my patron and confessor. For he himself washes me of my sins.' Íte prattles on.

'He's a little old for that, isn't he?' Darlughdach mutters.

If Íte hears it, she pretends not to. 'His holiness Bishop Patrick has taken it upon himself to ensure our safety. As we make our return. To Killeedy,' the woman says, each sentence broken and going up at the end, as though expecting Brigid to take over her tale. 'I have travelled all the way from Bishop Patrick's own church in Armagh. Where I have lived this past year. Under Bishop Patrick's personal tutelage.'

If Brigid had a lamb for every time Íte says Bishop Patrick, she could feed the convent for a year.

Íte gazes over at Patrick, who is slowly tearing into a chunk of bread. 'What a man. He was once a slave, you know? Can you imagine?'

'I can't,' Brigid says, as flashes of dark memories pass before her eyes. 'Though many of the women here can.'

Íte doesn't acknowledge what Brigid has said. She continues her babbling praise of Patrick. 'He had to tend to sheep from dawn till dusk, rain come shine, and it was only God's word that saved him.'

'There are worse things to do than tend sheep,' Brigid says. She wishes Íte would stop talking. It is like the buzzing of a fly.

'I like tending the sheep,' Clodagh says. 'When it's not cold. Then I like working in the forge.'

'You have livestock?'

'Sheep. Cattle. Some wild boar and deer that come and go as they please,' Darlughdach says. 'We grow grain also. Vegetables. Though we mostly let the land do as it wills. When we first took it on, the Curragh had been over-farmed and the soil was dry and lifeless. It took us hard work and patience, but life is returning.'

'Ah, then it is true. The whole of the Curragh is yours? So much land.' Íte takes a small bite out of the bread and places it back on her plate.

'Five thousand acres,' Clodagh says proudly.

'Hmm. I was offered as much by the chieftain Senach,' Íte says. 'I accepted only four acres. That was more than enough for my needs.'

These words are like arrows, aimed for Brigid. 'Your needs must be humble then.'

'Humility is the greatest virtue of a nun – would you not agree?'

Brigid opens her mouth to answer that she believes charity to be the greatest virtue. But Íte leaves not so much as a breath for Brigid to speak.

'For we are but hand servants of God and of his representatives on earth,' Íte continues.

'And who are these representatives?' Darlughdach asks.

'The pope, of course, and his bishops.'

'Men?' Clodagh spits.

'Of course. Only men have the power to consecrate your order. To perform the Eucharist rites. You *do* take Communion, don't you?'

'What's Communion?' Indiu asks, her dark eyes wide. She has been hanging on every one of Íte's words.

'You don't know about the Eucharist? Then how can you call yourself Christians?' Íte's hand makes a swift sign of the cross. 'It is bread and blood become the flesh and blood of our Lord Jesus. He commanded us to partake of it, in remembrance of his sacrifice. "*He that eats my Flesh and drinks my Blood has eternal life.*"'

'You drink blood?' Clodagh asks, her nose crumpled in disgust. 'That sounds pretty pagan.'

'No . . . I mean, yes, but . . .' Íte splutters, flustered.

'Can't we just eat bread and wine?' Indiu asks.

'It must be sanctified. By a priest. A man,' Íte says, her lips tightening again. 'The mysteries of the Mass are not ours to understand. We must humbly follow the instructions of the Church Fathers. For only through them may we come to Christ.'

'You would have us submit to Patrick then, have him consecrate us, as you have done?' Brigid asks.

'Oh, no, not Bishop Patrick himself, oh, no. He is select in those he brings to Christ.'

If the stories Brigid has heard about Patrick are true, he has baptized every man and woman he has come across, whether they wanted it or not.

'Maybe one of the other bishops there.' Íte nods at the men sitting either side of Patrick. 'They are Patrick's own nephews and most dear to him.'

The one on his right has a bright pink face, round as a pig ready for slaughter; the one on his left is as lean as a dog in winter, with eyes that dart side to side as though ready for attack. Gold crosses hang at both of their necks, though theirs lack the intricacy of Patrick's. The third brother, a freckled young man, looks away quickly as Brigid glances in his direction, and becomes deeply interested in his bowl of food. His clothes are the simplest of the four, his cross two pieces of wood bound together with twine.

The thin man is deep in conversation with Patrick, while the round one happily fills his bowl for a second time. If they are dear to Patrick, as Íte says, none of that shows on Patrick's stone-chiselled face.

'Bishop Moel is to set up a church at Mag Tulach.' Íte points out the rosy-cheeked one, who is happily spooning stew into his mouth. 'While Melchu . . .' The thin-faced man is whispering in Patrick's ear. 'Well, some say he will take over from Patrick at Armagh, when God calls him home.' She makes the sign of the cross again, her hands fluttering like wings. 'You could receive the veil from his hands, perhaps?'

Íte talks as if this rite Patrick performed on her was a kind of conjugal act, one that she would not have him share with other women.

'Are we not consecrated?' Indiu asks.

'You are not,' Íte answers before Brigid can. 'Only a man can carry out the ritual. That you have tried to call yourselves brides of Christ without having taken the veil is . . . I don't want to say sacrilegious . . .'

'Then don't,' Darlughdach says, fixing Íte with a warning stare.

'I would like to take the veil,' Induae says.

'Me too,' Indiu adds.

'I will think on it,' Brigid says, putting her spoon down. Suddenly the stew tastes bitter as though too much bay has been added.

Brigid is jolted by the feel of a hand on her shoulder. She turns to see one of Patrick's men, the young one with the sun-kissed skin. He is bowed so low she can see a scatter of freckles on the skin of his tonsured skull. 'His holiness would speak with you in private,' he says.

Brigid looks over to see Patrick's grey eyes fixed on her. Why could he not have come himself, or simply called across the room?

'Very well,' she says, pushing her stool back from the table, grateful for the excuse to be away from Íte and her constant chatter.

Lommán stands to join her, but she lays her hand on her shoulder. 'Stay. Finish your food. All will be well.'

She and the freckled man weave their way through the

tables. He is tall and broad, though he walks with a slight stoop, as though trying to keep himself small.

They wait at the back of the refectory for Patrick to join them. The bishop is slow to stand, and Brigid sees that it causes him pain. One of the other men tries to help Patrick up, but he pushes him away with a bark.

He makes his way towards Brigid with slow, stiff strides. As he walks, he throws his staff in front of him, before leaning heavily on it with each pace. There is a hitch in his step she knows from other elders who have come to her, as one who has been struck by an illness and learned to walk again.

I could heal him. But why do I think that would anger him?

'We met once,' the man standing beside her says.

She half-turns to him. 'We did?'

'It was quite some time ago in Faughart, I am not surprised you do not remember me.' He laughs and Brigid remembers that laugh, from a lifetime ago.

'Brendan?' she asks, peering into the man's eyes.

He smiles and she sees now it is Íte's ward, the young man she shared a few hours with in Faughart. His skin has turned the colour of aged leather and his hair has been bleached blonde in the sun. He has grown into his ears, and his jaw is wide and strong.

'I see you got your sanctuary,' he says.

'I did. And tell me, have you travelled the world?'

'To some of it,' Brendan says, standing taller. 'Though there is still so much to see.'

Their conversation is cut off by a sharp cough. Patrick stands before them, his lips pursed in disapproval. 'Am I interrupting?' he asks.

'No, Bishop Patrick,' Brendan says, bowing low, shrinking in on himself again.

Outside the refectory, dusk has settled and the evening

wind has a bitter chill. Brigid wraps her cloak around her, but sees that Patrick faces into the wind, as though challenging it to do its worst.

She has read of holy men who seek to be closer to Christ through the mortification of their flesh. Does Patrick hide scars of his own making beneath his cassock? Does he starve himself till he sees visions of God?

She pauses before deciding where to take Patrick. She does not want him to see inside the library tower or oratory, does not want him to see the true extent of their work. Neither does she wish to take him to the small room she has had built for herself, raised up over the dormitory, for this man would fill the whole space. She decides on the forge. Safe, quiet, and besides, it will be warm in there.

Patrick has to duck under the doorway to avoid hitting his head on the blackened lintel. He looks around, taking in the tools and fire, which glows faintly in the hearth. Brendan stands in the doorway, head bowed still. It irritates Brigid to see him like this. As though Patrick were his master and he a slave.

'So, my dear lord bishop?' Brigid says, pouring sweetness into her voice. 'What is it you wish to speak about?'

'I did not want to disturb the women.' He waves his hand in the air as though shooing away a fly, and Brigid suspects his care for the women is less than it might be for an insect. 'But you should know: there has been a most evil, most horrific attack on Christians by a chieftain called Coroticus and his villainous soldiers.'

This is a Latin name, not one of a man from this island. 'Is Coroticus a citizen of Rome?'

Patrick's face flushes red and he spits over his shoulder. A pagan protection, if ever Brigid has seen one. 'He is a citizen of demons! For he has made his home among the apostate

Scots and Picts in Britain, from where he raids the coasts of Ireland. Innocent men and women, newly baptized by myself, the anointing cross still on their foreheads, were cruelly slain or taken as slaves by these sons of the Devil.'

Brendan makes the sign of the cross, as if warding off the very mention of the Devil.

'My heart breaks for you and for your children in Christ,' Brigid says, reaching out a comforting hand.

Patrick draws away from her. 'I have not come for your sympathy.'

He stretches his hand out behind him and Brendan places a scroll into it.

'I understand you can read,' Patrick says, a sneer in his voice. He hands the scroll to Brigid without waiting for her answer.

She glances over at Brendan, who is gazing up at the rafters. Has he told Patrick she can read thanks to him? She thinks not.

She unrolls the scroll to see a sheet as long as her forearm covered in swift, sharp writing.

'I have had copies made of this letter to be sent to the soldiers of Coroticus, so that they might turn against him. And sent to all Christian communities, so that none of the holy and humble of heart will offer any hospitality to Coroticus and his men till they have made their penance, and set free the men and women of God they have taken.'

'I see,' Brigid says, scanning the writing. 'And what do you wish me to do? For we have no dealings with the Scots or Picts here.'

'It is a warning, woman!' Patrick roars, spittle freckling Brigid's face. 'You and your . . . holy sisters are in danger of such a raid. I have come to offer you my protection, for you too may also come under the sword or be taken for slaves.'

'The walls of Cill Dara are high and thick,' she says.

Patrick chews on his cheeks and runs a tongue over his gums. 'I had been told you were a holy woman. I see you are a sinner like all others.'

Heat bubbles in her palms, her teeth grind against each other. 'And what might my sin be?' she asks.

'Pride,' Patrick says.

Pride? She looks at Patrick's gold cross and embroidered tunic, stares into his arrogant eyes. He has come to her home and *dared* to call her a sinner?

Oh, I will show him pride.

She could make his already crumbling joints turn to dust. Break his spine and see him bow before her.

BE CAREFUL, LITTLE ONE.

She closes her eyes and forces away the images of Patrick bent in pain before her. 'I thank you for your offer,' she says, calm again. 'But Cill Dara does not need your protection. We already have the patronage of a king. And besides, God watches over us.'

THAT SHE DOES.

'You and your men can sleep in here tonight,' she says, 'For we would not wish you to be tempted into sin. It is a long way to Killeedy – I expect you will need to be gone before sunrise. May God protect you on your travels, Bishop Patrick. I hope we meet again.'

She walks away, leaving Patrick and Brendan in the forge. Brigid has always told the truth. Even when it earned her a beating. Even when it hurt others to hear it. But her parting words to Patrick are a lie.

31

Patrick, Íte and the others are gone before the women rise to break their fast. Brigid is glad to see them go, for their visit has cracked the shell-like peace of her sisterhood. Whispers spread through the convent like a blight.

'If we're to be a holy order, shouldn't we be a part of the holy church?'

'Íte said there's no way into heaven for us if we're not blessed. What if we die tomorrow?'

'What good is it us taking a vow if it's not consecrated? We might as well be throwing wishes into the well. And what good has that done us?'

Others are angry at the idea that Patrick or any man should have any say in their life.

'Sure, didn't I come here to escape the rule of men like him. Why should I care what they think now?'

New words join their vocabulary. Words that meant nothing to them days before now seem to mean everything. Consecration. Purgatory. Salvation. And the veil. Many of the women seem to want to take it. Some start wearing scarves over their hair as Íte and her companions had done.

'The women are restless,' Ciara tells Brigid a week later, as she, Darlughdach and Ciara sit in the sun, scraping leather for vellum. 'They seem to think they need a man's approval for the life we're building here. I've tried telling them that men are only good for one thing, but most of them being true virgins have no idea what I'm on about.'

'They're not alone,' Brigid says, ignoring Ciara's crude joke. 'The texts agree.'

She has been reading everything they have in their library, and all say the same. Only a man may carry out holy rituals. There are references to scrolls and gospels that hint at another way, but they are on the list of books decreed heretical.

'Then what's to be done?'

Brigid has already decided. She has already written to Bishop Moel at Mag Tulach and received his response that morning. She retrieves the letter from inside her skirt and hands it to Ciara.

Ciara scans the response, her lips moving as she reads. 'He sounds a little too excited at the idea,' she says, handing the letter back. 'So you're going to do it then?'

'I am.'

'Well, if you're to take the veil, then I will take it with you,' Darlughdach says.

Brigid laughs at her friend's loyalty. 'But you don't even believe in Christ.'

'I don't know. He's warming on me.' She looks up at a crucifix hanging on the wall behind them. One of the older sisters carved it, and though the cuts are rough, it has captured the depth of Jesus's despair. 'Besides.' Darlughdach looks back to Brigid, her gaze softening. 'I believe in you. And if you're to take this veil, then I will be right behind you.'

'Same here,' Ciara says.

Indiu and Induae have been hovering behind Brigid, listening in with their keen ears.

'Can we take the veil too?'

Brigid turns and sees many of her sisters gathered around. So many versions of what it is to be a woman: young things, faces smooth as river rocks, barely old enough to call themselves woman; old mothers, skin like bark and eyes that have seen too much. Women as tall as the warriors of the old tales, or as small as a child. Young, old, fat, skinny, princesses, paupers, the faithful, the fearful. And yet they have come to have a resemblance to each other as sisters do, for they share one thing. Hope.

'I will take seven women with me to receive the veil from Bishop Moel.' She scans the group, looking for three more to join the four already decided. She can tell those who wish it more than the others. But she must be careful who to select.

Her eyes pass over Lommán, who shakes her head. In the end, Brigid selects Orla, Clodagh and Cinnia. Clodagh is now a young woman, strong and broad, who has trained under Lommán to become a fine smith. They stand alike, swing the hammer alike and even look somewhat alike, as parent and child. Brigid often wonders at the closeness of their bond, and whether Clodagh knows Lommán's secret. Orla now has splashes of grey in her once auburn locks, and the haunted look she carried with her for so many years has passed. Cinnia, the princess, who came to them as though walking on a cloud, has grown fat and soft and swears almost as much as Ciara. They are all popular, and least likely to stir envy.

The eight women set out early the next morning. A white cow is brought down from the fields and strapped to a cart. Brigid and Darlughdach sit up front, while the other women squeeze themselves into the box behind and they head out. The sky is pewter grey; rain will not be long coming.

'Are you all right?' Darlughdach asks after a while, for Brigid has remained silent, staring at the landscape unrolling before them.

Brigid sighs. 'I was remembering a morning not unlike this one, when I was ridden out, wearing a veil, ready to submit to a man. I had hoped I would never experience the same again, and yet . . .' She turns back to Darlughdach and shrugs. 'Here we are.'

'At least with this ceremony we won't be returning with a useless hunk of meat,' Orla says.

'Do they give you meat when you get married?' Clodagh asks.

'She means we won't be coming back with a husband,' Cinnia explains, ruffling Clodagh's hair.

Clodagh pushes her hand away and flattens her dark hair. 'Give over, I'm not a baby.'

She is no longer the youngest member of their community, and yet many of the women still treat her as the daughter they never had or the ones they left behind.

'It will be fine,' Darlughdach says, though Brigid can hear the edge to her tone.

Brigid takes Darlughdach's hand and interlaces their fingers. 'You are right. I am fretting for nothing.' And yet she does not let go of her hand.

It is past noon when they arrive at Mag Tulach. It is a small fort, barely a homestead, with a sparse outer wall and shallow ditch. In the centre stands a small church made of wood, with a tall, angular roof.

A man stands on the steps, his hands hidden inside the deep cuffs of a blue tunic. A strip of white material falls across both his shoulders and meets in the middle of his chest, before falling in a single line down to his knees. He removes one of his hands and holds it out before them, two fingers pointing upwards, the rest curled in on themselves. And with it, he carves out the shape of a cross, as though blessing the air before them.

She remembers the druids doing the same, with wands of mistletoe in their hands. Ritual and magic and power.

'Well met, O holy Brigid. Oh, well met indeed. And to your sisters.'

Moel's round cheeks have flushed bright red in the presence of Brigid and her women.

'Thank you for receiving us, Bishop Moel,' Brigid says.

When she approaches, Moel reaches out his hand for her, fingers dipping before her face. A bright gold-and-ruby ring is wrapped tightly around his plump fourth finger, which he pushes a breath away from her mouth. A small cross has been carved into the stone.

Understanding dawns. Brigid leans forward and presses her lips against the ring. It is cold, like kissing ice.

Moel sighs, content. 'Come, holy Brigid, that a veil may be sained on ye.'

Brigid glances back at her sisters, seeing Ciara and Darlughdach suppressing smiles, and follows Moel inside the church.

Upon entering, it is as if she has crossed over into another world. Outside, it appeared a simple structure, but inside, everything shines.

Gold. Gold everywhere. Gold leaf wrapping around the pillars. Gold chalices on the altar. Gold candlesticks. She has never seen so much gold in her life. How many people could it feed? How many slaves could it free? Just a single cup would be enough to buy ten cumals.

'Oh, yes, ours is a beautiful church, don't you think?' Moel says.

They are not alone, for a small gathering of people are standing on either side of the altar. Among them a man with a long nose and sharp sneer. Bishop Melchu, Patrick's other nephew. He stares at them as though they have trod cow dirt in with them.

'Come, come forward,' Moel says.

'You're late,' Melchu shouts as they file towards the altar. 'You've missed Mass.'

'It is a long journey from Cill Dara,' Brigid says, pouring sweetness into her voice, but all she feels is a sharp bitterness towards this man. 'But we have been praying the whole journey here.'

Melchu sniffs, his thin nose twitching like a rat.

Why must everything be a battle with men like him?

'They're here now, brother.' Moel retrieves a book from the altar and starts to flick through the pages. 'Where is it? Where is it? Women . . . women . . .where are the women?'

'Have you not done a woman before then?' Ciara says, a twinkle in her eye.

Moel blushes deeper. 'Oh, well, I mean, that is to say, I have baptized women. But the veil . . . no.' He flicks the pages back and forth in his book, trying to find the right passage. 'Ah, here it is. The Rite of Consecration to the Life of a Virgin.' Moel ignores Ciara's snort and looks up at the gathering. 'Who will go first?'

'I'll be your first,' Ciara says, stepping forward.

Brigid throws her a look, telling her to behave. But Ciara has always enjoyed the discomfort of men. And this one is no different.

Moel clears his throat. 'Kneel.'

Ciara takes her time, lowering herself down while not taking her eyes from Moel's. She is enjoying this teasing far too much and Brigid pities the poor bishop. Moel flushes a deeper shade of red.

He reaches a shaking hand over Ciara's head and reads from the book. '"*Receive, daughter, the sacred veil that you will need to present without blemish to the tribunal of our Lord Jesus Christ, before whom every knee in heaven, on earth and in hell shall bow.*"'

A white cloth is placed over Ciara's head. Moel begins to adjust it, and Ciara leans into his hand like a cat. She grins as he snatches his hand away, as though she had bitten him.

Indiu is next to take the veil. Induae after her. Words are spoken and they are transformed.

'Do you feel any different?' Indiu asks her sister as they walk, hand in hand, back from the altar.

'I think so. I don't know. I feel . . . lighter.'

Orla and Cinnia follow. Cinnia resists kneeling at first, the last scrap of the princess in her, opposing the indignity of subjugation. But she kneels and is veiled. Orla practically throws herself to the flagstones, believing perhaps that this consecration will wipe away the pains of her past. Darlughdach is next to be called forward. She hesitates, her feet dragging on the wooden floor. She glances to Brigid, and there is such sorrow in her eyes that Brigid almost steps forward and stops the ritual, stops her friend from quenching the last of the light of the old gods in her. Darlughdach smiles, shakes her head and lowers herself to her knees. She bows her head and like the others, receives the veil.

Apart from Brigid, there is only Clodagh left. The young woman stands with her legs crossed over each other, arms folded, chewing on the inside of her cheek.

'You know what,' she says. 'I'm good as I am.'

There is a gasp of outrage, a hissing of disgust from those who watch. Clodagh looks around, confused. She has always been allowed to speak her mind without fear of consequences.

'Don't worry, Clodagh, no sister of Cill Dara will be forced to do anything against her will.' To the onlookers Brigid says, 'She is young still.'

'Well, I suppose that only leaves you, holy Brigid.' Moel reaches out his hand and gestures for Brigid to come forward.

Brigid takes a step and kneels before him on the cold stone. And at once she is kneeling in soft grass, in a grove, on a cold damp day before Imbolc. Pain itches in her cheek and she remembers needle teeth puncturing her flesh. My first gift. Here she is, kneeling again, waiting for another man to change her status with words. She resisted it then and does so now. Why should she not be equal to this man? Why should she not have his power to change matter with words? Wine to blood. Woman to nun.

You are more than equal.

A gust of wind rushes through the door and up the aisle, sending leaves swirling, the pages of Moel's book flap and fly like birds flushed from a bush.

Moel squints at the book, flicking back and forth through the pages, his podgy fingers rough with the vellum. 'Where is it now?'

'Can't find the right spot, father? Perhaps you'd like a steady hand to guide you?' Ciara purrs.

Moel's blush reaches all the way to his temples. 'I . . . think it was this one. Yes, this was it.' He doesn't sound certain.

Brigid hardly notices that the words he reads out are different from the ones he read before. Though she catches the whispers and angry inhalations of those watching. Whispers that become shouts. Time seems to slow as Moel reaches out his hand and places it on her head with his final words.

'"*Pour forth upon this chosen one the power that is from you, the governing Spirit whom you gave to your beloved Son, Jesus Christ—*"'

When a hand is laid on her head, she is brought back to the church. Time moves again as Melchu rushes forward.

'Stop!'

He pulls Moel's hand away from Brigid's head and pushes his brother away.

Brigid feels as though liquid gold is pouring from the crown of her head, over her forehead and neck, down, down over her face and to her lips.

'What have you done?' Melchu shouts.

'I . . . What, I have given Brigid her orders?' Moel says.

Melchu pulls the book out of Moel's hand and reads the text. 'You fool. You've read the ordination for a bishop. A woman can't be a bishop.'

They both look to Brigid and they see the light coruscating from her, as though reflecting off a diamond.

When she stands, she feels taller. Or has the world around her – the people, the pews, the church itself – shrunk? Power courses through her. She felt this before, when we met in the darkness and she was undone and made whole again.

'Brigid, are you . . .' Darlughdach reaches out a hand to touch her friend's arm and snatches it away. She looks down at her fingers. They are bright red as though burnt.

'Let me.' Brigid reaches out for Darlughdach's hand.

The woman pauses, curling her wounded fingers into a fist, resisting Brigid's burning touch. Brigid gently uncurls Darlughdach's fingers, hands now cool as marble, and lifts them to her mouth. She kisses each fingertip as gently as she might kiss a sleeping baby. Darlughdach breathes in sharply, her chest shuddering at the delicate touch.

Brigid reaches inside her for the light, and for the old words to heal. When she releases Darlughdach's hands, the skin is pale and soft once more. Darlughdach brings them to her own mouth, brushing her fingers against where Brigid's lips have touched and Brigid feels her own lips burn.

'What have you done?' Melchu demands again.

'It . . . it wasn't my doing!' Moel says. 'The pages . . .'

Brigid blinks, looks to Melchu, her head cocked to one side. Does this same power flow through his blood? If so, why is he so afraid? So ill at ease? Brigid has never felt more herself than she does in this moment.

A bishop. She has the power to ordain the rest of her women. To conduct Communion. Her dream of a world without men is within her grasp.

'Worry not, brother,' she says to Melchu, noticing how he flinches as she addresses him in the informal way. 'This is God's work.'

Yes, yes, it is.

32

Word that Brigid has been ordained a bishop reaches Cill Dara before she does. She walks through the gates to the ringing of bells and stamping of feet.

'If only you'd ridden home on the back of a donkey, they'd be throwing palms at your feet,' Darlughdach says, with a smile that shines less bright than usual.

Brigid has noticed her friend watching her on the journey back, quick glances out of the side of her eye as though afraid to look at her face on. She has also kept herself bodily away, choosing to sit in the back with the other women and telling Ciara to take her place up front. Brigid realizes then that she has missed Darlughdach's casual touches and the press of the woman's hips against hers on the cart. *Strange, how you only notice something when it has gone.*

Ciara, for her part, has chatted the entire way back about how different she feels. 'Like the way I felt after a man first lay with me, only in reverse. Does that make sense? I feel like a virgin again.'

'You can't become a virgin again,' Darlughdach says, annoyed with Ciara's chatter.

'Why not?' Ciara says, turning around to look at the woman. 'Sure, God can heal wounds and lift curses, I've seen him do it through Brigid. Why should this be any different? Losing your virginity is just another wound.'

'Well, I don't feel any different,' Darlughdach says. 'It's only in your head, Ciara.'

'Sure, isn't everything?'

Darlughdach doesn't respond, which is unlike her. She would usually rise to the argument and more often than not beat Ciara into submission with her words. She might not feel any different, but she is acting different.

I will talk to her. I will win her back to me. But for now, she has work to do.

'Sisters,' Brigid says, standing up on the cart. 'You have worked so hard to build our home, our sanctuary. And that work has been seen and recognized by God. For as a bishop, I now have the power to declare Cill Dara a true church. A powerful church. One equal to Patrick's church in Armagh.'

This declaration is met with whoops and cheers.

Darlughdach jumps off the cart and stomps away. The hem of her white robe catches on a splinter of wood in the door frame. She yanks it free, tearing a strip of white cloth that flutters in the wind like a scrap of flesh.

'You'd better hope himself doesn't hear about you becoming a bishop,' Ciara says, as she and Brigid clamber down from the cart.

'God?' she asks, confused, for doesn't God hear of everything?

'No. The next best thing. Patrick.'

Brigid goes to find Darlughdach. She must talk to her, she must ease this tension between them, for she needs her friend. More than ever.

She finds her by the river, throwing stones. Her veil lies on the ground in a heap. Brigid picks it up and folds it in a neat square, which she tucks in her pocket. 'What has the river ever done to you, Dara?'

Darlughdach startles and releases the stone too early. It bounces off a boulder and rebounds, clipping the side of her head. 'Ouch,' she says pointedly.

'Hush, it was only a pebble,' Brigid says, standing next to her friend. 'Let me see.' She takes the woman's head in her hands and pulls it forward so that she can look at the crown. 'Not even a scratch.'

Darlughdach shrugs away.

'What is wrong?' Brigid asks. 'Are you not happy to have taken the veil?'

Darlughdach picks up another stone and rolls it around in her hand. 'You know, I used to be one of the greatest bards in Ireland.'

'I do,' Brigid says.

'And now, what am I?' She throws the stone. It misses the river and lands on the bank on the other side. 'There is nothing special about me any more. I used to wear robes of rainbows, and now, I wear . . . this.' She tugs at the white tunic. 'The same as everyone else.'

'You are special to me,' Brigid says.

'Am I?' Darlughdach at last meets her eye.

'What do you mean? You are my own dear Dara. My oak. My friend.'

Darlughdach takes a step closer. Brigid can smell the sweetness of her breath, feel the warmth of her skin. 'Are we not more than that?'

'You are my anamchara,' Brigid says.

'Your friend of the soul?'

Brigid doesn't answer. She doesn't know what question Darlughdach is truly asking and it scares her not to know.

'But not . . . the body?' Darlughdach reaches out and strokes Brigid's arm with the back of her finger, the gentlest of touches leaving a trail of warmth dancing in its wake. Brigid's flesh vibrates like a bell that has been struck.

'When you kissed my hands today, I felt something. I thought that perhaps you felt it too?'

Brigid brushes her fingers against her lips. They thrum as though she has been eating nettles. She finds herself staring at Darlughdach's lips. How has she never noticed how red they are, the colour of a blackberry on the edge of ripeness? She wonders if they might taste as sweet. She sees a trickle of sweat fall down Darlughdach's neck and gather in the dip of her throat, before rolling down beneath her tunic. *Oh, were I that droplet.*

Brigid gasps in shock at her own desire, closes her eyes against the image of her and Darlughdach, wrapped in each other's arms, flesh pressed against flesh. And in the darkness behind her eyes, she sees the contorting bodies from the dreams that haunted her childhood. Humans become like worms, writhing against each other.

She steps away, holding her hand up as if warding off a curse. 'I love you, Dara. I need you.'

'You need me?' Darlughdach's voice is a sigh. She reaches out, takes a fold of Brigid's tunic between her fingers and draws the cloth towards her.

'As the earth needs the sun. As a body needs a head. A heart,' Brigid says, feeling the material drag against her skin. 'But no. Not this.'

Darlughdach lets her hand drop to her side. 'I had hoped that one day . . . But no. I see.'

She throws a stone into the air and catches it, once, twice, before handing it to Brigid. 'Ah, well. Sad endings always make for the best stories.'

She walks away, leaving Brigid holding the stone. It is shaped like a heart.

'I do love you. Please know that,' Brigid says, calling after her.

The stone digs into her hand as she squeezes it tightly, as though it were her friend she was trying to hold on to. She can feel something slipping away but can't seem to find the words to stop it. Feelings she does not understand, does not know the name for, swirl in her chest. She wills them to be still, to be silent. But they squirm in her belly like eels.

Darlughdach's head drops but she does not turn around. 'Yes, I know you do. In your own way. And I will love you in mine.'

33

Over the next few months, Brigid ordains all of the women who choose it. They take the veil and become dead to the world of men, but alive in this world of women. She has new robes made for the sisters: sturdy undyed linen and cut to the ankles. They are women who work, not fragile brides, and should dress accordingly.

'Look,' one of her new sisters says, hands thrust deep into the side of the robe. 'It even has pockets.'

As summer turns to autumn, Brigid smells something in the air. Burning. None of the other sisters can catch the scent on the wind.

'It's likely a farmer razing his land for crops,' Ciara says, after sniffing the air. 'You shouldn't worry so.'

The next day, Brigid understands that it has been a sign. A letter comes, sent to every church where people call themselves Christian. Rome has fallen.

'What do you think this will mean for us?' Darlughdach asks, when Brigid tells her of the letter and how a Barbarian king now ruled in the Eternal City.

They are together in Brigid's cell, a small, square room with a low cot pushed against one wall, rows of rough shelves on the other, and a single window with thick glass to keep out the wind. In the middle, a desk piled with papers and books. The room smells of ink, goatskin and, for the moment, Darlughdach's musky honey scent. It is the first time since the riverside that she and her friend have been alone. Despite her fear around the news from Rome, Brigid is grateful for the excuse to talk with her.

'We've never had any dealings with Rome, so I don't see why that should change now the barbarians have taken over,' she says. 'The imperial insignia has been sent to Emperor Zeno in the east and Pope Simplicius remains in Rome, safe.'

'For now,' Darlughdach says, chewing on the inside of her cheek.

Brigid leans back in her chair. 'Do you know why the Romans never conquered Ireland?'

'Because we have no wealth for them to ravage?'

'They believe us to be savages who lead a miserable existence because of the cold. That we slay and eat our fathers and sleep with our brothers.'

Darlughdach cocks an eyebrow. 'Well, maybe in the west . . .'

Brigid laughs, though it is a little forced. She is trying to recapture some of their old intimacy, but finds it slips away each time. 'We are on the very edges of the world. No one will bother with us here.'

'So, we just keep ourselves to ourselves?' Darlughdach says, a coldness in her voice that makes Brigid shiver despite the heat of her room.

Within weeks of receiving the letter, a steady flow of travellers pass by the gates of Cill Dara, coming from the ashes of Rome. A convoy of ships had landed on the southern coast, looking for new lands to settle and markets to trade. There are shapes of faces Brigid has never seen before, and all colours of skin. All look weary, with blank eyes, as though a light has been snuffed out within them.

'What should we do?' Ciara asks.

'Give them food and whatever help we can,' Brigid answers.

Ciara sighs, though Brigid has learned not to take her

complaints seriously. Ciara may grumble, but her heart is as soft as any of the sisters in Cill Dara.

'Oh, and Ciara,' Brigid says, as Ciara turns to leave. 'See if they have any books.'

Word spreads that Cill Dara is handing out food, clothing and even gold in return for books and Brigid has to be watchful that the leather-bound tomes they buy contain more than lists of accounts or even hastily squiggled nonsense on vellum, being passed off for the word of God.

She assigns Ciara to this role who takes to it with relish, for though her ability to read text is poor, her skill at reading people is better than any in the sisterhood. Brigid sometimes worries that Ciara spends a little too long chatting with the men, laughs a little too loud.

Each day, Ciara drags her new haul to Brigid in the library and together they go through them.

'Not bad today. Another copy of the Sinai Bible. A somewhat dull commentary on the Epistle to the Romans. Some Plato.' Ciara lays them all out on a long table by one of the windows, as the last rays of the day illuminate the texts. There are small, leather-bound books, piles of scrolls, single sheets of parchment. Many are soot-stained or torn.

'This one is fake,' Ciara says, throwing one of the scrolls aside.

'How can you tell?' Brigid asks.

'You can still smell the cow dung, see?' She holds the scroll under Brigid's nose. Ciara is right; it stinks. 'They dip the parchment in shit to try to make it look old. But we can scrape it clean and use it again anyway.'

Brigid picks up a small codex and opens it to the centre pages. The writing is like none she has ever seen before; a series of curved lines and dots flowing into each other with no breaks. 'What is this one?'

Ciara sniffs. 'Looks like nonsense to me. Another fake no doubt, by someone who can't even write.'

Brigid looks closer at the book. The leather is some of the softest she has ever felt and the craftsmanship of the writing exquisite. There are no illustrations, save for patterns around the edges of the pages. This book must come from the furthest edges of the world. Arabia or the Orient perhaps. Maybe one day, a woman who can read and write this beautiful script will come to Cill Dara and translate it. Until then, she will keep it safe.

On warm days, the library is Brigid's favourite place to be. Dark and cool, even when it is hot outside. She sits in one of the windows and listens to the *scritch, scritch* of swan quill against parchment as the women work from dawn till the candles burn out in the evening, capturing words from around the world.

The room smells faintly of rotten eggs and cider: the scent of the ink made from crushed oak apples, iron sulphate and vinegar. Brigid oversees the making of the ink herself each month. She dips her fingers in the pots and presses them against a scrap of calfskin, checking for the right consistency. Her fingers are now permanently black. She also oversees the making of the vellum, walking between the rows of calfskins hanging from frames, stopping every now and then to stretch a skin out further, or talk to one of the parchmenters. She finds herself walking with her hands clasped behind her back and remembers that was how her father would walk when assessing the work of his slaves. She tears her hands apart and shakes them by her sides, as if trying to shake any shared bit of him out of her.

Indiu and Induae have found a new gift in addition to their cooking. The making of inks. They experiment with everything they can find. Plants. Fungus. Rocks. Trying to replicate the colours in the books that are brought to them.

'We can't get a green as rich as this one,' Indiu says, pointing to a swirling letter that starts a page.

'What of the copper you found?' Brigid asks.

'It starts off bright but fades after a few days. See.' Induae passes her a scrap of paper with the word 'Sanctus' written over and over in different shades of ink. None are as vibrant as the originals.

'Keep trying,' Brigid says, gazing out of the tower window.

Beyond the walls, she sees a man leading a donkey, both are weighed down by leather bags. His head is shaven in the Roman manner, leaving a crown of hair around his scalp, and he wears the robes of a priest, worn though they are. He waits his turn to receive, and when he is handed a small loaf of oat bread, he pushes it into his sleeve. She has spied many travellers on the roads these past days, but he is the first Roman monk she has seen.

She calls out to him in Latin. '*Frater!*'

The man looks around, trying to find the source of the shouting. When he at last looks up, he sees Brigid and points to himself.

'Yes, wait for me.'

She clambers down the ladder and exits through a small door, rather than have the gates opened. The man is skinny, with a bent back and a restless energy. He rocks back and forth on his heels and his hands flap like birds, as though he is on the verge of taking flight.

'Brother,' she says. 'Are you well?'

'Oh, quite well,' he says in fluent Irish, though his accent has the edge of one who has been speaking another tongue. 'Well, as well as can be expected after days on the road.'

'You have come from Rome?'

'I have. Though I was born not far from here, in the mountains, over . . . there.' He spins around, to face the afternoon sun. 'No, no.' He spins again and faces the rising hills in the north. 'Over there. Though I have been in Rome these last . . .

oh, ten, fifteen years. And now I am on my way to a monastery in Scotland. Or that was the plan.' He scratches his tonsure with long nails. 'The boat was blown off course, or that's what the pirates I paid for my crossing told me, though I think they lied. So now I am trying to walk there. Is it far?' He looks at her, his nose scrunched on one side, eyes blinking as though he has just awoken.

Brigid can't help but smile at the strange man. 'It is very far, I am afraid. And you will need another boat to take you there.'

'Ah, well, I am sure God will provide.' His fingers work by his ears, rubbing against each other like cricket's wings. She sees black marks around his fingers, much like on her own.

'You were a scribe?' she asks.

The man stops his movement and stares at her, locking eyes for the first time. 'But how can you tell?'

'The ink.' She points to his hands.

He stares at the backs of his hands as if he has never seen them before. The fingers on his right are stained black. 'Well, would you look at that. Yes, indeed. I was a scribe. But now I am a beggar, for I have no other skills.'

He turns his hands so they are facing upwards. They are covered in deep red scars.

'How did you get the burns?' she asks him, holding his wounded hands in hers.

'Odoacer's men set fire to our church scriptorium. I tried to save as many of the books as I could.'

'Books?' Brigid says, her eyes wide with delighted curiosity.

He pulls the cloth away from the donkey's back, revealing saddlebags stuffed with books and scrolls.

Brigid brushes her fingers across them. There are codices here she does not even recognize.

'Could we buy these from you?' she asks.

'Buy?' He turns his head away, eyes squeezed as though disgusted even to look at her. 'Oh, no, no, no. I have been tasked with the preservation of these texts by God himself. I have made a holy vow. I couldn't sell them. No, no, no.' He shakes his head, like a dog shaking water from its fur. 'I have come to see if I could get some from you? I have been told you have many holy texts here.'

Brigid looks to the man. He is small, weak, she could easily overpower him and take these books for herself. For the church. But she looks once more to his hands, and pity overwhelms her.

'We do have many books. But none are for sale,' she says, stepping away from the donkey and its load, for fear the desire might overtake her once more. 'You should be on your way. But first.'

She takes his hands in hers, feeling the scaly roughness of his burns. She closes her eyes and searches once more for the words to heal. They do not come as easily as they have before, and she has to chase after them, like a cunning trout slipping through her fingers. The skin of her palms grows hotter as though holding them before a fire, and she sees light glowing from them.

'There,' she says, letting go.

The man holds his hands out before him, turning them back and forth, wiggling the fingers as though weaving the air. The skin is pink and fresh as a baby newly born.

'A miracle! A true, real-life miracle!' He lets out a squeal like a piglet, then digs around in one of his bags.

He pulls out a sheet of paper and leans it against the donkey's hind. From within his robes, he extracts a quill and with a light, dextrous hand, he draws an angular cross and a swooping letter P, the Greek letters for Chi and Rho. Brigid recognizes this symbol from the margins of texts as a way of referring to Christ. He finishes it with a dramatic dot, causing the donkey to bray in protest.

The monk laughs, a surprised shriek of delight, and writes three more. When his ink has dried, he returns the paper and quill to the bag and turns to Brigid. He falls to his knees before her, pressing his head to the ground.

The gesture embarrasses her. 'Please, please, get up.'

He looks up at her through eyes filled with tears. 'How may I thank you?'

'I only returned to you what God intended. That is all.'

'Then you must have this.' He stands and digs around inside the bags and pulls out a thick book. He drops it into Brigid's open hands. It is the largest she has ever seen. Written on the front in gold lettering are the words: *De Civitate Dei Contra Paganos.*

'*The City of God Against the Pagans* by Augustine of Hippo,' she translates.

'It is not a holy text, though it was written by a holy man, and so I think it is outside the vow I have made.'

'I cannot take this,' she says. The book must be worth more than any she has in the library.

'Of course you can. It is yours. I will make others. Now you have returned my hands to me. Oh, I will make so many others. But now I must be on my way to Scotland. Which way is it?'

Brigid smiles and gestures north with her chin. 'But perhaps you do not need to go all the way to find what you are looking for.'

'Oh, that is a good point, I suppose. Perhaps God is here too.' The man does not meet her eyes and speaks instead to the sky or the ground.

'God, I am reliably informed,' Brigid says, 'is everywhere.'

The man pauses as if about to reply, then turns his donkey around and walks away, taking his books with him.

34

The harvest is a poor one. The summer saw too much rain and not enough sun, and the crops rotted in the fields. A blight struck the barley and now their stores are depleted. The sisters wait for Brigid to perform another of her wonders, turning rocks to bread or grass to wheat, but none come.

'We may have to sell some of the cattle,' Ciara tells Brigid, showing her a record of their accounts. 'More is always going out than coming in.'

'I am grateful you have a head for numbers, Ciara,' she says, looking down at the rows of marks. 'But I am sure all will be well.'

'You're always sure all will be well,' Ciara says, slamming the ledger closed with a huff.

Brigid flinches at the thud; she has had a headache brewing all day. A pile of letters lies unanswered in front of her. There seems to be a constant flow of demands landing on Brigid's desk; each one feels as though it's taking a pinch out of her.

'And isn't it always so?' she says, pushing aside the letters.

'And what about the beggars who turn up every day? We've barely enough to feed ourselves, Biddy,' Ciara says. 'Let alone every hungry mouth in Ireland. I see some of them get to the top of the queue, fill their pockets, only to join the back of the queue again. We've hardly enough water.'

'Then serve them beer. We have more than enough of that in our stores. And tell the women that we will be fasting for the next forty days, food and drink to be consumed after sunset only, in memory of when Jesus was lost in the desert. That should help the food stretch a little further.'

'And what when the beer has gone?' Ciara scoffs. 'Will you turn puddles of piss to wine?'

Brigid meets Ciara's eyes with a cold, steady gaze. She does not like to be made fun of. 'Then God will provide.'

'And what about King Dunlaing? Didn't he promise to protect us?'

Brigid had, in fact, written to Dunlaing asking for aid, only to learn that he was raiding in the north, for his grain stores were as empty as theirs. When the answer came, Brigid felt a flutter of delight that she would not need to rely on him after all.

'God,' Brigid stresses, 'will provide.'

Ciara grumbles and mutters, but Brigid knows that she will do as she is told. 'Don't forget, it's your turn to watch the flame tonight,' Ciara says. 'Don't be passing it off to one of the others again.'

'I won't. I promise. In fact, I will go up there right this moment.' Brigid grabs her cloak and leaves the pile of letters for another day.

The sun is setting in a clear sky as Brigid climbs the hill to the grove.

'I am here,' she says, as she steps through the whitethorn hedge that surrounds the flame. The hedge is thick with red berries and as she brushes against them, they fall to the ground like hail. She reaches into her cloak and slips out a small jar with a wax stopper. She pulls the cork out and pours fresh oil on to the flame. A secret that only she knows. It flickers as it is fed anew.

She sits before the fire, legs crossed, and stares into the flames. Within, she sees the women they once were dancing, wild and free.

'I hope I have done what you asked,' she says, looking to the oak tree.

She waits for a reply, but I give her none, for I am resting.

The green of summer has been replaced by the gold of harvest. A group of jays settle on the branches, clicking and chirruping while a woodpecker thrums against the bark. Mice snuffle though the piles of fallen leaves. A column of ants spiral around the trunk, heading ever upwards. Life all around her, readying themselves for the death of winter.

As twilight creeps in, a sound catches her ear; a whistling as of a bird. Something comes shooting over the hedge wall and lands, thudding into the ground, a few feet from where she is sitting. She stares at it, hardly able to make sense of what she is seeing. A long stick, ended with the white feathers of a swan.

An arrow.

She is gazing at it dumbly, wondering what magic has brought this thing here, when screaming fills the air.

She jumps to her feet and starts to run towards the noise. Her way is blocked by a man standing inside the hedge, where no man has stood before. He carries a bow and a quiver of fresh arrows tipped with white fletchings. The hilt of a dagger juts from his belt. His teeth flash white and he reminds Brigid of an illustration she once saw of the devil.

The warning bells of the oratory sound and above them more screeches and cries from her sisters. Like lambs being slaughtered.

She moves to pass the man, but he draws his knife and circles around her. The reflection of the sacred flame catches in his blade and it looks as though it is on fire.

An old fear catches her throat, turns her limbs to stone. She wants to scream, to run, but she can barely move.

'No man may be here,' she says, forcing her lips to open.

The archer straightens and takes a step towards Brigid, licking his lips as though thirsty. The sounds of screaming have stopped, and Brigid does not know if this should fill her with fear or relief. She imagines her sisters dead, or worse.

'Who sent you?'

'What makes you think anyone sent me?' he says with a smile, though she can tell he is lying. There is purpose in him being here.

'You should not have come,' she says, her voice cold and steady.

'And are you going to make me leave?'

'Yes,' we say together.

This man's trespass has woken me from my slumber.

'You must be so thirsty,' Brigid says.

The man licks his lips again, forces down a swallow. He tries to take one more step closer and stops.

'So thirsty.'

He blinks, as though confused, and then his hands go to his neck. He opens and closes his mouth, like a landed fish.

'Water,' he chokes, barely able to get the word out. 'Water.'

Brigid tilts her head and smiles. She imagines fire. Imagines hot oil pouring down this man's throat.

He drops his dagger, falls to his knees, eyes bulging out of his head, fingers dragging across his throat as though trying to tear it open. He reaches out for Brigid, grasps at the skirts of her tunic. She yanks them free and squats before him, staring into his eyes which are turning red as blood vessels burst.

'You should not have come,' she says again.

His last breath is a wet gurgle as he drowns on lungs full of boiling blood. It is as sweet as birdsong.

'Brigid.'

She does not recognize her name at first, but it is called again.

She turns to see Lommán standing in the entranceway, a wooden cudgel in her strong arms. It drips crimson. Her hands and face are also covered in dark blood.

Brigid runs to her, traces her hands over her face, wiping it clean. Beneath it, she sees no cuts, no wounds. Lommán is unhurt.

'The blood is theirs,' Lommán says.

'What happened?'

'Raiders. Ten, maybe twenty men. I did not stop to count them.'

'You killed them?'

Lommán looks away, as though she is ashamed to meet Brigid's eyes. 'Some of them. Clodagh fought too. All of the women fought, and the men that lived ran.'

Relief washes over Brigid like sleep. It is done. They are safe. For now.

'Are any of the sisters hurt?'

Lommán looks down at the floor. Tears fall from her eyes. 'Laoise.'

Brigid struggles to put a face to the name and then remembers a young, skinny thing who had joined them just the week before. Her arm needed splinting from a beating her father had given her.

'And Orla,' Lommán continues.

This comes like a punch in her stomach and takes the breath out of Brigid's lungs.

'She thought it was her husband returned. She took up a scythe, but she wasn't strong enough. One of the men snatched it from her hand and—'

Brigid holds up a hand to stop Lommán. She does not need to hear, for behind her eyes she sees Orla, the soft grey material of her brain spilt on the floor.

'The man who killed her was the first to fall to my cudgel,'

Lommán says, lowering her head. 'But it wasn't enough. I couldn't protect them all.'

'You have done so well.' Brigid goes to take Lommán's hand, but she moves out of reach, as though even this small kindness is too much. She has no words of her own to comfort, so reaches for the words of the Bible. '"*If a thief is caught breaking in at night and is struck a fatal blow, the defender is not guilty of bloodshed,*"' she says.

Brigid looks back at the body of the archer. She has seen many dead bodies in her years, but never one whose life she has taken. She looks down at her shaking hands, which are glowing with a soft light. She clutches them closed and tucks them inside her tunic and hopes that there is some truth in what she has said.

'I must go and see to the sisters. Will you stay here and guard the flame?' she says to Lommán who is still standing on the threshold.

'I cannot enter,' Lommán says.

'Why not? It is only men who cannot enter without punishment.'

'But I am . . . In my soul. I am a man.'

Brigid stares at Lommán in confusion. 'I do not understand.'

Lommán raises her head and at last meets Brigid's eyes with a steady, sure gaze. 'Neither do I, Brigid. Only that I know it as surely as I know I am standing here, as surely as I know there is sky above me and ground beneath me, that if I step into the grove, I will die, as that man has done. For I am a man.' Lommán takes a deep breath and holds it for a moment before releasing it, as though a pain has left her.

Brigid remembers the tales of old gods, who changed their bodies as mortals changed their tunics. Is it possible that a woman might become a man through will alone? She looks again at Lommán, as though for the first time. How square her jaw is. How blue her eyes. And yes, perhaps she is looking into them at a man's soul.

'God loves you whether you are a woman or a man. As do I,' Brigid says, laying a hand on her friend's shoulder. 'Come, let us see to our sisters. The flame can watch itself for one night.'

The women stand in small huddles outside the oratory. Their white nightshifts glow like silver in the moon. Brigid can see that some of their tunics are torn and others splashed with blood. She scans their faces, which bear signs of the fight: bruises, cuts, blood. Many are weeping, arms wrapped around one another, giving what comfort they can. Others stand alone, their bodies quaking.

Darlughdach and Ciara stand side by side, squeezing each other's hands so tightly that Brigid can see the white of their knuckles. Blood pours from Ciara's nose down her chin and on to her neck, though she seems not to notice. Darlughdach's fingernails are painted red. Brigid sees that one of the bodies of the raiders is missing his eyes.

Oh, what warriors my women are.

Two of her women are dead. Four of the raiders. She bends over the body of one of the men and rolls him on to his back. The front of his scalp is shaved completely bare and he has a thick beard, plaited and bound with beads.

'Fucking Picts,' someone says, followed by a loud spit on the ground.

This man may be a Pict, but the one who came for her in the grove was not.

'What are you doing?' Darlughdach asks.

Brigid is rifling through the man's clothing, looking for proof of who sent them. She pulls a pouch free of his belt, opens it, and pours its contents on to her hand. Twenty silver pieces stamped with Roman lettering.

'These were not desperate men,' Brigid says.

'Some fucking bastard paid them?' Ciara says, her lips curled back in a snarl.

'Why?' Indiu says. 'Why would anyone want to hurt us?'

For the same reason any man hurts a woman. For power. Control. Fear. Brigid knows the women do not want to hear this. They want soothing words but she has none to give.

'More raiders may come,' Lommán says.

'Then we will be ready.'

'What shall we do with the bodies? Shall we bury them?' Indiu asks.

Brigid looks at the men who dared to hurt her sisters. She wishes she had the power to bring the dead back to life, if only so she could cause them a lifetime of pain.

'They do not deserve a burial. Cut them into pieces and feed them to the pigs.'

35

The shadow of the attack hangs over the convent. Brigid hears women screaming at night, horrors haunting their dreams. She herself is afraid to sleep, for in her dreams the archer comes again, and she finds she is powerless against him as he punches his blade into her belly over and over. The pain wakes her each time, and yet she finds she is wet between her thighs but not with blood.

Work becomes her only escape and she spends the dark nights of winter transcribing the Book of Judith, even though it is counted among the apocryphal texts. She has Cinnia, who has become her finest scribe, illustrate a full page of Judith slicing off the head of her enemy Holofernes.

'You have a way of making the most brutal things beautiful, Cinnia,' Brigid says, when the work is completed.

Cinnia shrugs off the compliment. 'Why do the fathers of the church want this story hidden away?' she asks.

'I don't know,' Brigid says. 'Perhaps it scares them, for it shows how fierce a woman's revenge can be.'

She has almost finished her transcription of the book, when one morning there is a thudding from outside her window. It repeats over and over, as though someone were chopping wood with a blunt axe. She goes to tell them to stop, for the pounding is vibrating behind her eyes and distracting her from her work. It is Lommán, stripped down to breeches and a thin shirt, swinging a cudgel over and over against a wooden fence pole. Each breath sends a thick cloud into the cold air.

Darlughdach sits near, wrapped in a thick blanket, back

pressed up against the wall, shouting encouragement. 'Come on, give me ten more.'

Brigid moves to the side of the window, so that she can watch them without being seen should they look up.

'You give ten more,' Lommán says. Despite the cold, Lommán is red-faced and sweating.

Winter has been cruel and long and a heavy coating of snow covers rock-hard ground.

'I do battle with words, my dear. You're the one with the big stick!' Darlughdach says, and then laughs, deep, throaty.

Jealousy jabs Brigid like a thorn. How easy they are in each other's company. How happy. *Darlughdach and I used to share that ease.*

Lommán goes to work on the pole again, putting all of her remaining strength into each strike. *His* strength, Brigid corrects herself. His. And she realizes it is easy to think of Lommán as a man. Even if he is not like other men. Not like the men who came to hurt them.

He swings his cudgel over and over. Lommán still blames himself for the women's death: each blow of wood on wood is a flagellation of sorts. But he should be proud of what he did. There is no sin in killing to protect, Brigid is sure of it.

She sees again the archer, fingers clutching at his throat, remembers the swell of excitement she felt deep in her groin at his pain. She knows she has the power to keep them all safe from any man who comes here, but at what cost?

She cannot even bring herself to think. 'I killed a man.' Better believe the Divine Vengeance that struck the archer came from somewhere else, somewhere ancient.

I MAY HAVE GIVEN YOU THE POWER, MY LITTLE ONE. BUT YOU CHOOSE HOW TO USE IT.

Brigid looks again to Lommán. His swings have become slower and he is hardly able to lift the cudgel above his shoulder.

At last he stops, head leaning against the post, body heaving, whether with sobs or gasps for breath, Brigid cannot tell.

Darlughdach stands and wraps a comforting arm around his shoulder. Brigid puts her hand to her stomach where a pain spears. It must be hunger, for she cannot remember the last time she has eaten.

'You're getting stronger,' Darlughdach says.

'Not strong enough,' Lommán replies.

Brigid risks moving to see them more clearly through the glass. Darlughdach takes the cudgel and struggles to raise it above her shoulder, all her usual grace gone. She swings at the pole, misses and spins away. Lommán catches her before she can fall, his hand against the curve of Darlughdach's waist.

Someone knocks at the door and opens it without waiting for Brigid's permission.

'We can't afford to feed the animals,' Ciara says, not even bothering to say good morning. 'Some of the women have taken to eating insects and grass.'

Brigid turns quickly away from the window and hopes that the cold hides the blush in her cheeks. 'I will write to Dunlaing again.'

'Dunlaing is still in the north. They say his raiding does not go well. Even if he could send aid, it might not come soon enough.'

Brigid rubs at her forehead, trying to push away the pain that sits behind her eyes.

If only I could sleep. If only I could stop.

She drops her hand. 'Then slaughter what cattle we can store and sell the others.'

'That's what I said,' Ciara says. 'But Buach won't allow it.'

Buach is their cowherd, who loves each and every one of the cows as though she had birthed them herself.

'I will speak with her,' Brigid says, sitting again at her desk.

'Today?' Ciara says. 'Tomorrow might be too late.'

'Today,' Brigid agrees.

Ciara sniffs her approval. 'What were you looking at?'

Brigid doesn't look up from the text. 'Hmm?' she says, attempting to sound at ease.

'The window, what were you looking at? I've never seen that expression on your face before.'

Brigid breathes in and meets Ciara's eye. 'And what expression is that?'

'Guilt,' Ciara says.

Brigid does indeed speak to Buach that same day, for she is glad to be away from the convent, where she might encounter Darlughdach or Ciara again.

'There has to be another way,' Buach says, after Brigid has explained the need for the slaughter.

She is a large woman, with thick arms and wide hips, though her flesh hangs loose from her bones now.

'It is the cows or your sisters,' Brigid says softly, giving the woman the choice.

It looks as though it is not an easy choice to make. Buach stares out at the skinny cattle who stand around empty troughs. 'May I keep just one?' She points at a dark-brown cow with a streak of white down its back. 'She's good luck. And a fine milker.'

Brigid nods. 'Yes, one. But the rest must be put to the knife today.'

Buach cries over each corpse.

The meat only lasts so long and soon fasting becomes an act not of remembrance, but of survival. Though some of the women relish the chance to follow in the footsteps of Christ, and take to the starving of themselves with a fervour that troubles even Brigid.

Indiu has to be forced to drink weak broth after Brigid learns she has not eaten for nearly two weeks. Imbolc comes and goes with no celebration.

'Have you abandoned us?' Brigid asks me, as she watches the flame one night. She picks a handful of snow from the ground and throws it into the flame. 'I thought you were the goddess of spring, then where the hell are you?' The flame hisses but keeps burning.

SOON, MY CHILD. I AM RESTING.

At last, the snow melts and the land comes to life. The redwings can be heard in the hedgerows and swallows cut through the clouds above. By April, the Curragh is alive with colour: primroses, buttercups and marigolds burst in thick clusters and the women gather golden furze to place on the doorsteps and windowsills for protection.

'We'll need more than flowers should the raiders come again,' Ciara says. 'Even Lommán has wasted away and can hardly lift his cudgel.'

He will need a sword, Brigid thinks. Armour too. Perhaps all the women need swords and armour, if raiders are to come again.

With the warmth of the sun comes food. The women go foraging and come back with baskets filled with sea beet, sorrel and wild mushrooms, and even a handful of strawberries tempted by the warmth. Wild onions and leeks and garlic burst through the soil in the convent gardens. They mate their last remaining cow with one of King Dunlaing's bulls, and it gives birth to twins. Buach the cowherd cries again, but this time they are tears of joy.

They give praise to Jesus in their daytime Masses. And praise to me in their night-time prayers.

Beltane arrives, bringing life back to the land and to the convent itself.

'To celebrate the arrival of summer, we shall have a feast!' Brigid announces to the gathering after Mass.

There is cheering and clapping. It has been too long since Brigid looked down on her congregation and saw smiles.

'With feasting?' Indiu asks.

'And dancing?' Induae, adds.

'Yes. And song and storytelling,' Brigid says, looking at Darlughdach. 'Do you still have your old harp, Dara?'

'I do at that.' Darlughdach smiles back and Brigid feels that it is not only the snow that has melted.

They have earned each scrap of happiness she can offer them, and Brigid gives in to their every demand. Except one.

'We could save ourselves the effort and go to Tara. King Lóegaire puts on a fine feast,' Ciara says.

'Oooh, yes,' Clodagh agrees. 'I used to go when I was a little 'un, and it was the best. He has the biggest fire in the whole of the land.'

'And not only the biggest fire, from what I hear,' Ciara says, winking at Clodagh.

Brigid fears what might happen to the women alone out in the world. Only here can she keep them safe, even if that means robbing them of these snatches of joy. 'What need have we of the king's fire, which only burns one night a year, when we have a flame of our own that burns eternally?'

It is decided. The women gather food and drink and climb up the hill to the grove, singing as they go. Some have brought coloured ribbons which they tie to the branches of the old oak as they did when they were just girls, making wishes on the wind. They want so much and yet ask for so little. Their singing wakes me and unseen I walk among them, listening to their prayers.

They take it in turns to leap over the flame, skirts hitched up to their hips. Though why any of them would wish fertility for loins they have forsworn from men, I do not know.

It is a cloudy night and in the far distance the clouds scudding across the horizon glow red. King Lóegaire's giant Beltane bonfire has been lit on the Hill of Tara.

As they gather to watch, they see a second burst of light in the sky, even bigger than the first. A bright column of light piercing the sky.

'Has the king lit two fires?' Ciara asks.

'Perhaps it is a trick of the eye?' Darlughdach says. 'The reflection of the fire caught in the clouds?'

The women gaze at it in wonder, but Brigid feels only fear. She imagines her skin blistering and bubbling, as though she were standing within the column of fire, feels the pain of the heat stripping her down to bone.

THIS DOES NOT BODE WELL.

'Brigid,' Darlughdach says, brushing her arm. It is the first time she has touched her since their talk by the riverside.

Brigid flinches at the gentle touch and looks to see her skin untouched and unblemished, though it shimmers with sweat.

'What do you need?' Darlughdach asks.

What she needs in that moment is to have Darlughdach's cool hand smooth over every part of her body, to quench the fire. She pulls away.

'Nothing.' She regrets her sharp tone and tries again. 'All is well. Come, play your harp, sing us a song.'

Darlughdach hesitates before plucking a string on her harp. The women continue their dancing as on the horizon the light burns into the night.

36

There are many heavy heads the next morning. Ciara has her head in a bucket, vomiting yellow bile.

'The sloe wine must have gone bad,' she says through retches.

'Oh, for sure,' Darlughdach says, holding her head in her hands. 'And my skull feels like it's going to split open because of the onions I ate. Nothing to do with all the ale I put away. We have only ourselves to blame.'

'I swear to God,' Ciara says. 'I only had a cup or two.' She retches again.

Brigid lays her hand on her old friend's forehead and reaches for the healing light within her. She whispers a word.

'That's better,' Ciara says with a long sigh.

'What about me?' Darlughdach asks. 'Where's my healing?'

"'*Whoever suffers in the body is done with sin*,'" Brigid says.

Darlughdach responds to this by blowing on her tongue, making the sound of a wet fart.

For days, the women do not stop discussing the meaning of the two fires. The older women believe it to be an auspice, a blessing on the year to come. While others see it as an omen. Brigid keeps dreaming of the light, sees herself standing within it, her flesh bubbling like a spit pig.

It takes almost a week for the news to reach Cill Dara, passed from farm labourer to trader to merchant and at last to Darlughdach.

There is a gentle knocking at her door, a rhythmic *rat-a-tat-tat*. Only one woman knocks like that.

'Come in, Darlughdach,' Brigid says.

She enjoys these little tricks, not magic, just observation, though for many of the women in the sisterhood, it's the same.

Darlughdach's face is pale as ash as she steps inside and closes the door behind her. 'It was Patrick.'

'What was?' Brigid asks.

'The column of light we saw, was from the hill of Slane. Patrick himself lit it.'

'Why would Patrick light a Beltane fire?'

Darlughdach takes a seat on the small bed in the corner. How long has it been since Brigid shared a bed with another body? Not since the second winter when they took to sleeping three to a bed to stay alive.

Darlughdach twists the rough sheets in her shaking hands. Her voice is steady, but Brigid can see she is having to fight back anger. 'They say he is calling it a Paschal fire, that it was in honour of the resurrection. King Lóegaire is spitting teeth but they say he dared not move against Patrick, for fear of bringing down whatever remains of Rome's power on himself. Lochru, however . . .'

Brigid knows that name: King Lóegaire's druid priest. She had seen Lochru once, at a gathering of Maithgen's. She remembers he was a small man with a big voice, who wanted to fight everyone. She had thought he must be dead already.

'What is the old fool up to now?'

'He challenged Patrick to a battle.'

'That sounds about right,' Brigid says.

'His magic against Patrick's miracles. They say Lochru summoned lightning and made the earth quake and lifted all watchers a foot into the air.'

Brigid doubts Lochru has the powers for such magic as this, but she doesn't interrupt Darlughdach.

'And Patrick, he just smiled.' Darlughdach herself smiles at this, but her mouth is twisted as though she has tasted something bitter. 'A fierce gust of wind blew Lochru off the cliff and he fell to his death, his head dashed against the rocks below. Patrick didn't so much as raise his staff.'

Brigid closes her eyes and sees the man's small body broken on black cliffs.

'They say King Lóegaire bent the knee to Patrick after that and swore his oath to Christ.'

'He is not as stupid as I had believed then.'

Darlughdach sighs. 'There is more.'

'Go on.'

'This is not the only story I have heard of Patrick's persecutions of pagans. I've heard it said he is responsible for the deaths of hundreds of druids and the destruction of hundreds of sacred wells. He has set himself against what he calls the black laws of heathenism and the spells of witches, wizards and smiths.'

'Smiths?' Brigid asks. She doesn't know whether to laugh or weep. 'What can he have against smiths?' It's true that Lommán and his smith apprentice, Clodagh, have yet to convert, but she has never seen them casting spells while smelting iron.

'They make the weapons.'

'Ah,' Brigid says, understanding. 'And why have you not told me of this before?'

'Because you and Patrick follow the same God. I was not sure you would believe me.'

It is as though Darlughdach has struck her. How could she ever think that? 'I will always believe you, Dara. Always.'

Darlughdach stands and brushes her skirt flat. 'Well, believe me on this. I would not trust Patrick as far as I could piss him.'

'Thank you, Darlughdach. I will think on this.'

Let Lóegaire and Patrick fight. Let the whole world of men outside these walls kill each other for all I care, as long as they do not set their sights on Cill Dara.

The next day, a letter arrives for Brigid. It had been sealed with green wax, pressed with the rough shape of a harp. But someone has broken the seal already. Brigid sighs. She's not even allowed to read her own letters first any more. If it got to Ciara, she would have opened it out of a meddlesome curiosity. If it was Lommán, it would have been out of protection. Either way, Brigid is annoyed. Surely they can see it came from King Dunlaing.

She opens it. It has been written in Latin. Poor Latin at that, and she wishes the men of Ireland would hold on to their native language rather than try to follow Rome in all things. Though in truth, Irish does not fare so well in written form. The clean lines of Roman letters seem to crush the lyricism of it. Irish is a language best spoken and heard – not trapped in ink. All the same, though, they could try.

"*King Dunlaing of Leinster does entreat the lady Brigid, holiest of women, most blessed of God's creatures . . .*"

She closes her eyes. A letter that starts with this much honey will soon have a sting.

"*. . . for her blessing that he will be victorious in a battle against the pagan forces of the Airgíalla tribe of Fermanagh, evildoers who raid his lands and take hostage his people, both Christian and pagan alike. King Dunlaing is preparing to gather his forces and ride to Fermanagh and strike mighty fear into their hearts. With the blessing of the holy Brigid, he asks that she ensure his victory through an intervention to God, to whom she is closest and of whom most beloved.*"

She winces. Now they believe she has the power of one of the old gods, to decide the fate of battles. If she had that, she would have no need of men like Dunlaing.

'Lommán,' she calls out.

The door opens almost before she has spoken the second syllable of the name. He must have been the one who opened the letter and has been standing outside the door waiting for this summons.

'What do we know of the Airgíalla tribe?' she asks.

'Their chieftain is a violent, vicious man. They say he killed his own father to take power. And since then has conducted cattle raids in Cavan, Tyrone and even across the Ulster border into Meath. And was two days ago seen a day's ride from here.'

'Do you think it was his men who raided us last autumn?'

Lommán chews on his cheek. 'I do not. The men of Airgíalla favour spears, not bows. But that does not mean they do not have plans to.'

'Has he raided Armagh?' Brigid asks.

'He has not. For fear that Patrick would set the hosts of God upon him.'

'And yet he plans to raid my land,' Brigid says. 'Does he not fear *my* wrath?'

Lommán does not answer, though the twitching of his hands speaks for him. He is afraid of this chieftain. Afraid of what might happen if King Dunlaing's warnings prove true. He still has only a cudgel to protect them and though he trains every day, Brigid can see he has not fully recovered from the famine of winter. His clothes hang loose on his shoulders and there are dark rings under his sunken eyes.

'Ready your horse. I will have a reply for King Dunlaing within the hour.'

Lommán bows and leaves Brigid. She takes up a quill, turns over the letter Dunlaing sent to her – for why waste good paper – and writes her answer.

He will have her blessing and he will be sure of victory against the Airgíalla. She asks for one small payment in return, as proof of his devotion to God.

She pauses, brushing the feather end of the quill against her lips as she considers what this payment should be. She smiles and finishes the letter. Folds it over and calls once more for Lommán.

'Here,' she says, handing it over. 'Take it to the king.'

A man on horseback carrying King Dunlaing's green-and-gold banner arrives a week later. Brigid goes out to meet him, Lommán and Ciara by her side. The messenger has a raw, red scar across his cheek and his face is splattered with mud and blood. Behind him, across the saddle, is a sack large enough to carry a man.

'Have you come from the raid on the Airgíalla?' she asks.
'I have.'
'And what news of King Dunlaing?'
'Victory was his. The chieftain of the Airgíalla is defeated.'
'Dead?'
The man nods. 'And the remains of his men sent scattering.'
Brigid fights back the flutter of delight this image brings her. Christ told his followers to hate violence, to turn the other cheek. But Christ was not a woman.

'A shame,' she says, making the sign of the cross. 'If only wars could be fought with words alone.'

'The king sends his humble thanks to you, for your blessing. And as promised . . .'

The man clambers off his horse, his movements stiff and slow. Brigid suspects he nurses a broken rib or two beneath that armour. He unties the sack. It falls to the ground with a loud clanging, and there is a glimmer from within.

The man drags the sack over to Brigid, upends it and tips

out a tangle of golden metal on to the grass. The sun flashes in Brigid's eyes as she tries to make sense of the shapes.

'Is that a suit of armour?' Ciara says.

'The king's own. As promised,' the rider says.

Streaks of blood across the patterned breastplate, and dents and scratches, speak of a fierce battle.

Ciara steps forward and bends down. She picks up a greave and stares at it, the reflected light turning her face bronze. 'This will feed us all for a year,' she says in delight. 'I know the perfect man to sell it to.'

'No,' Brigid says. 'It's not to be sold.'

'Melted down then,' Ciara says. 'For the manuscripts?'

'Not melted down either.'

'Then what?' Ciara demands to know.

'Lommán,' Brigid says.

Lommán steps forward, already bowed. 'Yes, Brigid.'

'This is for you,' Brigid says. 'As a sign of my thanks for protecting us all these years.'

'But—' Ciara starts. Brigid silences her with a twitch of her hand.

Lommán looks at the armour, mouth open in disbelief. He bends down and picks up the breastplate, holds it to his own chest.

'Take it to Clodagh,' Brigid says. 'She can hammer those dents out and make it fit you. Tell her to make you a sword, too.'

'I'm not worthy,' Lommán says.

'You said it yourself,' Brigid says, laying a hand on her old friend's shoulder. 'More raiders may come. Now you can meet them like the warrior you are.'

37

Another visitor comes from Mullaghmast within the week and again Brigid and her women walk out to meet them.

'What is it this time?' Ciara asks. 'Silver torcs for the geese? Maybe some crowns for our pigs?'

'Hush,' Brigid says, for she cannot hear one more complaint about Lommán receiving the armour.

If Lommán, who wears the armour every day, knows this barb is meant for him, he pretends not to notice.

Their visitor is a woman, dressed in reds and blues, wearing a thin gold band around her head. She is flanked by two men in leather armour and trailed by four young handmaidens, each more beautiful than the last. But their beauty is nothing in comparison to the woman who leads them. It is not just her face which is fair, it is the way she carries herself: as though the world belongs to her.

Brigid takes a moment to recognize her as the pale young woman who stood beside King Dunlaing on the day she was given the Curragh. Cuach, King Dunlaing's wife and Queen of Leinster. Today, she looks like a queen, which she had not those years before. It has been so many years, Brigid reminds herself. We have both changed.

'Queen Cuach,' Brigid says.

'Mother Brigid,' Cuach replies. She takes Brigid's shoulders in her hands and kisses her twice on both cheeks, before stepping back and taking Brigid's hands in hers. Brigid is not used to this physical closeness and confidence in a stranger, and she has to fight back the instinct to tear her hands away.

'I have come to thank you for the aid you provided my husband in his battle against the Airgíalla,' Cuach says.

'That was God's work, not mine.'

The woman smiles, as if acknowledging a shared lie. She bounces Brigid's hands up and down, as though they were girls playing a game, and then slips her arm under Brigid's and walks with her. 'I thought it was well overdue that we got to know each other. After all, we're the two most powerful women in Leinster. We should be friends.'

'Indeed. Then please, come in. Your handmaidens may accompany you, but your men must stay here.'

The men move as though about to protest, hands going to the hilts of their swords, but Cuach holds up a finger, as though hushing them. 'Stay.'

Brigid leads the way back through the gates, and as they walk Cuach squeezes her arm. Brigid looks down at it, wondering what the meaning of all this touching is about. The two women walk, their entourage silently following a few steps behind like the trail of a dress dragged on the ground. Brigid's arm, pinned under the queen's, feels as though it no longer belongs to her. Yet she does not take it back. This is some kind of test, between women who live in a man's world.

'Oh, it's even more magnificent than the stories say,' Cuach says, as they step inside the gates.

'Would you care to see the library?' Brigid asks, for this is where most visitors wish to see.

Cuach blows out her cheeks. 'Oh, I cannot read, so I am sure that most of it would be lost on me.' She leans in and speaks softly so only Brigid can hear. 'Perhaps somewhere quiet, where we can talk.'

'Let me show you my private room,' Brigid says.

They walk and Cuach does not wait till they are inside to

begin her talking. It is endless, flowing, and strangely soothing. Like the sound of water over rocks.

'What a place you have built,' Cuach chatters as they walk.

'Thanks to your husband and his patronage,' Brigid says, playing along with whatever game Cuach has set.

'Oh, he was raging after he passed the Curragh over to you, he might have hidden that well enough . . .'

He didn't.

'. . . but he kept hissing and puffing for at least three days after. But then he prayed on the matter and came to see that your glory is truly the glory of God. And any good you do with his land . . .'

His land?

'. . . will in God's eyes be seen as his own work. He tells everyone about you, you know, Blessed Brigid, Mary of the Gaels.' The woman pauses for a moment in her stream of chatter to look at Brigid. 'Do you know they call you that? Mary of the Gaels?'

'I have heard it before.'

'The Milk Mother of Christ, that's the other one. Though how any of that makes sense when he died hundreds of years ago is beyond me. Your religion is a strange one.'

'You're a pagan?' Brigid asks, stumbling as she tries to stop walking.

'Is that what it's called now? Anyone who follows the old ways. A pagan? Strange that there is now a word for what once simply was.' They continue to walk through the courtyard, slow as though taking a stroll on a summer's day. 'But no, I am not a pagan,' the queen declares loudly. She then lowers her voice and leans in close to Brigid. 'At least as far as my husband and his Christian allies are concerned. But in my heart . . .' She touches a space between her breasts.

Brigid does not need any more explanation. She too carries secrets.

'It took Dunlaing almost ten years, but he finally got me to convert.' Cuach laughs, throwing her head back and booms out three loud *har-har-har*s. Brigid is so used to the sound of women's laughter it has become like listening for birdsong. Even through the walls of her room, she can pick out the laughter of the other women. Cinnia's laugh that is like rain. Indiu's, that starts as a hissing and then explodes. Darlughdach's laugh that is like a donkey. But she has never heard a laugh such as this one.

They arrive at the door to Brigid's room, and at last Cuach frees her arm.

'You can wait here,' Cuach says over her shoulder at the handmaidens who have followed. 'I am sure no danger awaits me here beyond a nasty paper cut! Oh, what a cosy room, I really should get . . .'

Brigid nods to Ciara. 'See that our guests are comfortable.' Once they are inside and the heavy door is closed, Cuach's nail-sharp smile fades. She breathes in, holds the breath for a moment, and then lets it out with a long, heartfelt sigh.

'Now,' she says, with a warm, inviting smile, 'we can truly speak.'

Brigid finds herself laughing. 'And we weren't speaking before?'

'That,' Cuach says, moving around the room, taking in the walls and papers strewn on the desk, 'was chatter. What is expected of a woman.'

Almost everything about Cuach has changed. Her voice is lower, softer. Her movements slow and considered. She even seems to take up more space.

'And what have you come to truly speak about?' Brigid asks.

Cuach takes a seat on a low wooden bench. 'Dunlaing was injured in the raid against Airgíalla.'

Brigid had not heard of this. 'Have you come for my blessing?'

Cuach shakes her head. 'Even if you were to heal his wounds, it is only a matter of time before age comes for him. He is not a young man. Our son, Aillil, has sent word from Tara that he will return and take the throne for himself. If Aillil is king . . .'

'Then Cill Dara is in danger.'

She nods. 'And Aillil is not the only one you should be wary of. I hear rumours. Read my husband's letters. The wolves are circling, Brigid.'

'I like wolves.'

Cuach laughs. 'Of course you do.'

Brigid leans back in her chair and crosses her hands before her chest. 'Then what would you suggest I do?'

'I can see it's not in your nature to run?'

Brigid shakes her head. 'It is not.'

'Then you must start to make new alliances. Find a way to turn your enemies into your allies.'

'You don't mean Patrick? He has sworn to convert every pagan in Ireland and those who will not convert he will kill. I suspect that he wishes me dead, too.'

'Not dead,' Cuach says. 'He wishes you . . . gone.' Cuach waves her hand as though brushing aside a cobweb. 'I suspect he would be quite happy if you were to go and live in the mountains in a nice dark cave as a hermit of some kind. You scare them. The power of Cill Dara scares them. And you know what men do when they are scared?'

Brigid knows well enough. As do many of her women. 'I have kept away from the messy business of politics.'

'Then it's about time you got your hands dirty, Brigid. Power is politics.'

SHE IS NOT WRONG.

'You cannot hide away inside these walls, Brigid. You must make yourself seen. And by Patrick most of all. He is as powerful as a king now – even more so, perhaps, for kings bow to him. You do not want him as your enemy.'

It has been years since Patrick came to her doors, though he has rarely been far from Brigid's thoughts. She can still see the fire in his eyes when he called her a sinner. Was this a man who could ever become an ally?

'Thank you for your counsel, Cuach. I will think on this. But tell me these letters to your husband that you read. Are they written in Latin?'

Cuach smiles. 'Perhaps.'

'You are a fascinating woman, Cuach. Should you ever tire of the royal life, we would welcome a woman of your wit and wisdom here.'

'So it is true that pagans are welcome here?' Cuach asks. 'That you worship the new god and the old god the same.'

'All in need are welcome here,' Brigid doesn't quite answer.

'Then perhaps I will join you one day. When my husband is dead and my son is king. For he is sure to bring about much misery and I would prefer not to be there to see it.'

There is a knock on the door. 'Queen Cuach,' a weedy voice shouts through the keyhole. 'We must go.'

'Ah,' Cuach says. 'Duty calls.'

The women stand and Cuach embraces Brigid. She welcomes it.

'I wanted to give you this,' Cuach is whispering now. She reaches under her robes and pulls out a silver necklace, with a heavy pendant on it. She holds it up and it spins in the low light.

On one end, there is a silver apple, the size of an acorn, perfect in every way. On the other, the figure of a woman with large, heavy beasts, rolling belly and thighs, and hair wrapped in intricate patterns on a round, eyeless head. It is the most beautiful thing Brigid has ever seen.

Cuach places it into Brigid's hand. It nestles perfectly in her palm. The weight shocks her: it would buy a herd of cows.

'May the goddess watch over you,' she says, in a whisper.

Oh, I will.

The women embrace again. As Cuach walks out, Ciara walks in. The queen bows her head to the woman who was once a slave, though Ciara does not return it.

'I assume you were listening?' Brigid asks her when they are alone.

Ciara doesn't try to deny it. 'What will you do?'

'I don't know yet.' Brigid hands the silver necklace to Ciara. 'Put this in the chalice box.'

Ciara gazes at it in wonder. 'It's the most beautiful thing I have ever seen.'

Perhaps one day you will see the real thing. Then you will know true beauty.

38

A troop of warriors are spotted on the border of the Curragh a month later. They walk in single file like ants around a fallen plum. At their head, a single man rides on horseback and even across the distance, Brigid recognizes him. Aillil, come home.

King Dunlaing, Cill Dara's patron, must be dead.

'Wolves,' she says, watching them from the top of their tower.

'What's that?' Ciara asks.

The woman has had a clammy pallor to her skin of late, so Brigid has confined her to working only in the library till she recovers her health.

Brigid leans against the window frame. 'Tell me, Ciara, if you had to win over a man, what would you do?'

Ciara waggles her eyebrows.

'Not like that!' Brigid says.

Ciara puts aside her quill and stretches out her back. 'Well then, I would probably work out what he wants and how I could give it to him. Not like that,' she says, after Brigid fixes her with another disapproving glare. 'Like if I go to trade sheepskins in the market, I don't accept the first offer I get. I chat a little, all casual like, and find out that your man has the hots for your woman, and I say I will have a word with her. Or he says he has a hankering for honey ale, but the brewer won't sell to him after they had a falling-out last winter, so I offer to be a go-between. And he's so grateful that he buys every skin at full price. Everyone gets what they want and I go home with the convent's purse jangling. It's like a dance.'

Brigid has taken Queen Cuach's advice and though it took her three days to write it and she felt sick with every word, she wrote to Patrick, asking him to become the new protector of Cill Dara. There has been no response. 'And how can I find out what Patrick wants?'

'Well, you could ask him. I hear a synod is taking place in Dunlavin next month. And that all the leaders of the church will be there.'

Brigid had received word about this synod also. It is to discuss the shifting power struggles of the Church and the issue of confession. She had no plans to go, for she cares little about the messy squabbles of bishops. But perhaps, as Cuach said, it is time for her to get her hands dirty.

The next day, they have gathered in the refectory for their morning meal. Brigid finds she cannot eat, for nerves squirm in her stomach like eels. She pushes the plate of oats aside and stands. The chatter falls away like melting snow. Brigid rarely addresses the sisters other than in the oratory, and then she reads the words written by those gone before her.

'A synod is taking place,' she says, her voice weak at first. 'A gathering of the leaders of the Christian Church, to discuss the unfolding nature of our new religion. And I, as a leader, intend to be there. While I am away, Darlughdach will lead the services and oversee the running of the convent.'

Darlughdach looks up from her food, her mouth hanging open over her spoon. Brigid had not consulted with her, for there is still some distance between them that she doesn't know how to cross.

Their eyes meet as Brigid continues. 'For there is no one I have more faith in than Darlughdach. She is the best of us.'

There is cheering and beneath it, from some of the more zealous sisters, a low grumbling. Darlughdach might attend every service and no one can deliver the gospel like her, recited from memory for she still refuses to learn to read, but many believe she still holds tight to the old ways.

The women on either side of Darlughdach nudge her and give their congratulations, but she has not taken her eyes away from Brigid. They burn, questioning and challenging. At last, Darlughdach smiles. Her old, easy smile. A wave of warm relief passes through Brigid, melting the last of the ice that has crackled in her veins for months.

If my going brings about no good other than this, it will be enough.

Though she wishes she did not have to leave the safety of Cill Dara.

She does what she always does when she is uncertain: she sits down to work. She is in the middle of translating a passage from St Luke, searching for the words in Irish to capture the Latin. Latin, she finds, is controlled, precise. There is always the perfect word. Irish, this is never so. Even the word for a single mote of flour, cáithnín, can also mean a grain husk, or a speck in the eye, or a snowflake, or a pinch of butter. *Perhaps this is why the Irish never built an empire beyond our own land; we were too busy discussing the meaning of things.*

She writes this down in a separate, private book, where she keeps words that do not belong to others. Her own thoughts and ideas, though she knows she will never share these with anyone else. She waits for the ink to dry and then returns to her translation.

The sky has turned the colour of slate when her door slams open and Ciara bursts into the room. The shock makes Brigid jolt, and her quill leaves a black splash across the page.

She sighs. 'I have been working on this one page for three days and now it's—'

'Where is it?' Ciara says.

'Where is what?' Brigid asks, pinching the bridge of her nose.

'Don't play the fool,' Ciara spits. 'The silver necklace the queen gave you.'

Brigid is used to Ciara's outbursts; they come quick and blow quicker, like a rain cloud in spring. But she has never seen her this angry. It scares her. 'A woman came to the gates starving and asked for help. I gave it to her.'

'What about feeding us!' Ciara shouts. 'When did you last look at the women right here?' She holds out her hands, wrists up, as if Brigid is to see bones beneath her pale skin. 'We're all half-starved and our robes are wearing away. I was going to sell that necklace at the market in Dunlavin and get the best price. It could have seen sixty women clothed and fed for a year. And you've given it away to one woman! God save me, I never wanted to think of your father as long as I lived, but he was right. You are mad, giving everything away. And yet Lommán – fucking Lommán – is walking around in gold armour that would buy enough food so we could all die fat and happy!'

Brigid stands shaking her head. How many times must they go over this? 'This greed does not become you, Ciara.'

'Greed? Oh, fuck you,' Ciara shouts, and Brigid has never heard so much anger in her voice. 'Fuck you, Brigid. It's not greed to want to eat. To want firewood so we're not freezing our fucking tits off every night. Maybe it's because you were raised the daughter of a chieftain, born with wealth beyond dreaming, that you think it's fine to give everything away. But when you were born a slave, charity does not come so easy.'

Brigid's legs buckle as she struggles to stay standing, as though the ground beneath her is uneven, but when she looks, the slabs are smooth and flat. She and Ciara have often argued over the limits of their giving, but she did not realize her old friend's resentment went so deep.

'Charity is everything,' Brigid says. 'We have all we need — the rest we must give away.'

Ciara shakes her head, back and forth. Her lips are pursed tight as a walnut shell, her hands curled into hard fists. 'Well, you might be able to live on air and God's blessing, but the rest of us need bread. You'll heal every mute, leper and limping idiot that comes to those gates, and let the rest of us . . . rot . . .' She cannot finish, for her words are broken by great heaving sobs.

Brigid has only ever seen Ciara cry once: when she broke the bowl in Dún Ailinne. She has not shed a single tear since. Not when they were starving and cold, or when the raiders killed her sisters. And yet she wails now.

Brigid rushes to Ciara and takes her face in her hands, wipes away the tears. 'This is not about the necklace. Tell me, Ciara, what ails you?'

Ciara meets her gaze and Brigid sees something she has not seen in her friend's eyes since they left the walls of Dún Ailinne behind them. Fear.

'You are scaring me. Please, what is it?'

Ciara steps back and hitches up her tunic, and Brigid is expecting to see a rash of some kind on her thighs, or warts on her vulva, something that would explain the panic. Many of the women come to her with concerns about their dark places, asking for Brigid to heal them. Sometimes she does. Other times, she sends them to Ciara for an ointment or an education on what is normal for a woman. But now it is Ciara's turn to be showing her most intimate parts. She pulls the tunic up all the way to her chest, revealing the gentle swell of her belly.

It takes Brigid a moment to understand what she is seeing, *how* she can be seeing what she is seeing.

'You are pregnant?'

Ciara lets out a strangled scream. 'I'm fucking pregnant!'

Brigid staggers back, staring at Ciara's belly, at the faint lines rippling like roots across her skin. How can this have happened? 'Was it one of the raiders? Did they force themselves on you?'

'No,' Ciara says, throwing her robes back down. 'Nothing like that.'

'Then . . . how?' Brigid asks, but what she wants to ask is why. Why has Ciara done this thing?

'The usual way. It was a trader in the market. He gave me apples and I . . .' She raises a shoulder in a half-shrug.

Brigid runs her hand through her hair, wanting to tear it out. 'How? After the way men treated you, how could you have lowered yourself to lie with one?'

'Brigid, please.' Ciara falls to her knees, and presses her face into Brigid's skirts. 'Please forgive me. I will do whatever penance you ask to make up for this sin and every other sin of my entire life.'

'This was not the first time you have lain with a man since taking the veil?' Brigid asks, pulling away from Ciara.

Ciara stays kneeling. She gazes up at Brigid and then starts to laugh. 'Oh, Biddy, how is it you have visions and yet you can't see what's right in front of you. Of course I've lain with men. And when it has been my choice, I have enjoyed every second of it.'

Brigid wants to be sick, but there is no food in her stomach, only acid. How could Ciara do this? How could she allow a man to . . . How could any woman allow a man to perform such violence on her. And to enjoy it? She paces up and down the room, but it is so small she can barely take two strides before she has to turn around and it feels faintly ridiculous.

'But I promise, I swear on my life, on every god there is and will ever be, I will never lie with another man if you help me.' Ciara reaches out and grasps Brigid's hand, forcing her to stop her pacing. 'I'm too fucking old, Brigid. I don't want this baby. It will likely kill me coming out of me. I don't want to leave my life here. I love Cill Dara. I love you and the sisters—'

'But you can't stay.' Brigid shakes her hand free. 'What will the women think when they realize?'

'Then help me.' Ciara rises, though she has to lean on the edge of the desk to help herself up. 'Take the baby away.'

Brigid shakes her head. 'I'm not a midwife. I don't know the herbs.'

'I tried that. And obviously it did not work.' Ciara gestures to her belly. 'I don't need weeds and witchcraft, Biddy. I need your magic. I need this baby gone.' She strikes herself twice in the groin with her fist.

Brigid understands what Ciara is asking of her, but she doesn't know if she is capable of it.

'I know you can do it.' Ciara says, for she could always read every one of Brigid's expressions. 'You healed Cinnia.'

Cinnia had come to Brigid almost a year ago and had stood, as Ciara had done, and lifted the hems of her robes, showing Brigid her breasts. One of which was lumpy and misshapen. They had prayed together and all was well.

'This is different,' Brigid says, turning her back on Ciara. If she doesn't have to look at her, she might be able to refuse. 'A baby is not a disease.'

'Isn't it?' Ciara says. 'Because as far as I am concerned, it's a lump of flesh growing inside me that will kill me. I know it.'

She closes the gap between her and Brigid. Leans her head on her friend's shoulder and wraps her arms around her waist. Brigid cannot resist and returns her friend's embrace. The two hold each other as they did when they were children.

'It's not murder,' Ciara says, whispering in her ear. 'I have not felt the quickening. It doesn't have a soul.'

'You must do penance. Only bread and water till Yuletide.'

'I will do it.'

'And you must swear you will never lie with a man again.'

'I swear!' She squeezes Brigid so tight, her ribs crack. 'By every god there is, I swear it!'

Brigid pulls away. Grabs Ciara's face in her hands, feels the power tingling within her. 'A binding promise, Ciara. Of the old ways. If you break it, you will be cursed.'

Ciara looks deep into her eyes. 'I swear,' she says.

Brigid hugs her again quickly before pulling away. 'Lie down,' she says.

Ciara sits and then lies on Brigid's bed. Brigid sits next to her and places her hand over her friend's stomach.

It doesn't have a soul. She repeats Ciara's words. For now, it is only an animal. The killing of it no more than wringing the neck of a rabbit. But even this she has not been able to bring herself to do in the past.

Instead of killing it, what if it simply ceased to be? She imagines a fire burning to cinders, ashes blowing away in the wind. Her hands begin to heat like meat on a spit. Ciara squirms, bites down on her lip, groaning behind clenched teeth. She twists and turns, crying out in pain like an animal in labour, kicks her legs and buckles under Brigid's hands.

And then . . . it is done. Ciara's stomach deflates beneath her hands, as though she were pushing air out of a linen when washing, returning to its small, soft swell.

Ciara sits up. Places her hands over her belly, pushes against her muscles. 'It's gone.'

Brigid shakes her hands. They ache with pain. 'It's gone.'

39

Brigid leaves for the synod before dawn the next morning. Ciara has insisted she will come with her, 'to stop you selling the whole bloody monastery'.

Despite what they went through together the day before, despite Ciara's gratitude, she is still angry about the necklace. But Brigid knows that all of Ciara's moods are quick to pass. She has made no more mention of the pregnancy and though Ciara walks slightly bent over, hand pressed against her side, she is whistling with a lightness that is unusual for her this early in the morning.

Lommán is awake too, having lit the torches and readied Brigid's cart. His golden armour glimmers in the flickering flames.

'I have loaded the sheepskins, as you asked,' he says.

Piles of cream and black hides lay piled up in the cart, for there will be a market in Dunlavin, and Ciara plans to sell the skins.

'Thank you, Lommán. I am sure Ciara will get a fine price for them.'

'I won't come with you,' he says, brushing his hand down the nose of the horse to settle it.

Brigid had not asked him to, but it still surprises her that her guardian has chosen to stay behind.

'Dara may need me.'

Hearing her own name for Darlughdach on his lips feels like a wound.

'She will, I am sure,' Brigid says. And feels a churning, twisting in her stomach.

'Come on, the sooner we're on our way, the sooner we'll be back,' Ciara says, crossing the courtyard and climbing into the back of the cart. She winces as she sits.

'Does it hurt?' Brigid asks.

'A little. You drive. I'll sleep till we're across the Curragh.'

Ciara curls up in the piles of sheepskins and is snoring before Brigid clicks the horse's reins to set it moving.

It is noon before Ciara emerges from her fleecy nest. She yawns, stretching her arms over her head, fists balled as though around invisible ropes pulling her upward.

'Good sleep?' Brigid asks.

'The best I have had in years.'

'And your pain?'

Ciara pats her womb. 'Better every hour. Where are we?' She clambers over to sit next to Brigid.

'Near Narraghmore,' Brigid replies.

'That far? You should have woken me.'

'I tried. When we left the Curragh. And again, as we crossed the Tully river. Your snoring was so loud it kept away any robbers at least – they must have thought I had a dangerous beast in the cart with me.'

Ciara elbows Brigid. 'Oh, give over. I don't snore that loudly.'

'The only thing louder than your snoring is the rumbling of your stomach,' Brigid says, as Ciara's belly gurgles loud enough to be heard over the soft clopping of the horse's hooves. Away from the convent, an unnamed heaviness lifts from Brigid's spirit. She remembers when she and Ciara were girls, with no more responsibilities than milking the cows and staying out of her father's way. *But you are free now*, she reminds herself. *Free, but burdened with cares.*

'My stomach thinks my throat's been cut,' Ciara says, rubbing at her belly. 'Did we bring food?' She rifles through their bags.

'I didn't think to.'

'You never think about food, Biddy,' Ciara says, giving up her search. 'Ah, but God has answered.'

The cart is passing under an apple tree, heavy with green fruit. Ciara stands up and plucks three apples from the branches. She bites into one and offers another to Brigid, who shakes her head.

'What of your penance?' Brigid asks.

'Oh, I looked it up. The text says, "*If a woman by her magic destroys the child she has conceived of somebody, she shall do penance for half a year with an allowance of bread and water.*"'

'Precisely.'

'Well, it wasn't *my* magic now, was it?' She bites again into the apple, grinning as the juice runs down her chin.

'You are as slippery as a salmon, you know that, Ciara?'

'I try, Biddy. I try.'

They ride for a while longer, the silence only broken by Ciara's crunching of apple flesh.

'So, what will be discussed at this synod of yours?' Ciara asks, as she wipes juice from her chin.

'The date of Easter, I think. Whether priests are subject to the law of their land or only to the law of the Church.'

Ciara makes an unimpressed *huff* and bites into the apple again.

'Mainly, I think it will be about the role of private confession versus public penance.'

'What's confession?' she asks, a mouthful of white flesh.

'Telling your sins to a priest.'

'Why would you do that?'

Brigid laughs at Ciara's bluntness. 'So, they can cleanse

your soul and you can feel . . . lighter, I suppose. Unburdened.'

Ciara throws the apple core over her shoulder. 'But why tell a priest? When I want my soul to feel unburdened, I tell a friend.'

Brigid glances across at Ciara. The woman has always been wiser than she lets on.

'Not that you would ever have anything to confess though, Ciara,' Brigid says, smiling.

Ciara smiles back. 'But of course.'

They ride on a little longer and Ciara eats the second apple. 'Do you think Patrick will say yes?'

'To what?'

'To being Cill Dara's protector. That's why we're really going, isn't it?'

Brigid glances at the woman out of the corner of her eye. In another life, Ciara would have made a fine queen: she understands politics in a way Brigid does not.

'Yes,' Brigid says, looking back at the road. It vanishes around a tight corner ahead. 'And I don't know.'

'Appeal to his vanity,' Ciara says. 'Make him feel like the big man, protecting the poor little women.'

'And have him think us weak?' Brigid says, yanking on the reins so tightly that the horse whinnies.

Ciara spits out an apple seed. 'Who cares what he thinks, as long as we get his money.'

Brigid laughs. Ciara makes it all sound so simple.

'Will Bishop Brendan be there?' Ciara says, licking her fingers clean of the apple juice.

'I . . . I don't know,' Brigid answers. 'Perhaps. Why do you ask?'

'Oh, just that he was rather pleasant on the eyes.'

'Ciara, you swore!' Brigid says. She cannot believe that her friend has forgotten so soon. 'A binding oath.'

'And I will keep it! By Jesus, I will. But it's not a sin to look, is it?'

Brigid raises an eyebrow at her friend. 'In some writings, they say that the sin of the mind is as bad as the sin of the flesh.'

'Well, that's bollocks,' Ciara says. 'You're telling me thinking about wanting someone dead is as bad as actually murdering them? Bollocks.'

Brigid laughs. 'Perhaps you should be the one speaking at the synod, with such a fine grasp on . . .' Her voice trails off as they see a large group of people on the road ahead making their way towards a small homestead.

As the cart nears the back of the crowd, a man is in the middle of telling a joke. He holds up a scrap of bread, and pretends to offer it to his friends, as one giving the Eucharist. 'Body of Christ. Body of Christ,' he says, bobbing the bread before one man and then the next. 'Christ, what a body,' he says, when offering the bread to an invisible third party. The people gathered around him howl with laughter. And he is invited to tell the joke again.

'What's going on?' Ciara asks a woman.

'Bishop Melchu,' the woman says.

'What's the fool done this time?'

'There's a woman, she's accused him of being the father of her child.'

'Oh, this I've got to see.' Ciara jumps down and ties the reins of the horse around a tree branch.

Brigid does not follow. 'Ciara, this is not our business. And we don't have time . . .'

'Come on,' Ciara says, grabbing Brigid by the wrist and dragging her off the cart and through the throng of people.

They push their way to the front. Ciara has a way of making even the biggest men step aside by fixing them with a stern look.

On a wooden platform stands Bishop Melchu and next to him, Bishop Moel. On the other side of the platform is a woman. She is strikingly beautiful. Young, perhaps barely in her twenties, wearing the simple robes of a farmer's daughter. And in her arms, a wriggling, screeching baby. Her face is pale and her eyes dart left and right, as an animal trapped. The crowd watching this sport are jeering and every now and then, there is a wet *thwack* as a rotten cabbage or handful of muck is hurled towards her. She turns, protecting her child, and takes the blows on her back. Her dress is already wet with dark stains.

Bishop Moel holds up his arms. 'Silence, silence. We are gathered to hear the accusations that this woman has made against his holiness Bishop Melchu.'

'That he put his bastard son in her,' someone in the crowd shouts out.

This is met with much laughter, while Melchu stares out into the crowd, peering down his long nose, looking for the location of his tormentor.

'Come now, you all know Bishop Melchu—'

'Not as well as the girl knows him.'

More laughter. This is all sport to them.

'The bishop is innocent,' a woman standing next to Brigid cries out. 'The girl is a seducer and harlot.'

'He is a man of God,' a deep voice cries out. 'He would not sin in this way.'

'You would say that,' someone sneers. 'He's your cousin!'

More rumbling. Hot, sweating bodies press in around Brigid. She wants to be out of the crowd. Away from the noise and heat and stink of so many people.

'Ciara . . .' she says.

'Yes, I know. Let's go.'

Ciara takes Brigid's hand and starts to pull her from the

stage. But before the women can fight their way free, Brigid hears her name being called.

'Mother Brigid?' Moel shouts. 'It is you! Oh, praise the Lord.'

Brigid freezes and slowly turns back to the stage. People around her make space, stepping away as though she is a pebble dropped in a pond. But all are staring.

Moel rushes forward. 'It is surely divine providence that you are here at this time.' He grabs her hand and drags her upward.

Ciara still holds her other hand and for a moment, Brigid is stretched between the two, like a lambskin pulled across a frame. Moel wins the tug of war, and Ciara lets Brigid's hand go. She is yanked up on to the stage, scraping her shin on a splinter of wood.

'Mother Brigid here is known throughout the land for her piety and wondrous powers,' Moel declares.

Whispers spread throughout the crowd.

'Is it her? Can it be her?'

'She looks younger than I thought.'

'If anyone can prove my innocence, it is Brigid, she whom God has raised up,' Melchu says, his stare brimming with menace.

And whom man can bring down, is the threat he speaks only with his dark eyes.

THIS MAN IS A FOOL, BUT A DANGEROUS ONE. BE WARY.

'What has occurred, Father?' Brigid asks.

'This woman, this . . . succubus!' Melchu shouts, pointing at the young woman, 'has accused me of evil baseness.'

Brigid turns then to the young woman. 'What is your name?'

'Áine.' Her voice is raspy and her eyes are red-ringed from crying.

She rocks the baby back and forth, back and forth, trying to soothe it, but it wails and wails, a desperate, hungry wail.

'Tell me, Áine, what is your charge against Bishop Melchu?'

'He has done me a great evil,' she says. 'He came to my parents' house and preached the word of the Lord and then he told me that there was a way that all my sins could be forgiven. If I were to lie with him—'

'Liar!' Melchu's hollow face crumples in disgust. 'I have never touched this woman or any woman! She should be hanged for this. Surely the Devil is in her, for look at the beast of a child she has born. It can only be Satan's spawn.'

'This child is his,' Áine says. 'And now I have been cast out by my family and no one will help me.'

Brigid pulls aside the cloth wrapping the baby. It's a frail thing, skin like the inside of a shell, lips almost blue. It has a fine coating of soft brown hair across its body which she has heard can happen with babies, but she has never seen before. It also has a shock of hair on its head, the same deep red as Bishop Melchu's.

The eyes of every man, woman and child here are on Brigid, watching what she will do, whose side she will take. Her every instinct is to side with the woman – as she has always done. Áine is the one without power here: young, unwed, abandoned. And yet, Cuach's words ring in her ear: *"Make alliances."*

If Brigid declares the baby Melchu's, it will sour him even further against her. He has Patrick's ear; she saw that when they came to Cill Dara. But if she is to take Melchu's side, it would mean betraying this woman. A woman who needs her help. What, though, is the need of one woman, against the hundred who live in her community?

Behind the walls of her convent, her word is never questioned, never doubted, but out here, in the world, how much weight does the word of a woman truly carry? She looks at Áine; innocence glows from her for any who have eyes to see, and still she is not believed. In truth, she would be safer if Melchu were not the father. If it was some lowly man from another province; even a raiding foreigner would be better than a man with power who will do anything to protect it.

Brigid has always seen the world in sharp contrast: good, bad. Man, woman. Slave. Free. But was she not herself once half free, existing in the liminal? Perhaps she can find that same space between states now.

She leans down and kisses the baby on its forehead, stilling its cries. She twists her head, so that her ear is close to the babe's mouth, feels its weak breath on her cheek.

'It is speaking,' she says.

There are gasps of wonder at this magic Brigid has performed.

There is no doubt in her mind that Bishop Melchu is the child's father. She straightens up. 'Bishop Melchu is not the child's father,' she says.

There is a moment of shock and silence before the crowd erupt in screeches and cheers, Bishop Melchu claps his hands in triumph, while Áine stares, open-mouthed, unable to say a word. She glares at Brigid. Hatred, betrayal, confusion all dancing across her young face. She is trying to speak, to protest her innocence, but no words will come. Tears flow down her cheeks and drop on the ground like rain.

Brigid has to turn away from her for she cannot bear to see the pain of her betrayal.

She sees Ciara in the crowd, standing arms crossed, nostrils flaring. How can she explain that it had to be like this? That she had to make a choice. To sacrifice one woman to protect them all.

Words a-plenty come to Melchu. 'See! She lies! She is

nothing but a harlot!' the bishop shouts, his face red, spittle flying from his wet lips. 'She should be whipped.'

'Whip her! Whip her!' A chant starts up from the crowd.

Áine backs away, clutching her baby to her breast. 'No, no,' she says, her voice drowned under the shouts. 'I did nothing. I did nothing!'

She looks to Brigid, her eyes daggers.

Guilt bites at Brigid's gut, as sure as any blade. *What have I done?*

The crowd are pulsing forward, any moment one will break and leap up on to the stage. She holds her hands outstretched, as though she were calming spooked cattle. And from the stage, that is how the crowd appear to her: an unsettled herd, ready to stampede at the sound of a twig snap.

'Good people,' she says. 'Peace be on you all. And peace be on this young woman. Do not judge her for this sin, for only God may do that. Instead, let her do penance. Six months with only bread and water. Once she has completed that, her sin will be washed clean.'

Grumblings like the moos of cattle move through the crowd. They had come for entertainment, and now all they are getting is a sermon.

'She seduced my husband,' a woman shouted from the crowd. 'She cannot pass by him without his eyes jumping out of his head.'

'Then look to your husband on that,' Brigid says. 'For he is the owner of his eyes, not her.'

A crowd are like a beast with one mind. She must give them something else to focus on, or else they might still demand to see this woman whipped. 'Pray with me.'

She holds her hands out, as she would when blessing her sisters in the oratory at home, and begins to recite the Lord's Prayer. Those that know it mutter along; those that don't slip away, bored with the new entertainment. When she has pronounced her last 'Amen', the heat has left the gathering and all go about their business.

Brigid turns back to Áine. *Go*, she mouths. The girl looks at her as though she wishes Brigid were dead, but heeds her instruction and slips away.

Moel approaches. 'Mother Brigid, a million thank-yous, a fine thing you have done today. We are in your debt.'

Melchu is still red-faced and puffing. 'That is as may be, but I have no doubt that the truth would have been seen in the end.'

'I have no doubt about that at all,' Brigid says. 'Did Luke not say, "*There is nothing concealed that will not be disclosed.*"?'

She and Melchu stare at each other. A secret kept has strength. *And so we trade truth for power.*

'How,' he says slowly, 'may I repay your kind deed?'

'Tell me, will Bishop Patrick be at the synod?'

'He will,' Melchu says.

'I would speak with him. To discuss some matters of Cill Dara.'

Melchu sucks in air through tight lips. 'He is a very busy man. Every bishop at the synod will be demanding his ear.'

'But as his dearest nephew, his own flesh and blood, I am sure you will be able to ask for a moment of his time.' Brigid smiles, wide enough to show her teeth, but her eyes remain cold.

Moel stands looking from one to the other, a happy, shiny look, as though he were watching two people engaged in a game of fidchell.

Melchu swallows, his sharp Adam's apple rising and falling. 'I will see what can be done. Come, Moel, we must be leaving.'

'We will meet again soon, my dear Bishop Melchu. Bishop

Moel.' She nods at each man and walks away as Ciara slides in beside her.

'What the fuck, Biddy? Why did you—?'

'Go, find Áine,' Brigid says quickly. Ciara's admonition can wait. 'Tell her to leave this very night and make a new life away from here. Away from Melchu, for as that boy grows up all will see that he is Melchu's son.'

'Then why didn't you reveal him for the dirty bastard he is? Why didn't you help her?'

Brigid grasps Ciara's hand. She must make her understand. 'Because I needed him on my side. On our side.'

Ciara shakes her head. She has always challenged Brigid, fought her on almost every matter of how Cill Dara should be run. But she has never been disappointed in her till now. 'There must have been another way. That girl will have to live with the shame of that for the rest of her life.'

'Shame can be washed away. For the right price. Give her all that you have in your money pouch.'

For once, Ciara doesn't argue. She pushes through the crowd in search of the young woman.

Brigid watches Bishop Melchu walk away. Bishop Moel wraps an arm around him, to comfort him for all he has been through.

This is the cost of power, then? Betraying those lone souls most in need, in order to protect a community. Weighing the worth of one life against the needs of many.

Her decision sits in her throat like a stuck fishbone.

40

Ciara refuses to talk to her for much of the journey to Dunlavin. She stares out at the changing landscape, back turned.

'It was better this way,' Brigid says when she can no longer stand the silence.

Ciara spins around in her seat. 'How? How exactly was betraying that girl better?'

Brigid yanks the reins and stops the cart. 'What do you think Melchu would have done had I declared him the father?' she shouts. 'Do you think he would have taken her and her baby into his home? Raised the son as his own?'

Ciara looks down, hands twisting in the folds of her skirts. And Brigid realizes that this is not about Áine and her child, but Ciara herself and what life could have been for her had Brigid not helped her. 'No, but . . .'

'Áine is safe now.' Brigid flicks the reins again. 'And that is more than many women get.'

They don't need to ask for directions to Dunlavin for a trail of white-haired men in long grey and purple robes lead them all the way up the hill and to a new church that has been built on the ruins of a ring fort. The men talk too loudly in Latin, and jostle and slap each other on the backs.

'They're all so old,' Ciara says, as they leave the cart and slip into the moving huddle of men.

'Political power takes time to accumulate,' Brigid says.

And that's what these men have: power. She can almost

smell it on them. It is not like the scent of the old power she catches on the air when there has been rain after drought or when walking across the Curragh at night – that smells of dirt and lightning and blood. They smell of rich food and rare dyes and anointing oils. And if smugness had a smell, they would smell of that too. For each man she sees looks far too pleased with himself.

Will I become like them, now I have started to play their games of influence?

'And wealthy. Look at all the gold.'

Ciara is right. Each man wears a golden cross around his neck. Brigid rests a hand on her chest: she has never worn a cross before and suddenly feels the absence of it. Will they judge her for not declaring her faith to all who see? Will they laugh?

She glances to a small river that runs beside them. Fresh green reeds line the bank.

'What are you doing, Biddy?' Ciara asks, as Brigid begins to tear the reeds from the soil.

'How did Dara do it again?' she says, folding a reed across another.

She fails the first and second time, throwing the discarded reeds away, but at last her fingers find the pattern as she folds reed across reed, turning ever clockwise. When it resembles a cross, she wraps each end with a strip of grass, pulls a thread from her cloak to act as a chain and hangs it around her neck.

'There,' she says.

'It's not gold,' Ciara says, shaking her head at Brigid's woven cross.

'Then it will remind them that I am a humble woman.'

They join the procession of men, ignoring the hisses and tuts directed at them as they all file through into the hall, like a herd of sheep moving into a pen and there . . . their shepherd.

Patrick stands at the front of the gathering, his long,

hooked staff glimmering in the soft light. A woman stands beside him, the only other woman here apart from Brigid and Ciara: Íte of Killeedy. She flutters around Patrick like a moth, trying to encourage him to take a seat, but he shakes her off. Every man who passes Patrick genuflects before him on creaking knees, and he waves a hand over their heads.

Íte sees Brigid and the smile she had been flashing at the men slides from her face like rotten meat from a plate. She bustles over, weaving between the men who treat her presence as they might a wasp: an irritation.

'What are you doing here?' Íte asks. She glances at the cross made from reeds around Brigid's neck and curls her lip in disgust. Around her own neck hangs a cross made of gold and rubies.

'Are you not happy to see us?' Ciara says.

'This is a council of bishops,' Íte says, ignoring Ciara.

'And Brigid is a bishop. Ordained by Bishop Moel himself,' Ciara snaps back. 'Go and ask him if you don't believe me.'

Ciara nods across the room. Moel and Melchu have arrived ahead of them. Moel is beaming at everyone who passes, his full cheeks rosy. Melchu stands with his chin tilted, trying to look down at the other men, though he is a foot shorter than many gathered. He makes the sign of the cross over some who pass, but Brigid notices they do not stop to receive his blessing. The righteous bishop, passing judgement over all he sees. If only the men gathered here knew his true nature.

Melchu meets Brigid's stare and quickly drops his hand. He nods at her, a tiny gesture of recognition and Brigid cannot deny the shiver of pleasure that passes through her as she realizes he is afraid of her. But afraid enough to have put her request to Patrick?

'Well, of course, that was a mistake,' Íte prattles on. '*Everyone* says it was a mistake.'

'God does not make mistakes,' Brigid says, not even looking at Íte. She is looking at Patrick.

He stands, a full head over any other men here, though Brigid suspects that is because the men bend themselves so as to be beneath him, as men do before a king.

He stands stiffly, with his back to her, but she senses that he knows she is here. She recognizes a man talking to Patrick by his sun-bleached hair and tanned skin. He now wears the pectoral cross of a bishop.

As if feeling her eyes on him, Brendan turns. His freckled face erupts in a smile. 'She has arrived. Our Mary of the Gaels!'

One by one, heads turn in her direction and the chatter that had filled the hall stops. And suddenly, every gaze is that of her father, every sneering mouth is that of her brothers. She is a small girl once more ready to receive punishment for some perceived infraction. Her hands start to shake, her stomach roils. She can hear her heart pounding in her ears and every fragment of her wants to run, out into the fresh air and away from the eyes of these men.

She had come here to be seen. But by so many men? All at once? Each stare feels like a slap. She steps backwards, once, twice, is about to turn and run, when she feels Ciara's hand on her shoulder.

'Stand your ground,' her old friend whispers in her ear. 'You're more powerful than any man here. You deserve to be here.'

I ALWAYS LIKED THAT GIRL.

Brigid focuses on Ciara's strong grip, steadying her. Some of Ciara's certainty flows into her and I add a little of my own. She can almost feel it pour into her spine as she lifts her head, pulls back her shoulders, and stares defiantly at the men.

She locks eyes with Patrick. Eyes grey and sharp as spearheads. What damage he could do with just those eyes.

Brigid clears her voice and stretches out her hands as she does every time she takes Mass. 'Blessings on all gathered here today.'

Not saying whose blessing, you sneaky thing.

Men bow their heads, receiving her blessing. Many cross themselves, in protection or in acceptance of her power, she does not know. Her fingers tingle and she fears light might burst from them. It is one thing to claim her right to be here as their equal, but another to reveal how inferior their power is to hers.

'And blessings on you, Sister Brigid,' Patrick says. 'Now, shall we get down to the reason we are all here? God's work.'

And that is it. If this has been some kind of test, she has passed.

'Remember who you are, Brigid of the Fothairt,' Ciara says, practically shoving Brigid forward. 'Mother of Cill Dara. Protector of the lost and broken. God has chosen you for this.'

Ciara leaves Brigid alone. All the bishops take their seats, while their vassals and servants leave. The heavy doors boom shut, shaking dust from the rafters.

Only Patrick and Brigid remain standing. Their eyes meet again over the heads of the congregation and a look of annoyance flickers across Patrick's face before it returns once more to granite.

He may be annoyed by me, but he cannot ignore me. She sits down.

Patrick clears his throat, as though dislodging a crumb, then begins. 'To the matter of confession . . .'

The discussions begin. Whether man (*man*, always *man*) can be cleared of his sin through private confession or if he must do public penance as is the current tradition. Rome believes one, the majority of the bishops of Ireland another.

'But it says in the Didache, "*Confess your sins in church, and do not go up to your prayer with an evil conscience,*'" a bishop who speaks Latin as though biting into a rock says. 'For your sins to be forgiven, they must be spoken in public.'

'What of those who fear to expose themselves?' one of the Irish bishops says. 'Like a man who contracts a disease in his more shameful parts and will not seek help. Is he condemned to perish because of his bashfulness?'

"'*I am the way and the life,*'" Melchu proclaims, as though he is proving a point, though what it is, Brigid does not know. "'*No one comes to the father except through me.*'"

Brigid rolls her eyes, for what has this to do with penance?

'Perhaps Sister Brigid has something to add?' Patrick says, his sharp eyes fixing on her. 'How is forgiveness bestowed at Cill Dara?' He says the name of her home as though spitting a curse.

Brigid refuses to be afraid of this old man. She forces herself to stand. 'At Cill Dara, we avoid the whole issue of confession,' she says, trying to hide the quake in her voice. 'By simply living a life without sin.' She sits again.

This is met with mutters of outrage, though from somewhere in the gathering she hears the familiar chuckle of Brendan.

Patrick goes red around the cheeks. "'*If we say we have no sin, we deceive ourselves, and the truth is not in us,*'" Patrick says, quoting from John.

Brigid opens her mouth and is about to say that by the grace of God, Mary remained free of personal sin. Instead, she bites down on her lips. She has come to ask Patrick for help and arguing with him will not benefit her community.

'You are correct, Your Grace,' she says, bowing her head and sitting again.

A satisfied smile spreads over Patrick's face. The debate continues, back and forth, as bishop after bishop quotes from increasingly obscure tracts, some that not even Brigid has read.

'It is agreed,' Patrick says at last. 'We shall follow the teachings of Cassian. The recitation of sins and the performance of penance will be between the sinner and their confessor only.'

Patrick slams his staff on the stone floor to silence the sudden outbreak of disagreement. 'It is agreed,' he repeats. 'And now, let us take Mass.'

'We can have it here, your holiness,' Melchu says.

Patrick looks up at the roof above their heads, and the steam from the hot breath expelled over these past few hours collecting there. 'I prefer to hold my Masses in the fresh air, where God can better see what we're up to.'

Brigid and all the other bishops stand and follow Patrick out. The cool air from the open doors is welcome, even if it is already drizzling. It carries on it a taste of salt, though they are far from the sea.

Brendan comes to stand beside her in the doorway. He closes his eyes and lets the rain kiss his face.

'It reminds me,' he says, without opening his eyes, 'of being at sea. It even smells like it.' At this, he glances at one of the bishops squeezing past him.

The man was one of the most vocal of the Roman bishops and the stress and sweat of his protestations has stained his robes. Brendan catches her eye and Brigid turns her face to hide her smile. It wouldn't do to be laughing at a time like this.

Brigid remembers when they first met and how he wanted to know if the Christian God was the right one. 'Tell me, on your travels, did you find a better God?'

Brendan smiles, then looks over his shoulders as though checking that they cannot be heard. 'In truth I found something else.'

Brigid waits for his answer.

'That all gods are the same god.'

They move outside. Patrick stands before a large rock, over which has been thrown a simple white cloth. She and Brendan sit at the back.

'Congratulations on your appointment as bishop,' she says, nodding at the golden cross of office he now wears.

'Oh, they will make anyone a bishop these days,' he replies. 'Even a woman.'

She opens her mouth to protest, but sees by the twinkle in his eye that he is teasing her.

'I do not yet have a ministry,' Brendan says. 'So I am bishop in theory only. Whereas you are a true leader of the Church. I should be bowing to you.'

'Oh, don't worry,' Brigid says. 'I would never compel you to bow to me.'

'You are a woman who could compel a man to do anything, Brigid.'

Brigid doesn't meet Brendan's eyes, though she can feel him looking at her. *This man is another life.*

Patrick is staring at them both. He clicks his fingers in the air.

'Ah, I must attend,' Brendan says. 'Good luck, Bishop Brigid.'

He joins Moel and Melchu behind the altar. Patrick lifts his hands to the sky. The rain clears and sunbeams punch through clouds like blades.

NICE TRICK. BUT MY ONE WOULD DANCE ON THOSE SUNBEAMS SHOULD SHE WANT.

Patrick holds out his hands. 'In the name of the Father and of the Son and of the Holy Spirit.'

The congregation reply, some speaking, others singing. 'Amen.'

Patrick joins his hands before his chest and says, 'I will go to the altar of God.'

Brigid responds in time with the voices around her. 'To the God who gladdens my youth.'

Patrick starts the service the same way she does, with the antiphon, but his words soon differ from hers. His prayers talk of shields and swords, whereas she chooses to preach of love and charity. He talks about the end of days, while she promises a life to come. The side of his mouth droops the smallest amount and some of his words are lisped.

The sun beats down on Brigid's back, adding to the weight of the long journey here. How long has it been since she slept? Ate? She looks for Ciara in the congregation but cannot find her. Perhaps she is in the market, bartering with their sheepskins.

Loaves of bread are passed from hand to hand. Brigid takes a crumb and brings it to her lips, before passing it on. A cup is next, with only a swirl of wine in the base. She wets her lips with it and tastes vinegar and rust.

She tries to focus on Patrick, as he opens a bible to read from the Gospel, but she finds herself thinking about the quality of the binding, wondering at what illuminations it might have and whether he would allow her to take it with her to be copied. Or at least study it here, so that she could lock it into her memory.

He reads from St Paul. Of course. His Latin is stilted, his voice monotone. There is so much poetry that he is failing to find. Brigid's eyelids grow heavy; the bark of the tree pressed against her back feels not unlike her bed back at home. And before Patrick even gets to his homily, she is asleep.

41

She dreams of home. Of Cill Dara. As it is now, and as it will come to be. She sees her women working to raise the city up, growing old and dying, and new women taking their place. And then she sees a flock of black birds descend on Cill Dara. They settle on every surface, eating every speck of grain, carrying off every scrap of cloth. Their wings become the pages of books, flapping away into the sky, until they burst into flames, shrieking.

The screeching of the black birds becomes the coughing of a man.

WAKE UP.

Brigid opens her eyes to see a tall figure standing over her, blocking out the sun.

'Did my Mass bore you, Sister Brigid?' Patrick says this with a small, broken smile, but his eyes are cold as winter. Melchu stands slightly behind him, head bowed.

The rest of the bishops have returned to the cool shade of the church. Only she, Patrick and Melchu remain outside.

Brigid wipes dribble from the side of her chin. 'No, I was . . .'

She needs to make this man her ally, not her enemy, for if he sees the threat in her, he could take away everything that she has built.

'I had received a vision from God.'

CLEVER GIRL.

Patrick's nostrils flare and his jaw tightens. 'And tell me, what did you see?'

Brigid stands up and looks into his grey-slate eyes. They have clouded a little since their last meeting, but they still shine with a dark, dangerous intelligence.

'I found myself standing on a high mountain', she begins, unsure where she will take this tale, ' with all of Ireland in my sight, and from every part of it I saw bright flames that joined together and burst into the sky. I looked away, and when I looked back, the land was covered with black birds, snuffing out the fires with their wings.'

She finds her mouth has gone dry and wishes for another sip of the communion wine.

'All became ash,' she continues. 'I shut my eyes and wept, but when I opened them again, I saw a great steady bright flame shining in the north, and another in the east. And both flames then spread, till the whole of the land was lit up again once more.'

Patrick does not say anything for a moment, though Melchu's mouth bobs open and closed, as though he has words he is desperate to say. 'Father, does that not sound like your own vision?'

'A little,' Patrick says, his lips pursed like a walnut. 'I spent Lent on the top of Cruachan Aigle fasting, as Our Lord did. And as I fasted, I was tormented by a demon in the form of a flock of crows. But I defeated it by ringing my bell that drove it back into its cave.'

YOU DID NO SUCH THING. FOR THAT WAS MY SISTER, THE MORRIGAN, YOU FACED. AND SHE SENT YOU RUNNING, BOY.

He moves aside his cloak to reveal a bell strung to his belt. A dull, pewter thing that might hang around the neck of a bull. It has a large crack in it. Brigid sees that Patrick's knuckles are swollen with rheumatism. Ciara would prescribe a compress of comfrey twice a day for that. Brigid herself could heal it with a touch, should he ask. Though she knows he never would.

'Once I was freed of my tormentor,' he says, 'I was visited by a vision. In it I saw all of Ireland illuminated by a great light. The light of faith.' Patrick strikes his staff on the ground with each of his last words.

'Ah, perhaps it is the light of our two churches that we have seen?' Brigid says. 'The light of the new faith.'

'In *my* vision, there was only one source of light,' Patrick says, his voice as sharp and hard as granite.

Brigid smiles. An old smile she used to use on her father. It feels uncomfortable on her, like wearing an old pair of shoes that she has grown out of. 'But what if one light was to go out? Would having two not safeguard the faith?'

Patrick's eyes narrow. 'In my vision, it was made clear that the light of my church will never extinguish.'

Brigid sighs. She is bored of talking in metaphors. Bored of this dance. 'I am no good at this game,' she says. 'So let me be clear. You once offered me your protection. I may have need of that now.'

Patrick grins, and Brigid sees he is missing his back teeth. 'Tell me, do you still dance at Imbolc?'

He is better at this than she is, but she will not be cowed. 'We do. At Imbolc, Beltane, Lughnasa and Samhain. And I am sure if Christ walked these green lands, he would join us in those celebrations. Does it not say in the Acts of John that he led his disciples in song and dance?'

'The Acts of John has been declared heretical by Rome,' Patrick says sharply.

'Ah,' Brigid says with a sigh, 'another book that must burn.'

Patrick's eyes flash, and for a moment she sees reflected there the fire he set on the Hill of Slane.

'You should be careful, Sister Brigid, of allowing the heretical ways to poison your . . . convent.' He is careful not to use the word 'church', she notices. 'The pagans are savages.

They still believe in human sacrifice and the Irish pagans are the worst savages of all.'

Brigid can still taste the metallic Communion wine on her lips. The blood of Christ.

'Tell me,' she says, 'if you hate the Irish so much, why did you choose to build your church here? I would have thought having escaped us once, you wouldn't have been so keen to return.'

Patrick grinds his teeth back and forth. 'God called me to lead this land towards the Faith.'

'As he has called me also.'

'It is a sin for women to preach,' Patrick says, his nostrils flaring. 'As Paul said, "*I do not permit a woman to teach or to have authority over a man, but to be in silence.*"'

'It's fortunate then that the women of Cill Dara do not preach. We merely share stories.'

'Stories?' Patrick says, a thick eyebrow raised in suspicion.

'Christ's parables,' Brigid replies. 'Among others.'

This seems to appease Patrick a little. The flare of his nostrils softens and the muscles around his jaw unclench.

FOOL, THIS SHOULD SCARE HIM MORE. FOR DOES HE NOT KNOW THE POWER OF STORIES?

He sucks air through his teeth, as if freeing a morsel of meat trapped between them. 'I hear that you have brought many female sinners to God's light?'

'This is true,' Brigid says, though she winces at the use of the word female, as though he were talking about an animal.

'And you ask for my protection to aid you in your work?'

Brigid lowers her head. *Must I do this?*

IT IS THE ONLY WAY.

She swallows the taste of sick that has risen in her throat and meets his eyes. 'I do.'

'And in return?'

Brigid remembers Ciara's advice: '*Work out what he wants.*'
'What would you suggest?'

'That you vow to bring the sinners of this land towards God's light,' Patrick continues, as though he were preaching from the altar now. 'And if they will not convert and put aside their evil practices and spells, they should be driven out like the snakes they are. But for those who follow the true light, God will grant them peace.'

So this is the deal Patrick is offering her: that she convert or drive out any who follow the old ways. And in return, she will have his protection.

'I will see to it that every soul who passes through Cill Dara is brought to God,' she says.

Patrick nods, pleased with himself. '"*Anyone who believes will be saved; anyone who does not believe will be condemned. God has spoken.*"'

NOT GOD. JUST YOU.

'Amen,' Brigid says, bowing. Something poisonous swirls in her stomach, as though Patrick's snakes had found their way inside her and were trying to get out.

'I must say, I was most impressed by Cill Dara. And I hear it has grown since my visit.'

There is a hook to these words. 'A little, My Grace.'

'I have been told you have a library that is the envy of the Roman world. Greater even than the Imperial Library of Constantinople.'

Who is Patrick's spy within her community? 'Hardly,' she says. 'We have only a small collection.'

'Of course, the Imperial Library was destroyed by fire when you were just a child,' Patrick says, looking up at a patch of dark cloud that has passed over the sun. 'That is the danger of so much fragile parchment in one place: so easy to catch light.'

Brigid lets out a small huff. So it has come to this. Threats within threats.

Patrick looks down at his fingernails, as though examining them for dirt. 'It would be a shame for anything to happen to your collection, before it was *properly* catalogued.'

Brigid remains silent, waiting for Patrick to get to his point, but she can feel her palms burning. She pushes them into her pockets.

'I have some of the finest scholars at Armagh. I would like to send them to assess your library. Ensure that the codices are being properly taken care of.'

That word again. Properly.

Still she stays silent. Her hands burn so fiercely inside her pockets, she fears her skirts might catch fire.

'A bishop should be appointed to oversee it,' Patrick says, looking over at Melchu, who has remained silent throughout the whole exchange, only his eyes moving from Brigid to Patrick and back.

'Oh, yes, Your Excellency. Perhaps Moel or—'

'We already have a bishop,' Brigid says, through clenched teeth.

'Oh, I mean a proper bishop,' Patrick says, looking down at Brigid. 'A man.'

The words land like an anvil on her chest. She knew he would want to bargain, but she did not think he would sink this low.

'Cill Dara is a community for women . . .' she starts, struggling to find the words.

'And you have been without guidance for too long. It's only a wonder Cill Dara is still standing. I will send you a list of suitable men to become bishop. It will be your choice, of course.' He smiles, a small, satisfied smirk. 'Well, it is getting late. Come, Melchu.'

Melchu bows and takes Patrick's arm, aiding him as he walks away.

Brigid is unable to move, unable to find the words to protest. Her mouth feels as dry as ash.

'Oh, your brother sends his greetings,' Patrick says, without turning around.

Brigid blinks, struggling to process the change of topic. 'My brother?'

'Beccan. I ordained him as priest myself last month.'

Brigid stares at Patrick's back, at the slight curve at the top of his spine. She remembers Beccan, of how she made his eyes bleed, and wonders if she could do the same to Patrick?

'I'm sorry to hear about your mother, though,' Patrick says, looking over his shoulder.

She had forgotten this man knew Broicsech, had been the one to convert her. No, not forgotten, but chosen not to think about, for she does not think of her mother at all.

'What about her?' Brigid says. She hates how much power Patrick has over her. If this is a game they are playing, he is winning.

He looks back at her over his shoulder. 'You don't know?' he says, as though there is something amusing in her ignorance. 'She is dying.'

The world stops. A lock of Patrick's hair dances in the wind, the sunlight reflects in Melchu's golden cross. In the distance, Ciara returned, head thrown back in laughter as she talks to Brendan. Then all goes white, as if she has been struck by lightning. Pain erupts behind her chest. A spear plunged into her heart and twisted, around and around, and she feels herself wrapped around the source of that pain like a whirlpool. She thinks of the stabbing ache as smoke, black and tar from a charcoal fire, and imagines it become harder, like coal, harder still, a diamond rock. And this she buries in a dark place within her.

She forces her burning anger to snuff out. But the ember of it stays glowing in the space between her ribs.

'It has been some time since I have returned to Dún Ailinne,' she says. 'I have been busy.'

'Haven't you just,' Patrick replies. 'Well, I will pray for her. Though I hear that it will not be long before she is with Christ.'

'We should leave now, Your Excellency,' Melchu says, his voice barely above a whisper.

'Yes,' Patrick says, still looking at Brigid. 'Yes, we should go. It has been . . . illuminating talking with you, Brigid. I will pray for every Christian soul at Cill Dara. And the bishop who joins you will be a fortunate man to have you serve him.'

Patrick's staff beats out a steady rhythm as he strides away.

42

Brigid is too angry to speak on the journey back. She tries, but the words come out in hisses as she forces the rage back down deep into her belly.

'Not even your father got you this riled up,' says Ciara who has not been able to extract from Brigid the full details of what Patrick said.

Brigid attempts to answer, but she can't make it make sense. 'He dared . . . Me! Serve!'

'You're scaring me now, Biddy,' Ciara says. 'And for God's sake, don't take it out on the horse.'

Ciara extracts the reins from Brigid's hands. She has been using them to whip the horse forward, wishing it could fly and they could be away.

Brigid leans back in the seat and closes her eyes and imagines waves lapping against a shore. She tries to breathe in time with their ins and outs. In and out. All will be well. In and out. You are a free woman. In and out. You are chosen. And yet, in the susurration of the imagined waves she keeps hearing Patrick's words.

'*Have you serve him. Have you serve him.*'

'My mother is dying,' she says at last.

She can feel Ciara's eyes on her, though she looks away. She cannot bear to see any kindness, for she knows it will break her resolve. She must return home to Cill Dara. Patrick has made his move and now she must plan her next.

The cart jolts forward as Ciara snaps the reins. She turns the cart and snaps the reins again.

'What are you doing?' Brigid asks. 'Cill Dara is that way.'

'We're not going to Cill Dara,' Ciara says. 'We are going to Dún Ailinne.'

'No, I swore I would never return there.'

'Oh, get over yourself, Biddy,' Ciara says. 'You've been a fool too long.'

It has been eight years since Brigid last saw her mother. The same number of years they were separated when she was a child, when they had been torn from each other, as a heifer and its calf. Then, her heart ached every day at the absence and she longed to be reunited. Now, she wishes it could be another eighty years. As each acre they cross brings her closer to Dún Ailinne, closer to her mother, she feels only nausea.

'Stop,' she says, as she sees the dark walls of Dún Ailinne in the distance. 'I feel sick.'

Ciara ignores her and urges the horse on. 'That will be your pride. Swallow it.'

Dún Ailinne looks smaller than Brigid remembers it. In her mind, it was a giant fort, impenetrable and ancient. But it is just a simple fort, made of stones, and raised on a small hill. And she had thought her father's retinue at least a hundred strong, but as they ride through the gates, she sees only fifteen, maybe twenty, men and women at work.

One man stands in the doorway. His hair has gone the colour of ash and his eyes shimmer with clouded grey. His back is bent, his arms hang loose by his side. She would not have recognized him in a crowd had it not been for the sword hanging from his belt. The sword that bought her freedom.

'Father,' she says, climbing down from the cart. She stands before him, and his head comes to her own. *Has he always been this small? Or is it I who has grown?*

'I wondered if you would come,' Dubhthach says. And even his voice is weak.

'Can I see her?'

He nods and steps aside.

The hall is dark; damp drips down the walls, and the tapestries that once hung from roof to floor are so moth-eaten, they look like lace.

'Was it always this . . . shit?' Ciara asks.

'You've aged, Ciara.' A woman's voice comes from the shadows. Breachnat steps out, dressed in heavy furs wrapped around a frail body.

'Who is here?' A man stumbles out from behind Breachnat. He approaches, staring at Brigid with squinting eyes. He wears the tunic of a priest and has his hair shaved in a strip from ear to ear. He coughs, spits on to the floor, and Brigid knows him.

'Beccan.'

Her youngest brother blinks, takes another step forward and squints his eyes tighter. 'You,' he says at last. 'I had hoped I would go fully blind before I ever saw you again.'

'Good to see you too, Brother. You're a priest then?'

He pulls his shoulders back. 'I am. I was ordained by Patrick himself!'

'Then you should kneel,' Ciara says. 'For you are addressing a bishop.'

Beccan looks from Ciara and back to Brigid. 'So, it is true then? I thought it was yet another lie about you. Well, I don't care what the prophecy said, I won't be kneeling to you.'

KNEEL, we say.

There is a *crack* as Beccan's knees hit the granite slab of the ground.

'No! It cannot be.' Breachnat wails, a long, pained screech as her most feared prophecy comes to pass. Her child kneeling before Brigid.

Breachnat drags her nails against her cheeks as Brigid

makes a slow, drawn-out sign of the cross over Beccan's bowed head. In her mind she imagines she is holding a blade, and is quartering him, head to groin, shoulder to shoulder.

'Peace be with you,' Brigid spits, turning back on both her brother and stepmother. 'Where is Broicsech?'

'Through there,' her father says, nodding to a door at the back of the hall. He ignores the pathetic sobs of his youngest son as he leads the way.

The room stinks of death. A sweet sickly decay. There is a small bed on the floor, and in it lies a body. Brigid cannot believe that there can still be breath in it, for it looks more like a skeleton than a woman. Grey skin is stretched across cheekbones and her eyes are sunken deep into their sockets. Brigid approaches and tries not to recoil at the stench.

'Mother?' she says.

There is no response. No flicker of her eyes.

Brigid kneels next to the bed and takes her mother's hand. It is cold and heavy as a day-old fish and her skin feels like autumn leaves.

'I think we're too late,' Ciara says.

Brigid refuses to hear. 'Get me some beer.'

'We have no beer,' Dubhthach says.

'Then get me water,' Brigid shouts.

Ciara runs and returns a moment later with a cup of water. She passes it to Brigid, who covers the rim of the cup with her hand for a moment, and then holds it to her mother's cracked lips. Golden-brown liquid pours down Broicsech's chin. Not a drop is drunk.

Brigid puts the cup on the floor and wipes her mother's mouth with the sleeve of her tunic. A red stain marks the white. She brushes a grey strand of hair away from her mother's forehead and places her hand on her chest below her neck, feeling for a heartbeat. It is there, faint and unsteady.

It is not too late. She reaches inside herself to find the light and the words of healing, but finds only darkness and silence. She loves her mother, she is sure of it. But the bitterness she felt on the day her mother chose Dubhthach over her has wrapped itself around her soul like roots around a stone. She can find no softness within, only a broken heart.

'Please,' she says, a tear falling down her cheek and falling on to her mother's hand. 'Please, help me.'

THIS IS NOT MY DOING.

Suddenly, her mother gasps; her clouded eyes become clear and she stares ahead as if looking at something in the far distance. Her body becomes stiff, the tendons of her neck standing out like strips of leather. Then she lets out a slow crackling hiss of breath and falls back on to the bed. All life has gone.

Brigid pulls her mother's limp body into her arms and rocks it back and forth as her mother did to her when she was a child.

'I forgive you,' Brigid whispers into her mother's ear, before letting her go.

AND WHO, I WONDER, WILL FORGIVE YOU?

43

The sun sets behind them as they leave the hills around Dún Ailinne and drive back towards the flat, still lands of the Curragh. Ciara watches her in glances, but doesn't speak, and Brigid is grateful for the silence. For what is there to say? She keeps hearing the hiss of her mother's last breath, but in her mind it becomes the sucking of air between Patrick's teeth. This is his fault. For it was Patrick who told Broicsech to subjugate herself to a man. And now he would have Brigid do the same. Her whole life, men have demanded that she kneel to other men. Patrick is no different. She will not have it. She will not give up the home she has built. She will not die a useless death like her mother.

They rest the horse for a while at a stream and Ciara fills two bowls with cold barley pottage she retrieved from the kitchens in Dún Ailinne. She hands one to Brigid.

'To think they once had feasts, and now all they have is this . . .' Ciara dips a spoon into the pale grey sludge and brings it to her lips. 'Doesn't even have salt.'

Brigid does not touch hers. Her stomach is too full of acid to eat.

'Oi! You there!' Ciara shouts.

A man walks on the road towards them, back bent beneath the weight of a sack strung across his shoulders. At its open neck, a glimpse of white shimmers in the last rays of the setting sun.

'Is that salt?' Ciara asks, jumping down from the cart. 'It's salt, Biddy! God truly does provide.'

The man scrabbles his hand over his shoulder and closes the neck of the sack. 'Salt? Oh, no, this is rocks.'

'Rocks?' Ciara asks, an eyebrow arched.

'Yup. Just rocks. Now I'll be on my way.'

'We only wanted a pinch for our pottage,' Ciara says, moving to block the man's escape. She holds up her hand, thumb and forefinger pressed against each other. 'Just a pinch.'

'Well, best of luck to you.' The man moves, trying to sidestep Ciara. 'Better get these rocks to where they need to be.'

'Wait!' It is the first word Brigid has spoken since they left her mother. The man freezes, as though caught in mud.

Brigid slides off the cart and approaches the man. 'Rocks, you say?'

The man nods. 'Aye, aye, lots of rocks.'

'They must be heavy.' Brigid takes another step forward.

Heat flares between her breasts, deep in her chest, as though there is an ember where her heart should be.

'So very heavy.'

The man's back bends forward even more and he lets out a groan.

'Crushingly heavy.'

He falls to the ground, the weight of the sack crushing his back. Brigid can almost hear the crunch of his spine under his screams of pain.

'Biddy!' Ciara cries. 'Stop it!'

Brigid blinks. The man lies on the floor, sobbing. His sack has fallen over and white crystals of salt spill out around him like snow.

'Jesus,' Ciara says, pulling Brigid back on to the cart. 'He was just a fool of a man.'

'All men are fools,' Brigid says.

It is dark when they drive through the gates of Cill Dara and the torches have been lit. The sisters cheer and shout, overjoyed to see their abbess returned. They bustle around her, asking what happened at the synod, who did she see, what was said? She does not stop to talk to any of them, and instead strides away and towards her room.

'What happened?' Darlughdach asks Ciara, though Brigid does not hear the answer.

Inside the dark coolness of her room, behind the thick wooden doors, alone now with the silence and the scent of cedar and ink, she falls to her knees and screams. For the death of her mother, for the lost years of bitterness she put between them, and for all that could have been. She tears at her hair, beats the floor with her fists till her knuckles split and bleed. She screams against Patrick's easy threats. She imagines that the slab beneath her is his face. She and her women have built this place with their bare hands. Women she loved and thought of as sisters died to raise the tower to the sky. She is not going to let a man take it. Patrick may have power outside these walls, but within Cill Dara, she is sovereign. She screams again. If anyone hears her, they do not come.

When her throat is raw and her hands throbbing with pain, she rises, brushes the dust from her skirt and sits behind her desk. She picks up a quill with a shaking hand and begins to write. The lines are thick and heavy, the words running into each other without gaps. She does not even know what she is writing, only that after she has filled three pages, she feels lighter.

There is a gentle knocking on the door. A soft *rat-a-tat-tat*.

'Come in, Dara,' she says.

The woman opens the door a crack and slides her slim body inside, before turning her back on Brigid to close it gently. She then turns, leans against the door and speaks.

'Go on then. What did the old bastard have to say?'

This makes Brigid laugh, despite the anger still fizzing. Ciara will have told Darlughdach about her mother, but her friend somehow knows this is not what she will want to talk about. Not today, maybe not ever.

'That a man needs to be bishop at Cill Dara. He does not approve of women ruling themselves. He does not approve of women doing much of anything for themselves. And I fear if I do not accept it, then he will take Cill Dara from me. From us all.'

'Can he do that?' Darlughdach sits on the opposite side of the table from Brigid.

'I think he can do almost anything.'

'He's powerful then?'

Brigid nods.

'As powerful as you?'

Brigid chews on her lower lip, almost afraid to say it. As if the arrogance of speaking it out loud might pull the stones of Cill Dara down on her head.

'No,' Darlughdach answers for her. 'Then why worry?' She leans across the table and takes Brigid's bruised hands.

It is as though she has plunged her hands into warm water. Tingles dance up her arms all the way to her neck.

'Let him send some man,' Darlughdach continues, gently stroking the back of Brigid's hand with her thumb. 'And then bend him to your will, as you bend the very stars.'

Brigid snatches her hands free of Darlughdach and slams them on her desk, shaking an ink bowl. Splashes of black fleck her hands. 'I swore that I would never bow to a man.'

'You wouldn't be bowing to him. You'd only be letting him believe he was in control.'

'I could not bear it, Dara!' Brigid shouts, the smoking anger sparking into flame once more.

'But you will have to learn how,' Darlughdach says, standing. 'We have built this life here, a sanctuary, and I will not stand by and allow you to have it taken from us because of your damn pride.'

'Pride?' Brigid shouts. 'I have no pride!'

'You are filled with it, Brigid. As you have every right to be. Look at what you have created.'

'I have created a world without men!'

Darlughdach laughs. 'No men? Then what is this?' She grabs a scroll from the desk. 'Who wrote this?'

Brigid blinks in confusion. 'Augustine.'

'Men,' Darlughdach shouts. She grabs another. 'And this?'

'Aristotle,' Brigid says.

'Men. Every book of the gospel, written by a man.' She grabs book after book from Brigid's shelves and throws them down in from of her. 'Men. Men. Men. Everywhere, the words and thoughts you have fought to preserve are those of men. What is one more man if it means saving your sisters? Do not let your hubris be your downfall.'

Darlughdach's words ring in the air. Seeing her own anger matched by her friend's passion has helped soothe it.

'Hubris?' Brigid asks. 'You've been reading Aristotle?'

'You know I can't read,' Darlughdach says, some of the heat leaving her voice. She sits before Brigid, her shoulders rising and falling as she returns to herself. 'I have Indiu read it to me. Better than the bloody Bible again.'

Brigid finds herself laughing as she has not laughed in months. Darlughdach is right. She is letting her own pride go before the needs of their community. Perhaps Íte was right all those years ago: a little humility could do her good.

So she will need to find a man. A man she can present to the world as ruling by her side, but who would in truth be her servant. A man who she can bind to her.

Brendan could be a good choice. He respects her and she enjoys his company. But no, his desire to spread the word beyond the boundaries of Ireland would keep him away.

She looks at one of the books Darlughdach threw before her. *The City of God Against the Pagans* by Augustine of Hippo. The gold illuminations shine like salmon skin in springtime. The blues are like the deepest, darkest parts of the sea. And the letters themselves, more crisp and perfect than any written by any of the scribes here. She has seen this book before, read it many times, it is one of her most treasured. But now she sees it in potential.

'Tell me,' she says. 'Do we know what happened to that monk who came from Rome?'

44

The monk's name, Brigid is told, is Conleth. He never made it to Scotland, indeed, he never made it beyond the border of Leinster, and has made a home for himself on the banks of the Liffey, not more than an hour beyond the walls of Cill Dara.

At the first light of dawn, Brigid sneaks out alone for she does not want any of the sisters to know of her plan. Not even Darlughdach, for the shame of what she must do hangs heavy on her. She walks, following the path of the river, listening to the birds singing. As a child, she knew the names of all the birds, but now finds it harder to tell the difference between the nuthatch and the bullfinches.

She arrives at what looks to be an abandoned shelter, little more than a pile of sticks tied together and strewn with a patchwork of animal skins. But when she approaches, she sees signs of life surrounding it. A fresh animal hide hangs from a rope hung between two willows. Brigid reaches up to rub one between her fingers. Goat's skin, and as fine as any they have in the library at Cill Dara. There is also the smoking remains of a turf fire, and over it hangs a heavy metal cauldron. Brigid bends over it, expecting to see the remnants of a stew inside, but instead she sees a glittering liquid. She runs a finger across the rough insides of the cauldron and stares in wonder at gold flakes that cling to her finger. A gentle drifting wind picks them up and they blow away like leaves.

A twig snaps behind her and she looks around to see a man. She hardly recognizes the shaven, fresh-faced man who had turned up at her door carrying the weight of the world's knowledge on his donkey. He has grown a beard long enough that it hangs almost to his navel, though where his beard starts and his hair ends, she cannot tell, for the two have melded together in great mats. Over his shoulder he carries a dead baby goat, its throat a red gash. Blood still pours from it down his back, dripping on to the ground.

'Are you Conleth?' she asks.

He throws the limp carcass to the floor and throws his arms open. 'Brigid.'

Above his dark, dirty beard, he smiles and his teeth are white as pearls.

'What an honour to have you here. What an honour. Come, come, sit.' He looks around for a chair, but there is only the muddy bank of the river.

'I'm fine standing, Conleth. It has been some time.'

'Fourteen months and twenty-seven days, if we are to measure on the new Roman calendar. I, myself, prefer the Thracian system, much more precise.'

'Thracian?' She has never heard of this. Could it be a language of one of the texts that lie unread in her library?

'Oh, yes, let me show you. Come, come.' He pulls aside one of the animal skins and ducks inside his shack. 'I have it here somewhere.'

Brigid follows. Everywhere, books lie in small piles, and there is a pyramid stack of tens, maybe hundreds, of scrolls. There is also an old chest filled with books and unbound pages.

'Where did you get all of these?'

'Oh, my old friends from my time in Rome seek me out, and they bring me gifts.'

Conleth squats down before the scrolls and runs a long-nailed finger along the rows. 'Of course, we have the Julian Calendar now. You know what they said when they designed that?'

Brigid tears her eyes away from the texts and back to the small man. 'I don't.'

'Times must change!' He laughs at his own joke. 'Oh, yes, they must. And the calendar was very clever. But not as . . . elegant as . . . Alpha, Beta. Here we are.' He slides a scroll out, and waddles over to Brigid, knees still bent. He then drops down, crosses his legs and opens the scroll.

Brigid sits beside him. On the page is a series of circles, intersected with sharp, thin lines. And in the centre are two circles overlapping by a breath.

'Ingenious, isn't it? It uses both the sun and Jupiter for its calculations. Divided into twelve constellations, each of which they named after an animal. See, a dog, a boar, a mouse, a snow lion, not sure what that is, a rabbit, a dragon . . .' With each name he taps at a different segment. 'I got it off a spice trader I travelled with for a while.' Conleth rolls the scroll back up and smiles at Brigid. 'I've made a copy, of course.'

He springs up and walks to a stack of pages lying on a tree stump. He rifles through them and pulls out a page. It is a perfect copy of the calendar, only even more beautiful. He has added intricate scroll work and where there was block text she could not make out, there is now tiny, almost too tiny to read, Latin script.

'You made this? Here?' Brigid looks around the shack.

'Oh, yes, I have everything I need.'

There is a plank of wood, propped up at an angle by a small pile of rocks. A few upturned shells holding paint and in a beautiful golden goblet, a whole cockerel's worth of quills.

Brigid picks up the goblet. It is exquisitely engraved with swirling patterns and light as an egg. 'Was this another gift from your friends in Rome?'

'Oh, no, that I made.'

Brigid almost drops it in her shock. 'You truly are a master craftsman.'

Conleth's nose hitches up to the side, and he blinks. 'Oh, well, I had a lot of gold, you see, but only needed the tiniest amount for my manuscripts. So, I thought, what could I do with what was left? I had an idea about creating locks and chains for the books, like I had seen in Rome. But then, I thought, why lock away words?'

He opens a wooden chest. There is a folded purple robe embroidered with exquisite needlework, and nestled on top of it is a row of tiny, beautiful golden cups.

'So I made these instead. No idea what to do with them. Would you like them?'

He smiles up at her.

'You should know, if you were to gift these to me, I would only give them away to the poor.'

'Oh, what a good idea. Yes, that's what you should do.' He scoops them up and presses them into Brigid's arms. 'Yes, yes, give them to the poor.'

Brigid stares at the man. He gives away wealth as easily as she does. Easier even, for she knows the worth of it, but for him, it is no different from his giving her a feather he had found or a smooth rock.

'Would you like to see our library at Cill Dara?' she asks.

'Oh, I have heard such things of your library. I've heard that you have over three hundred books.'

'Double that figure.'

He rubs his finger against his lower lip, as though tasting something luscious. 'Oh, my.'

'Will you come?'

'But I thought only women were allowed inside.'

'Times must change.'

'Ha!' He waggles his finger at her.

'Will you come?' she asks again.

'I will indeed.'

'And would you stay?'

'What do you mean?' he asks.

'Continue your work, but alongside my scribes. Teach them your skills, your languages. We have a whole smithy that would be at your disposal to keep making whatever you wish to make.'

Tears fill his eyes. 'Is this a vision?'

It is. One in which Brigid can hold on to her power at Cill Dara and grow the library and the walls even greater. With this simple man by her side, Patrick cannot threaten her.

45

'You promised us a world free of men,' Clodagh says the day after Conleth is ordained as Bishop of Cill Dara.

'I promised you a world where you would be safe from men,' Brigid says. 'And Conleth is no threat to any of us.'

'But now that he is here, more men will come,' Clodagh says.

Brigid doesn't argue. She is weary of the deal-making and compromises that she has to make. She no more wanted a man within these walls than Clodagh or any of the other sisters who carried scars, hidden and otherwise, from their dealings with men. But this is the lesser of two evils.

'You should explain it to them,' Darlughdach says, following Brigid as she strides away. 'Explain why you had to do this.'

'I am abbess here,' she says, snapping, 'I should not have to explain any decision I make. Besides, this was your idea. You explain it.'

She trudges through the mud back to her room, feeling Darlughdach's hurt eyes following her the whole way.

A few days later, Ciara delivers a letter. She opens it to find text written by a familiar, if shaky, hand.

"*I, Patrick, am but a humble sinner, who has been appointed Bishop of Ireland by the same good God who will soon call me to his side—*"

She scans over his waffle, till she finds the meat of the letter.

"*As it pleaseth the Lord, so it pleaseth me, to learn of Brother Conleth's appointment as Bishop of the Church of Cill Dara, which is now welcomed into the arms of the Roman Church. As such, Cill Dara will receive the protection of Armagh, for the paltry sum of thirty silver ingots a year, paid in quarterly sums."*

Brigid doesn't finish reading. She crumples the letter up and throws it at the wall.

Ciara bends over, retrieves the parchment and flattens it out on Brigid's table. 'No good wasting vellum. We're going to need to save every scrap we can.'

'You read the letter then?'

Ciara nods and takes a seat in front of Brigid. 'He wishes to extract taxes.'

'As though he were a king!' Brigid says, her fists curled into tight balls.

Ciara blows her nose on a square of cloth and tucks it back into her sleeve. 'He's as good as.'

'The deal was I appoint a man as bishop and he would offer us his protection.'

'Protection. Not money,' Ciara says, a weary half-shrug.

Brigid stares at the letter, wishing she could make it burst into flames. 'What should we do?'

'Pay him. Look at his writing,' Ciara points to the letter and the weak, shaking handwriting. 'Patrick is old. He says it himself. Let's hope the angels come for him soon.'

Brigid closes her eyes. She had not wanted to do this, but what other choice does she have? 'Sell Lommán's armour.'

Ciara stands and though she has told Brigid to do this since the day the golden armour arrived, she looks saddened.

'Have you told the sisters yet about the festivals?' Brigid asks, as Ciara reaches the door.

Patrick had written a week before forbidding any celebration of the seasonal festivals. The only feast that would be permitted was Easter.

'Ha, not a chance. I'm not telling them.' Ciara wags a finger at Brigid. 'I don't want to be hated.'

Brigid tells the women at the next Mass and Ciara was right, they hate her for it.

'No!' they shout, outraged.

Cinnia stands, her pretty face crumpled in an angry snarl. 'But it's the way it's always been!'

'The one thing that keeps us going throughout the year!'

'The crops will fail, just you see,' Buach says, crossing her thick arms.

'Why don't you stand up to him?' Clodagh says, from the back of the oratory.

All eyes turn from Clodagh back to Brigid.

Why don't I? Oh, how sweet it would be to tell him to keep his protection and his bishop and have nothing to do with him ever again.

But the answer is simple enough. This is a man's world. Brigid and her women may have carved out a small corner for themselves behind their walls. But outside, men with swords and spears await.

She forces a soft smile. 'Bishop Patrick offers us his protection in return for this simple sacrifice.'

'Don't we make enough sacrifices?' Indiu says.

Brigid is surprised that even Indiu, one of her most devout sisters, is protesting.

'You could always make his eyes explode.' She does not see who says this, for it comes from one of the pews at the back.

'There is still Easter,' Brigid says, ignoring the ripple of laughter.

'It's not the same,' Indiu says.

No. No, it's not.

Another year passes and both Brigid and Patrick hold to the promises they made. She pays the taxes to his Church and no raiders come to their walls. She allows the world beyond to believe that Conleth rules at Cill Dara, and she is permitted to rule within the walls.

Conleth hardly leaves the library, though he has been given a room on the far corner of the convent. He sleeps under his scriptorium, and on the nights when Brigid is to watch over the sacred flame, she can see a smaller light burning in the window where he sits, scribbling all through the night. She is both envious of his focus and glad that he is here. Her own skills at transcribing have departed from her, for she is too agitated to write: her line work is shoddy because of her shaking hands. Her precision ruined by her impatience.

Of late, all she seems to feel is anger. Like a searing coal behind her chest.

46

A terrible, screeching wail disturbs their prayers one morning. Brigid fears more raiders have come. If they have hurt one of her sisters, there will be no end to the pain she will bring them.

She and her sisters rush out of the oratory to find the source of this agony. It is not one of the women wailing. It is Conleth. He is on his knees, rocking back and forth, tearing at his tunic and hair. Tufts are coming away in clumps.

Brigid takes his hands in hers, to stop him from doing more damage to himself. 'Conleth, what has happened?'

He wails, spittle spraying, and she cannot make out the word he is saying.

'*Padre?*' Lommán asks. 'Is he saying *padre*?'

Clodagh moves Brigid aside and slaps Conleth around the face. The man blinks, shock shaking him to his senses.

'I've wanted to do that for an age,' Clodagh says.

'Tell us,' Brigid says, giving Clodagh a stern look. 'What has happened?'

'Patrick,' Conleth says, the word coming out at last.

'Has he sent men?' Lommán asks, grabbing his cudgel. 'Are we under attack?'

'No,' Conleth says, a bubble of snot popping from his nose. 'He is dead!'

Gasps, shouts and more wailing. Women join Conleth in keening and tearing at their hair. The great father of the church is dead.

Brigid staggers away, wanting to put space between her and the noise. Ciara, Darlughdach and Lommán gather around her. They seem to be the only ones not keening for Patrick.

'What does this mean?' Ciara asks, turning to Brigid.

'Are we safe now?' Lommán asks, lowering his weapon.

'Brigid,' Darlughdach says, taking Brigid's hand. 'You are shaking.'

The earth beneath her feels as though it is sinking, as though it might swallow her up.

'I need . . . I need.' She walks away, unable to find the words to express what she needs. But she has to be away from the women and their worried eyes, away from the wailing for a man she had come to hate.

Patrick had been old when she had first met him, and yet she somehow believed that he would never die. She had prayed for this day to come, had expected joy to fill her heart, but all she finds is an emptiness she cannot explain.

She tries to remember life before Patrick came to Cill Dara. Were things simpler then? Were they as carefree as in her memory? Could it return to what it once was? Or with him dead, will some new man take his place and try to steal from her all that she has built here?

She allows Conleth to lead the service they dedicate to Patrick, for she knows she could not force herself to speak of his holiness. The service goes on for three hours, as Conleth recites from memory every passage from every bible that he believes will help soothe the great heartache of the congregation.

'Patrick's name shall be remembered for all eternity,' Conleth promises. 'He is on the right hand of the Lord now, and his light shall shine till the end of time.'

A month passes without Patrick and Brigid sometimes catches herself feeling as though she is falling, as if Patrick were a door she had been pushing against, only to find that now it is gone, it has opened into an abyss.

Every day, letters come addressed to Conleth, which she makes sure to intercept. They come from Benignus, the new Bishop of Armagh, and every other bishop in Ireland. And even from Rome. While the bishops from Rome call for Conleth to abandon Cill Dara and return to them, Benignus suggests that the relationship between Armagh and Cill Dara be deepened further, for it to become a sister church of their own. *"Let me, Brother Conleth,"* Benignus writes, *"take on the burden of managing Cill Dara, so that you may dedicate yourself to the translation of God's works."*

She reseals those letters that she decides it safe for Conleth to read, the rest she burns.

Easter arrives and is celebrated at Cill Dara. But as the sun sets, she sees some of the women sneak up to the hill and hears the pounding of drums caught on the wind. The sky turns red and gold, and for a moment she hopes she is seeing the bonfires of Tara lit once again. But it is only the clouds.

The flow of women who come to ask Brigid for her help – her blessing, her protection – is never-ending and for the first time in her life she wonders if she may have given all that she has to give.

'We have to stop taking in strays.' Ciara comes to complain to her one day, as she works in the library alongside Darlughdach. 'We have no more room.'

'Then build more rooms,' Brigid says, not lifting her eye from her page. Conleth has taught her a new technique for flowing letters into one another to speed up the writing, and she is trying to master it.

Ciara laughs. 'Simple as that, is it?'

Brigid looks up from her work. It is poor and she will need to scrape the ink off and start again. 'Yes,' she replies. And for her, it is that simple. Women need a place to be safe, then she must build it.

Darlughdach leans forward and blows gently on the parchment she is working on, her breath warming the glue, just enough so it is ready to brush with gold flakes. Another technique Conleth has taught them. 'Do we have the money for that?' she says.

'Exactly,' Ciara says, throwing her hands into the air. 'Unless you can magically milk gold from the cows?' She mimes tugging at udders.

'I will write to Bishop Benignus,' Brigid says, pressing so hard against the parchment that the nib of her quill splits and black ink speckles her work.

'And what will he ask in return?' Ciara says. 'The skin off our backs?'

'We should send word to the new pontiff, His Holiness Pope Felix,' Conleth says.

He sits bent over a desk behind them. He has never joined in the discussions around the running of the convent before and hearing his low, soft voice is such a surprise that all the women stop to look at him.

He sniffs, his nose hitching in that strange mouse-like way. 'If it's money you need, tell his Holiness the Pope of the work and wonders we are doing here. I am sure he will send aid.'

The women look now to each other. How had they never thought of this before?

'Why go to Armagh, when we could go straight to the source?' Darlughdach says.

'Cut out the middleman,' Ciara agrees, nodding. 'I like it.'

I DO NOT.

'I will write to Pope Felix,' Brigid says.

'Let me do it,' Conleth says, returning to his work. 'I served His Holiness when I was in Rome. He will remember me.'

Rome does not send gold. They send an envoy.

47

A group of men on horseback are spotted on the edge of the plain riding towards them.

Brigid has become used to a stream of visitors coming and going, trading foods and news. But most come on foot, by donkey or ox-driven cart. These men ride warhorses.

As Brigid stands with Ciara watching them ride closer, a broom falls behind them, clattering to the ground.

'Trouble's coming.'

As if Brigid needed a broom to tell her that.

It will be an hour still before the men arrive and she has work to be done. The flax needs harvesting before the rain comes in. She hitches up her robes and joins the women already out at work in the fields. The rain turns from a shower to a downpour, and by the time the riders arrive at the gates, she is drenched to the bone.

She trudges through the mud to meet the men. Three ride large horses that have a sheen of white sweat on their flanks, so they must have been ridden hard. One, a man dressed in the simple linen tunic of a slave, rides a small hinny.

'God bless you on this day,' Brigid says when they draw near.

'God bless you, child,' the lead rider says. He is dressed in the fine purple robes and white cross cloth of a bishop. A heavy golden crucifix hangs from his belt and she wonders how he managed not to be robbed on the road, showing off wealth like that. Since Rome fell, she has become accustomed to seeing men and women of different colours, and some of her sisters have skin the colour of autumn leaves, but she has never seen a man as dark as this. So dark as to be almost blue.

'What brings such an esteemed father to Cill Dara?'

'I have come to speak with the head of your order. Will you send word that Bishop Gelasius has come to speak with him?' He speaks his Latin in soft, flowing tones, with just the hint of a clicking at the back of his throat.

'You have just told her,' Brigid says.

The man looks down at her muddy feet and soaked robes. 'Abbess Brigid?'

She nods.

He stands up in his stirrups and then in a swift, dance-like movement throws his leg over the saddle and lands on the soft ground with both feet.

'My instructions from His Holiness were to speak with Bishop Conleth,' he says, looking over her shoulder at the fortifications behind them. 'But my guide here . . .' He looks then to the man on the hinny. Brigid recognizes him as one who has worked the fields for her at harvest. 'He tells me you are the real power at Cill Dara.'

Brigid merely smiles. 'Come, let us both get out of what's left of the rain.'

The downfall is light now and beams of sunshine break through the clouds overhead.

The man looks up at the sky, letting the drops fall on his face. 'Where I was born, it rains so rarely that when at last it comes, we see it as a blessing from God.'

'Ireland must be truly blessed then.'

She nods to the men still on horseback and the guide. 'There is a river there where you can water your horses and rest your feet.'

They look to Gelasius for approval. The man nods and they lead the horses away.

Brigid leads Gelasius to the gates. When he steps through, she watches his face, for she loves to see the effect of Cill Dara on visitors. This man's expression does not change. His eyes or mouth do not open in wonder. He simply nods as though everything is as he expected it to be. On their walk towards her cell, she sees him scanning the buildings as though he were counting every brick and stone, assessing the quality, the cost. He reminds her of a man at a cattle auction and if Cill Dara were a cow, he would be feeling her udders.

The sisters at work in the yard stop to stare at the man. Some cover their mouths as they whisper to the nuns beside them, others blush and look away as he meets their eyes.

This is why we don't have men in Cill Dara. Not men like this anyway.

Ciara sits on a stool, plucking handfuls of feathers from a cockerel, whose red neck swings back and forth, though her eyes are fixed on Gelasius.

'Ciara,' Brigid calls over.

She has rarely seen Ciara move so quickly as she throws the bird to the floor and races over. 'Well, hello,' she says.

'Tell me, where is Bishop Conleth?'

Ciara doesn't take her eyes off Gelasius. 'He is in the lamb shed, selecting which of the lambs to skin.'

'Ah, perhaps you will meet him later then,' Brigid says, gesturing for Gelasius to walk ahead. Before passing, she whispers to Ciara, 'See that Conleth stays there.'

Once inside, she unwraps her cloak and throws it towards a bronze hook by one of the windows and goes to take a seat behind the table.

She sees Gelasius gazing at the cloak. 'You know,' he says, 'I met a man once who told me you hung your cloak from sunbeams.'

Could that man have been Brendan? For he had said that to her when they met as children.

'If I did that, my cloak would get dirty.'

Gelasius turns to her. 'You're not what I expected.'

'Oh, and what was that?' Brigid asks.

He looks around the room, taking in the plain furnishing, the piles of paper. 'In truth, a virago, draped in gold, man-hating and power-crazed.'

'Do I not seem powerful then?'

He tilts his head to the side, fixing her with his brown eyes, as though he is measuring her as he had measured the bricks and stones. 'Powerful, yes. Man-hating . . .?' He rocks his head back and forth, as if undecided. 'But not crazed.'

'Tell me, Bishop Gelasius, why have you come?'

He takes a seat in front of her and crosses his legs, something she has never seen a man do before. 'Bishop Conleth wrote to His Holiness telling us of the glory of Cill Dara and asked for the Holy Father's patronage to continue his work here.'

His work? Brigid opens her mouth to protest.

Gelasius coughs quickly and corrects himself. 'The work of the community here.'

Brigid raises an eyebrow. This man is sharp indeed. 'We have more women seeking sanctuary here than we have gold to feed.'

'I see. You ask for Rome's help?'

Brigid pauses before answering. She can feel a swell of pride bubbling in her chest, a desire to refuse the help of this man – and all men. But she thinks of her sisters, sleeping two to a bed, fasting not only on Fridays but on Sundays also, to make the food last. She must remember them.

'We do,' she says, through tight, resentful lips.

Gelasius moves, uncrossing his legs and leaning forward in

his seat. 'I have heard you are assembling a library of some of the rarest texts in the world. They say that all the lost knowledge of Rome passes through your doors.'

Brigid bows her head. 'I have been tasked with this mission.'

'By God?'

'Mmm-hmm,' Brigid replies, not meeting his eyes, slippery as ever.

'May I see it?' he says, voice level. And she knows this is not a request, but a demand from a man who is used to being listened to.

She looks up. 'Our library?'

'Yes.'

She considers him. He is so still, his movements measured and controlled. And yet, she senses threat in every gesture. What choice does she have?

'Very well.'

She leads him to the tower and waits as he climbs up the ladder to the doorway. His movements are so swift and graceful, the rungs barely bend under his step. She follows after.

Inside, all is quiet, save for the scratching of quills on parchment and the turning of pages. He stares around at the shelves upon shelves of books and scrolls, and at last his eyes widen in wonder. 'This . . . is a miracle.'

Brigid tries to hide her pleasure.

'Come,' she says, her voice low. She leads him towards the largest table where Cinnia is at work, head bent over the page.

'We are working on a great gospel,' Brigid says. 'Though it will be many, many years before it is finished. Perhaps we will not be alive to see it.'

If Cinnia is surprised to see a man other than Conleth within the confines of the library, she does not say so. Though the other women stop their work to stare. Gelasius bends down to examine the page. It is an illustration of the Mother

Mary, the Christ child held lovingly in her arms. Cinnia has captured her staring out into the distance, as though weary from the burden she carries, while the baby stares up at his mother, eyes full of love. Intricate patterns frame the figures, and lines of scripture weave in and out of the patterns like ivy.

Gelasius sighs. 'It looks as though it were created by angels.'

Brigid pats Cinnia on the back. 'In a way, it has been.'

Gelasius fires questions at Brigid as they walk through the room. How many books do they have and how did they come to acquire them? How many scribes do they have, making how many copies? How do they make the inks, the parchments they use, even down to the angle at which they cut their quills?

'You know much about the art,' she says.

'A little,' Gelasius replies, and it is not false modesty Brigid hears in his voice. 'It is why His Holiness chose me for this mission.'

'So this is not merely a courtesy visit?'

Gelasius smiles, but does not answer.

They clamber back down the ladder and out into the sunshine. The women who pass stare open-mouthed at the sight of another man within the inner walls of Cill Dara. Buach spits a curse at him.

'Forgive my sister,' Brigid says. 'She is . . . unaccustomed to men.'

'Well, she will have to become accustomed to them.'

Brigid stops to stare at Gelasius as he continues to walk ahead. 'What do you mean?'

Before he can answer there is a high scream of delight.

'Oh my, oh my, oh my!' Conleth comes running towards them, his strange half-skipping, half-hopping run. His white tunic is stained with the blood of lambs.

'A visitor from Rome! Well met, Brother.' Conleth almost

crashes into Gelasius as he comes to a halt. He grabs the man's left hand and kisses the golden ring.

'Bishop Conleth,' Gelasius replies, bowing. 'His Holiness received your letter.'

'He did! Oh, how wonderful. And does he remember me?' He hops back and forth, like a crow on a branch.

'He does, with great fondness.' He pats Conleth on the hand and Brigid is surprised by the gentleness there.

'When did you arrive? Have you seen the library? Come, I must show you what I am working on.' Conleth takes the man's hand and tugs at it.

'Abbess Brigid has already shown me.'

'Oh,' Conleth says, his face crumpling like a discarded sheet of paper. 'Then we must sit and talk, for I miss the stimulation of the conversation of men.'

'Fear not, Brother Conleth,' Gelasius says. 'For soon, you are not to be the only man in Cill Dara.'

'What do you mean?' Brigid asks again.

He turns to face her. 'What you have built here is truly a wonder.'

Brigid waits.

'And Rome will offer you her protection.' He takes a small step forward, closing the gap between them. 'But a glory such as this cannot be protected by women alone. It cannot be . . . hoarded by women alone.'

'But Conleth—' Brigid says, pointing at the small man.

'Is but one man. His Holiness would have Cill Dara become a place for men and women.'

'Oh, wonderful.' Conleth claps his hands together in delight.

'But that would be impossible,' Brigid says, ignoring Conleth.

'Oh, on the contrary,' Gelasius says. 'There is already a

dual monastery in Gaul, built by a man named John Cassian, which is now thriving. And we are certain that Cill Dara will thrive also.'

'Oh, we shall, we shall,' Conleth says, giddy.

Gelasius looks around at the yard. 'We will send brothers to you, good men who can advance your work while also offering you their physical protection. I have heard you have had trouble with raiders. With men here, the raiders would not dare to come.'

'Isn't this wonderful?' Conleth says, rocking back and forth on his toes.

Brigid looks at the blood staining his arms, from the tips of his fingers all the way to his elbows. *I should never have let him write to Rome. I should never have let him take any part in the running of Cill Dara.*

'Of course, Rome would also provide you with additional funds to build the new quarters for the men and feed and clothe them. Cill Dara will become the richest monastery in Ireland. Greater even than the monastery in Armagh.'

Brigid never wanted this. She never wanted to outshine Patrick, merely to maintain what she had.

DID YOU REALLY THINK YOU COULD ASK FOR HELP AND THEY WOULD ASK FOR NOTHING IN RETURN?

'I will not allow it,' she says, stamping her foot in the dirt as though she were a child.

Gelasius takes a small step forward and looks down on her, blacking out the sun. 'Of course, we could simply save ourselves the effort of building new quarters for the men by taking the ones already built for the women.'

'And where would the women go?' Brigid asks.

'The souls of women are not the concern of Rome.' He looks up at a passing cloud. 'For there is even debate as to whether a woman has a soul.' He looks back down at her. 'For my part, I believe they do. Although logically a woman's soul must be weaker, just as a woman's body is weaker.'

Gelasius's eyes scan her, up and down, and Brigid has not felt as small, or as powerless, since she was a girl.

SHOW HIM.

The heat rises in her hands; she stares into his eyes and imagines blood pouring down his face, as it once poured down the face of her brother Beccan.

LET HIM SEE HOW STRONG YOU TRULY ARE.

She will send a message to Rome that she cannot be controlled. A message to all men that Cill Dara belongs to women alone.

And yet another, cooler, thought rises in her mind like a branch floating on a lake. Rome will only send more men. Men who would come with more than words. And what would become of Cill Dara then?

She lowers her gaze. 'Very well.'

THEN YOU HAVE FAILED.

48

Within a month, fifty monks arrive. Brigid watches them from the window of her raised chambers, staring down at the bald patches on their heads as they file through the gates. She has fought to keep men out of Cill Dara, and now they walk in as welcome guests.

The women withdraw to the dormitory and watch them through the windows. Many make the sign of the cross as the men pass. Even Ciara scowls and hisses curses. Buach holds out her hand, making a ward against evil. Brigid hopes none of the men know its meaning, for they might report her back to the Holy Father for heresy. These men are not only invaders; they are spies.

Conleth is overjoyed, shaking each brother by the hand and guiding them to the stables, where they will be sleeping till their new rooms are built.

'Welcome brothers, oh, what a joyous day, welcome,' Conleth says, again and again till Brigid is sick of it.

He shouts orders and directs the men around, though he points to the stables and calls it the forge and to the kiln and calls it the kitchen. He even walks differently now he is surrounded by men, with his chest puffed out and his shoulders drawn back.

'I wish I had left you in the forest,' she says, though he does not hear.

The men come bearing chests of gold; more than Brigid has ever seen. She knows it is needed, but it makes her queasy as though she were looking at a pile of vomit.

'Lock it away,' she tells Ciara and hands her the only key to the chest, for she cannot trust herself not to give it all away.

The men also come with plans drawn by Gelasius. Where there was one oratory, there are to be two. Two dormitories. Two refectories. A mirror of each other. Brigid makes one addition with a single stroke of her quill. A wall, twenty foot high. There will be a man's side and a woman's. Only the library and oratory will be accessed by all.

The men get to work. With every stone laid, Brigid feels as though it has been placed on her heart.

The news that men are now living at Cill Dara spreads faster than blight, and within a week men join women in begging at the gate for Brigid's blessing. Each morning she goes out to greet them, joining her sisters in handing out what little they have.

'The men take more than their fair share,' Ciara says bitterly. 'See how they push the women aside and grab the bread for themselves?'

'And why is it only the sisters who serve the poor?' Clodagh asks. 'Why are none of the monks out here freezing their arses off every morning?' Clodagh huffs, her breath making a cloud in the cold air. 'Lazy bastards, if you ask me.'

Brigid has thought both of these things herself, but has no solution. 'The men are here. We must learn to live with them.'

Some of the women do not mind the men's presence as much as the others. As Brigid is returning to her rooms late one evening, her eyes tired from a day's transcribing, her shoulders aching from bending over the desk for so long, she sees one of her nuns, couched down on the floor, her lips pressed against the wall that divides the two sides of the monastery.

'Sister,' Brigid says, for she does not know the nun's name.

The woman jolts and scrambles to her feet. 'Mother Brigid, I . . . I was just . . . I have to—' She turns as if to go.

'Wait.'

The woman freezes at Brigid's command, then slowly turns around to face her. Brigid looks down at the wall, to where the woman had been pressing her face, and sees a small hole about two foot off the floor. No bigger than a mouse hole.

The woman lowers her head and bites her lips. Brigid knows this expression from the times she has taken confession. Shame.

Slowly, Brigid bends down and presses her eye to the hole. Through it, she can see a pair of sandal-clad feet with thick yellowing toenails and hair sprouting from the toes.

'Fiadh?' a man's voice whispers through the hole. 'Is that you?'

He bends down and meets Brigid's eye. Through the hole, she sees his eye widen in shock and a moment later his feet scuttle away.

'We talk, Mother Brigid,' Fiadh says, pressing her hands together in supplication. 'Only talk. I swear.'

Brigid stands. 'And what is it you talk about?'

Fiadh's eyes dart left and right, as though looking for the answer on the walls of the small corridor. 'Life, I suppose.'

'Life?' Brigid says, looking down again at the hole.

She thinks of Pyramus and Thisbe from Ovid's tragic tale, speaking words of love through a crack in a wall. Perhaps she will have Fiadh translate it from Greek into Latin or Irish as penance? Perhaps writing of their tragic deaths over and over will teach her that no good can come from such trysts.

'You may go, sister,' Brigid says.

Fiadh bows as though Brigid were an altar and runs away back to her dormitory.

How many other women come to this wall to whisper to

the men on the far side? Brigid bends again and looks through the hole. There is another world on the other side of those bricks. One from which she must keep her women away.

She puts rules in place about interactions between the two sexes. No man or woman to sit beside each other in the library or at Mass. If a man should speak to one of the sisters, she may not respond, for no words may be exchanged between men and women.

'Would you have us be a silent order then?' Darlughdach says. 'Like Íte's?'

'I would keep my women safe,' Brigid says, irritated by being challenged yet again.

Darlughdach shakes her head. 'You would keep them caged.'

The sisters continue to meet those begging at the gates, though Brigid joins them to ensure the words passed between her sisters and any of the men are kept to a minimum.

One morning, two male lepers arrive. The other beggars move aside, not wanting to brush shoulders with them. Brigid hands over a single oatcake to the first leper.

'Go with God,' she says.

He takes the offering but does not move. 'Do you not remember me?' he asks. 'You were a runaway girl and we shared our scallops with you.'

Brigid looks into blue eyes in a scarred face. 'Caíndelbán?' she asks. The leper she met on the beach. It cannot be possible. It has been almost fifteen years.

'The very same! Though I do not blame you for failing to remember me, as there's not as much of me as there once was.'

He is telling the truth. His wounds have deepened and he is missing many of the fingers from his left hand.

'And I see another old friend with you,' he says. 'You're

looking mighty well there, Lommán. One might not even know you were a leper at all.'

'Hello, Caíndelbán,' Lommán says, his voice as deep as the day Brigid first met him.

'They say you're a healer?' the other leper says to Brigid.

Brigid does not recognize him, though he could well be one of the other men from that day.

'Oh, more than that, Fergal,' Caíndelbán says. 'She's a wonder worker.'

The crowd of people who have all come for the same purpose gather behind Caíndelbán, listening in.

'God has been kind to me,' Brigid says.

'Well, now, would he be so good as to be kind to me and my friend here?'

There's an edge to Caíndelbán's words that jabs at Brigid. But the man is right; he showed her kindness when she needed it and she has plenty of kindness to spare.

'Come,' she says, leading him down to the river.

'I remember the day when you washed my feet, Brigid. Do I need to wash yours now? Is that how the magic works?'

Brigid shakes her head. Since her mother's death, she has not performed any healing. She has not even tried, for the light feels so far away from her. She has carried something back with her from Dún Ailinne, an illness perhaps.

She takes a cloth from her waist and hands it to Caíndelbán. 'Wash each other,' she instructs.

The two men look at each other. Caíndelbán shrugs. He tosses the cloth to the other man. 'Come on then, Fergal, me first.'

Caíndelbán strips off his clothing, revealing a body eaten by disease. Great holes are missing from him and his thighs are shrivelled. He steps into the water and holds his arms out, as though he were readying himself to be nailed to a cross.

Fergal begins to wash Caíndelbán's body. Where the cloth passes, skin flakes away, falling into the water beneath him, revealing pink flesh, as fresh and new as a baby's. As he runs water over the stub of Caíndelbán's hand, fingers regrow. He is hurrying now, throwing water over Caíndelbán's body like a child splashing in a stream, while Caíndelbán stands, head thrown back, laughing.

Fergal stands back and stares at his friend. 'It's a miracle.'

Caíndelbán looks down at his body; he holds up his regrown arm in front of his eyes, wiggles his fingers.

'You did it. You glorious wonder-worker, you did it.'

'It is God's work,' Brigid says.

'My turn,' Fergal says, ripping off his clothing and jumping into the river beside his friend. He presses the cloth into Caíndelbán's hands, holds his arms out, and squeezes his eyes shut.

Caíndelbán steps back, looking at Fergal's body in horror.

'I'm not touching him,' he says, throwing the cloth to the ground. 'Now I'm healed? Not a chance. I don't want to get infected again.' He leaps out of the water and pulls his robe around him.

The burning coal sparks in Brigid's chest once more at Caíndelbán's ingratitude. At his defiance of her grace. He should be on his knees praising her name. He should shout her glory from the mountain tops. How dare a man deny her.

'Then I will wash you, Fergal,' she says, turning to the leper with a forced smile.

She picks the cloth up and places it against Fergal's shoulder. As water trickles down over his chest, her own shoulder explodes in pain. She moves the cloth to his back and feels as though someone is dragging a hot brand across her spine.

She has healed a hundred people, but never before has it caused her such agony. She clenches her teeth against it and continues to wash Fergal. With each pass of her cloth, the sickness washes away like dirt, and he is whole once more. And yet her whole body feels as though it is on fire. She looks to her hands, expecting to see them covered in leprous sores. There is nothing but the old calluses from her work.

When she has finished, Fergal falls to his knees and grasps Brigid's skirts. 'Oh, my lady, how may I repay you?'

'Dedicate yourself to Christ.'

'I will. I will!'

'And you?' She turns to Caíndelbán, who is rubbing his hands over his body lovingly, as though it were the body of another.

'What?' Caíndelbán asks.

'Will you convert?'

'Ah, well, now . . . I can't be doing that. But I do thank you, sure enough.'

The rage flares.

Caíndelbán falls to his knees, crying out in pain. His body bends and buckles as he writhes on the floor, screeching in pain. And Brigid smiles.

'Enough, Brigid,' Lommán says.

But Brigid cannot hear him. All she can hear is the sound of flames.

'Enough!' Lommán grabs Brigid by the arm and spins her around.

How dare he? For a moment, she imagines Lommán's flesh on fire, sees his skin peel away like a page of vellum caught in flames. The horror of the image breaks the spell. The rage subsides. Brigid is herself once more.

'Take this man away from here,' she says. 'And see that he never steps foot near Cill Dara again.'

49

A late spring snow falls, and Cill Dara looks like a fresh sheet of parchment with only the black footsteps of the sisters tracking between the dormitories and the oratory to mark it. Could she confine them to their rooms, just for one day, maybe two, so that the snow could settle?

A knock on her door pulls her out of her musing. She does not recognize it.

'Come in.'

It is a man, one of the young monks. His face burns pink with embarrassment – and with good reason. Men are not permitted within the women's quarters. He opens and closes his mouth, no words coming out.

'Speak, brother,' Brigid commands. For the rules of conversing with men do not apply to her.

'Bishop Conleth wishes to see you,' he says, rushing the words out.

'He knows where to find me,' Brigid says.

'He says you are to come to him.'

'Does he now?' Brigid says, standing.

The monk shrinks away.

'Very well,' Brigid says. 'Let's go and see him, shall we?'

The monk rushes ahead, leading her through the small door in the dividing wall. She has not been on this side of the convent since it was built. It smells different from the women's side. Of damp and cabbage.

Monks scatter in her wake as she strides down the narrow passageways, or close their eyes so as not to watch her pass, as though even looking upon her might be a sin. The young man leads her past rows of small doors, till they arrive at one at the end of the corridor. He knocks on it and does not wait for an answer before rushing away.

Brigid does not wait either. She opens the door.

The room is a mirror of her own, although she sees that Conleth has filled it with many comforts. Soft pillows lie on the bed and there is a thick sheepskin lying over it. There are, as she had expected, many, many books. Some she is sure should not be removed from the library. Once Conleth only slept in the library, but now he has made himself a bedchamber worthy of the bishop he has become.

He sits behind a desk. Fresh gold rings are wrapped around his fingers and he is wearing the purple robe from his chest. It is embroidered with swirling patterns in golden thread and she can smell the mildew on it from across the room. He has even shaved his tonsure, which he rarely does, though he has done a bad job of it: trickles of blood leave tracks across his head from small nicks on his scalp. He is smiling like a giddy boy, showing the rotting black teeth at the back of his mouth.

'You wanted me?' she says, her voice like ice. If Conleth knew her better, he would know to fear that tone. But the man does not seem to notice.

'A messenger came. Pope Felix himself has requested my presence in Rome!' Conleth says, his words skipping over each other in his excitement.

He holds up a letter and Brigid can see it has been marked with the seal of Rome. How did this letter get through to him without her knowing? How was a messenger let in?

She snatches the letter from his hand and reads it. 'You can't go,' she says, throwing it back on the desk.

'But . . . Pope Felix.'

'You're needed here,' Brigid replies. 'Rome has interfered enough with the running of Cill Dara.'

'Interfered?' Conleth laughs.

Brigid does not like to be laughed at.

'It's not interference. It is a blessing!' Conleth says. 'His Holiness says he wishes to reward my work here.'

'Your work?' Brigid says, heat rising in her belly. '*Your* work!'

She has suspected this for some time now. That his pride has grown along with his belly and that he would soon take credit for all her work here. She should never have invited him in.

'Well, yes, I mean, the scriptorium . . .' He waves his hand in the direction of the tower.

'I forbid you to go,' Brigid says. Her leg twitches with the effort of standing still, for she wants to stamp her foot like a child. She wishes she could stamp on Conleth himself, as though he were an ant.

'You cannot give me orders,' he says, blinking at her as though she were the sun. 'For *I* am the Bishop of Cill Dara.'

'I am bishop,' Brigid says, her voice suddenly high-pitched.

Conleth chuckles, and for a moment Brigid sees herself reaching over his desk and tearing his tongue from his throat. 'You know women can't be bishops. You are of course a woman of great power and I am a lucky man to have your support. But even so, you can't overrule the Pope, Brigid.' He seems amused by her, and speaks as though explaining something very simple to a child. 'He is the father of our order. The rock upon which our very church is built.'

'Our church wasn't built on some Roman rock,' Brigid replies. 'It was built here, on Irish soil, by Irish hands and with Irish blood. Irish *women's* blood.'

'And I will be sure to tell His Holiness—'

'I will not allow it!' she roars.

Conleth rocks back from the force of her voice.

She has surprised herself. She tries again, keeping her voice lower, though it quakes with the effort. 'You understand, don't you, why I brought you here?'

'Well, to oversee the scriptorium. Because you said you respected my craft and—'

'I brought you here, gave you everything your heart could desire, because I needed a man. Any man would have done, but I chose you. So, remember, Conleth, who is the power here. And know this – if you leave to go to Rome, you will not be permitted to come back.'

She spins on her heel and returns to her room. She lies on the ice-cold stone floor and waits till the fire that has bubbled under her skin finally cools. *He cannot leave. He will not leave.*

She hears the next morning that Conleth has left for Rome.

'He left before dawn's service. Him and his chest and one of our donkeys,' Ciara says.

Brigid does not look up from her work; slowly copying a passage from Matthew.

"Beware of false prophets, which come to you in sheep's clothing, but inwardly they are ravening wolves."

She goes over the last two words with her quill again and again and again.

The next day, Lommán finds her in the library. 'Brigid,' he says. 'I am sorry.'

Brigid does not turn around. She remains standing, staring out of the small square window at the courtyard below. The women are about their work, breaking the ice covering the water butts so that the animals may drink.

'It is Conleth,' Lommán says.

'What about him?' Brigid asks. Her voice is cold as the ice below.

'His body was found on the road. What with the snow, the wolves were starved. He never even made it to the coast. They wouldn't have recognized it was him were it not for the purple robes he was wearing.'

'His travelling chest,' Brigid asks, still not turning. 'Is that safe?'

'I . . . I think so. But Brigid, Conleth is dead.'

Brigid says nothing. Does not move. Simply stares out into the misty grey morning.

Lommán moves to stand behind her, the floorboards creaking under his weight. 'Brigid, are you well? I know things with him were tense of late, but he was your friend once. Will you not step away from the window? It is so cold in here.'

Lommán touches Brigid's shoulder. His fingers feel like fire.

'Make sure the chest is returned to Cill Dara.'

A strangled noise catches in Lommán's throat. He slowly removes his hand. 'I will.'

Brigid does not turn for she does not wish Lommán to see that she is smiling.

50

Brigid spends most of her days responding to the countless letters that come from the men of the Roman Church. Their words are honeyed, but she can taste the poison beneath. They offer up good men who can replace Conleth and warn what might happen to the monastery without a man to rule. She has written back, managed to persuade them that all is well at Cill Dara. She will appoint a new bishop from the men already within her community and everything will continue as it was. She writes to Brendan, asking him to intercede on her behalf, only to hear back that he is on another journey, this time to the west searching for undiscovered lands.

The letters come and go and through her will and words alone, she keeps the bishops at bay. But she does not know for how long she can keep it up. She barely leaves her room, eating and sleeping there (what little she sleeps and eats), for when she leaves, she feels as though she is drowning in demands. Only inside the small room, with the four cold walls and heavy oak door, does she feel safe. She has not taken her turn watching the flame in many months and in the rare moments she listens for my voice, she finds only silence.

The sound of splintering wood does not wake Brigid for she has not been sleeping. She has not, in fact, slept at all in many nights, for an unease has been scratching at her mind, as though she has been waiting for this.

She rises slowly from her bed, straining her ears for any sound. Perhaps she imagined it, for there is only the wind howling through the trees. It comes again: a sound like wood being broken for firewood. And then, a sudden cracking as though a tree has been blown over by the wind.

It is just a storm. It will pass.

A howling sound, like a wolf cry. But she knows it is not an animal that makes that sound but a human. A man.

She pulls her cloak over her shoulder and runs, barefoot, through the corridor, down the stairs, and collides with the young nun called Fiadh coming the other way. The girl is breathless and her face pale as bone.

'Raiders!' she says. 'Raiders have come!'

'Ring the bell,' Brigid says, pushing her aside. 'Tell the sisters to lock themselves in the oratory and not to come out.'

Brigid rushes out of the door to see shadows pouring through the shattered gate, hulking figures dressed in fur, the light of their torches gleaming in their weapons. The women shriek, scrambling for shelter, but there is nowhere to hide. The raiders are upon them.

They whoop and holler like boys, but they have the strength and weapons of men. They strike down women, blood spraying on the snow, but the worst screams come from the sisters the men throw over their shoulders and drag away.

Brigid looks to the wall that divides the monasteries. Where are the men? Where are our brothers who we were told would protect us? Are they hiding in their cots listening to our screams?

She will tear that wall down and crush every man here beneath the stones. She places a hand against it, feels the stones vibrating under her touch, feels the mortar crumble and fall like hail around her.

A high whooping laugh cuts through the air as a white horse leaps through the broken gate, its hooves clattering down on the flagstones. Astride it sits a man, bearded, wrapped in strong leather armour, a glimmering sword in his hand. Is it King Dunlaing, come to save her? But Dunlaing is dead. The brow is the same, the nose, but his eyes are weak, his mouth a thin slash across a round face. It is Aillil, his son, now a man and come for his revenge at last. His teeth shine white in the gloom. He will be the first to fall, she thinks, as the stones under her hands rumble.

A boot scrapes behind her, but she is too focused on Aillil to turn, too caught up in her anger to see the cudgel raised above her.

Pain explodes in her head. She falls forward, all strength driven from her. She has never known agony like it. A wetness pours from the back of her head to the snow around her. She has no more strength than a newborn. She cannot move, she cannot see, she can only hear: the screams of her sisters, dying, pleading for mercy, before her blood fills her ears and the darkness takes her.

She looks for me there, in the blackness, cries out my name over and over. But I do not answer.

51

'Biddy,' a soft voice calls to her from far, far away, as though carried across the waves of the sea. 'Biddy!' It is louder now, more determined. Hands shake her roughly, fingers pinch at her skin.

Bright sunshine blinds her when she opens her eyes. She lies on clean linen sheets that smell of lavender and beneath that, she can smell rust. No, blood.

She turns her head to see that she is lying in the infirmary. Every bed is occupied by a sister. Some are sitting up, being given sips of water or ale by other sisters, others rock and moan, blood-seeping bandages wrapped around limbs or heads. Others again lie completely still.

The simple act of moving her head sends a lightning of pain through her skull.

'Take it easy, Biddy.' Ciara sits next to her, tearing veils into bandages. 'You took a nasty blow.'

Brigid forces the pain down as she sits up. 'How many?'

'Twelve dead. Five taken. Clodagh and Indiu among them,' Ciara says. She tears into another sheet of cloth with her teeth, as though she were ripping the skin from one of the raiders. 'And they took all of the cattle, too.'

'We should go after them!' a man shouts outside. 'We should beat their heads bloody.'

Brigid does not know his name, for she has made a point of ignoring all of the new men at Cill Dara.

'If we let them get away with it,' another man says, 'they may come again.'

'Yes, they have struck us, we must strike back harder.'
'We should hunt them down!'
'Get our cattle back.'
'Kill them.'

Brigid closes her eyes against the men's shouting. Why must men's voices be so loud?

Where were you last night? Where were you when we needed your so-called strength?

'Now, now, brothers,' a man says. 'What does Jesus say about violence? That we must turn the other cheek. These men may have been starving, let them have the cattle. We can buy more.'

'And what of the women?' This is Darlughdach now. Brigid can hear the barely suppressed rage in her voice. 'Will we buy more of them?'

They descend into bickering.

Brigid forces herself to stand, to walk towards them, though the room spins around her and she has to steady herself against the doorway.

'Brigid!' Darlughdach comes running towards her, holds her face in her hands. 'Thank the gods, you are alive.'

Brigid takes Darlughdach's hands away, for even her gentle touch causes her pain. 'Where is Aillil and his men?'

'They were last seen camping on the other side of the Liffey,' Lommán says. His face is coated in dry blood, and purple spreads beneath his eyes like paint dipped in water. One arm hangs loosely by his side, the other is wrapped around his waist. 'If I leave now, if I take a horse, I could catch up with them.'

'And what would you do in your state?' Brigid asks. 'Die before you could raise your sword? No. Get Ciara to see to your wounds.'

'But—'

'I said no!'

Brigid tilts her head as if listening for birdsong on the breeze. She can hear the lapping of water against rocks, the splashing of salmon in the river, and mocking laughter.

'No,' she says more softly this time.

'You have a plan?' Darlughdach asks.

'Yes,' Brigid says. 'We wait.'

'But our sisters? We can't just leave them. Who knows what could be happening—'

'We wait!' Brigid snaps. Pain knifes her head and her vision is blurred. Nausea twists her stomach and she has to force her legs to move, for they feel like lumps of wet clay.

She limps off to the library and sits before a blank page. She dips her quill into blue ink and for the rest of the morning, she paints curling waves around the corners of every page.

Exhaustion creeps up on her like a rising tide. If she can rest for just a moment... She lays her pounding head down on the desk, and sleeps. And as she sleeps, she dreams of water.

She is walking by the shore of a river she knows to be the Liffey, though it is not the Liffey of home, but an older, deeper river. Wide as twenty trenches and stretching as far as she can see into the distance. On the other side she can make out a gathering of men, standing in a circle, as though a ritual were about to begin. On the ground in front of them five women are huddled together, hands bound.

Brigid looks into the river. It has become still as a pond, its surface like polished bronze. She sees not her own face in its reflection, but the face of every woman she has ever known, coalesced into one.

I smile up at her.

Brigid bends, dips her fingers into the water. Her touch makes no ripples, as though she were not even there. She hears her name, one of the women on the opposite shore calling out to her. She must help them. She must punish the men who took them. She starts to walk into the water, up to her ankles, up to her knees, trailing her hands across the surface. The water is warm, although it is late January and the Liffey of her home is patchy with frost.

One of the men laughs. Aillil. His laugh is the laugh of her father, of her brothers. Of every man who has snorted or sneered at her. They will be punished.

Beneath the surface, her hands become fists and the water around them bubbles as though a hot stone has been thrown in. The still river starts to ripple, to wave, till it is rising and falling around her, like a sheet caught in the wind. Like her cloak, when it covered the whole of the Curragh.

A cape of water rises up around her and then charges, like a stampede of horses, towards the men. Above the rushing wild waves, she can hear her own laugh.

She awakes to a bell ringing, light and clear.

'They've returned,' a woman cries. 'The cattle have returned!'

Brigid rubs her eyes and stands to look out through the library window. Just on the edge of the Curragh, she can see a herd of cattle trundling their way home.

Brigid follows the rush of women who flow down the ladder and out through the gates to greet the cattle. The pain in her head has gone and her vision is clear. She looks down at the hem of her tunic and sees it is soaked with water to the knee.

Buach runs, faster than Brigid would expect from such a large woman, and reaches the herd before the others. She throws her arms around the first cow's neck and bawls. The cow moos in reply. She moves quickly through them, running her hands over them, lips moving as she counts.

'They're all here!' Buach says. 'Twenty cows and the bull. All unhurt.'

A cow nuzzles against Brigid's shoulder. She strokes its nose, whispers into its ears. 'Good girl, well done for coming home.'

'What is this?' Darlughdach asks, pulling something off a cow's horn.

It is a scrap of fur, soaking wet.

'Here too,' Lommán says, untangling another strip of cloth from the horns of another of the cows.

'What happened to the raiders?' Ciara asks.

They look to Brigid. She swallows and puts her hands behind her back, for they are covered in blue ink.

'They drowned.'

All turn to see Clodagh. And behind her Indiu and the three other women who were taken. Their hair falls around their faces, dripping with water as though they have been bathing. And though their eyes shine with a haunted darkness, they are unharmed.

Induae howls as though keening and throws herself at her sister, pulling her to the ground in her evaporating grief. The sisters fold in on each other, sobbing.

'Did they hurt you?' Lommán asks Clodagh through his teeth.

'Only enough so that we would comply,' Clodagh says. 'They bound our hands and feet. They said they were going to play bones for us: to see who got the first pick.' She spits on the ground.

'We pleaded with them,' another of the women says, a small, bird-like creature. Brigid tries to find the woman's name in her mind, but it escapes her. 'We reminded them that we were holy sisters, your chosen ones. And that if Mother Brigid did not have her revenge, then God would.'

'Aillil laughed,' Clodagh says. 'He actually fucking laughed.' She spits again, and this time, she spits out a tooth.

'How did you escape?' Lommán asks.

'As we lay there, the men squabbling over us, there was a sudden sound like thunder. And then, a wave the size of a fort came rushing towards us. It crashed down on the men, thrashing them against the rocks, breaking their bones as though they were driftwood caught in an eddy. It washed over us and the cattle and when the wave passed, the men lay dead and naked.'

Brigid can feel Lommán's eyes on her, though she refuses to look at him.

'Aillil?' Brigid asks, brushing a strand of hair out of Clodagh's eyes.

Clodagh nods. 'He is dead. It was as if the Liffey herself rose up against them.'

Lommán looks to the blue ink on Brigid's fingers. 'Brigid?'

Strange that one word can carry so much meaning. Brigid, did you do this? Brigid, are you responsible for these men's deaths?

Brigid doesn't answer directly. She pushes her hands deep into her pockets. And quotes from the fourth Beatitude. '"*Blessed are they that hunger and thirst after justice: for they shall have their fill.*"'

Once again she returns to her writing. And for the rest of the day, she works in red.

52

'Cinnia is dead.'

Brigid had not even realized the woman was ill. She had been so occupied with the matter of appointing a new bishop, she had not spoken to many of the women in weeks.

'What happened?' she asks Ciara who has come to deliver the news.

Ciara shrugs. 'Nothing serious. Just death.'

'Such a loss,' Brigid says, shaking her head. 'She was our best illustrator.'

Ciara snorts. 'That's it? A woman you have known for twenty years dies, and you worry about the loss of her skill, not her soul?'

'I have lost women before and will lose more to come. If I shed tears over every death, the salt would turn the Curragh barren,' Brigid says, her words clipped. 'Cinnia's soul is no longer my concern, for she is with God now.'

Ciara gazes at her, head tilted. 'You know, I sometimes wonder if you truly believe that.'

Brigid reads the burial rites as they lay Cinnia to rest in the land behind the oratory and a stone cross is carved to mark where she lies. One of the older sisters keens for Cinnia, singing of her kindness and beauty in a high, undulating voice. Keening does not belong to the Christian rites, but to the older ways. All the same, Brigid allows it. She sees a time to come, where crosses grow out of the soil like a forest. A time when she too will lie here, her body turning to dust beneath the earth.

The women cry, tell stories about Cinnia that make them all laugh, and then life goes on, while snowdrops grow over Cinnia's grave.

She is heading back from service, head bowed, when Brigid hears her name being shouted.

'Brigid, you're needed at the grove!' Darlughdach shouts, breathless.

'What's happening?' Brigid asks. Have raiders dared to come again? She will destroy them. But this time, she will see that their deaths take decades. That they suffer beyond imagining.

'Just come!' Darlughdach runs ahead.

She carries a small lantern, and Brigid stumbles after the flickering light in the darkness, tripping over unseen stones and uneven earth.

I will kill them. Tear their limbs off and reach inside their chests and crush their hearts. I will strike them with eternal thirst and agony . . .

The way up is steeper than she remembers; her legs protest as she climbs and her breath leaves her quickly. She realizes that she has not, in fact, taken her turn to watch over the flame for over a year now. There was always something more important to do and she appointed younger sisters in her stead each twenty-one days, making it sound like an honour. Would tonight have been a night she should have been there? She has lost track of the days, months.

She pushes herself on, fear and rage fuelling her as she takes the last few painful steps to the top.

When at last she reaches the hole in the hedge protecting the oak and the flame, breathless, sweating, dizzy, she sees lights moving inside. She pushes through, her hands already alight with fire.

She sees not raiders, but her closest sisters. Darlughdach, Ciara, Indiu, Induae, Clodagh. They stand in a circle, hair free of their veils, white robes falling to the floor, each carrying a small candle in one hand and a cup in the other. And they are smiling, faces she knows better than her own, creased with childish delight. Even Lommán is there, standing on the edge.

'We thought you might have forgotten what night it is,' Darlughdach says, her grin even wider than all of them.

You have forgotten.

'It's Imbolc!' Ciara shouts and thrusts a cup into Brigid's hand.

Brigid takes it weakly. She looks down to see only water and her reflection in the dark surface. She cannot remember the last time she looked at herself. Her eyes are sunken, cheek bones jut out of pale skin, she hardly recognizes herself. When did she get so old?

'We were out of beer,' Ciara says. 'But we thought you might . . . you know?' She laughs and the other women laugh along.

Brigid looks up at all the expectant faces, glowing in the light from the flame. They raise their cups. Indiu and Induae grab each other with crossed hands and start to spin. And from beneath the oak tree, she sees the darkness moving, as though something is forming in the shadows.

A great unease comes over her. A greasy, sickening feeling deep within. She cannot name it, only that it has sat in her for many years now, like a toad growing and growing. And now she feels as though it will burst out of her.

'You think I have time for this? For dancing? Drinking?' She throws the cup of water into the flame. It hisses and flickers, sending sparks up into the darkness. 'You wish me to use my power for your . . . your merrymaking?' she shouts. 'You would have me perform tricks like some court magician? God gave me this power to heal, to save people, to protect us!'

Have you forgotten which god gave it to you?

'No!' Brigid screeches, pressing her hands against her ears to block out the voice. But she knows it comes from within her.

'Brigid, we thought—' Darlughdach reaches out to her.

Brigid slaps her hand away. 'Oh, you . . . You would have us abandon everything and return to the old ways, to the old gods? You never truly believed, did you, Daughter of Lugh?'

'Brigid,' Darlughdach says, her voice sharp as a bite. 'Stop it.'

'Come on, Brigid, let's get you—' Lommán tries to take her elbow, to lead her away.

Brigid lashes out, slaps him across the face. 'Don't you touch me. Get away from me. Away from here. How dare you, in this place, this holy place. If you want to be a man, then leave! In fact . . . Yes.' Brigid has found the source of this oily, greasy unease that is swelling up in her like a bubbling swamp. 'All men must leave Cill Dara! I created this space for women, and men have come in and . . . poisoned it. But no more. Go and tell the men they must leave tonight or I will make them leave!'

Lommán stands blinking, his hand pressed against his cheek. Darlughdach stares at Brigid, her face completely still, completely cold. Worse than if she shouted back. Worse than if she had struck her in return.

Brigid turns and walks away, steady at first but her pace quickens till she is running down the hill, faster than she can ever remember running in her life. She has to get away from the grove, back to her room. As soon as she shuts the door, she retches, vomiting yellow bile on to the stone floor. It's not enough. There is something foreign and toxic inside her, she has to get it out. She reaches a finger into her throat, pushing it deeper, deeper till her teeth are biting into her flesh. She wants to push her hand all the way down into her belly and pull out the cancer that is in there. But all she does is retch again, bringing up only foam. She falls to the cold floor, writhing as an acid burning eats at her.

Footsteps sound on the gravel outside her window. Crawling on her belly, she drags herself over to it, pulls herself to standing and presses her ear against the glass, listening.

'What will you do?' It is Darlughdach, her voice so low as to be barely a whisper.

'What can I do but leave as she has ordered.' It is Lommán's voice, hushed and cracking.

'But she's not herself. She hasn't been since Conleth's death. We need to help her.'

'She has not been herself for some time, Dara. Since before Conleth. Not since she returned from the synod. I don't know who she is, but she is not the woman I swore to protect. She has become so . . . so obsessed with holding on to power. This building, her fucking books, matter more to her than any of us.'

'She has lost her way. I know I can bring her back.' Darlughdach's voice is muffled and Brigid imagines her friend's face pressed against Lommán's chest.

'It's too late,' Lommán says.

'Please stay.'

'Come with me.'

There is a moment of silence, in which Brigid is sure she can hear her own heart creak and splinter like a stone in a fire.

'Come with me,' Lommán says again, his voice surer, stronger. 'Dara, you are my life. You are the pulse of my heart. I love you more than anything. More than her.'

'Don't say that.'

'Let's leave tonight. We can go far away from here and have a life together. Together, Dara.'

'She is my best friend.'

'Tell me you don't love me.'

Darlughdach does not answer. For the longest time, she does not answer.

Lommán speaks again. 'I understand. I will wait for you outside the wall at dawn. If you do not come, I will know your answer.'

Heavy footsteps move away. Stillness, and then the softest sobbing, as though coming from a thousand miles away.

Brigid presses her face against the wall and wishes she could strip off her skin and slide through the cracks between the stones, to fall like a shed snake's skin before Darlughdach's feet.

She cannot leave me. She can never leave me. None of them can ever leave me.

Brigid waits till the crunching of Darlughdach's footsteps fades away. Waits till the convent is silent apart from the scurrying of rats. When she is sure no one is outside, she opens her door and drags herself out. The cramps racking her body prevent her from standing, so she half-crawls, half-skitters across the flagstones like a spider to the dormitory.

Darlughdach is deep asleep. Curled up in her cot, her back to the door. Her shoes lie next to the bed, neatly lined up against each other. In the morning, she will slide those on and she will walk away, Brigid is sure of it.

Brigid stands and looks down at her friend. Her dearest, most beloved friend. She was always able to sleep anywhere, no matter what was happening in the world around her or in her own heart.

Her face is pale, the cheeks under her eyes a touch red, and her dark hair is splayed across her pillow like a river running over rocks. Brigid reaches out a shaking hand and strokes a single strand. Darlughdach does not stir. She barely breathes; only the subtle cloud of her breath on the icy air gives any sign that she is alive.

Brigid considers sliding into the bed next to her, of wrapping her body around Darlughdach's as they did once, back in the winter that took many lives. She remembers the smell of her, the warmth of her body. The softness of it.

A small coal fire is burning in a stove close to going out. Brigid breathes on it to stir it to life once more. She does not want her friend to get cold in her sleep.

The coals glow deep red. Brigid reaches out and plucks a small piece between two fingers. She stares down at her fingers. Flesh hisses and she can smell burning skin, but she does not feel any pain. She places the coal in one of Darlughdach's shoes. Takes another from the fire and places it in the other. She does not want her friend to have cold feet when she rises for morning prayers, which she judges by the sky she can see through the window is less than an hour away. It is a deep, dark blue and reminds Brigid she must get more woad for ink.

She returns to her room and waits for the bell. It rings, cold, clear. And is soon followed by screaming.

53

Brigid walks slowly, ever so slowly, towards the screaming. Her sisters run through the corridors, hair wild and loose from their sleep. They throw quick glances as they pass her, but she keeps her pace steady.

Indiu and Induae sit on either side of Darlughdach, holding her up like midwives helping a mother through a birthing. Darlughdach lies on the floor next to her bed, twisting, writhing and thrashing her legs as though she were trying to shake her very feet off. She reminds Brigid of a fox she saw once, caught in a snare, chewing through its own leg to escape.

The soles of Darlughdach's feet look as though the skin has been flayed from them and the room is filled with the smell of burnt flesh.

'Brigid,' Indiu says. 'Thank God. Heal her, please.'

Brigid does not move. All eyes turn to her, pleading, questioning. Darlughdach looks at her and the agony of her body is, for a moment, superseded by something else as realization stabs through her heart.

'You?'

'Leave us,' Brigid snaps.

The twins hesitate. They do not know what is happening, only that they have been given a choice. Between their sister and their leader.

'Leave!' Brigid roars.

The instruction is no longer a choice. Indiu and Induae's limbs move without their own will. They march out of the room like puppets controlled by a child.

Brigid takes a step closer to Darlughdach. She kneels down on the floor, pulls her sleeve back and places her hands above Darlughdach's feet. Not touching. Not yet.

'You did this?' Darlughdach fights to get the words out. Her breath is heavy, sweat and tears pour down her face, blood stains her teeth. She must have bitten her tongue or cracked her teeth.

Brigid meets her friend's eyes at last. Were they always this blue? Could they always see into her so clearly?

'Why?' Darlughdach asks.

'You were going to leave,' Brigid says simply.

Darlughdach stares at her as though she does not know what she is looking at. And then she laughs. Even through her agony, she laughs.

'Stop it!' Brigid shouts. She covers her ears to block out the mocking laughter.

'You first!' Darlughdach screeches back. 'Heal me.'

Brigid tries to find the old words in her mind, words she has used to heal over and over, but there is only silence. 'I . . . I can't.'

Darlughdach swallows, then snarls at Brigid, lips pulled back over her bloody teeth. 'Lommán was right, I don't know who you are.'

'I am your friend.' Brigid looks down at her, eyes filled with tears. 'Your anamchara.'

Darlughdach scoffs at the word, turns her head away. 'Soul friend? You have no soul left,' Darlughdach shouts. 'Look at you. The great Brigid, Mary of the Gaels.' Her breathing is ragged, her voice raw with pain. 'You . . . you've become so hungry for power. You lie and manipulate and . . .' Darlughdach struggles to finish but Brigid knows what she wants to say. Knows what has been whispered about her since Conleth did not return, and knows the truth of it. Killer.

'Hurt people,' Darlughdach says with a heavy sigh. 'People you have sworn to protect.' There is none of Darlughdach's usual kindness in her words. There is only pain and rage. And Brigid knows that she has lost her.

'Get out,' Darlughdach screams. 'Get out!'

Brigid runs from the room, pressing her hands against her ears to block out Darlughdach's curses that follow her.

There is only one place she can go. Though she will not find forgiveness there; forgiveness belongs to the new god, not the old.

She does not see the smouldering coal that has rolled from Darlughdach's shoe to under her bed. Does not see how its smoke dances beneath the straw mattress. But I do.

54

Brigid returns to the sacred grove as the sky turns from inky black to soft grey. A blonde woman sleeps, curled up in a blanket beneath the flame. For a moment, Brigid believes it is Cinnia, and then remembers she is dead and feels the woman's loss as though for the first time. So many women have died and Brigid did not stop to mourn them. Did not feel the need.

Brigid cannot remember this girl's name – she is one of the novices who joined only a few weeks before. So many names these days she fails to remember. Who should have been watching the flame tonight but has delegated to this youngster?

And then she remembers. It was her.

She lays a hand on the girl's shoulder, shakes her only a little.

'A little longer, Mam,' she mumbles, still half-asleep.

'Come now,' Brigid says, shaking her a little harder.

The girl's eyes snap open and she scrambles to her feet. 'Mother Brigid, I am sorry. I . . .'

'Hush. All is well. It was my night to watch the flame. You return to your own bed.'

She glances to the flame and back to Brigid.

'This is not a test,' Brigid says. 'You have done your duty for the night. Go.'

The girl gathers up her blanket and backs away, bobbing and bowing with each step. When she has passed through the hedge, she turns and runs back down the hill.

Brigid walks around the flame three times, hands

outstretched. The fingers which plucked the coal from the fire sting with pain still. The flame looks smaller than she remembered, as though a gentle wind might blow it out.

She takes the bottle from within her robes, adds oil to the fire, then sits under the great oak and stares back at the fire as it grows.

'Goddess,' she whispers. 'Goddess, are you here?'

I do not answer.

'Goddess, please, I need you.'

Silence. Let her wait.

'I did what you asked of me. What more did you want of me? I gave you everything and you take even more? You would take my mind, my sanity? Take every one I love? Is that what you want?'

She stares up at the sky, wishing lightning would strike, but only clouds float by. She turns then to the earth, throwing herself to the ground and beating the soil with her fists, over and over, like a child in a tantrum. She looks at last to the hole beneath the great oak. She longs for the darkness within. The silence she has not known for too long. She crawls towards it on her belly, tries to push herself inside it, but meets only mud and roots.

'Please.' She is sobbing now, her face pressed into the dirt. The soil tastes like blood. 'Please tell me what to do.'

She lies there as the creatures of the earth move around her. Worms weave through her hair, earwigs march across her skin. She listens for the gentle rustle of a snake and hears only the slither of insects. Doesn't she know? There are no more snakes in Ireland. For Patrick and his God – her God now – drove them all out.

Brigid rolls over on to her back, her face painted in mud like the druids of old, and stares up at the sky. The last stars flicker out as the sun rises.

'Have you truly abandoned me, you old hag?' she says, closing her eyes.

'Hag, is it?' I say, as we meet again in the world.

I stand before her in the body of a woman, ripe and fertile and bursting with life. A rainbow of light coruscates from my body, as though my skin were made of gemstones.

Brigid holds her hand up to shield her eyes from my light, which shines brighter than the flame.

'Where have you been?' she asks, dragging herself to her feet.

'Here,' I say, gesturing to the earth beneath us. 'And everywhere. Everywhere I have been needed.'

'I have needed you,' she says.

I raise an eyebrow. 'Have you now? Seems to me you have been carrying on quite well on your own.'

I sit against the tree, naked, feet together and my knees splayed out. 'Tell me, then, Brigid of the Fothairt, Mother Brigid of Cill Dara, what do you want?'

Brigid opens her mouth to answer, but finds there are no words to express the depths of her need. Not in any language she knows. All that she knows is that she is lost in the darkness.

'You gave me a purpose once,' she says. 'I ask that you do so again.'

'You have the same purpose you always did.'

'But I don't understand. I have built this library.' She looks down to the tower. The glow of oil lamps shine from the windows as her scribes begin the morning's work. 'I kept the knowledge safe. From all over the world, I protected it even as darkness has taken over the Empire of Rome. The lights burn here still.'

'And what a thing that is to have done,' I say. 'I am proud of you. You have made a fine start.'

'Start . . .?' Brigid tilts her head, confused. 'Is that not everything you asked of me?'

'Remember,' I say.

'I do remember!' she says, frustrated. Tired. She rubs tears away, unwilling to let them fall. 'I have never once forgotten.'

'But you have. You have forgotten so much. It was not knowledge I tasked you with protecting.'

Brigid's brow furrows as she tries to drag the memory from her mind. 'Wisdom? But what is the difference?'

I reach out and touch her forehead. 'Knowledge lives here.' I draw my finger down her face, her collarbone, and to the space between her breasts. 'Wisdom lives here. In your heart. A heart, my sweet child, that you have worked so very hard to turn to stone.'

'What should I have done?' Her hands claw at the air as though she wants to drag her nails against my flesh. She curls them into tight fists. 'Let myself love, knowing I would only be hurt? Let the ache of my mother's death bring me to my knees? Let the pain of the world break it over and over and over?' She pounds on her chest.

I smile at her. 'Yes. All of this and more.'

She drops her hands to her sides. All the anger, all the frustration flows out of her. 'I . . . I don't know how.'

I stand up, stretching my body. It has been a full year since I walked the lands above and I have much to see. 'You will learn.'

'But what do I do now?' Brigid asks.

I place my hand over her eyes. 'Listen,' I say.

In the darkness beneath my touch, Brigid hears a bell ringing. Each peal becomes a flash of light as her mind cracks open to my vision.

She can see a bell in her hand. It is square, made of bronze, and has a crack in it. She shakes it. Instead of a clang, it lets out a loud, high-pitched caw. Something black bursts from inside and into the air. She remembers Patrick's story of how he used a bell to drive demons back into the darkness. But instead of driving birds away, hers is creating them. With each swing a bird, large and black, bursts out of the bell and up into the sky. She looks again and the bell has become a beating heart, bloody and raw. The birds circle overhead, then swarm down to feast on it; even as she holds it up to them to be devoured, she knows it is her own heart. When at last the birds are done, they evaporate like mist and she holds a single heart-shaped stone. Cracks run along its surface like spiderwebs.

The bell will not stop ringing. On and on. Frantic.

She opens her eyes to see I am no longer with her. The sound, she realizes, has not been in her head. It is coming from the monastery. Raiders? She listens closer.

Not raiders. Fire.

55

Cill Dara is alight.

Black smoke and yellow fire engulf the women's dormitory, pouring out of the windows and doors. Wood cracks like bones and the roar of the flames is like an animal, insatiable.

Women and men rush back and forth, their grey robes turned black from the smoke, carrying buckets of water from the wells and throwing them desperately at the fire. But they might as well be trying to drain the sea with an acorn cup.

The library tower is standing still. For now. As Brigid walks closer, slowly as though in a dream, she sees dark figures in the top windows appearing and disappearing, throwing out everything they can. Pages flutter in the wind like autumn leaves, spiralling downward to where a group of nuns and monks have stretched out a sheet, to catch the manuscripts like fish in a net. Others retrieve what has fallen, gather them up in their skirts and robes, and run to the walls, where they stack them up. Then they come running back for more.

Brigid stops one of the women as she races by. 'What happened?'

'We don't know. It started in the dormitory.' The woman runs on, carrying her cargo of books.

'The dormitory,' Brigid whispers. She caused this. Her jealousy and her fear caused this.

'Darlughdach!' Brigid starts screaming. 'Darlughdach!'

She runs towards the building, pushing past the water carriers. The heat of the fire is like a wall. She covers her eyes with her arm and presses forward, pushing against the waves of heat. Thick smoke blinds her. She cannot breathe. She can almost feel her skin being peeled from her flesh as she pushes closer and closer, all the time calling the name of her friend.

She left Darlughdach crippled, unable to walk, unable to escape the flames. The woman she loves is dead and it is her fault. She pushes against the heat, wishing to join Darlughdach in death.

Arms encircle her waist, dragging her back. She tries to fight against them, but they are even stronger than the fire. 'Darlughdach!' she screams.

'She's safe,' the woman holding her says, and Brigid recognizes the voice as Clodagh's, husky from smoke though it is. 'I got her out.'

Brigid goes limp in Clodagh's arms, folding over as the woman pulls her away from the fire.

'Where is she?'

Clodagh points over to the well, where Darlughdach is sitting, back propped up against the wall.

'I'm here, you fucking idiot,' she says.

The skin around her eyes is angry raw, and the whites of her eyes have turned red, but she is staring back at her friend. Brigid runs, though it feels as if she is floating, flying towards her. She throws herself to her knees and pulls Darlughdach into her arms. The woman cries out in pain. Brigid releases her slowly, looks down at her friend's feet. The soot has coated them too and Brigid could choose to believe Darlughdach were merely wearing black socks. But she has been turning away from the truth for too long. It is time to face what she has done.

'So are you going to—' Darlughdach's words are cut off by a spasm of pain. 'Heal me or what?'

Brigid hovers her hands above Darlughdach's feet, then pulls them away, curling them into tight balls. 'I don't know if I can.' Brigid's voice has never been so small. 'The goddess . . . I think she has left me.'

I will never leave you.

'Try,' Darlughdach says, her voice a whisper, her face twisted in pain. 'Please.'

Brigid lays her hands on her friend's feet. Darlughdach cries out from the pain of the contact, tries to pull away, but Brigid holds firm. She turns her focus inward, following the path within. There, a trickle of energy, small and faint as the first glimmers of dawn. It starts in her belly and then moves up through her chest, through her heart, up, up her neck and settles on her tongue. The words for healing return.

Darlughdach's moans of pain quieten. Her panting slows. And when Brigid at last takes her hands away, the soles of Darlughdach's feet are soft and white as a snowfall.

Brigid becomes aware of pain in her hands, looks down to see the skin of her palms flayed as though she has placed them in a fire. She curls her fingers around the pain, hiding them.

Darlughdach crosses her legs and grabs hold of her feet, touching them, squeezing them.

Brigid knees back on her heels, head bowed. 'If you leave now, Lommán may still be waiting . . .'

'You are so stupid, Brigid. I chose you. I wasn't going to go with Lommán. Do you understand that?' She bites down on her lip. 'I chose you. Despite your stupidity. Despite your ambition. Despite it all. Fuck knows why, but I chose you. I chose Cill Dara. I chose you.'

A feeling bubbles up within Brigid's stomach which she cannot at first name but slowly she recognizes it. Selfishness. And it is delicious as the sweetest of strawberries.

She pulls her sleeve down over her wrist and uses it to wipe away the dirt from Darlughdach's cheeks and forehead. 'Will you forgive me?' she asks.

'I thought only God forgave?' Darlughdach says, not cruel, only curious.

'Fuck God,' Brigid says. And Darlughdach's gasp sends a thrill through Brigid as delicious as any prayer ever has. 'I can deal with him when death comes. For now, it is only your forgiveness that matters.'

'I am not a priest,' Darlughdach says.

'Not of Christ,' Brigid says. 'You are more than that. You are my anamchara.'

Brigid bows her head before Darlughdach and waits. She shivers as Darlughdach places a hand on her head.

'I cannot forgive you, not yet. But . . .' Darlughdach says, before planting a kiss on Brigid's forehead. 'Until I can, I will keep on loving you.'

Brigid takes Darlughdach's hand and together they get to their feet.

All around them, Brigid watches as the men and women of Cill Dara work side by side. There is no one telling them what to do, no orders being shouted as to who can scoop water into the buckets and who can throw it on to the flames. They know instinctively how to work together. And their efforts become like a dance. They have given up trying to save the women's dormitory as it was doomed anyway, and all have turned their efforts to the tower. But it will not be enough.

Flames are now licking the base, getting closer and closer.

'We need more water,' someone shouts.

'The well is empty,' comes the reply.

Brigid turns and looks to the silver snake of the Liffey in the distance. Moonlight glints off its slow, dark surface.

'Get everyone out,' she says, not taking her eyes off the river. 'Get everyone out of the tower and get them to the grove. Save as many of the books as you can, but save yourselves first.'

'What are you going to do?' Darlughdach asks.

'I am going to save what I can.'

Darlughdach passes on the order. Some, too deep in their focus of the task, are reluctant to listen. But Darlughdach shakes them and points them back to the grove.

Brigid stands before the tower. It rises high above the land, like a fist punching out of the earth to the sky. Smoke pours from the window at the top like a beacon fire, a light to warn of invaders. But this time the danger has not come from without.

She knows what she must do. The only thing that has a chance of saving everything she has built. But she does not know if she has the power.

It is within you. You just have to let it go.

She senses it deep, deep within her: the spark. It is so weak. Around it she has built a wall, and she has covered it with every emotion she was too afraid to feel. Everything that made her human, she had extracted and discarded, for she did not see the use of it. Every soft part of her, she turned to stone.

She walks to the riverbank, keeps on walking till she is standing up to her waist in the freezing, rushing black waters. The rapids pull at her skirts and she has to fight to stay standing. She dips her fingertips into the water and lets herself feel.

Feel everything she has denied herself. Rage, envy, fear, lust. All the messy, confusing emotions she found so disgusting, she allows to rush through her. She throws her head back and screams.

And I scream along with her.

The waters of the Liffey rise up around her like a cloak caught in the wind. Higher and higher it rises, higher than the waves that beat against the coast, higher than a tidal wave, high as the tower now. All the water of the Liffey from here to the sea rises up under Brigid's command.

And then, Brigid lets go.

56

The flood water is up to her ankles as she wades through it. Burnt wood and lone pages spiral in her wake. The smell is overpowering, like burnt honey and stagnant water.

So much lost. And yet she looks up at the tower, standing still. So much remains.

The rain has come now, heavy and hard, which will do for any remaining embers. The sisters stand in quiet huddles, arms wrapped around each other. The brothers too, stand side by side with them. They are exhausted, baffled, heartsore. But she counts them; they are all safe. The same cannot be said of the library. Of the thousand books they had gathered, perhaps one hundred remain. They lie in messy, smoking heaps.

She picks one up from the sodden ground. The binding and edges are blackened with a thick, sticky soot. Scared of what she will find, she opens the book. Bright white pages, colours still as fresh as the day they were first painted. The words are untouched. She closes the book and hugs it to herself, presses her face against the cover. Her instinct is to fight back the tears, but instead she lets them flow, cutting tracks through the soot on her face. She cries as she has never cried before, as she has never allowed herself before. And soon her sobs become laughter. Catharsis. To cleanse or purge. Just as Aristotle said.

'Mother Brigid?' Indiu says. No, it is Induae. Brigid can hardly tell beneath the dirt. 'Are you all right?'

Brigid cannot stop laughing now. She grabs Induae's hand

and squeezes it, trying to form words, but all she can do is laugh.

Induae starts laughing, too, Brigid's mirth infecting her. Her twin next. And soon, it spreads through the sisters and then the brothers. Laughter like bells, ringing out. They hug each other, slap each other on the back, point up to the wreck of what was once their home, and then slap their thighs. Delirium has taken them as surely as had they drunk from a lake of beer.

'What in God's name are you all laughing about?' Ciara asks, standing over Brigid.

She too is covered in soot. Her hair is free from its veil and stands up in all directions like a thistle. The laughing takes over Brigid again.

'You're a mad bitch, Biddy,' Ciara says, though she is laughing too now.

Brigid looks around at the faces of all her sisters: they are tired, injured, their eyes are filled with tears, and yet they laugh.

A man stands behind them, head bowed low. His clothes are so covered in burns, they barely cling to his narrow shoulders.

'Lommán,' Brigid says, closing the gap between her and the man. 'You returned.'

'I know you told me to go,' he says, still not lifting his head. 'But I saw the flames and . . .'

Brigid bows her head before him. 'You came to protect us, just as you have always done.'

Lommán's eyes are red and raw, from smoke or crying, Brigid is unsure. His hands are black with soot. She takes both and kisses the back of each. 'I am sorry for my words, Lommán,' she whispers. 'So very sorry.'

Words to wound. Words to protect. And words to heal. These are words of healing.

But there is still so much healing to be done. So much harm she must undo. She gazes at the blackened shell that was once their home, a home she and her sisters built together. Then turns again to her old friends, those who have always looked to her to lead. Who look to her now to tell them what to do, but she does not know herself. The only certainty she has left is that she needs these people more than she has ever needed anything.

'I don't know what to do next,' she says.

She once had such a clear vision of what she wanted for Cill Dara, she could see every stone of every building, every doorway and window. Now, all she sees is ash.

'We start again,' Darlughdach says, taking her hand, their fingers entwining with each other. 'Only this time, we do it together.'

57

There is nothing but ash left of the old wooden dormitory, and many of the women declare they're glad to see the back of it: it was always too cold in winter and too warm in summer. Brigid orders the wall between the monastery and convent knocked down for the stones; these are put towards building a new dormitory for the sisters, with beds raised up off the floor and windows facing the setting sun.

Barely a tenth of the texts have survived, fewer still of the scrolls, and of those only a handful are of any great quality. Brigid sorts through them all, assessing the damage and choosing which can be saved, and which must be discarded. She wonders if she could bury the books that must be abandoned in the field behind the oratory, for some feel like dear friends.

She picks one from the pile: a small, tattered book slightly larger than her hand. The leather binding, once soft from the touch of hundreds, perhaps even thousands, of hands, is now stiff and brittle as bark. She risks opening it. The binding cracks and falls to the floor. But the pages inside are untouched.

'Is that . . .?' Darlughdach asks, picking the fallen scrap of leather from the ground.

'Yes,' Brigid says, turning a leaf-thin page. 'It's the copy of St Paul's Letters to the Corinthians which Brendan gave me thirty years ago. Where it all began.'

'And where it can begin again,' Darlughdach says, squeezing Brigid's arm.

Brigid brings the book to her lips, kisses it gently, and places it on the pile to be saved.

It takes a full year before the library is restored, brick by brick, book by book. They have added new windows, made the roof higher, and what was once a place of candles and shadows is now filled with light. Brigid spends her time there reading the work of the Greeks on how a society should be run. She learns a new word – *dēmokratia*. A flawed system, but she can find no better.

She puts it to the test. After service, she pauses before dismissing them. 'I have something to ask of you all. Who should be our new abbot?'

Every face stares back dumbly, as though she has asked them all to take to the air and fly.

'Come on,' she says. 'You must have an opinion?'

At last, Ciara raises her hand. 'Ninnidh.'

All eyes turn to a monk sitting in the middle of the congregation. A young man, with a face like one of Cinnia's painted angels.

'Why do you cast your vote for him?' Brigid asks, eyes half-closed with suspicion, for she knows her old friend too well.

'Because it would be nice to look at his pretty face every Mass.'

The explosion of laughter breaks the tension. Ninnidh's face turns crimson as the monks around him josh and tease.

Ciara winks at Brigid.

'Aidan gets my vote,' a man says, after the laughter has subsided.

'Aye, he's a good one.'

'How about Cathal?'

And so the voting begins.

After that, they are given the choice to vote for everything.

How to distribute food, divide the labour, use surplus resources. There are days Brigid wishes to return to when she made every choice, for often these votes turn into squabbles. But in the main, the choices made are wise, and if not, then at least the consequences are shared among them all.

Five years after the fire, almost to the day, Ciara dies.

She was, Brigid is told, in the infirmary, teaching a young novice the use of healing herbs and plants, when the young woman held up a large root in the shape of a man's member and asked, in all innocence, 'And what might I do with this?'

Ciara laughed so much that she stopped breathing and collapsed on the floor, a wide grin on her face.

Her body is committed to the ground and the land behind the oratory grows another white cross. Brigid allows herself to cry for her oldest friend. Allows her heart to break a little more without fighting the pain.

Lommán is the next to go. He goes out foraging one day and does not return. He is found sitting with his back against a mossy tree, as though he is asleep. Brigid and Darlughdach see to his anointing and he is buried with the men. Clodagh melts down his sword to make a cross.

For each member of her community she loses, more come. A cycle of life and death and life again. Brigid's red hair turns grey, and flesh that was once firm becomes soft. With age has come a sort of ugliness, the kind she once prayed for. She finds freedom in it.

'When did we get so old?' Darlughdach asks ten years after the fire, as she sits on the edge of their bed, waiting for the dizziness she gets now when she sits up to pass.

Brigid has caught Darlughdach squinting at herself in a bronzed mirror Ciara gave her before she died, tracing the lines on her face, running fingers through her thinning hair.

'I like being old,' Brigid says, looking at her reflection next to Darlughdach's, their faces framed like an illustration of saints. 'The beauty of youth was wasted on me.'

'You are still beautiful,' Darlughdach says, turning and kissing Brigid on the corner of her mouth. 'You will always be beautiful.'

Brigid has no words for what their relationship has become. Are they lovers? Friends? Anamchairde? Perhaps it does not need a name, for it is what it is, and she is grateful for it. She returns Darlughdach's kiss.

She used to count the passing of time in cycles of months, with each full moon and each coming of fresh blood. But her menses stopped many years back and so now she measures it by the twenty-one days before it is her turn to guard the flame again. Though each of her sittings seem to pass quicker each time and the hill seems to get steeper. As she climbs up to take the watch, the night before her eightieth birthday, she has to stop three times before reaching the top and can feel her heart flittering like a bird trying to escape a cage. Of late she has felt a tightness in her chest and a pinching pain in her jaw and neck.

There is a spot under the oak where she likes to sit, her back supported by the soft roots. The oak is now the height of twenty men, its trunk as wide around as three women lying head to toe. She takes her seat under the branches, wrapped in her cloak which has been repaired so many times over the years, she wonders if there is still a thread left from the cloak that once covered the whole of the Curragh. But it is still as warm as it ever was.

She stares into the flame, feels her mind drifting as though floating on the sparks that dance up into the sky, back to when she was young. Her mind drifts a lot of late, time loosening its hold on her, and she returns surprised to find herself looking down at wrinkled hands, speckled with liver spots; at first she mistakes them for ink stains.

As the darkening sky above turns a deep inky blue, there is a rustling and steady *tap, tap, tap*.

'It's freezing, Dara,' Brigid says. 'You shouldn't have come.'

'I wanted to check you hadn't fallen asleep.'

Darlughdach walks into the grove, a thin stick reaching out before her, for she has been blind for over a year.

Brigid takes her free arm and helps her sit down.

'I'll need your help to get back up,' Darlughdach says. 'My hips are giving me hell.'

'We can help each other up.'

They sit in silence, hands held tightly. Dawn comes, a bead of light flashing across the horizon.

'It is Imbolc tomorrow,' Darlughdach says.

'Yes, it comes so quickly.' Brigid watches as the sky turns from pewter grey to the colour of fresh lambswool. 'I won't see another.'

'What do you mean?' Darlughdach turns her head to face Brigid, as though she could still see.

'I will die soon,' Brigid says. 'Tomorrow, I think.'

'Hush.' Darlughdach pats her hand. 'You'll live for ever.'

Brigid leans her head against Darlughdach's shoulder. 'I want you to take over as abbess when I am gone.'

Darlughdach gently strokes Brigid's hair, twirling the strands between her fingers and bringing them to her lips. 'When you die, I will die too.'

'Don't be ridiculous,' Brigid says, straightening up to look into Darlughdach's face.

'I am not being ridiculous,' Darlughdach scowls. 'I am telling the truth. My heart won't take it. It's already flickering out.'

'Well, hold on for one more year then.' Brigid returns her head to Darlughdach's shoulder. 'To see things in order. I have left notebooks filled with my thoughts and instructions.'

'You know I can't read.'

'Get one of the sisters to read them to you then. Indiu still loves to read and her eyes are sharp as ever.'

'Then get her to take over,' Darlughdach says, hitting the ground with her stick.

Brigid smiles at the outburst, though she knows Darlughdach would be annoyed if she could see it. 'You can appoint her as your successor. I'm appointing you. No arguing.'

Darlughdach takes a deep breath in and out, her chest rising and falling, and Brigid can hear a soft rattling in her lungs. 'There can be no Cill Dara without Brigid.'

'Brigid is just a name. And names can be passed on.'

Darlughdach makes a noncommittal grunt.

More silence. The sun rises slowly, fighting its way through a thick coverage of clouds that has come in from the north.

'Is it beautiful?' Darlughdach asks, clouded eyes turned towards the light.

'It is,' Brigid says.

'Describe it to me.'

Brigid has never been good at finding the right words. Writing down those of others, yes, but creating her own, that was Darlughdach's skill. But she tries.

'The sky is grey—'

Darlughdach tuts. 'You can do better than that.'

'The sky is the colour of freshly washed vellum.'

'Better.'

'And the clouds, there's the hint of light inside them, like wool kindling set to light. A flock of linnets are flying past, heading south.'

Darlughdach turns her face, seeking out the light of the rising sun. 'I wish I could see it one more time.'

Brigid has tried healing Darlughdach's eyes before but has failed each time. 'Let me try again.'

Brigid leans over and kisses the delicate, wrinkled skin of Darlughdach's eyelids, first the right, then the left. And with each brushing of her lips, she pours love into them. She used to believe that healing came from pity, from kindness, but now she knows that it has always come from love.

'Open your eyes and see.'

Darlughdach blinks her eyes open. 'I can see the Liffey!' she says, though she is facing away from the river below. 'Ah, see how it shimmers. And look at the golden barley, catching the last of the sun's rays.'

The barley field is green with fresh shoots. Brigid knows Darlughdach is lying, but she loves to hear it.

'Oh, Brigid, it's so beautiful to see it one last time. If only we had another lifetime together, a thousand lifetimes.'

'We do,' Brigid says. 'We will.'

'And now,' Darlughdach says. 'You may close my eyes again, for I see the light of God better in the darkness.'

Brigid laughs. When Darlughdach plays at being a nun, she always goes too hard.

'Very well then.' Brigid places her hand over Darlughdach's eyes, wipes gently across them.

'Ah, yes, darkness once more.'

The women stand – though Darlughdach was right, it takes them a few tries – and hand in hand they walk back home.

Brigid was also right. The next night, death comes for her.

She has felt a tightness in her back all day, as though her ribs were bound with cloth, and finds each breath comes harder than the last. Clodagh finds her sitting at the foot of the ladder to the library, unable to stand, and without saying a word, helps carry her to her bed. She then sends word to the others that the time has come.

Brigid is not afraid to die. Her only sorrow is that there will be no more days with Darlughdach, no more meals eaten with her sisters, no more books to read. If she had a hundred lifetimes, she would still not have read all that she wants to. Could heaven, whether it is the one above written about in the Bible, or the one below from the old tales, be something like a library?

Ninnidh arrives, flustered, carrying the holy oil and his bible.

'Am I too late? Has the Lord taken her?'

After many years, he has become abbot, and though he is still called 'Ninnidh the fair' by many in gently teasing tones, little of his cherubic beauty remains.

'Not yet, father,' Brigid says. 'The Lord must be busy elsewhere.'

Ninnidh prays over her, anoints her head with oil, and once the rites are delivered, he bursts into tears.

'I will never,' he says, his chest heaving, 'wash this hand again.' He stares at the fingers that touched Brigid's skin while snot runs down his chin.

'Oh, give over,' Clodagh says, and shoos the man out.

It is only the women now. Brigid is surrounded by her sisters. Darlughdach by her side, Indiu, Induae and Clodagh. And in the shadows, she is sure she can see the faces of Ciara and Lommán, Orla and Cinnia, and all the others she has lost. She even believes she can see her mother.

'Sleep,' Darlughdach says. 'We will all be here.'

She closes her eyes, takes one last long breath, and before she can let it out, slips into the embrace of sleep.

In the darkness, I wait for her. She is young again, as when I first met her, and it being the first dawn of Imbolc, I am young too.

'At last, my little one,' I say. 'Welcome home.'

I take her hand and we walk together into the light.

In time, we will be joined by the other Brigids; abbesses who rule over Cill Dara in the years to come, dedicating their lives to keeping the sacred flame alight. And though, centuries and centuries from now, men with swords will strip the convent of its wealth to feed their rapacious king from across the sea and the fire will at last be quenched, the light will burn still. The light of wisdom and curiosity and kindness and sisterhood will continue to glow in the heart of every woman who is brave enough to ask, 'What if?' 'What if there was another way?' To live. To love. To rule. What if? And though the stones of Cill Dara will crumble and the bell be silenced, the call to prayer, to gather, to dance, sister hand in hand with sister, will echo for eternity. And my light, my flame, will never go out.

Acknowledgements

There's a common phenomenon in publishing known as 'the difficult second novel'. You're now writing under contract, with deadlines and expectations. It can be punishing. And if it wasn't for the support of my many, many friends and publishing colleagues, I may well have ended up like the salt seller who tried to lie to Brigid: crushed. Thanks to your kindness, encouragement and unwavering support, I made it through and I am so very proud of this book.

Thank you to:

Ruth Atkins, my editor, your brilliantly insightful notes were a shining North Star that kept this book on course and guided it home. There just aren't enough ways to say thank you.

Vasilisa Romanenko and Jon Kennedy for being so open to my design requests and creating a truly stunning cover.

Mary Chamberlain for your eagle eyes on the copy-edit and Bea McIntyre for taking such good care of Brigid in the last stages of publication.

Rachael and Tom for the care and craft in bringing the story to life in audio. And Simone, I could listen to your beautiful voice all day.

Everyone else in the Penguin Michael Joseph and Penguin Random House Ireland teams for getting this book into the hands of readers.

Sarah Devine and Lisa Paasche. Good friends will help you move house. Great friends will help you move a body. You're definitely the first people I will call if I have a body to move.

Amy McCulloch, as ever, for your untiring moral support and for being my first reader. I couldn't have made it through the slump times without you.

Bex Levene and Caroline Lea for your early reads, edit notes and words of encouragement. Making time when deep in your own books means so much to me.

The PMJ authors chat group, for keeping me sane when the brain weasels went to work

Mum, Dad, my sisters and niblings. The fact you're proud of me makes me proud of myself.

Chris, my husband, partner and best friend of nearly thirty years. We do alright.

Domino, I'm sorry that sometimes I have to write rather than rub your belly.

And to my readers, I hope this book wraps you in a loving cloak of curiosity, kindness and wisdom. And that if anyone looks at you in the wrong way, their eyes explode.